## OTHER BOOKS BY CLARK HOWARD

The Arm

A Movement Toward Eden

The Doomsday Squad

Last Contract

Siberia 10

The Killings

Summit Kill

Mark the Sparrow

The Hunters

The Last Great Death Stunt

Six Against the Rock

The Wardens

Traces of Mercury

Zebra

American Saturday

Dirt Rich

Quick Silver

Brothers in Blood

Hard City

Love's Blood

# CITY BLOOD

## A Novel of Revenge

# Clark Howard

OTTO PENZLER BOOKS
NEW YORK

**OTTO
PENZLER
BOOKS**

Otto Penzler Books
129 West 56th Street
New York, NY 10019
(Editorial Offices Only)

Simon & Schuster
Rockefeller Center
1230 Avenue of the Americas
New York, New York 10020

Book design by Richard Truscott /PIXEL PRESS

Manufactured in the United States of America

10   9   8   7   6   5   4   3   2   1

Library of Congress Cataloging-in-Publication Data

Howard, Clark.
City blood : a novel of revenge / Clark Howard.
p.   cm.
1. Police—Illinois—Chicago—Fiction.   2. Chicago (Ill.)—Fiction.   I. Title.
PS3558.O877C58   1994
813'.54—dc20           94-14820
CIP

ISBN 1-883402-39-5

## To more of the next generation

Robert Lee Stoneking
Ashley Nicole Stoneking

# O N E

As the unmarked Chicago police car slowly cruised the night streets of the lower West Side, the faces of the two detectives in the front seat were shadowed except when they passed under a streetlight, or went by a cocktail lounge with a twist of neon in the window or above the entrance. The vapor lights overhead cast their features in a clammy gray that made them look embalmed, while the neon brought them back to life with brief lines of carnival colors. As the car was guided along its aimless way, the two detectives conversed in quiet tones.

"I don't believe this," said the man in the passenger seat. He bobbed his chin toward the sidewalk, where a ferret-like little man was skulking down the street. "Pete Fingers. The son of a bitch must have made parole."

"Wonder why those assholes in Corrections didn't send us a release notification?" the driver asked.

"Who knows?" his partner replied indifferently. "What the hell do they care if the pickpocket stats at the Stadium go up?" He watched the little man disappear into a building.

"Maybe they didn't notify us because he's rehabilitated," the driver suggested.

"Yeah. And maybe I'll win the fucking lottery next week."

*The car passed the mouth of an alley. Down that alley, in the murky light of a single bulb above the rear entrance of a topless go-go club, a young woman in a terry-cloth robe was flailing with her fists at a man who had backed her against the wall of the building.*

*"Cut it out!" she said. Her fists seemed feeble against his solid chest. "Stop it! Leave me alone, you son of a bitch!"*

*"Son of a bitch, am I?" The man's words were soft but offended. He slapped her, a hard, stinging blow.*

*"Goddamn you—!" The woman tried to claw his eyes but he grabbed her wrists, jerked her forward, and slammed her against the wall. Her head bounced off the brick and she moaned.*

*"Little bitch," the man said, so quietly it was like an obscene breath.*

*"No, please—look, I'm sorry, okay?" the woman begged. She gave up her physical struggle and tried words. "Wait—I'm sorry—" From one of the club's partly open back windows, the sound of muted go-go music underscored her plea. "Please, don't—"*

*A hand shot out of the shadows and slapped her again, viciously, across the mouth. Groaning, she slumped helplessly back against the building. The hand jerked open her robe. She was wearing red bikini panties with a fringe trim, and a matching half bra with tassels on it: a dancer's costume with breakaway Velcro closures for easy removal on the stage. The hand seized the bra's breakaway between the cups and pulled it open, exposing the young woman's buoyant, starkly white breasts to the hazy light.*

*"Fucking little slut—" the man's voice said from the darkness, harsher now.*

The detective on the passenger side of the unmarked car was Joseph Patrick Kiley, a fourteen-year Chicago PD veteran. He was a third-generation Irish-American whom women found attractive if not exactly handsome. His features were clean, even, honest; the kind of a face a woman—or a man—could talk to. It was a face that showed interest easily, even though its most memorable feature, his clear, light blue, very direct eyes, were most of the time completely without warmth. Still, strangers tended to start conversations with him, quickly confiding in him, trusting him, which frequently served him well as a cop. If he had paid more attention to wardrobe and grooming, he would have been charismatic; as it was, he often passed for ordinary. His hat said it all: It was inexpensive, nondescript; under it, he had thinning brown hair that cried out to be styled but never would be. He was the kind of cop who always carried a backup piece.

The cruising car passed a seedy little bar called the Down-and-Dirty. A young Haitian man with bulging, wild eyes leaned in its doorway, surveying the night street.

"Bert Bombier," the driver remarked with a soft grunt. "Three times the son of a bitch has been in a lineup in front of his rape-robbery vics, and three times he's walked."

"Sure," said Kiley. "The women take one look at those voodoo eyes glaring out at them, and they lose their memories. Never mind what he *did* to them. Nobody wants to finger a fucking psycho and have him get out in five years and go on the prowl for them."

"I'd like to catch him in the act sometime and have him make a run for it," the driver yearned. "I'd put one low in his spine, just far enough down to cripple him."

The driver was Nicholas Dominic Bianco, twelve years on the force, a swarthy, sensuously handsome Italian-American, also third-generation, whose hat was a Burberry snap-brim that covered a head of lustrous, healthy black hair. He too was the kind of cop who carried a backup pistol.

"Listen," Bianco said, abruptly changing the conversation from police to personal, "you're still on for Saturday night, aren't you?"

"Sure, I'm still on. I've never passed up Stella's manicotti yet, have I?"

*In the alley, the young woman's nose was bloody; mascara-darkened tears streaked her cheeks, giving her the look of some painted primitive. She continued to plead to the background of faint go-go music.*

*"Please, stop—I'm sorry—please, no more—"*

*"No more?" the harsh voice said indignantly. "I haven't even started on you yet, you tramp!"*

*The hand began slapping her face back and forth: sharp, cracking blows, like the sound of slow applause.*

It was Kiley who watched the streets more closely as they patrolled, Kiley who scrutinized people, cars, doorways, shadows, looking for something wrong, something out of place, something presently or potentially *bad*. Kiley was like a doctor checking a patient's bloodstream; to him the streets were the bloodstream of the city, and he was supposed to recognize the germs in that bloodstream. Not that Bianco was a flake; Bianco was a good cop too. But Bianco had a house in the suburbs, a wife, two little girls. What Kiley had, mainly, was his job.

Crossing the street in front of them at the next corner was a shapely black woman in a tight dress, with highly glossed, thick, prominent lips.

"When did Power Lips start working west of Damen?" Kiley asked.

"Who the fuck knows?" Bianco said, shrugging. "Hey, know what Alvin told me about her?"

"Alvin who?"

"Alvin Washington, the spade that partners with Charley Norris. He said that Power Lips practices her technique by sucking marbles through a piece of garden hose. He knows the pimp she hustles for, and the pimp told him."

Kiley shook his head in mild disgust. "You've got a dirty mind, you know that? And just when were you talking to Alvin Washington?" There was a barely perceptible edge to the latter question.

"I wasn't exactly talking to him," Bianco explained. "I was with some other guys in the locker room who were *listening* to him."

Kiley watched Power Lips strut her stuff down the street. She had a fine, dark body, but Joe Kiley did not particularly like blacks in any form. There were too many of them in the department these days, thanks to the god-damned mayor's insatiable hunger for federal funds, and Kiley had lost out on a couple of promotions to them. Most of the white cops he knew felt the same way, that it was reverse discrimination. Bianco was a little more liberal, a little more tolerant.

"Better stay away from Alvin Washington unless you want to get a bad rep," Kiley reminded him quietly. He held one wrist close to the dash-board light to look at his watch. "Let's go for some coffee."

*In the alley, the young woman no longer begged for mercy. She was being beaten by two hands now. Closed into fists, they punched out of the shadows, delivering blows to her eyes, nose, cheeks, ears. Finally, in the wake of a sadistic chuckle, the fists be-gan beating the young woman's full, bare breasts, methodically drubbing them like a boxer working on a speed bag. The chuckle became a laugh as the attacker's en-joyment increased.*

*After a while, the young woman's head fell limply to one side, but the fists went right on pounding her breasts.*

# TWO

**B**ianco pulled into a NO PARKING ANYTIME space in front of the Midwest Hotel and Athletic Club, and the two detectives went into the corner drugstore of the building and sat at the lunch counter. Bianco carried their portable police radio and set it on the floor between his feet. They were General Assignments detectives, working out of the Warren Boulevard station; they patrolled rotating selected segments of the precinct, just as uniformed officers did in marked cars. Their job was to respond to felony calls so that the uniforms could stay on regular patrol.

At the lunch counter, over coffee, Bianco swiveled his stool around to check out, for about the sixth or seventh time since their shift had begun at four that afternoon, Kiley's new suit. "I can't believe you bought another gray suit," Nick said in mild exasperation. "Your other two suits are gray."

"Gray doesn't show the dirt," Kiley replied. "My mother taught me that when I was a kid."

"Where'd you buy it at?" Bianco asked. "I'll bet in one of those warehouse stores where everything's hung on metal pipes, right?" Bianco himself was wearing a snappy double-breasted number, navy blue, with a fine pinstripe, European cut. "How long I been asking you to come down to Maxwell Street with me to get your suits?" he asked. "Look at this one I'm wearing: It's a Valentino, retails for eight-fifty. I got it for two."

Kiley nodded knowingly. "One of these days," he warned, "you're going to get caught buying hijacked suits and it's going to be good-bye badge."

Bianco shrugged. "I'll be the best-dressed cop they ever fired. Anyhow, look who's talking. Where'd you get that set of silverware for your sister's wedding present six years ago? Maxwell Street, that's where. And what was it? Hot, that's what."

"That was different," Kiley rebutted. "That wasn't for myself, it was a gift."

"Oh, I see," his partner derided. "Well, just think of my suits as gifts too: from me to me." He took a sip of coffee, then added, "Wait'll I tell

5

Stella you bought another gray suit, she won't believe it. Wear it Saturday night so she'll know I'm not putting her on. Only do me a favor, get a nice red tie to dress it up, will you?"

Kiley's eyes narrowed suspiciously. "Who else did Stella invite to dinner?"

Bianco looked away. "I don't know. Stella takes care of all that stuff."

"Who else?" Kiley pressed.

"Hey, I said I don't know."

"Forget it then," Kiley said. "I'm not coming."

"All right, look," Bianco admitted, "it's a gal named Arlene. She's a fire-man's widow, goes to our church."

"Christ," Kiley said irritably. "I can't believe this, Nick."

"Listen, this one is primo, buddy," his partner promised. "Brunette, nice bod, no kids—*and* a city pension."

"Stella's got to cut it out," Kiley complained. "I'm serious, Nick. This shit has got to stop."

"She's just trying to find you somebody nice to socialize with."

"Somebody nice to marry and settle down with, you mean. Tell her I'm not coming."

"For Christ's sake, Joe, what the fuck's your problem anyway? What, are you gonna live alone in that ratty little apartment of yours until you die?"

"*Ratty* little apartment?" Kiley snorted. "It's good enough for you to use as a home address so you can live in the suburbs and be on the city pay-roll. What you seem to forget, Nick, is that I—"

Kiley's words were halted in mid-sentence by a beep from the radio at Bianco's feet. Bianco picked it up and put it to his ear. After listening in-tently for ten seconds, he pressed a button and said, "Ten-four, dispatch., Tac Eight will respond." To Kiley he said, "We got a situation with a dead woman in the alley behind the 4-Star Lounge."

They each put a dollar on the counter, left the rest of their coffee, and hurried out to the unmarked car.

At the rear of the 4-Star, several shadowy figures were standing around something still and white on the ground when Kiley and Bianco got out of their car, folding badge cases over the breast pocket of their coats so that their badges showed outside. As they walked toward the body, a large rat scurried out of a garbage can and disappeared. Bianco went directly to the spectators and began corralling them. "Okay, everybody move back a lit-tle, right over this way, come on, let's go—"

Kiley knelt next to the woman, shining a flashlight on her. Under an open robe she was wearing some kind of Frederick's of Hollywood getup. Red hair spread out from her head, and she had freckles on her forehead, probably on the rest of her face too, and her breasts, but he couldn't tell because the former was close to being pulp, and the latter were covered with blood so completely they might have been spray painted. Trying her wrists first for a pulse, Kiley found none, so he put two fingers in the slick blood on her neck but didn't find life there either. As long as his fingers were already bloody, he gently turned her face by its chin for a better look at what had been done to her. When he moved her head, the flesh on her face shifted like gelatin that hadn't set. Laying the flashlight down, he used his clean hand to feel in her two robe pockets but found nothing, not even Kleenex. He retrieved the flashlight and played its beam slowly along her body all the way to the feet. She had a gold ankle bracelet on one leg, two hearts engraved on it but no names, no initials.

Kiley rose, put the flashlight in his coat pocket, and cleaned the blood from his fingers with a handkerchief, which he carefully folded, blood inside, and also put in his coat pocket so the crime scene techs wouldn't find it and think it was evidence. Stepping over to Bianco, he handed him the flashlight and said, "Okay." Nick went to kneel beside the dead woman to make his own observations.

"Who found the body?" Kiley asked the five men that Bianco had herded back under the single bulb above the club's rear entrance.

"Th-that was me," said a short man wearing bib overalls and a sweatshirt. "I c-come out the back door to t'row out the t-trash an' there she was—"

"You the one called us?"

"No, that was me," another man said. He was bigger, with a belly that pulled at the buttons of a plum-colored silk shirt.

"What's your name?"

"Max Getman. I'm part-owner of the 4-Star. Wally here," he gestured toward the shorter man in bib overalls, "is my janitor. That there girl on the ground is one of our dancers—"

"*Was* one of our dancers," a black man next to Getman corrected. He too wore a silk shirt, with pearl buttons.

"I'll get to you in a minute," Kiley told him evenly, pointing his ballpoint at him. It was another way of saying shut up, and both Kiley and the black man knew it. "Go on," Kiley told Getman.

"That's all, I guess," the club owner said. "Wally found her and come right away to tell me. I come out and took a look-see, then went back in my office and called the station."

Kiley nodded and turned to the black man who had spoken out of turn. "All right, who are you?"

"Ed Laver," the man replied coldly, obviously miffed by Joe's blunt rebuff. "I work for Max. Club manager."

"What do you know about this situation?"

Laver shook his head. "Just what Max and the janitor said."

The other two men didn't know anything either; they were both customers, both black, who had been in the men's room and became curious when they happened to see the activity in the alley.

"Okay, I'd like all of you to stay right where you are for a minute while I get my partner," Kiley told them. "Then we'll speak to you individually and let you go. Don't walk around the area, and don't leave."

Kiley went over to the car where Bianco was now sitting with one leg in, one leg out, using the radio. "—morgue wagon, deputy coroner, homicide team, and two squad cars to block the ends of the alley." After his request was confirmed, Nick added, "Nell, call Stella for me, will you? Tell her I might be a couple hours late."

Bianco stood up out of the car and Kiley asked, "What'd you get from those guys?"

Nick, who had out a spiral notebook of his own, shined the flashlight on it and said, "The vic's name is Ronnie Lynn, dancer inside, hasn't been there long, was working eight-to-two tonight. The three guys connected to the club don't know what she was doing out in the alley." Nick leaned closer to Kiley. "What the fuck's a white girl want to take off her clothes and dance in front of a bunch of spades for?"

"How the fuck should I know?" Kiley said almost curtly. He was still irritated about the Saturday night dinner setup. "Come on, let's get some of this situation worked up before the Shop boys get here." The "Shop" was Chicago Police Department headquarters at 11th and State streets; it was from there that the team of Homicide detectives would be dispatched, along with evidence technicians and others needed to process the crime scene. Kiley, Bianco, and other General Assignments detectives in the precincts had little use for the "Shop cops" from Homicide, Robbery, Burglary, Auto Theft, Bomb and Arson, Organized Crime, Gang Intelligence, and the other titled commands, members of which were the cops who always seemed to get their names in the newspapers—and snared the attendant promotions and commendations—while, as everyone above the level of Mongoloid idiot knew, it was the GA cops who did most of the real work in the city, the scut work, the grunt stuff that kept the streets from turning *completely* into a swamp. The only time a GA cop admitted to any possible worth of a Shop cop was when the GA cop got promoted to a command—something to which they all, or *most* all, aspired. Prior to promotion, however, GA cops did nothing but denigrate Shop cops.

As Kiley and Bianco went back toward the men waiting at the club's back door, the detectives saw there were only four there now instead of five. "Didn't you tell them to stay put?" Nick asked.

"I told them," Kiley said tightly. Glancing at his spiral notebook, he walked up to Max Getman, the club owner. "Where's the other guy, the guy named Laver?"

"I sent him inside to do something for me," Getman replied blandly, looking away with an attitude of "so what?"

Kiley and Bianco exchanged glances. "Step over to the car with me," Nick said to Max Getman. "You other three," he told Wally the janitor and the two customers, "stay right here." As Nick led Getman to the car, Kiley went in the back door of the club to find Laver.

At the car, Nick said, "My partner told all of you to stay put. Why'd you send that guy inside?"

Getman gave Bianco a dubious look. "What'd you say your name was?"

"Detective Bianco. B-i-a-n-c-o—"

"Well, look Bianco, you ain't dealing with a street punk here, okay. I mean, I know my rights, okay. Now maybe I sent my manager in to check if everything's all right in the club, okay. If that's something you and your partner are gonna start harassing me about, maybe I should be calling my lawyer."

Nick smiled a perfect, glowing smile that he had been using to charm, and disarm, people since he was fourteen. "No need to call your lawyer, sir," he said smoothly. "It was certainly not our intent to harass you, and I'm very sorry if we gave you that impression." He put a forefinger on his temple, the way he'd seen Peter Falk do as *Columbo*. "Excuse me, what was your name again, sir?"

"Max Getman. G-e-t-m-a-n. I'm part owner of the club there."

"Well, Mr. Getman, sir, I'm sorry if my partner or I created any misunderstanding. We'd very much like your cooperation in this matter."

"I never mind cooperating with the police," Getman declared self-righteously, "as long as I get treated with respect, okay. I ain't no street punk and I don't want to be treated like one, okay."

"I understand, sir." Bianco poised to write in his notebook. "Could you tell me how long Miss Lynn had been a dancer in your club?"

• • •

Inside the rear section of the 4-Star, it only took Joe Kiley a minute to find an open door into a small office, where Ed Laver was sitting at a desk with a phone to one ear, dialing a number he has reading from a Rolodex in front of his. Joe moved quickly through the door and up to the desk. "Who you calling, Laver?"

The club manager immediately put the receiver down and reached to close the Rolodex, but Kiley was too quick for him. The detective put a finger in the way to keep the file open.

"Hey, man, what the hell is this?" Laver snapped.

"That's what I'd like to know, *man*," Kiley mocked. He snatched the top card from the Rolodex and read the name aloud. "Phil Touhy." His eyebrows shot up. "Is this the same Phil Touhy who runs all the rackets on the North Side?"

"What if it is?" Laver replied smugly.

"Why are you in such a big hurry to call him?" Kiley asked, his icy light blue eyes locking onto Laver's brown ones. "He have something to do with that dead woman out there?"

"Mr. Touhy is part owner of the club," Laver said. "Max thought he ought to know about what happened tonight."

"What did happen tonight?"

"About Wally the janitor finding one of the dancers dead in the alley."

Kiley's lips pursed in thought for a moment as his eyes stayed riveted on Ed Laver. He noticed the black man had begun to sweat across his upper lip, which was a good sign to Kiley; he liked it when people he was intimidating began to sweat. Tossing the Rolodex card onto the desk, Kiley said, "You can call Touhy later. Right now, I want you to show me where the dead woman kept her personal belongings. She have a locker or something?"

"There's a dressing room that all the dancers share."

"Let's take a look." As Laver was coming around the desk, Kiley asked, "What was her name again?"

"Ronnie Lynn."

"Ronnie short for Veronica?"

"How the fuck should I know, man?" Laver said. There was no rancor in his voice, just the implication that it was a fact simply not worth knowing. Kiley's eyes hardened on Laver as the black man led him out of the office.

Kiley followed Laver past a curtain opening to the stage out front. Go-go music was playing over speakers somewhere out there, and because the curtain was partly open, Kiley could see a young white girl, who looked no more than sixteen, gyrating to the beat of the music, topless, her halter lying on the side of the stage floor, her thumb hooked enticingly in the Velcro breakaway at each side of her abbreviated bottom.

Laver opened a door without knocking and led Kiley into a dingy little dressing room. Two young women, one black, one Asian, were sitting at small tables with mirrors hung behind them, makeshift vanities, both women with sad expressions, one with tears in her eyes. The black woman wore a robe, similar to the one the dead woman had on; the Asian sat topless, a towel draped around her shoulders not quite reaching her small, dark-nippled breasts. Both were smoking. They looked apprehensively at Laver and Kiley as the two men came in. Glancing around, Kiley saw a variety of clothing, some for dancing, some for street wear, hanging from hooks on the walls. A disarray of makeup was spread on the tables, along with cigarettes, ashtrays, junk food, carryout cups; from one table, popcorn had spilled from a package onto the floor, been stepped on, and left there.

"Okay," Kiley said to Laver, "you can go make your call while I talk to these ladies." Laver frowned and gave the suggestion of hesitating. "Go on," Kiley told him evenly. "Then wait back outside like I told you to do in the first place." His words were clearly an order, to which Laver responded with a hard, mean look, then nevertheless obeyed.

Kiley closed the door behind him and went over to the women. "Sorry to bother you right now, ladies, but I need to find out a few things about Ronnie—"

When Joe Kiley stepped out the rear door thirty minutes later, he saw squad cars with red lights flashing blocking each end of the alley, a police photographer shooting pictures with a detachable strobe he kept holding at different angles, and a deputy coroner just getting out of one of the plain panel trucks that served as hearses for the county morgue. But no homicide investigators yet, the lazy pricks, Kiley thought; the longer it took them to get there, the more work they knew he and Bianco would have done for them. Kiley saw that Laver, the club manager, was now where he should be, with the other witnesses, which was lucky for Laver, the way Kiley was beginning to feel about him. Kiley went over to the unmarked car where Nick was still questioning Max Getman. Nick raised his eyebrows inquiringly as Joe approached. Joe bobbed his chin at Getman.

"He sent his boy inside to make a phone call to his partner in the club. Phil Touhy."

"Phil Touhy, the boss of the North Side?" Nick asked in surprise.

"That's the one."

Bianco smiled at Getman. "You didn't mention that Phil Touhy was your partner. Or that you sent your boy in to call him."

"Why should I?" Getman said with an elaborate shrug. "It's none of your business, and it's got nothing to do with the dead broad."

Turning back to his partner, Nick said with mock gravity, "Mr. Getman is not a street punk, Joe."

"He's not?"

"No, he's not. Also, Mr. Getman knows his rights, Joe."

"He does?'

"Yes, he does. And guess what else?"

"I can't imagine."

"Mr. Getman has a lawyer he can call if we harass him."

"No shit!" Joe feigned utter surprise.

Max Getman gave both of them scathing looks and said, "Oh, no. No, no. I don't have to take this shit from no fucking cops." He stalked away as fast as a man with a big belly can stalk. His boy, Ed Laver, broke ranks and followed him inside.

"You hurt his feelings," Kiley told Nick.

"I'd like to hurt his fat balls, if he's got any," Nick said abrasively. "Somebody kills one of his dancers, beats the poor fucking broad to death, looks like, and all this son of a bitch is concerned about is whether he gets treated politely. Fuck him. What'd you find out inside?"

"I'm not sure," Kiley said, putting a hand on his partner's shoulder and guiding him toward the back of the car, farther away from everyone now at the scene. Out of hearing, lowering his voice anyway, Joe said, "One of the other dancers inside, Asian girl named Amy, told me that about an hour before Wally the janitor came out with the trash and found her body, the vic got a call on the pay phone backstage. Wally answered it and knocked on the dressing room door to call her to the phone. She came out, talked a couple minutes to whoever had called, then went back in the dressing room and told this Amy that it was a boyfriend she'd just broken up with, he was going to meet her in the alley out here in half an hour. She told Amy that he wanted back an expensive ring he gave her, and she'd agreed to give it to him in exchange for some Polaroids they took with an automatic camera of themselves fucking and sucking. The vic got Amy to dance part of her gig for her, and in half an hour came out here to the alley. Another half an hour and Wally found her dead."

"We know who the boyfriend is?" Bianco asked.

"Only his first name. Tony."

Joe fell silent and watched Nick's face. The brilliant Italian smile was gone now, Nick's handsomely sculpted features absorbed with concentration. When Nick's mind was riveted in thought like that, it reminded Joe of a face on a coin or on one of the big statues at the Art Institute. Joe unwrapped a stick of Dentyne and put it in his mouth. He had barely chewed a little flavor out of it when Nick's face lighted up.

"Jesus Christ. Phil Touhy's got a kid brother named Tony. Punk in his late twenties about. Been in traffic court half a dozen times for speeding around in sports cars. You think it could've been him?"

"Could be. Let's see if there's a link." Kiley walked to the front of the car. "Hey, Wally! Come over here a minute, will you?"

The little janitor in the bib overalls and sweatshirt hurried over and Kiley led him back to where Bianco stood. Wally was a short, stocky man, at least forty, with an expression that advertised the dullness of his mind, the fact that he swept floors and emptied garbage not because he was stupid, but because his mind was simply slower than most.

"Wally," Kiley said gently, "when I interviewed the ladies inside, the other dancers, they all said that you were a real good guy; that you went and got sandwiches and coffee for them all the time, and that you always knocked on the dressing room door and never just barged in like Ed Laver does. I thought you'd like to know how much they like you."

Wally smiled slightly. "That's nice. I try to treat everybody good, you know. Sure am sorry about Ronnie," he said, looking sadly over at the body. "She hadn't been around long but she was a nice lady."

"Wally, when you answered the phone earlier and it was for Ronnie, did the caller say who it was?"

Wally nodded slowly and sniffed. "Yeah. Said tell her it's Tony."

"After my partner and I got here, when you were standing over there with Getman and Laver, did you happen to mention the call to them?"

"Yeah. I said to Mr. Getman, jeez, I couldn't believe Ronnie was really dead, 'cause I'd just talked to her a little while ago to tell her that her boyfriend Tony was on the phone."

Kiley and Bianco exchanged quick glances , as if communicating by look. Then Kiley patted Wally on the back and said, "Thanks for talking to us, Wally. There'll be some other policemen here later and they'll want to ask you about finding the body. Just tell them exactly what happened. You can go back and wait with the others for now."

Nodding, Wally shuffled away.

"What do you think?" asked Bianco.

"I think," Kiley said, "that when Wally mentioned the call from Tony, Max Getman sent his boy Laver in to call Phil Touhy to tell him his kid brother might be involved in a homicide."

"That part of it makes sense," Bianco said. "But why would the guy say who was calling? That's like announcing himself as a suspect."

"Maybe he didn't plan to do it; maybe it was an impulse thing: she wouldn't give him the ring, they got into an argument about something."

Nick looked around, on the alert for anyone who could overhear them. "The Shop boys aren't going to be able to put a last name to Tony, are they?"

Kiley shook his head. "Not unless Getman or Laver volunteer that Phil Touhy is a partner in the club—"

"Which they probably won't do—"

"Especially if the Tony that called *is* the kid brother."

Nick reached into Joe's shirt pocket and took a stick of Dentyne for himself. "So, next question is—"

"Do we give it to the Shop cops—"

"Or keep it for ourselves?" Bianco began chewing the gum furiously. "We don't have enough for a collar, right?"

"Right. All circumstantial. We need something physical."

They stared at each other for a moment; then, as if rehearsed, both turned at the same time to look at the deputy coroner, who was on one knee making a preliminary examination of the body before it was taken away. Without a word, the two detectives walked over and stood next to him.

"Hi, Doc," said Nick. The deputy coroner glanced up at them.

"Messy one, huh, Doc," said Kiley

"Somebody was pissed off at her, that's for sure," said the deputy coroner. He was an angular, balding man, with a toothpick between his lips. Kiley and Bianco knelt with him.

"Was something used on her, Doc?" asked Bianco.

"Can't tell for sure until we strip the skin off her face and check the bones."

"Could you just give her a feel, Doc?" Kiley asked. "Off the record?"

The deputy coroner threw him a sour look. "You'll have an official report in forty-eight hours."

"We could have this perp in custody by then, Doc. Come on, give us a jump start."

The deputy coroner sighed heavily and nodded toward the morgue truck. "There's a container of wet wipes on the seat. Get it for me."

Bianco hurriedly fetched a blue plastic container and stood holding it while the deputy coroner gently, carefully, put all eight fingers and both thumbs into the pulp that had once been Ronnie Lynn's face. Closing his eyes, he moved his hands about as delicately as if there might still be life left there to feel pain; lightly as a musician playing the softest of sounds. "No blunt weapon," he said quietly after a moment, almost as if talking to himself. Kiley and Bianco were mesmerized by him. "Knuckle impressions, very definitely." Then: "Not much bone trauma. Not brass knuckles; bare knuckles."

While the detectives were staring in awe, the deputy coroner finished and withdrew his fingers. He held them in place so that any blood or tissue matter would drip and fall back where it had come from. "Well?" he finally had to say to Bianco.

"Oh, sure, Doc, sorry," Bianco came awake and began handing him wet wipes to clean his hands.

When the deputy coroner finished, he handed Kiley a wad of bloody wipes, moved the toothpick to the other side of his mouth, and belched loudly. "I had a pastrami sandwich a couple hours ago that my digestive system is definitely not pleased with."

"Doc, whoever did this: bruised knuckles?" asked Kiley.

"Oh, yes."

"How about with gloves on?"

"What kind of gloves?"

"Driving gloves. Like you see on guys that drive sports cars."

"Not as severe, but definitely there. All eight fist knuckles. Matter of fact, if the attacker worked on the face and head first, it would have been painful as hell to punch those tits after." The deputy coroner rubbed his stomach, said, "Christ, I've got to get an Alka-Seltzer," and walked away with his container of wet wipes.

Kiley and Bianco moved around the perimeter of the crime scene, expressions somber. "So what do you think?" Bianco finally asked.

"Could work for us."

"We'd have to level with Parmetter after," said Nick. Parmetter, first name Dan, was commander of the GA cops.

"If it worked, he'd cover for us. It's not like it's an original idea. GA teams do it all over the city to raise precinct rates for collars."

"Yeah, they do it," Nick qualified, "but not on homicides much. Homicides can get sticky. Wonder who the Shop cops will be?"

"You'll know in a minute," Kiley said, bobbing his chin at a pair of headlights that had been let through the police line at the mouth of the alley. It was an unmarked car similar to theirs except newer. When it parked, they both squinted to see who got out. Presently a fireplug-shaped white cop who carried himself like a wrestler came out of the shadows, followed by a black officer who wore a turtleneck under his suit coat.

"Dietrick and Meadows," Kiley said scornfully.

"A dickhead and a spade," said Nick. "Wonderful." He looked soberly at his partner. "We go for it ourselves?"

"We go for it ourselves," Kiley confirmed.

Fireplug came up and said without preliminary greeting, "What have we got on this situation here?"

"Vic was a go-go dancer at the 4-Star named Ronnie Lynn," Kiley told him. "Doc says she was probably beaten to death. Little guy over there in the bib overalls, name's Wally something, is the janitor at the club and found her when he came out to empty the trash. Club owner's name is Getman—"

"Doesn't like cops *or* questions," Nick interjected. "You'll love him."

"—and the manager's name is Ed Laver; he's a black dude," Kiley's eyes flicked to Turtleneck, "who'll try to scare you to death with nasty looks."

"What have we got on the vic?" Turtleneck asked. Bianco took over.

"According to Getman, she's worked for him about a month. He thinks she's from somewhere downstate, or maybe Indiana, he's not sure. The dancers get paid cash by the shift; the joint doesn't really ask many questions."

Kiley cut back in. "According to one of the other dancers, an Asian named Amy, the vic had a boyfriend named Tony something who called her on the backstage phone earlier this evening. She was supposed to meet him someplace later tonight or something; it wasn't too clear."

"That it?' Fireplug asked when Joe stopped talking.

"That's it," Kiley said. Both he and Nick nodded.

"Okay, Meadows and me'll take it from here," Fireplug said. "Get a copy of the IR to us sometime tomorrow, okay?"

"Right," said Bianco. The IR was the Incident Report.

Kiley and Bianco went back to their car as the Shop cops began their official homicide investigation.

"What now?" Nick asked as they were let out of one blocked end of the alley.

"Now we try to get a line on Tony Touhy, find out where he is," said Kiley. "See if he's got bruised knuckles. If he has, his ass is ours, partner."

# THREE

K iley and Bianco came into the precinct just after noon the next day, almost four hours before their shift started. Eyebrows were raised. Cracks were made.

"Joey and Nicky are trying for brownie points again."

"Oh, lieutenant, dear, we have visitors from another shift."

"You mean another planet."

"Is there an exam for sergeant coming up?"

"Yeah, but whites are excluded."

"Hey, fuck you, honky!"

Kiley ignored them. Bianco shook his head and said, "Look at them. One step up from crossing guards."

The two partners went into a computer alcove and sat down at adjacent terminals in the farthest corner so that no one could walk by and see what they were displaying. In tandem, they accessed felony records and entered the name Tony Touhy. Momentarily the screen displayed:

Touhy, Anthony Francis
aka: Tony Touhy, Frankie Touhy

ACCESS RESTRICTED
ORGANIZED CRIME BUREAU ONLY

"What the hell's it got an OCB lock on it for?" Nick asked indignantly. "This punk has never been anybody."

"Every relative Phil Touhy's got probably has an OCB file," Kiley said. "Let's run misdemeanors."

This time the screen displayed:

Touhy, Anthony Francis
Drivers License T3068763

6-17-93 TC 109 FTS BF $250
4-10-93 TC 109 FTS BF $200
9-21-92 TC 109 FTS BF $150
4-19-92 TC 109 FTS BF $100
1-11-92 TC 109 FTS BF $100

"All traffic code violations for excessive speed, all failures to show in court, all bail forfeits," Nick translated aloud.

"And no license revocation," Kiley noted. "Must be nice to have a big brother who owns judges. Let's run the DL."

They accessed motor vehicle records and entered Tony Touhy's drivers license number. The screen displayed:

Touhy, Anthony Francis
DL T3068763

ACCESS RESTRICTED
ORGANIZED CRIME BUREAU ONLY

"I don't believe this," Nick said. "His fucking *driver's license* is classified?"

Frowning, Kiley accessed the Chicago metropolitan alphabetical telephone listings. He got:

Touhy, Anthony F.
Non-published

"Call Glenda at the phone company and get his number and address," Kiley said. Nick went over to the nearest telephone. While he was gone, Kiley accessed, in turn, municipal business license records, Cook County business license records, pending criminal actions, pending civil actions, Illinois state parole and probation records, real estate ownership records, and credit bureau records. Each response on the screen was:

Touhy, Anthony Francis
No Record

Sitting back, Kiley tried to think of another record sector to search. Juvenile criminal records was out, he knew; in Illinois, such records were automatically computer purged on the eighteenth birthday of the offender. Before Kiley could think of anything else, Bianco returned with a disgusted look on his face.

"Glenda says his listing is in what they call a Class X file. All those records are kept by a phone company officer in a locked cabinet. It's where they keep the mayor's home phone number, stuff like that. No way Glenda can get to it."

"Big brother Phil is keeping a tight lid on young Anthony," Kiley said thoughtfully. "Wonder if it's because he's a weak link in the Touhy chain?"

"What I've heard," Nick said, "Phil Touhy doesn't *have* any weak links."

"Bullshit. Everybody's got a weak link. Listen, you go work up the IR on Ronnie Lynn; that'll give us an excuse to call the Shop cops and find out what they turned up last night. I'll keep playing with this."

While Nick went out to his desk to type up the IR, Kiley resumed random accessing of every data base he could think of. He tried voters registration, board of education records, communicable disease records, even the birth section of vital statistics in case Tony Touhy was listed as the father of a legitimate or illegitimate child. Everything came back NO RECORD. Accessing the data base first of the *Chicago Sun-Times*, then the *Chicago Tribune*, he tried to find any mention of Tony Touhy in either daily newspaper during the preceding five years. Again, nothing. He even tried accessing Illinois state income tax records; they were confidential, but three years earlier a GA cop named Glogowski had accidentally got into the data base. For nearly twenty minutes, before the system monitor caught him, he had pulled up and printed hard copies of tax returns from his friends, relatives, fellow cops, city aldermen, mayoral appointees, and everyone else he could think of except the suspect he was investigating, whom he completely forgot in the excitement of the moment. Since then, every cop who sat down at a terminal tried to access state income tax records, just in case. So Joe Kiley entered Tony Touhy's name twelve times, just in case. But each time he received an ACCESS DENIED response.

Giving up on the computer, Kiley went out to their desks where Nick was just finishing the IR. Kiley read and, as senior officer on the team, signed the report, kept one copy for themselves, put a copy in the fax pickup box to be sent downtown to Homicide, and tossed what was left into the records distribution pickup. It was two o'clock by then, so Kiley called Homicide and asked for Dietrick, but was told the Shop cop hadn't checked in for his shift yet.

"Can I get his home number? This is Kiley, GA at Warren Boulevard."

"I'll refer it to the lieutenant," the duty clerk said.

Ten minutes later, the Homicide day watch lieutenant called Kiley back and gave him Dietrick's unlisted home number. With Bianco listening on an extension, Kiley called the Homicide investigator.

"Hey, Dietrick, this is Kiley. I just wanted to let you know that the IR on the Lynn case is on its way to your desk. Did you turn anything new last night?"

"Naw, nothing, Kiley," the Shop cop replied. "Everybody at the club looks clean. We're trying to nail down this Tony whoever, her boyfriend, but nobody seems to know his last name."

"Could be he's a customer she got cozy with," Kiley suggested.

"Yeah, could be that. Meadows might hang out in the joint for a while tonight, see if he can make somebody."

"Bianco and I'll check with our regular snitches in that area," Kiley said. "If we turn anything, I'll give you a yell."

When Kiley and Bianco hung up, Joe said with a grunt, "Meadows *might* hang out in the joint tonight. My ass."

"All's they're gonna do is paperwork," Nick said knowingly. "They don't give a shit about some bimbo dead in an alley."

"Better for us. Now, how the hell do we make Tony Touhy? We don't have any contacts in OCB; *nobody* has contacts in OCB. They've got tighter assholes than IA has got. I wonder if any of Tony Touhy's traffic hits were taken near where he lives? And if the uniform who hit him would remember it?"

"Listen," Bianco said, "I might have a better way for us. Let's run down to the Shop. We got time."

"The Shop? What for?"

"I'll tell you on the way," Bianco said. "Come on."

On the drive down to 11th and State, Nick Bianco said, "Before I did the IR, I made a call to a contact I've got in Central Records. A supervisor I know there might be willing to take a quick peek at Tony Touhy's OCB file, just for an address."

"Who do you know in CR that I don't know?" Kiley asked curiously.

"Sergeant Mendez." Bianco threw his partner a quick glance. "Gloria Mendez."

Kiley frowned. *Gloria* Mendez. A Latino female sergeant—that his partner knew but he didn't? Eight years they had been working together, and this was the first Kiley had ever heard of Sergeant *Gloria* Mendez. "Would you mind sharing with me," Kiley said acidly, "just how you know this sergeant when I don't, and tell me why you think she might violate department regulations for us by giving us information from a restricted file?"

"Look, Joe, this is a little embarrassing," Bianco said. "I mean, you're like one of my own family, you know? You and Stella are close, you're godfather to my youngest daughter—"

"Skip the guinea family bullshit and get to it," Kiley said.

"Gloria Mendez and I had an affair once," Nick admitted.

"What, you mean before Stella?"

"No, Joe. After Stella."

Kiley stared incredulously at him. *After* Stella? How in hell could a guy with a wife like Stella Bianco fool around with another woman? Kiley couldn't imagine it. He kept staring at Bianco in disbelief.

"There, see?" Nick said, seizing on the look. "That's what I meant about you being like part of my family. That look is exactly how my sisters, uncles, and cousins would look at me"

Kiley shook his head. "I can't believe this," he voiced his thoughts. "You asshole."

Nick shrugged. "It was a long time ago, Joe. Gloria and I worked Humboldt precinct together when I was in uniform. She worked in the property room and I worked the lockup." Nick's voice became subdued, a little woeful. "It wasn't something I went out looking for, Joe; I wasn't on the prowl for pussy like a lot of married cops we both know. I was just young, the kids hadn't come yet, Stella was working days and I was working nights. Gloria and I kept running into each other; I mean, like everywhere: coffee room, hallway, parking lot, until it finally got to be kind of a joke between us, you know? And one time I said to her, 'You know, I think I see you almost as much as I see my wife.' And she looked me right in the eye and said, 'Want to try for more?' That was when we both realized that it wasn't a joke, that there was something real between us. It was very strong and very good. I might even have split up with Stella over it—but the thing I didn't know was that Stella was already pregnant with Jennifer. So that was that. Gloria had been married once and had a daughter, so she knew how bad it was to have a family break up. She would have tried to take me away from just Stella in a minute, but not from Stella and a baby. So we kind of pulled apart, you know, even though the feeling was still there between us. It didn't mean that I didn't love Stella; I did. I never stopped loving Stella. But I loved Gloria too, in a different way."

Nick took a handkerchief from his inside coat pocket to wipe his hands, which had begun to sweat on the steering wheel while he was telling his partner the story. Kiley continued to stare at him, thinking of Stella, of how he always resisted her efforts to fix him up with other women. And *why*. Because none of them were like her, like Stella.

"Are you still seeing this Gloria?" Kiley asked bluntly.

"No, Joe, I'm not. Not for a long time."

"What makes you think she'll check Tony Touhy's record for you?"

"I just think she will, that's all. You'll understand when you meet her. She'll help me because she's that kind of woman, Joe."

Chicago Police Headquarters, the "Shop" at 11th and State, was a worn-out, decrepit, dilapidated old excuse for a building, some sixty years old but looking a hundred. As Kiley and Bianco walked along one of its grimy halls, in yellowish light from long-faded fixtures, through an ongoing foreign smell that made an outsider's nose hairs bristle, Nick shook his head in amazement and said, "This is the end of the rainbow here. This is where we all want to get promoted to. I can't believe how fucking dumb we are."

"If we were smart," Kiley told him, "we'd be with the FBI."

A fearless roach, from one of the world's largest colonies housed in the old building, scurried across their path and disappeared under a floor molding. Through open doors, the detectives saw uniformed desk cops moving about: ass-heavy men and women who had spread out after they got their tedious, boring, dull, dreary, monotonous, *safe* jobs in the Shop. Everyone seemed to move with a listlessness, almost an indifference to their duties, as if none of it really mattered. There were probably more bellies hanging over belts, and more high-riding asses, per capita in the Shop than anywhere else in the world except Tahiti. Considering the decaying building, its vermin population, the huge percentage of unattractive employees, along with the steady traffic of hoodlums, punks, hookers, snitches and, worst of all, slick or sweaty shyster lawyers who had business on the premises, some considered the most fortunate person at 11th and State to be the old man who ran the concession stand in the lobby—who was blind.

When the two detectives entered the reception area of Central Records, they found themselves surrounded on three sides by a long counter against which policemen and others who worked in the Shop were requesting or perusing hard copies of records. Nick looked around until he saw a woman wave at him from the door of an office deep behind the counter. She pointed to a gate in the counter and nodded to a clerk to buzz them through.

Gloria Mendez, Kiley saw as they walked toward her, was a bosomy, light brown Puerto Rican woman with upswept raven hair, not a hint of make-up, and delicate, beautifully shaped ears. There was about her an immedi-ate allure as well as a suggestion of sharp, steel edge, the one to attract, the other to fend off if necessary. In her starched blue blouse with its gleam-ing badge and sergeant chevrons, she was every inch a female as well as a police officer. "Hi," Nick said, walking up to her.

"Hi."

Awkwardly they started to shake hands, hesitated as if feeling foolish, then finally did it, although tentatively.

"Hey, you look great," Nick told her.

"Yeah, you too." Smiling, Gloria removed her hand from Nick's and ex-tended it to Kiley. "You must be Joe. I'm Gloria."

"Pleased to meet you," said Kiley, suddenly feeling awkward himself as he took her hand. *Pleased to meet you*? His mother had taught him that when he was eight; he hadn't said it in two decades. Now all of a sudden he found himself feeling like a kid in the presence of this woman he had al-ready made his mind up to dislike.

"How's Meralda?" Nick asked. Gloria rolled her eyes.

"Sixteen, shapely, and smart-mouthed," she said. "If I survive the next couple of years, it'll be a miracle. Your girls?"

"Growing like weeds. Both daddy's girls until this one comes over," he nodded at Joe, "then they're Uncle Joey's girls. Fickle, both of them."

"A few more years and you'll know what I'm going through," Gloria said, nodding sagely. "Come on in." As she went around her desk, Nick started to close the door behind him and Kiley, but Gloria said, "Leave it open. Looks better." The detectives sat facing her and she leaned forward a little, keeping her voice low. "So you want to look at a restricted access file? I presume it's important or you wouldn't have asked."

"It's important," Nick confirmed.

"You know, Nick, that when I pull up a restricted access file, there's an automatic record made of my terminal number, the date and the time. Anybody accessing the file after that can trace my access back to me. Then I could have to justify it to my superiors. I can always say it was an acci-dental access, but if there's been some kind of heat related to the subject, I might not be believed. Then I could be up on charges, you know? And there goes my career."

"Maybe it wasn't a good idea to ask you," Nick said.

"Friends are for friends, Nick," she told him, "but I need to know what's going down before I get involved. For my own protection."

Bianco looked at Kiley, who shrugged and said, "That's fair. Tell her."

"You know Phil Touhy, the mob guy who runs most of the North Side? Well, we think we can make his kid brother Tony on a homicide," Nick said, his own voice also very quiet now. "We think he lost his head and beat a girl to death last night. But we need to eyeball him before his bruised knuckles heal, and we haven't been able to make him anywhere: no home address, no business, no hangouts, nothing. We don't need his whole record; just some starting point so we can track him down."

"Whether I give you one line or the whole record," Gloria said, "I still have to pull it up. What are your chances of making a case?"

Again Nick looked at Joe Kiley. "High," Joe said, "*if* he's got bruised knuckles. Zilch if he hasn't."

"If you bust him, there's bound to be some activity around his record," Gloria said. "What are the chances you can get me a back-dated request for the file from the assistant state's attorney who handles the charge?"

"Probably eighty percent," Joe said. "We know most of the prosecutors; they're pretty solid."

Gloria gave it a long moment of deep thought, slowly tapping one forefinger on a notepad in front of her. Just as her face was without makeup, so were her nails without polish, but they were long and attractive nevertheless, Kiley noticed. And those pretty ears. And her *mind*; that good, logical, *cop* thinking; it was seductive as hell, better than if she'd unbuttoned her blouse. Kiley began to understand the mixed feelings Nick had spoken of earlier.

"Okay," Gloria finally said. "One time and one time only—just for you, Nicky." She swiveled around to a terminal beside her desk, inserted a key into a lock in its base, and turned it on. "Master terminal," she told them. "Accesses anything. It's always locked when not in use, and I'm responsible for the key one shift a day." When the screen came up, she asked, "What's the full name?"

Nick gave it to her and she quickly keyed it in. Within seconds, lines of data began streaking across the screen like laser beams. Because Kiley and Bianco were sitting at a forty-five-degree angle to the monitor, they could not read what was being displayed. Kiley took out his notebook and pen, poised to write. Presently Gloria began to read aloud, quietly.

"Subject resides at 3333 Lake Shore Drive, apartment 2201. Registered owner of a 1993 Jaguar two-door, plate number CZ372Y, color teal blue. Last known place of employment: Shamrock Club, 630 W. Lawrence Avenue. Club known to be owned by subject's brother, Philip Algernon

Touhy. Club has a suspected illegal card room on the premises. Only felony record against subject is a charge of receiving stolen property in July 1988, description of stolen property shown as miscellaneous jewelry, charge later dropped. End of record." Gloria went off-line and the screen turned black. "That's it," she said, swiveling back toward them. They were being told the visit was over.

"Listen, thanks, Glor," said Nick as he and Kiley rose.

"Hope you make your case." She looked at Kiley. "Nice meeting you, Joe."

"Same here," Kiley replied. He meant it, and for the split instant that his and Gloria Mendez's eyes locked, they both knew it.

"See you around sometime, maybe," Nick said self-consciously.

"Sure, sometime. Maybe." She reached for some papers on her desk.

Kiley and Bianco left. In the elevator of the dismal old building, they did not speak or look at each other. Both were glad to be leaving the Shop: because of the way the place was, but also because of the woman, Gloria Mendez. She had made both of them feel somehow immature.

But they had their information on Tony Touhy—and that was what counted.

# FOUR

**B**ianco turned out of the rush-hour traffic, pulled into a public parking area adjacent to Lincoln Park, and cut the engine. He and Kiley sat silently checking out the high rise at 3333 Lake Shore Drive, just across the wide, divided boulevard from the park. It was an upscale area, near Belmont Harbor, across from the Chicago Yacht Club, overlooking Lake Michigan. Apartment 2201, the detectives guessed, had to be a front corner.

"Clear day, the punk can probably see into the next time zone," Bianco said. He glanced at his watch. Six o'clock. They had been on duty two hours and had left the precinct patrol, a gross violation of department regulations, to drive over and check out where Tony Touhy lived. What they found was not very promising.

"Secure lobby, doorman, gated underground parking," Kiley said. "All he has to do is say no to the doorman and we don't even get to the elevator without a warrant."

"How about we park near the underground garage entrance on the side there and watch for his Jag. Then block his way."

Joe shook his head. "Building like this has got to have some kind of roving security. Unless we happened to get him in the first hour or so, we'd get made for sure. Security cops would run our plate, a report would be filed with the building management, they'd complain to somebody downtown, and we'd be called in."

"We could probably cover the joint on Lawrence Avenue, that Shamrock Club, a lot easier," Nick suggested.

"Yeah, but that's a longer shot than this," Joe figured. "He can probably stay away from the Shamrock Club as long as he wants to, but this is where he sleeps. And he thinks this place is safe." Kiley looked around the public area where they were parked. There was a telephone booth on the street nearby. "Thing to do is cover *both* places—at the same time. Me here, you over at the Shamrock. For a full shift."

"Come on, Joe, we can't stay out of the precinct for a full shift, we'd get made for sure—"

"We do it on our day off, tomorrow. In our own cars. Keep in touch by phone every hour or so."

"I'm supposed to take Stella and the girls to a big flea market tomorrow, then to dinner and a movie—"

"Tell them you have to work, Nick. They know it happens."

"I hate to disappoint them," Bianco said with a pained look.

"Did we decide to do this or didn't we?" Kiley pressed.

"Yeah, we did," Nick shrugged.

"Listen, we make this punk on a homicide, it'll be a major collar. You'll get a promotion *and* a commendation."

"Me? What about you?"

"What about me?" Kiley asked shortly, on the edge of irritation. "You think I'll ever get a promotion, with my record? One more reprimand and I'll get a fucking *de*motion. I'm doing this for you, you retarded wop!"

"Well, I don't like it!" Nick snapped back. "I don't like you putting your job, which is all you've fucking *got*, on the line so I can maybe move up in the department. You should be looking out for yourself!"

"I *am*! I'm making an investment in you, stupid. The higher you go in the department, the more payback I'm gonna expect. When I get tired of the street, I'm gonna want a nice cushy job someplace, preferably in one of the better divisions and not in that rathole Shop downtown—*and* I'm gonna look to you to get it. Someday you'll be a lieutenant, maybe even a captain. I plan to be right there riding your coattail." Kiley's voice quieted. "You're gonna take care of me, right?"

Nick swallowed, feeling self-conscious now. "Yeah, sure. Right. It's different when you put it that way."

"Good," Joe ended the argument. "Now let's make some plans to nail this punk."

"Okay, okay. You want to do it tomorrow?"

"The sooner the better. The punk's knuckles won't stay bruised forever. Look, just tell Stella you've got to work for somebody that's sick. Come home after the flea market, then leave the house at the regular time and drive over to the Shamrock Club. Find a good place to stake it out; it's a busy street, you won't have any trouble. Meantime, I'll come down here and park close to that phone booth over there; you get close to an outside phone too, should be easy. I'll stake out the building garage; if the Jag comes out, I'll tail him. Wherever he goes, I'll call you from. If he shows up there, you call me. If we work both places from four to midnight to-morrow, we've probably got a good chance of nailing him. What do you think?"

"Yeah, that's a good plan," Nick said. Some interest came into his ex-pression now and he moved Stella and the girls to a lower rung in his mind. "Once we get him somewhere, what do we use for cause?" They were supposed to have probable cause, some legal reason other than mere speculation, for approaching Tony Touhy to look at his hands.

"If we can see his knuckles and they're bruised, we bust him on suspi-cion for the Lynn thing," Kiley said. "If his hands are covered, like if he's wearing those faggot racing gloves, we pull a simple identity check on him, ask to see his driver's license. Probably he can't get the license out of his wallet with gloves on, so he'll have to take one of them off. We'll find a way, don't worry. Have to, I'll drag the punk son of a bitch into an alley and do it by force."

"No, we're not going to let it come to that," Nick said firmly. "You've got enough shit on your record already. One more disciplinary hearing and you'll be back in uniform. Have to, *I'll* drag the punk son of a bitch into an alley and do it by force."

"Whatever you say, Macho Dago," Kiley told him with a grin. "So, we set?"

"We're set," Nick confirmed.

"Pull over to that phone booth," Kiley pointed, "and we'll get the number."

At four the following afternoon, Joe Kiley parked his own gray Buick close enough to hear the booth phone ring, and at the same time in position to keep under surveillance the gated side entrance to the underground garage in Tony Touhy's apartment building. Scotch-taped to Kiley's steering wheel was a slip of paper on which was printed the license number of Touhy's teal blue Jaguar: CZ372Y. On the seat next to him was a pair of 750-power binoculars. Joe took a moment to focus the binoculars on a street hydrant very close to the garage entrance. Just as he got the focus locked in, the phone rang in the booth. Kiley was out of the car, with the binoculars, answering it on the fourth ring.

"Yeah?"

"Joe, I'm out here," Nick said. "The joint's on the corner of an alley. It's got a parking area behind it, for about a dozen cars, but it's all marked private and no public parking all over the place. I'm across the street by a deli with a pay phone outside it. From here I can see the front entrance, the side entrance, and one end of the alley. But I can't see *down* the alley, and a car could get in and park behind the joint from the other end. What do you think?"

"You're covering three out of four," Kiley told him, "so stay there. Maybe about every hour take a quick walk down the alley to see what's parked in the back. Get license numbers; if the Jag doesn't show, we can at least find out who else has parking privileges. Hold on—" He raised the binoculars to look at a car exiting the garage, but it was a green Mercedes. "Okay, false alarm. What's the phone number where you're at?" Bianco gave it to him. "Okay, call me if he shows, or every hour otherwise. I'll only call you if I'm on him. Got it?"

"Got it, right."

"Stella and the girls pissed about dinner and the movie?"

"They've been happier."

"We collar this punk, we'll have a big party for your promotion; they'll be happy then."

"I still don't feel a hundred percent right about this, Joe. I mean, if this thing works for us, me probably getting most of the benefit from it."

"Will you drop it, please? After being down at the Shop yesterday, I wouldn't even *take* a promotion now. I've decided that all I want to do is continue serving the people of Chicago in the humblest position possible—"

"Oh, fuck you," said Nick, and hung up.

Grinning, Kiley went back to his Buick and settled in. On the floorboard in front of the passenger seat he had a small cooler containing a sliced beef sandwich wrapped in foil, a plastic cup of macaroni salad, and two cans of regular Coca-Cola, the kind that still had caffeine in it. Next to the cooler was a thermos of black coffee that would stay hot for six hours. Removing his hat, loosening his tie, adjusting the big revolver on his left hip, he removed his second, smaller gun, an automatic, from an inside-the-pants holster near his right kidney, and slipped it under the seat.

Cars arrived at and cars left the garage at 3333, and Kiley raised the binoculars to his eyes if one of them even remotely looked teal blue and had sleek, Jaguar-like lines. He had, he felt, a better chance of making Tony Touhy than Nick had. If Tony was a typical low-life hood—and Joe had no reason to think otherwise, the punk's big shot big brother notwithstanding—then he was almost certainly a night crawler, a frequenter of clubs, lounges, illegal gambling dens, fancy cathouses, sporting events, whatever was going on between sundown and sunup. The way Kiley figured it, Tony would probably get out of bed some time mid-afternoon and hit the street in his fancy car between six and seven. Joe had no idea where the punk would head: maybe someplace to eat, maybe to pick up his steady squeeze if he had one, maybe to check in with big brother Phil to see if there were any errands that didn't require a minimum of high school intelligence. It would be too much to hope that Tony would come tooling out of the garage in his Jag and go directly to the Shamrock. Turn into that alley right under Nick's fine Italian nose, with Joe right on his ass. Have Joe and Nick right there when he parked, have him get out of the Jag ungloved with eight big, blue, swollen fist knuckles. Hold it right there, punk, you are under fucking arrest. You have the right to remain *silencio*—

Yeah. Too much to ask. But even a GA cop could dream, couldn't he?

By seven o'clock, on Lawrence Avenue across from the Shamrock Club, Nick Bianco was leaning on a stand-up counter next to the window in the deli, sipping black coffee and toying with what was left of a small antipasto salad. It was all he planned to eat during his shift because there was left-over manicotti at home that Stella would heat up for him when he got there, which by his estimation would be quarter of one at the max. That would be if neither he nor Joe made Tony Touhy and decided at midnight to call it a shift. Of course, if they *did* make the punk, there would be some transportation and booking time involved, but even if they made him as late as eleven, Nick would still get home to the manicotti on time. There was always the chance that they'd make him *after* eleven, but Nick felt that was remote. Night crawlers were usually set down somewhere by then, in an illegal card game or crapshoot, still at the Stadium watching the fights or at some bar after a ball game at Comiskey Park, or in some cunt's silk-sheeted bed. Wherever they were by then, chances are they would be there until they packed in for the night and headed home—which would be after he and Joe called it a night.

Nick knew that Joe had taken the most likely make for himself, giving Nick the least likely of the two chances for an encounter. Joe frequently did that on whatever situation they worked: put Nick less in harm's way than he put himself. It was because of Stella and the girls, Nick knew: *his* family, but of which Joe Kiley felt such a close part. At first Nick resented it, feeling that he was a man and should carry his share of whatever risk the two of them faced. But when he braced Joe about it once, Joe reminded him that it was the senior detective's prerogative to call the shots in any situation. Joe explained that he put himself through doors first because he *liked* it that way, he liked being on the edge, challenging the situations, and it had nothing to do with Nick's wife Stella, whom Nick suspected Joe had a much deeper feeling for than either of them could ever discuss; or Nick's oldest daughter Jennifer, who was ten and always acted the little lady for her Uncle Joey; or his youngest, Teresa, seven, to whom Joe was godfather and who clung to him like a little primate every time he came over. It had nothing to do with any of them, Joe said; it was just *him*: He thrived on the risky moment, flourished on the peril of it all, got off on the uncertainty of living or dying on a given night.

Nick halfway believed Joe Kiley. Of course, he *wanted* to believe him; wanted to think that it had nothing to do with Joe trying to shield him from primary danger; that it was all Joe's character, his nature, his disposition toward jeopardy. Nick knew that over the years Joe had been taken to task on a number of occasions for his actions—or *reactions*—in field situations, the line of fire, judgment calls. He had two serious disciplinary actions in his folder, both of which had resulted from formal complaints and for which he had been given thirty-day suspensions without pay; and he had half a dozen or more reprimands which had come in the wake of informal complaints. Joe was right: He'd never get promoted. But Nick *could*. And when he did—Joe was right again—Nick would take Joe right along with him, to whatever good job he got.

Joe Kiley was Nick's partner and his friend, his best friend, actually his only *real* friend. Nick was glad he had finally leveled with Joe about Gloria Mendez. Keeping that from Joe had been a thorn in Nick's conscience for a long time. Now it was no longer a secret between them and Nick felt much better about it.

Finishing his coffee and what was left of the salad, Nick went back out and sat in the car again. It was beginning to get dark. He looked at his watch and decided that in fifteen minutes he would take a walk down the alley to see if any cars were behind the Shamrock yet; then he would call Joe at the other stakeout. In fifteen, maybe twenty minutes.

Right now, he wanted to think some more about seeing Gloria Mendez again yesterday. About how it had felt: so warm, so good. So very good.

The two detectives maintained their respective stakeouts for more than seven hours, without a make.

On West Lawrence Avenue, Bianco did not even *see* a Jaguar throughout the entire shift. Nine times he left his car and walked into the alley to check the parking area behind the Shamrock, but he had not seen a single car parked in any of the private spaces at any time. Each time that

Nick called to check in with Kiley, his voice carried more and more of the disappointment he was feeling. The shift, Nick finally decided, was a bust.

Over on Lake Shore Drive, Kiley was beginning to feel much the same way. Joe *had* seen Jags that evening, a number of them, mostly the common colors: black, white, red, a couple of beige ones. Three came out of or went into the building at 3333, and even though in the well-lighted garage entry, where the vehicles had to pause while the gate slid open, all of them were clearly of a different color than Kiley was looking for, he nevertheless focused his binoculars on the respective license plates just to be sure. But nothing.

Finally, at eleven-twenty, frustration set in completely and Bianco called Kiley, saying, "This neighborhood's practically shut down, Joe. Shamrock's only got a couple customers left. I think we struck out tonight."

"Looks like it," Kiley reluctantly agreed. "Okay, let's wrap it up. Come on over; I'll wait for you here."

Fifteen minutes later, Bianco pulled up and parked behind Kiley and got in the car with him. "What do you think?" he asked. "Just bad timing?"

"Maybe. Or maybe we're really on to something: Maybe he's purposely dropped out of sight because he's dirty and he knows there's an outside chance he can be connected. Maybe big brother Phil put him in hiding."

"If he's hiding out, we'll never make him before his knuckles heal. He's probably not even in the city."

"Maybe not," Kiley allowed. "Maybe we'll have to lean on Phil a little to find him."

"Whoa, now," Nick demurred at once. "Fucking with Tony is one thing, Joe; fucking with Phil is something else. People who fuck with Phil Touhy have been known to step in something very soft and very deep. Let's think that one over, partner."

"Yeah, you're right," said Joe. "Let's sleep on it. Go on home."

"I'm gonna call Stella and tell her I'm on my way," Nick said, getting out of the car. "She's got manicotti for me tonight. See, Joe, if you'd find yourself a good woman, you'd have somebody waiting at home for you with a nice meal ready. Come on out and meet this Arlene on Saturday night. What have you got to lose?"

"Goodnight, Nick."

"You're a fucking hardhead, you know that?"

"Close the car door," Kiley said. Nick slammed it.

"Asshole," he said, loud enough for Joe to hear him through the window. "I'm putting in for a new partner. I give up on you."

As Bianco walked toward the phone booth to call Stella, Kiley started his car, rolled down the window on his side, and smacked a kiss at Nick as he drove by. "Goodnight, sweetheart."

"Fuck you," he heard Nick say.

Kiley rolled the window back up, smiling.

Kiley was home twenty minutes later. He lived in an old apartment building on the near North Side, where he had been for ten years. It was an eight-flat building; he was on the bottom floor, rear, with a private entrance on the side. The landlady was a little Jewish widow named Mrs. Levine, who considered Joe Kiley her own private policeman. In the decade he had been her tenant, she had never raised his rent, and in return he was always on call to handle any complaint about other tenants who might have tried to take advantage of her; neighborhood kids who occasionally got out of hand; neighbors with unleashed dogs that came onto her property and defecated; and any number of minor problems which can seem major to a widow living alone. "That Joey Kiley, he's like a son to me," she periodically reminded people. Kiley indulged her and was really quite fond of Mrs. Levine. He took care of her little irritations as a matter of course, without rancor to the troublemaker; but if anyone had ever seriously harmed Mrs. Levine in any way, Kiley would have hospitalized them.

Entering his apartment, Joe stepped over the mail Mrs. Levine had slipped under his door, and turned on the light. Hanging his coat and hat on a chair back, he saw that the telephone answering machine at one end of his old couch was blinking on and off, but he ignored it as he slipped his belt off and removed the one holster he still wore; his backup piece he had forgotten and left under the front seat. Putting the gun on a table, he went past the blinking answering machine into a tiny kitchen. Probably Stella, he thought, wanting to scold him for saying he wasn't coming over to meet Arlene on Saturday night. She would rag on him about settling down, just like Nick was always doing, and in the end he'd probably go over Saturday night and both he and Arlene would feel awkward all evening because they both knew what was going down. At the end of the evening, Arlene would promise to have Joe over for dinner sometime but never would, and Joe would promise to give her a call for a date sometime but never would. After a while, Stella would start a new search while Joe fell back into his comfortable bachelor routine of take-out food, watching the fights and the ball games on television, and drinking at the neighborhood bar when he felt like it, usually ending up in bed with one of the half dozen women who were also regulars there. They all thought he was good-looking, and liked it because he was tough as well. Joe had been to bed with each of them at one time or another over the years, and while none of them were raving beauties, they were healthy, earthy, factory women who gave as good as they got between the sheets and avoided personal commitment as conscientiously as he did. Kiley felt he had a good life; Nick and Stella just refused to accept that fact. Joe kidded Stella a lot about her matchmaking. "Find me somebody like you," he challenged. He wasn't certain whether she thought he was serious or not. He was.

From the freezer he took an iced mug and filled it with non-fat milk. In one long swallow, he drank half of it down, feeling its icy stream soothe and coat all the way to the duodenal ulcer he had been living with for a dozen years. Going into his little bedroom, past the rumpled bed which only got made on Saturdays when he changed the sheets, he went on to the bathroom and from a bottle in the medicine cabinet shook out his bedtime Tagamet, which would guarantee that his ulcer would let him sleep the night.

Back out at the couch, he sat and used the remote to turn on the late news, at the same time running the answering machine tape back to listen to his message. He was sipping the icy milk again when Nick's urgent voice came on, speaking very fast.

"Joe, listen, I'm back over at the Shamrock, you won't believe this, while I was talking to Stella that fucking Jag came out of the garage! I followed it back over here, it's parked out back right now. The whole fucking parking area behind the joint is full—Caddy Sevilles, Lincoln Town Cars, a custom Corvette! Something big is going on here, Joe, and that punk Touhy is part of it. Get over here right away, we've got this fucking punk, Joey!"

For a split instant, Kiley stared straight ahead, as if not comprehending what he had heard. Then he thrust the mug aside, sloshing milk on the end table, and dashed over to where he had laid his gun. *Jesus!* his mind prodded like a branding iron touching him. Snatching up his coat and hat, carrying them with his gun, he rushed from the apartment.

As Nick had told him earlier, the 600-block of West Lawrence was almost completely closed down. The only light when Kiley arrived, other than the vaporous streetlights, came from the far end of the block where a package liquor store was still open. Even the Shamrock, which could have re-mained open until two a.m., appeared closed. Nick's car was parked in front of the deli across from the Shamrock, near the outside pay phone Nick had been using, but Nick himself was nowhere to be seen. There were no other cars parked nearby.

Joe got out of his car and stepped into the darkened doorway of a shoe store next to the deli. While his eyes scanned the quiet street, he worked his belt in and out of trouser loops until he got both holstered guns into place. Despite the cold milk and the ulcer pill, he could feel his gut beginning to constrict, stomach acid churning. *Jesus, the fucking street was dead—*

Going back to his car, Joe reached in and got a flashlight, then walked briskly across to the Shamrock Club. There were no visible lights inside except for the night-light above the mirror behind the bar. No sign of any movement at all. Kiley quietly tried the side door; locked, as he expected. He made his way to the front door, finding it locked also. Out on the side-walk, he stood with his back to the building and again let his eyes scout the dark street for some sign of Nick. There was no movement, no sound.

Hurrying quietly along to the alley, Kiley stepped inside and paused there, deep in shadows, listening intently. Nothing. Just the stink of near-by garbage. Resisting the temptation to turn on the flashlight, he began edging farther inside. Nick had said there was a parking area in the rear, big enough for a dozen cars. Maybe Nick was waiting back there, staking out Tony Touhy's Jaguar—

Moving across the alley from the side of the Shamrock, Kiley made his way to a point where he could see, by the streetlight that came barely that far into the alley, a break in the building where the Shamrock ended; there was an open area there, probably the parking spaces.

Cautiously, Joe moved back across the alley, toward the space, wonder-ing why, if the club's rear door was there, it didn't have a night security light. Most bars, lounges, clubs, liquor stores had at least some kind of light above the rear door to discourage burglars. But the Shamrock Club had no light at all. Kiley wet his lips and chewed on the bottom one for a moment in thought.

When he got all the way across the alley, Joe was able to see that the parking area was indeed there: twelve spaces dead up against the back of the building, with the club's rear door facing the two middle ones. No cars were parked there. Kiley moved to the rear door and slowly, quietly tried the knob, half expecting to hear a burglar alarm go off. But the door was locked and he heard nothing. There was, he could now see, a bulb above the door, but it was not turned on.

For a moment he stood there, confusion mounting, mind in a quandary, feeling sweat on the back of his neck under his shirt collar, sweat in the hair just above his ears, sweat slicking the palm closed around his flashlight. What the fuck was going on here? Could he have missed Nick out on the street? Possibly—but highly unlikely that Nick would have missed *him*. Could Nick be *inside* the goddamned place? There was no light, no sound from the club, but there could be an inside room of some kind; Gloria Mendez had read from Tony Touhy's file that there was a suspected illegal card room on the premises. But why would Nick *be* inside; how could he have *gotten* in—unless somebody let him in. And there were no signs of anyone else around.

Maybe, Joe thought, for some reason Nick was on another part of the block, on foot, reconnoitering , checking out parked cars, something. He said he had followed Tony Touhy's Jaguar over here, but where the hell was it? Maybe the punk shook Nick off his tail, maybe—

Maybe any fucking thing.

For sure, standing there wasn't getting him anyplace. Shifting the flashlight to his right hand, Joe wiped his sweaty left palm on the front of his shirt inside his coat. He started back for the street, following the wall of the Shamrock now, seeing the outline of several metal garbage cans setting up against the building between him and the streetlights. He wasn't walking fast, but neither was he moving as slowly and stealthily as he had when he entered the alley. If he had been walking faster, he would have fallen when he tripped, instead of just stumbling. It was his right foot that caught on something as he passed the garbage cans. Stumbling two steps, he cursed softly: "Goddamn it—" He took two more steps then, after regaining his balance, before he stopped cold, realizing what it had been that he tripped over.

A foot.

Someone else's, sticking out from between the garbage cans.

Retreating, feeling his blood run cold before he even knew for sure, Joe turned on the flashlight and shined its beam down on Nick Bianco.

Nick, slumped half sitting up against the Shamrock Club wall, eyes wide but sightless, the front of his shirt under another one of those sharp Valentino suits completely soaked with blood.

Nick, dead.

# FIVE

**B**y noon the next day, Joe Kiley looked like he had been on a five-day drunk. His eyes were red and swollen from lack of sleep—and from a modicum of crying that at odd moments he had not been able to control. It was a strange thing to be crying: He had not cried since he was a kid, except once, at his mother's funeral; yet now, when he was alone—in the men's room at the Shop, or in the interrogation room waiting for the next round of questions—the tears would suddenly be there before he could stop them. His red eyes, a nearly thirty-hour beard, and the early stages of sleep deprivation stupor, all simulated a massive hangover.

When Dan Parmetter arrived at the Shop early that morning, while it was still dark out, the General Assignments commander had been incensed at finding one of his detectives in an interrogation room like a common suspect. Parmetter, from the old school of up-through-the-rank cops, had escorted Joe into the offices of Internal Affairs. The commander of IA, Allan Vander, had said, "We're not finished with him yet, Dan."

"You're finished with him in the interrogation room," Parmetter said evenly. "My men don't get questioned in the same place you question hoods."

Vander's deputy, Bill Somers, explained, "I just put him in there for convenience, Dan—"

"Well, *I* took him out for propriety," Parmetter replied. "You can question him in here. Sit down, Joe."

Kiley slumped in a chair and Parmetter drew another close to sit next to him. After a moment of heavy silence, Parmetter said pointedly, "Well?"

"We're waiting for Chief Cassidy and Deputy Chief Ward. They're on their way over," Vander said.

Kiley turned his tired eyes to Parmetter. "Who went out to Nick's home, Dan?"

"Father O'Neill and Katie Muldoon."

Joe nodded. Father O'Neill was the department's Catholic chaplain, and Katie Muldoon was a lieutenant in public affairs who functioned as an aide to both the Protestant and Catholic chaplains in grief situations. Having lost both a husband and a son in the line of duty, she was uniquely qualified for the job. Kiley was glad Katie Muldoon would be with Stella—and he was glad he did *not* have to be. Inside he was sick almost to the point of vomiting about Nick's killing. It was all he could do to maintain a reasonably controlled exterior as his mind reeled with guilt and his ulcer drowned in stomach acid. He would as soon have put a pistol barrel in his mouth as face Stella Bianco just then.

Presently the office door opened and in strode Chief of Police John Cassidy and his deputy, Lester Ward. Accompanying them was Gordon Lovat, commander of the Organized Crime Bureau. After a round of good mornings, and Vander vacating his chair so Chief Cassidy could sit at the desk, Dan Parmetter asked Lovat, "What's OCB got to do with this?"

"Your man said he and his partner were after Phil Touhy's brother Tony," Lovat replied. "Anything to do with Phil Touhy concerns us."

"I authorized Commander Lovat's presence," Chief Cassidy said. He nodded to Vander to resume Joe's interrogation.

"All right, Kiley," said the IA man, "we've got all the details about how you and Bianco decided to conceal a lead from Homicide and try for a collar yourselves. And you have admitted that at least in your case you knew that you were violating department policy—"

Parmetter cut in, saying, "It's done all the time, for Christ's sake."

"We know that, Dan," said the chief. "We also know how zealously you protect your men, and that's commendable. But one of your men is dead this morning. Let's stay away from generalities and concentrate on specifics here. All right?"

"Yessir, Chief," Parmetter said. "I just don't want it sounding any worse for Joe than it really is."

Cassidy nodded to Vander and he resumed, saying, "Detective Kiley, were you the only one who had any contact with Bianco relative to this matter, the only one who had any conversation with him about it?"

"Yes," Kiley said wearily, lying. If Gloria Mendez's name came up later, he would have to try and deal with it then. For now, he intended to cover for her if he could.

"After you split up last night, the only contact you had with Bianco was the message on your answering machine, is that correct?"

"Right, correct."

"He said he was following Tony Touhy out of the parking garage at 3333 Lake Shore Drive?"

"Right."

Vander said, "You wouldn't mind if we went and got that answering machine tape, would you, Kiley?"

With a knowing glance at Dan Parmetter, Joe tossed Vander his apartment and car keys. "Have your boys search the place while they're there, Commander. You have my permission."

Vander reddened slightly and passed the keys to his deputy, Bill Somers, who left the office. Chief Cassidy leaned forward on the desk.

"I think we pretty much know what went down to get this situation started," the chief said. "Joe, what's your best guess as to what happened?"

"I'm not sure I have a *best* guess, sir," Kiley replied, sitting up straighter in the chair, giving Cassidy the demeanor and tone he deserved as chief. "I think it's safe to say that somebody made Nick; somebody must have seen him follow Tony Touhy up to the Shamrock. There was an illegal card game suspected on the premises; maybe it had a lookout. Maybe a card player who got there late saw him. It's even possible that Nick somehow got a look at Tony Touhy's knuckles, saw that they were bruised, and tried to take him down before I got there. Tony might have resisted and pulled a gun before Nick realized it—"

The chief shook his head. "Too many maybes, Joe. Too many might haves. You don't have anything solid?"

"I wish I did, Chief." There was agony in Joe's eyes.

"Kiley," said Gordon Lovat, the Organized Crime Bureau commander, "how did you and Bianco find out Tony Touhy's address so you could follow him?"

"I think we got it from an old traffic warrant on him," Kiley replied. Lovat's eyebrows rose.

"You *think?*"

"Nick got it," Kiley said. "What I meant was, I think that's where he said it came from."

"That's odd," Lovat said. "Everything on Phil Touhy's family, which would include his brother Tony, is supposed to be in the restricted access files of the OCB."

"I wouldn't know about that, Commander," Kiley said, careful to keep his tone neutral.

"I suppose a traffic warrant could have slipped through somewhere," Lovat admitted. "But tell me, how did you know about the suspected illegal card room on the premises?"

Kiley shrugged. "We did a little legwork in the neighborhood. The card room's no big secret." He and Gordon Lovat locked eyes for a moment, and it was clear to Joe that the OCB commander was measuring him, evaluating his words, trying to get a feel for whether Kiley was lying to him. Lovat was a clean-cut, conservatively dressed man not all that much older than Kiley. With degrees in Criminal Justice and Law Enforcement, he had moved up rapidly in the department, taking time off only to go to Vietnam with his reserve fighter wing and become a decorated hero. Everyone expected him to become chief someday, possibly even mayor. He had enjoyed much liaison with the FBI and other federal agencies, and was the department's acknowledged expert in organized crime matters.

Vander, the IA man, asked, "Detective Kiley, are you willing to sign a statement admitting that you and Detective Bianco violated department policy by withholding evidence from the command officers who took over the Ronnie Lynn homicide case?"

"Oh, for Christ's sake, Vander!" Dan Parmetter objected.

"This is *procedure*, Dan!" the IA man snapped. "Your men went out of bounds!"

"It's done all the time, for Christ's sake. It's a way for GA cops to get noticed, to get promoted."

"Well, it got one *killed* this time!"

Chief Cassidy raised a hand for calm and said to Parmetter, "It's imperative that we have this situation properly documented, Dan. I'm sorry."

"Will you sign the statement, Kiley?" Vander asked again.

Joe nodded. "For myself only. I won't sign anything with Bianco's name on it."

"May I ask why not?" Vander's eyes went cold; IA was very big on cops signing statements.

"Because," Joe said levelly, "I don't want some asshole bureaucrat trying to fuck up the Bianco family's pension by saying Nick was acting outside his authority."

"Which he was," observed Lovat of OCB.

"That's a matter of opinion," Kiley said, his voice taking on an edge of harshness. "We were trying to nail a punk for beating a young woman to death. The punk happened to be a member of an organized crime family.

Maybe if your bureau did a little better job, he wouldn't have been on the street in the first place."

Lovat smiled coldly. "That kind of immature, disrespectful remark is exactly why some records are restricted from ordinary officers, Detective Kiley. It's impossible for you to grasp an overview of what the Organized Crime Bureau is all about. Tony Touhy is on the street because we *want* him to be. We have plans to use him someday to testify against his brother."

Kiley grunted derisively. "You're having a wet dream, Commander."

"And you, Detective Kiley, are incompetent and undisciplined. You shouldn't be carrying a badge."

"Enough," said Chief Cassidy, pointing his finger, first at Kiley, then at Gordon Lovat. "Speaking of badges, do you know anything about Nick's?" he asked Joe.

"What do you mean, sir?" Kiley frowned.

"It wasn't on his body. Did he mention leaving it at home, or losing it?"

"No, sir." Kiley shot a look at Gordon Lovat. "Pick up Tony Touhy. You'll probably find that he's got bruised knuckles *and* Nick's badge."

"Yes, we'll go out and get him right away, Kiley," replied the OCB man, openly scornful. "We'll do it solely on your suspicion and forget all about reasonable cause and constitutional rights."

"I said enough," Chief Cassidy's usual calm tone now carried an edge that was a warning to everyone. The chief leaned back and sighed quietly. His lips pursed in thought, a signal to everyone that they should keep quiet. Cassidy had heard enough for now; he was mulling over a decision. There were a number of cracks to be filled here.

"All right," the chief was finally ready. "Dan," he said to Parmetter, "I'll send you two new GA men today from the uniformed ranks to replace Kiley and Bianco. Al," he looked at Allan Vander, "finish up whatever you have to do at your end and get the IA report and recommendations to me as soon as possible." His eyes went to the OCB commander. "Gordon, coordinate with the Homicide officers handling the Lynn and Bianco killings. If the Touhy kid is involved, I want him made for it, regardless of any future plans your bureau might have for him. We don't let murder go in order to plan organized crime strategy—especially when one of the vics is our own. Clear?"

"Yes, sir, Chief, clear," said Lovat.

"Les," the chief turned to his own deputy, "all statements to the media are to come from Public Affairs." His finger went up and he drew an imaginary line across everyone in the room. "No exceptions." Another quiet sigh, then: "Joe—"

"Yessir—"

"—you're on departmental paid leave until after Bianco's funeral. Stay away from the division. Don't talk to the press, not even for one of those so-called bullshit human interest pieces about how it feels for a cop to lose his partner. Nothing. Clear?"

"Yessir." Kiley would not have talked to the press anyway; he ranked reporters somewhere below defense lawyers, barely above child molesters.

"That's it for now," Chief Cassidy said. "This is a bad day for all of us, men. Let's pull together on this as a team. Remember, the good of the department takes priority over our personal feelings. We'll get back together after Detective Bianco is laid to rest. That's all."

Cassidy came around the desk and extended his hand to Kiley.

"I'm truly sorry, Joe."

"Thanks, Chief," Kiley said hoarsely.

His eyes filled with tears and there wasn't a goddamned thing he could do about it.

# SIX

**K**iley, along with Dan Parmetter and four other GA detectives from Warren Boulevard station, were pallbearers for Nick, sitting in a row at the church, across from the pew where the slain officer's widow, daughters, and other family members sat. Nick's parents were deceased, so it was his father's eldest brother, Uncle Gino Bianco, who stood in as head of the family and, with his wife, sat with Stella and the girls.

Joe felt as rotten and wasted during the mass as he had felt in Chief Cassidy's office, even though it was now four days later. Several times during the mass, Dan Parmetter had put a hand over to pat Joe's knee. In the intervening time since Nick's killing, Kiley had spent most of his time alone, in solitary drinking. He had been out to see Stella and the girls twice, had been at the wake, and had shown up for pallbearer practice, but for the most part, except with Stella and the girls, he had been remote, noncommunicative, unreachable. He felt zombie-like.

At the cemetery, when the pallbearers had fulfilled their final responsibility of placing Nick Bianco's casket on the lowering device above the open grave, Joe had moved back to stand in a line with the other pallbearers while Father O'Neill spoke his final words. But Stella Bianco suddenly said, "Joe," in a broken voice, through her tears, and held out a black-gloved hand to him. Kiley hesitated; it was all family over there. But Parmetter gave him a slight nudge and he self-consciously went around the casket and stepped to Stella's side. When she laid her sobbing face against his chest, he automatically put an arm around her, and with his other arm held the girls, Jennie and Tessie, close to him. For an instant, Kiley's eyes met Uncle Gino Bianco's and he thought he saw displeasure there; but it must be grief, he told himself, because Gino Bianco had always accepted Kiley as if he were a member of the family. Kiley had no time to ponder it anyway, because Father O'Neill finished speaking, the department honor guard fired its twenty-one gun salute into the air, and then, as the mourn-

ers began moving past the casket, the pipers of the department band began playing the funeral dirge. One by one, the department brass, led off by
Chief Cassidy, stepped up to the casket for the final time. Allan Vander was
there, the deputy chief Lester Ward, even Gordon Lovat. The OCB man
seemed to study Kiley curiously whenever he had a chance; twice Kiley
caught him staring at him, but refused to react to it.

Stella and the girls were the last to go up to the casket, and Kiley went
with them because Stella would not let go of him. Her pretty, olive-com-
plected face was not drawn as it might have been, but rather was puffy
from her head constantly being bowed over the past days, and the contin-
ual crying that drew liquid to her eyes. Her thick black hair was combed
straight back on top as always, pulled over her ears at the sides, and held
in place by a black comb that had belonged to her grandmother. There was
a black scarf over her head that was not as black as her hair. Jennie and
Tessie, with hair like their mother, wore similar scarves, but their little
faces *were* drawn, their eyes, especially of the ten-year-old Jennifer, hollow
and fearful.

Just past the casket, where Uncle Gino and some other family members
were waiting for Kiley to turn Stella and the girls back over to them, Stella said, "Joe, you're coming out to the house?"

"Sure." He hadn't meant to; he did not want to be in the mob of
mourners who would be there.

"Because I have something for you—"

"Sure," Kiley said, patting her hand.

Kiley rode back to the funeral home with Parmetter so they could talk.

"Where does it go now, Dan?" he asked.

"I don't know," Parmetter replied, with a shake of his head. "I can't get
a feel for it, Joe. A lot of it'll depend on what Lovat and OCB finds out,
and what Vander and his IA boys recommend. If you and Nick were right
about Tony Touhy, it'll be a big plus for you, of course. But if you were
wrong, if Nick was lost because you guys had a wild hair up your asses,
well, you can see how it'll look, you being the senior man and all—"

"Who'll be primary on Nick's case?"

"Homicide, I'd imagine," said Parmetter. "With IA and OCB very
strong secondaries. But Cassidy won't take it away from Homicide. He's
ex-Homicide himself."

"Can you get me TADed to Homicide, Dan?" Kiley asked. TAD was
Temporary Attached Duty, usually an assignment for some special reason.

"I can try," Parmetter said. "You're not exactly real popular in Homicide right now, holding back on them the way you and Nick did. But I'll do what I can."

Kiley knew Dan Parmetter would. He was the kind of cop Gloria Mendez was—although Parmetter would have hotly disclaimed such a comparison.

At the funeral home, Kiley got his own car and drove over to Nick's house, a neat, two-story Tudor model tract house on a middle-class suburban block—where Nick was not supposed to reside because he was a City of Chicago employee and was expected to *live* in the city. Moot point now, of course. Kiley had to park over a block away because cars filled Nick's block corner to corner on both sides of the street. Walking back, he encountered a number of children playing out front, and found Jennie sitting forlornly on the porch with two little girls her own age, cousins probably, just talking.

"Hi, Uncle Joe," she rose to greet him.

"Hi, baby," he said, gathering her into his arms. "You doing okay?"

"Sure," she said resignedly. She was like her mother: pragmatic, realistic, sensible. It was Tessie, the youngest, who was more like Nick had been: temperamental, impatient, excitable. "Mom and Tessie are somewhere inside," Jennie told Joe.

As he went into the poignantly familiar house, Kiley again felt an implosion of guilt. Nick was not there. Nick would *never* be there again. And it was his fault. Nick would never have tried to clear the Ronnie Lynn killing without Joe's urging. Despite his temperament, his occasional volatility, Nick had been the more cautious one of the team. Only when Joe was the instigator, the encourager, the leader, only then had Nick taken chances.

The house was wall to wall with people, as Kiley had known it would be: relatives, friends, neighbors, cops, priests, nuns—all drinking coffee, eating, talking in small groups. As Kiley inched his way through the family room, he saw Uncle Gino waving to get his attention from the patio outside the room's sliding glass door. Beyond the patio was Nick's brick barbecue and a big, aboveground pool he had put in for the girls and their friends. Kiley waved back to Gino and changed direction to thread his way to the patio.

"Joe, come join us," Gino said, coming over to meet him, putting an arm around his shoulders, guiding him to a group of men sitting at a picnic table. "You know Nick's cousins: my son Frank; my sister's boys,

Bruno and Carmine Bello; and these are my sons-in-law, Ray Rinni and Michael Russo."

Nick shook hands all around and accepted a small tumbler of home-made wine that Uncle Gino poured for him.

"We was just talking about you, Joe," said Gino's son, Frank Bianco. "How long was you and Nicky partners?"

"Eight years," Kiley said.

"That's what I told them. 'Cause I know you was partners before Tessie was born, 'cause you're Tessie's godfather."

"The cops, they gonna get whoever killed Nicky?" asked Carmine Bello. All eyes went to Joe.

"Yeah," Joe said, "they will. Eventually."

"You working the case?" Carmine's brother Bruno asked. Joe shook his head.

"Not yet. I'm on departmental leave until tomorrow. But I'm going to try to get assigned to it."

"Joe," said Uncle Gino, "there's something we're curious about. Understand, no disrespect is meant, but as Nicky's partner, how come you weren't there when he was killed?"

Joe became acutely aware that these six men were Nick's blood—Italian, all Calabrian—and he had only been Nick's partner—a shanty Irishman that Nick had somehow adopted as a surrogate brother. With Nick gone, Kiley realized, there was nothing between him and Gino Bianco anymore, no connection whatsoever to any of the Bianco men. Nick was dead—and Joe was being asked to explain why.

"I was on my way there," Joe said, working to keep his words even. "Nick and I had been on a stakeout and quit when our shift was over. Just after I left, Nick spotted the guy we were looking for and tailed him. When I got home, there was a message on my answering machine telling me where Nick followed the guy to. I got there as fast as I could, but—"

"Who's the guy you were following?" asked one of the others. Nick locked eyes with him.

"That's confidential information."

"Tell us, like, off the record. Maybe we could help the cops on this."

Kiley shook his head. "The department doesn't need any help."

"Nick sure as hell could have used a little."

Joe Kiley's light blue eyes hardened. "What was your name again?"

"Ray Rinni. I'm—"

"I know who you are, Rinni. Nick told me all about you. You fence hot car parts, don't you?"

"Just a fucking minute, man—" Rinni began hotly—but his father-in-law quickly put a tight hand on his arm.

"All right, Ray." Gino Bianco smiled at Kiley. "No need for that kind of talk, Joe. I hope we all have the same interest here. Ray would naturally like to know the name of anyone who might have been involved in Nick's killing, as we all would."

"Nick was a police officer. His killing is a police matter," Kiley said flatly, putting his glass of wine down. "It will be handled by the police department."

He turned and walked away.

Back inside the crowded house, Kiley made his way to the kitchen, which was where he thought Stella would probably be. He was right; she was putting two newly arrived dishes of food on an already crowded counter that was serving as a buffet. Three other women were helping in the kitchen: washing dishes, pouring coffee into cups on a tray, tending to all the logistics of feeding the mourners.

"Hi," Joe said, going up to Stella at the counter.

"Oh, hi, Joe—" She wiped her hands on a dish towel and embraced him, pressing her face into his neck for a brief moment and gripping his upper arms tightly.

"I saw Jen outside, but where's Tessie?" Joe asked.

"I got her to lie down for a nap, thank God," Stella replied as they separated. "How are you doing, Joey?"

"Good," he told her. "I'm doing good."

Stella took his arm and drew him to the farthest corner of the kitchen. "Is the department giving you a lot of heat?" she asked quietly.

"What do you mean?"

"For not being there to back Nick up. IA has been out, wanting to know if there was any trouble between you two, that kind of stuff. Are they on you?"

"A little," he admitted. Kiley studied her large, dark eyes, trying to see if there was in them the same thing he had seen in the eyes of Gino Bianco and the men on the patio.

"Joe, I want you to know that I'm not questioning it," Stella told him. "I know you loved Nicky like a brother. If you weren't there for him there was a reason."

"I was on my way, Stel," he said. "Nick was supposed to be waiting there for me. Something must have gone down before I got there—I don't know what—" Shaking his head, Kiley decided to level with her. "We weren't on the job, Stel. We were trying to make a homicide collar on our own—"

"Not on the job?" Stella Bianco's expression became gray. "You weren't signed in? You weren't on duty?"

"No."

"Christ, Joe, what will that do to my pension? I've got the girls to raise—"

"Your pension won't be affected. At least, I don't think it will—"

"You don't *think*? My God, Joe—"

"Everything's going to be okay," he assured, putting a hand on her arm. "I was senior officer; I can cover any question that comes up. If necessary, I'll say that Nick *thought* he was on duty, that I set up the operation on my own and he had no part of it."

"Will they believe you?"

"Doesn't matter if they do or not; they can't disprove it."

Stella covered Joe's hand with hers. "Then what happens to *your* career, Joe?"

"That's not important right now."

"Joey—" She spoke his name as a plea.

"Let me handle it, Stel. I'll see that you and the girls don't lose anything you've got coming." He leaned a little closer to her. "Just keep it to yourself about us not being on the job. Don't tell Uncle Gino or anybody else."

"All right, Joe." She patted his hand. "Come upstairs to the bedroom, Joe. I have something for you."

Joe followed Stella as she made her way through the clots of people between the kitchen and the entry foyer stairs. Along the way she had to pause a dozen times to accept condolences, hugs, kisses on the cheek, sympathetic handshakes, gentle touches. To each she responded with a sad but still beautiful smile. Her lips were a fraction too wide for the rest of her face, though not unattractively so; and her teeth were straight, perfect, matchless white; making her smile, whether in happiness or grief, a lucent, infectious thing. Just to see Stella Bianco smile, under any circumstances, made people around her feel better.

Upstairs, Stella quietly opened the door to the room her daughters shared, and looked in on Tessie, who lay sleeping, fully dressed except for shoes, with a light blanket over her. Closing the door again, Stella said quietly, "God, I hope she sleeps until these people clear out. She's so damned confused by all this; I'm not sure she even realizes Nick is *permanently* gone. Come on in here—"

She led Joe into the master bedroom. As soon as he looked at the big king-size bed, Kiley could not help thinking of Gloria Mendez and the incredible fact that Nick had been unfaithful to Stella with her. Joe wished to God that Nick had never shared that secret with him; he wished he could just erase it from his memory. How much easier it would be to remember Nick as a totally devoted, loving husband to a woman who returned that love and devotion full measure. Not that Nick's affair with Gloria Mendez made him a sleaze-bag like some of the married cops that Kiley knew, cops that actively scouted pussy every shift they worked, taking it from complainants, victims, co-workers, hookers, suspects, any woman who might put out for any reason: fear, intimidation, payoff, the need for help, or simply being a cop groupie. Nick had not been like that, far from it; still, he *had* cheated on Stella—and that tainted, ever so slightly, the memory Joe Kiley had of him.

Stella took something from a dresser drawer and brought it over to Joe. "Here, I want you to have this. I know Nick would have wanted you to have it."

It was Nick's dress watch, an expensive gold Movado that Stella had saved up for and given Nick for his thirtieth birthday.

"Stel, I can't," Kiley said. "The girls—"

"No," she insisted, "it's yours, Joe. If Nick and I had a son, it would be different, but we don't. This is yours, Joe, for being like a brother to him."

Her expression and voice were so insistent that Kiley could not bring himself to refuse. Nodding, he put the watch in his coat pocket.

As they came back downstairs, Joe saw that Gino Bianco was now in the living room, standing in a group with a coffee cup in his hand, watching him and Stella. Wanting no more of the extended Bianco family at the moment, Joe said, "Listen, Stel, I've got to go."

"So soon?"

"Yeah. A few things I need to clean up."

Coupling her arm in his, Stella walked Kiley out the front door. Jennie and her cousins were no longer on the front steps, and the kids playing out there had disappeared too. Joe and Stella walked down the driveway toward the street.

"Joe, will you come to dinner in a few days? For the girls? For me too, but especially for them, so they'll see that everything else is still the same."

"Sure. I'll call you once things settle down a little."

"I'm glad we've got you in our lives, Joe," she said, on the verge of tears. She put her arms around his neck, hugged him tightly, then hurried away.

As Stella ran toward the house, Gino Bianco came down the driveway to where Kiley stood. Turning to watch Stella go inside, he said sadly, "A beautiful young woman, Stella: so vibrant and alive. For her to lose Nick, to be without a man, is tragic. Tragic."

Joe studied at close range this man who was the head of the Bianco family. In his sixties, Gino Bianco was still lean and trim, with a full head of hair albeit mostly gray. To Kiley, there had always been something unlikably remote about him, as if he feigned friendship instead of feeling it. His business was used cars; he owned several large lots and employed his son Frank as well as his nephews and sons-in-law. Nick had been the only Bianco who refused to work for Uncle Gino, shocking everyone by joining the police force.

"Listen, Joe," the elder Bianco said now, "I hope you'll overlook that business with Ray out on the patio. Sometimes his mouth gets ahead of his brain."

"Forget it," Kiley said, knowing even as he said it that neither of them would.

"I wonder," Gino explored, "if you would take a little friendly advice from someone who's been around a while longer than you?"

"What's on your mind, Gino?" asked Joe.

"It's you and Stella," the uncle said. "A few people have commented on how she turned to you for comfort at the cemetery. And now they see the two of you doing a lot of private talking, a little touching, going up to the bedroom together—"

"What the fuck are you getting at?" Joe asked bluntly.

"Understand, I'm not implying that anything at all is improper," Gino emphasized, spreading his hands innocently. "I'm just asking you, for Stella's sake, to consider how it looks. I mean, first you're not there to back Nick up and he gets killed—"

"You're on thin ice, Gino," Kiley warned in a flat, hard voice.

"—and then you seem to be very, how should I say, *comfortable*, around Nick's widow. I have to tell you, Joe, it don't look good." Gino's expression changed from friendly to authoritarian. "I think maybe you should stay away from Stella for a while."

"Go fuck yourself."

"I would consider it a personal favor if you would show me your respect in this matter."

"Don't pull any of your guinea godfather shit on me," Kiley said. "You're all a bunch of assholes as far as I'm concerned, you and your son and your fucking nephews and sons-in-law, all of you. The only Bianco who had any brains or any balls was Nick." Joe made himself take a couple of steps away, to curb his temptation to get in Gino Bianco's dago face, to crowd him a little, let him know who he was fucking with here. "I was Nick's best friend," Joe continued very deliberately, "and I'll be Stella's best friend too, as long as she wants me to. You want me to keep away from Stella, you get Stella to tell me so. Meantime, *Uncle* Gino, you stay the fuck out of my business, *capice?*"

Without waiting for a reply, Kiley strode away, fuming, the ulcer in his duodenum starting to roil. But halfway down the block to his car, he was forced to ask himself an unavoidable question. Had Gino Bianco detected what was in Joe's heart and mind regarding Stella Bianco? Did how he feel about her *show?*

If so, then Gino was right.

It did not look good.

# SEVEN

Just before nine the following morning, Joe was riding the elevator up to Chief Cassidy's office at 11th and State. Dan Parmetter had called Joe at home the previous night and said that the chief wanted them both in his office.

"What's up?" Joe had asked his GA commander.

"Don't know," Parmetter replied. "I assume he's made some decision about you, but I wouldn't even guess what it is. I was waiting in his office when he got back from the funeral, and asked him about putting you in Homicide on a TAD. He asked me if that was my recommendation and I told him yes, it was. I said I thought you deserved a chance to help make your partner's killer. That's the best I could do for you, Joe."

"Thanks, Dan. You know I appreciate it," said Kiley.

"I know you do, Joey. I hope things work out for you."

Now, getting off the elevator and walking down the hall, Kiley was tense, apprehensive. The best he could hope for, he knew, was temporary attached duty in Homicide to help nail Nick's killer; the worse that could happen was that he would be brought up on charges of a violation of department standards and regulations which resulted in the death of a fellow officer—a move which almost certainly would cost him his badge. Whatever the chief ruled, however, Kiley had made up his own mind not to cooperate in any way that would incriminate Nick and jeopardize Stella's pension. He was determined to be very firm about that, whatever the cost to himself.

In the reception room, a secretary said, "Go right in, Detective," and Kiley knocked briefly and entered the large, well-lighted, tastefully decorated office of the chief of police. There were rich leather chairs, an oversize glass-topped desk, deep-pile carpeting, floor-to-ceiling bookcases alternating with floor-to-ceiling windows, a trophy case, a photograph wall. The place looked like a movie set and Kiley, never having seen it in his fourteen years with the department, found it difficult to believe that such an office was actually a part of the ignominious old headquarters building.

"Good morning, Joe," said Chief Cassidy from his desk. Already there were Dan Parmetter, Gordon Lovat of OCB, Allan Vander of IA, and Lester Ward, the deputy chief of police. Kiley became aware at once that the group had been there for a while; all of them had nearly finished their coffee. "Take a chair, Joe," the chief said. "How is Nick's widow doing?"

"Holding up, sir," Joe replied.

"Good. And you?"

"I'm all right, sir."

"Can I have my secretary bring you some coffee?"

"No, I don't think so, sir, thank you." Let's get on with it, Kiley thought edgily.

"Joe," the chief said without further preliminary, "I'm taking you off General Assignment and putting you on temporary attached duty in a command."

Kiley's tension eased at once. Homicide, he thought. Everything was going to be okay.

"You're going to the Bomb-and-Arson squad for a while," the chief said then.

Kiley glanced around at the other men in the office, saw satisfied looks on everyone except Parmetter, then met Chief Cassidy's eyes. "Are you serious, Chief?"

"I'm serious," the chief assured. "The investigation of Bianco's murder is already a very delicate and complex matter, involving not only Homicide but now, because of the information you and Bianco tumbled onto—and, frankly, how you handled that information—also involves Internal Affairs and the Organized Crime Bureau. If OCB ties Phil Touhy's kid brother to Bianco's death, this department is going to have the highest profile murder case in the past decade. It is going to be absolutely essential that you and Bianco look clean for a trial. Because if you *don't* look clean, the department won't either. And if some high-powered lawyer working for the Touhy organization can make you, Bianco, and the department look dirty, make us look like we're playing outside the rules—as you and Bianco *were*—then a cop-killer could go unpunished. I'll put up with a lot—but I won't put up with *that*."

"But I don't understand, Chief," said Joe. "Why bury me somewhere when I could help make Tony Touhy? Let me go to Homicide and—"

"Homicide wouldn't have you, Kiley," said Vander, the IA man. "As far as Homicide's concerned, you're *responsible* for Bianco's death."

Cassidy held up a hand to silence Vander. "That's not really the point. The controlling factor here is objectivity. You and Bianco were partners for eight years, Joe. You're godfather to his youngest daughter. It was you his widow reached out to for support at the funeral. You're too close to everything. I don't want you even remotely involved in the investigation."

Joe sat back, eyes narrowing a fraction. "There's more to it than me being too close, isn't there?" He looked at Vander. "It's IA's idea to bury me, isn't it? Teach me a lesson." His eyes switched to Lovat. "And Nick and I stepped on some elite toes in Organized Crime, didn't we?"

"I should think," Gordon Lovat said evenly, "that you'd be grateful just to be keeping your badge, Kiley. IA could have recommended that you be brought up on charges."

"IA *wanted* to recommend that," said Vander. "We just couldn't do it without the department looking bad."

Joe's eyes flicked back to Cassidy. "Why am I getting the feeling here that nobody wants me on this case because I might work too hard to clear it?"

"Joe," the chief said patiently, "you're a pretty good cop, all things considered. But we both know that there have been times in the past when you were—let's say, overzealous. You know as well as I do how many reprimands there are in your jacket. Just last summer you slapped a drunk driver in the mouth with your handcuffs after he'd run over an old lady, and knocked all his front teeth out—"

"He resisted me," Joe said mechanically.

"—and the time when you caught that pervert the Sex Crimes Squad was looking for and worked him over with a sap—"

Kiley sat forward. "That son of a bitch had raped—not molested but raped, *fucked*—six little girls all under twelve," he said, nodding righteously, obviously unrepentant. "He had it coming to him."

"Not from you, Detective!" the chief snapped. Cassidy's ire came like a crack of lightning; he'd had just about enough of this maverick cop. "You're not God, mister, and you're not a judge or a jury! That shield you carry doesn't give you leave to dispense justice, whether it's right or whether it isn't!" Cassidy jabbed a stiff forefinger down at his desk top. "The investigation of Detective Bianco's killing is going to be handled in a professional, efficient, and objective manner, by the book—and you are going to stay completely away from it! You are not to call Homicide to check on their progress, you are not to ask to read any reports, you are not to nose around on your own—you are not to do *anything*." The stiff forefinger that had been jabbing the desk top now came up and pointed threateningly at Kiley. "You go to Bomb-and-Arson—today! Report directly to Captain Madzak: he's expecting you. That's all, you're dismissed, Detective."

Kiley stood, the muscles of his jaw flexing involuntarily, stomach churning as he seethed inside, the back of his neck on fire. Without looking at any of the other men in the office, he turned away from Cassidy and walked toward the door.

"Kiley," the chief said as Joe's hand touched the knob. Joe stopped without turning around. "If I find out you're meddling in the Bianco homicide, I'll put you back in a prowl car—in *uniform*. If that doesn't work, I'll have you brought up on charges and take your shield away from you. And if you continue to give me problems after that, I'll have you busted and locked up like a common hoodlum. You understand the drill here?"

"Yessir, I understand," Joe said, still not looking back. His voice was dispassionate, but only because of the vise-like control he was able to exert on it. Even if it caused his fucking ulcer to perforate, he swore in that instant he stood there, he would not let the men in that room—bastards all, except for Dan Parmetter—see him wilt or crawl.

"All right, go on," the chief told him.

Kiley walked on out, the pulse in his throat throbbing as his blood pressure escalated.

On the elevator, Kiley pushed the button for Bomb-and-Arson. As the car started down, he suddenly frowned, a new thought splitting through the turmoil in his mind. Impulsively he pressed another button, for Central Records.

Gloria Mendez was out of her office, getting something from a bank of filing cabinets; she saw him crossing to the counter and came over to open the gate for him.

"Jesus, you look like you're hyperventilating," she said.

"They're not going to let me work on Nick's killing," he told her tightly but quietly.

"Why the hell should they?" Gloria asked without rancor. "Go sit down in my office."

Kiley did as she said and a moment later she came in and handed him a paper cup of cold water. Then she went into her purse and gave him a pill. "Take this."

"What is it?"

"Valium."

Joe swallowed the pill. "I didn't see you at Nick's funeral." It was not an accusation.

"I was there," Gloria told him. "Way in the back. That oldest girl of his: she really favors Nick, don't you think—" Her voice broke and she had to reach for a tissue. After she composed herself, she asked, "What'd they do with you?"

"Sent me to B-and-A."

"You're lucky they didn't bring you up on charges. How'd Nick end up dead?"

Kiley told her what had happened after he and Nick separated following their eight-hour stakeout of Tony Touhy's apartment building and the Shamrock Club. When he finished, Gloria shook her head dismally. "Jesus, what a lousy break. I guess there's a lot to be said for going by the book, after all."

"You're right about that," Kiley admitted miserably. "If it wasn't for me, Nick never would have tried to go after Touhy and he wouldn't be dead."

"You can't blame just yourself," Gloria said. "Nick was his own man; if he went along with it, it was because he wanted to. He told me on the phone before you guys came down the other day, he said, 'Glor, I've got a chance to do something to get a better assignment.' He sounded very enthusiastic. So he wasn't just following your lead; he wanted to do it."

"Listen," Kiley said, getting away from the subject of his own guilt, "I think you ought to know that Lovat, the OCB commander, has been in the meetings. Has he checked Tony Touhy's file to see if anyone accessed it?"

Gloria shook her head. "No way to tell unless I access the record again. If I did that, it would blow my excuse that the first access was accidental. All I can do right now is say it was all a coincidence and hang tough. Nobody on my watch will admit ever seeing you and Nick in my office, and you're not on the sign-in log. OCB and IA will know I'm lying, but they won't be able to prove it."

"You think your job's okay then?"

"Sure. I'm a double minority, Joe: female and Puerto Rican. I'd have to kick Chief Cassidy in the *cajones* to get fired." She paused a beat, then added, "Nobody can connect me to this but you."

"That'll never happen," Kiley assured her.

Gloria bobbed her chin at the open door. "You better beat it. The pill working?"

"Starting to." Rising, Kiley paused. "Listen, I—"

"I know," she said, not letting him finish. "We both are. So long, Joe."

"So long, Gloria."

Captain Leo Madzak, commander of the Bomb-and-Arson squad, clasped his hands together on his desk.

"I don't like this any better than you do, Kiley," he said to Joe, who sat facing him. "I said as much to the chief's deputy, Les Ward, when he called about you. Far as I'm concerned, you ought to be allowed to work your partner's homicide."

He doesn't know, Kiley thought. It was being kept under wraps that Nick was killed while they were off duty.

"A man's partner gets it, the officer should be allowed to help go after whoever gave it to him," said Madzak. He was older, probably nearing retirement, smelling heavily of cologne. "But I don't run the Shop, the chief does. So as of now, you're B-and-A, and I've got instructions to keep you busy. For the time being, I'm just going to give you scut work and gofer jobs. My instinct tells me you won't be here long, and I don't have the budget to send you to any training schools unless I know you're permanent."

"I'll work whatever you give me, Captain," said Joe. The Valium had kicked in completely by now. "I understand the position you're in, and I appreciate what you just said."

Madzak tossed a file across the desk. "This is a guy named Winston. We're holding him as a suspect in some city bus sabotage, but all we got is some weak circumstantial evidence and the guy won't cop to anything. We have to either charge him or cut him loose by three this afternoon. Go over to the jail and talk to the guy; see if you can come up with anything; if you can't, let him out. Then call it a day. I'll find you a desk tomorrow." Madzak stood up and extended his hand over the desk. "Welcome aboard, Joe."

"Thanks, Captain."

Kiley drove out to 26th and California to the Cook County Jail and logged in at the police desk, checking both of his guns and filling out a request to have detained person Winston, Harold Paul, brought down to the release pen. Then Kiley went into the pen and found a place to sit on a hard bench against the wall. The pen was aptly named: there were forty or fifty people milling around, some of them prisoners waiting release, others relatives, lawyers, cops, all involved in the release process. The room had half a dozen small cubicles for semi-private conversations; the rest of the people filled the big room like milling livestock. With his back to the wall, Kiley opened Winston's file and read:

CASE BACKGROUND: On four consecutive Thursdays beginning 5-6-93, small homemade bombs have exploded on Chicago Transit Authority buses idle in terminals after being parked for the day. The theory is that the bombs are being placed under a rear seat on one of the vehicle's last runs of the day on a route that does not operate between midnight and six a.m. Intent appears to be to damage vehicles, not to injure passengers.

BOMB ANALYSIS: Bombs are satchel-type packed in plastic baggie containers, timer detonated by small, ordinary, inexpensive Atlas brand alarm clocks. Damage to date has not been extensive, limited to several seats being destroyed, but potential exists for much more serious loss if device should detonate vehicle's fuel tank.

CASE ANALYSIS: Through cooperation of CTA officials and employees aware of the situation, the four acts have not been reported to the press or in any other way made public. This is to avoid any panic insofar as passengers are concerned, and also to deprive the perpetrator of any notoriety possibly being sought.

COURSE OF ACTION: Bulletin notification to all department, variety, and drugstores carrying the model Atlas alarm clock being used as a timer detonator. Request immediate notification to hot line number while sale in progress, sales receipt copies, charge card numbers, and any other information on purchasers of this clock if not detained.

UPDATE: On 6-1-93 hot line called by manager of Bolden Drugs, 10230 Arten, that a customer was in process of purchasing four of the specified clocks. Hot line relay to precinct patrol which apprehended purchaser, Harold P. Winston, shortly after he emerged from the store, purchase still in possession. Subject turned over to B&A for disposition.

DISPOSITION: Subject arrested suspicion of vandalism to public property. Record check showed no priors.

Joe closed the file and sighed quietly. His partner's grave was still fresh and the department had him working bullshit like this. He had helped kill Nick: He knew it and the department brass knew it. And they wouldn't even let him do penance by putting him on the job to help catch Nick's killer. Dirty bastards—

"Winston!" a jail officer shouted from the lockup door, and let in a thin, balding, very intense-looking man wearing wrinkled street clothes. He looked warily about at the activity in the pen.

"Over here, Mr. Winston," Kiley said, holding up the file. As Winston crossed the room, Kiley selected a semi-private cubicle occupied by a trashy looking white couple who both had dirty blond hair and tattoos. "Vacate," Kiley said, showing his badge. They left, giving him surly looks. "Sit down, Mr. Winston," the detective said, taking a chair on one side of the little cubicle. Still wary, Winston sat down. "We're releasing you this afternoon, Mr. Winston, and I have to complete the necessary forms—"

"Releasing me? You mean letting me go?"

"That's right."

"I'm not being charged?"

"No."

"But I thought—I mean, they *arrested* me—"

"Just on suspicion. No formal charge was filed."

"But I've been in jail two nights," Winston half protested. "How can I be kept in jail without being charged?"

"You couldn't have been," Kiley told him frankly, "if you'd asked for a lawyer. If you'd had legal representation, you'd have been out in four or five hours. But if you don't ask for a lawyer, we can hold you for up to seventy-two hours."

"That's not fair," Winston said, trying to marshal some indignation.

"Doesn't have to be fair," Kiley said, "as long as it's legal."

"I was positive I'd be charged," Winston said, as much to himself as to Kiley. His voice had a letdown note to it. Kiley studied him just long enough to think: *This asshole is guilty. And he's pissed because he's not being charged.*

"Look, Mr. Winston, if you want to be charged, why don't you just admit committing the crime?"

"Why should I?" Winston almost demanded. "You're *supposed* to put me on trial and *prove* that I did it."

"We don't have enough evidence against you, Mr. Winston," Kiley said patiently.

"I bought four of those alarm clocks," the irritated man asserted. "They're the same kind used in all of the bombs. Isn't that evidence?"

"Only circumstantial evidence; that's not enough in your case." Kiley cocked his head slightly. "How'd you know they were the same kind of clocks."

Winston smiled slyly. "Think you're clever, don't you? Well, the detective who questioned me yesterday said they were, that's how." He leaned forward a fraction in confidentiality. "Listen, off the record, can I sue for false arrest?"

"You need a lawyer to tell you that. Personally, I don't think so." A plan began to take form in Kiley's mind; a way for him to have some free time to continue pursuing Tony Touhy—because he was convinced that Touhy had either killed Nick or been involved in killing him. His and Nick's efforts to tie the punk to Ronnie Lynn's death had only been speculative; Touhy's connection to Nick's killing was, in Kiley's mind, a certainty. But knowing it and *proving* it were two different matters. Kiley needed time to work at the latter. "Look," he said to Winston, "let's get this form completed so we can both get out of here. Your address is 3312 North Kalvin, is that correct?"

"Yes, correct."

Kiley smiled briefly. "Small world. I live in that same general neighborhood."

Winston's eyebrows raised. "Oh?"

Kiley went immediately back to the form, leaving the subject hanging. "There was no place of employment listed on your booking slip, Mr. Winston. Where do you work, sir?"

"Why, I-I'm unemployed at present," Winston said, looking away.

Lying prick, Kiley thought. "Un—em—ployed," he said slowly as he wrote. "Let's see: height, weight, color of eyes—I can just copy the rest of this stuff. Come on over to the release desk, Mr. Winston, and I'll get them started processing you out."

After Joe had seen to Harold Winston's release, he returned to the Shop to see Leo Madzak.

"I think I can make this guy Winston, Captain," he told the B-and-A commander. "I think he's your bus bomber."

"Run it down for me," said Madzak.

"Okay, first of all, I don't think he's a loony; at least, not an *ordinary* loony. I think he's got a *cause*; I think there's some kind of planned reasoning behind what he's doing. Like he always bombs on Thursdays; maybe he was in some kind of an accident with a bus on a Thursday, something like that. The guy *wants* to be charged; I think he wants to be put on trial so he can have his say about whatever it is that's bothering him, whatever it is that he thinks wronged him——"

"You mean he's looking for a public forum? Maybe to attract some press coverage?"

"Yes, sir. Could be he bought those four clocks deliberately to get caught; I mean, it was a pretty dumb thing to do otherwise: Who the hell buys four alarm clocks at once?"

Madzak pondered the matter for a moment, then asked, "What do you need to make him?"

"Just time," Kiley replied. "Time for some surveillance, some street work."

"You want this guy full time, free rein?"

"Yes, sir."

Madzak held Kiley's gaze. "You know, Joe, if the brass catches you nosing into your partner's killing, they'll have your ass. Maybe mine too."

"Not yours, Captain," Kiley shook his head firmly. "If you get the bus bomber, there's nothing the brass can say about how you let me work. You give me this and I'll give you the bus bomber."

Madzak rose and walked around the office, one palm at the back of his neck as if he had a headache. "I had a partner get killed on me once," he said quietly. "We were trying to catch a prowler in an apartment building over on Jackson Boulevard. I took the front, my partner took the back. He wanted to call for backup, but I wouldn't listen to him. 'What for?' I said. 'It's a lousy prowler. Why share the collar?' Only thing was, this prowler was carrying. A little twelve-dollar Saturday-night special. Drilled my partner in the left eye with it; he was DOA at county hospital. That was more than thirty years ago, but I've never quite gotten over it." Madzak paused behind Joe and patted him briefly on the shoulder. "I want you in the office at least once a day for an hour. Aside from that, you're free to work as you please on the bus bomber case."

Kiley rose and they shook hands. "Thanks, Captain."

"Good luck, Joe."

# EIGHT

**W**hen Stella Bianco opened the door for Joe, her face was still badly swollen from crying, her large, usually lively eyes red-ringed and puffy, with dark hollows under them. She wore no makeup, and Joe realized that it was only the second time he had ever seen her without it; the first had been in Resurrection Hospital about two hours after Tessie had been born, seven years earlier. Joe had paced the maternity waiting room that day as nervously as Nick had, and after the baby arrived Nick had insisted Joe come in to see Stella and their new daughter with him. Always after that, Stella had kidded Joe that he was the only man besides her husband who had "seen me at my very worst." But to Joe she had looked beautiful that morning in the pale, drawn wake of labor, holding her new infant. This, the way she looked now, ravaged by sudden grief and an exhausting wake-and-funeral program—this was easily the worst he had ever seen her.

And still he thought her beautiful.

"Joe, come in," she said hoarsely, taking his hand. "I'm so glad you could come." She stood on tiptoe to kiss him on the cheek. "Go see Tessie; she's watching cartoons in the family room. Then come on back to the kitchen."

"Where's Jennie?" he asked.

"I got her ready for bed early. Maybe she'll come down later." Stella shook her head uncertainly. "She seems to be taking it so much harder than Tess—"

"She knew her daddy longer," Joe said quietly, squeezing Stella's hand.

In the family room he found seven-year-old Teresa on her stomach, chin propped in her hands, both feet up and wiggling, as she watched a Rug Rats cartoon. "Hiya, beautiful," Kiley said, sitting on the couch.

"Uncle Joey!" She was up and onto his lap in an instant, giving him a hug and a big smacker kiss, then settling familiarly, comfortably, back against him. "Jennie went to bed crying about Daddy," she said.

"Your mommy told me. She said you were being a very brave girl."

"I cry sometimes too," Teresa said frankly. "But I'm not crying right now."

"That's good. And for being brave, you get these," he pulled a bag of jelly beans, her favorite, from his pocket. "For *after* supper," he cautioned. Giving her another kiss, Kiley put the little girl back on the floor and went into the kitchen. Stella was at the stove.

"The spaghetti sauce will be a few minutes yet, Joe. Pour yourself a glass of wine."

Kiley got a fat bottle of dark red wine from a cupboard and filled two of the small, stemless, Old Country glasses that Nick's father had passed on to him from his own father, glasses that had come from the village of Bianco in the Calabria region of Italy, where the family originated. Kiley held one of the glasses out to Stella.

"Joe, I shouldn't," she protested. "I need to stay clearheaded for the girls—"

"You need it," Joe insisted. "It'll help you relax, help you get to sleep tonight. I can tell by your eyes you haven't been sleeping."

"I know I must look like hell," she said, pushing her hair back.

"You couldn't look like hell if you tried," Joe scoffed. He touched his glass to hers and they drank with only a silent toast. Then Stella sat wearily on a kitchen chair and suddenly tears came.

"Christ, Joe, what am I going to do—what am I going to do?" she asked in anguish.

"You're going to go on living, Stel," he said, sitting around the corner of the table from her. Seeing her begin to tremble, he took the glass of wine from her hand and set it down. "That's all you *can* do," he told her in the softest voice he could command. "Go on living—for your girls and for yourself. Work at getting through it one day at a time. That's the only way."

"I keep waiting for it to start getting better," she wept, "just a little bit, but it doesn't, it only gets worse—"

"Maybe it's too soon to start getting better," he said. "Maybe grief has to peak, like pain, before it starts getting better. But it *will* start, Stel."

She fluttered her hands like a broken-winged sparrow. "I keep reaching for him in bed. I get so cold at night, Joe—"

"It'll get easier," Kiley promised, taking her hands to still them.

"Hello, Uncle Joey," a voice said, and they both looked around to see Jennifer, the ten-year-old, come in. She had on a nightgown and robe, her hair mussed from being in bed.

"Hello, sweetheart," Kiley said, opening his arms as she came to him.

"Did you have a nice rest, baby?" Stella asked, brushing Jennie's hair back with her fingers.

"It was okay," Jennie said, hugging Joe. "May I eat dinner with Uncle Joey?"

"Of course you can. Go wash your face and comb your hair, then get your sister."

"Tessie's eating jelly beans," Jennie said as she left the room.

"Oh, not before dinner," Stella moaned.

"My fault," Joe quickly alibied his goddaughter. "I forgot to tell her not to."

"All she's eaten since the funeral is junk," Stella said, taking a sip of wine. "Oh, well. I guess it won't hurt her. But I've *got* to get some kind of order back in this house—" She stirred the sauce, then resignedly sat down at the table again.

"Listen, Stella, if there's anything I can help you with around here," Joe offered, "just let me know. Seems like Nick was always talking about fixing this, fixing that—"

"I know," Stella smiled cheerlessly. "His favorite saying was—"

"It's always something," Joe finished it for her.

"Yeah. He got that from Gilda Radner. That's what she used to say, right up until she died of cancer." Stella thought about Joe's offer. "Actually, there's nothing that needs doing right now. Nick's cousin Frank has been dropping over every day to see how we are. He fixed one of Tessie's dolls whose arm came off. And he said he'd seed the lawn for me when it gets warmer. You know Frank, don't you? Uncle Gino's son. Sells cars at one of Gino's lots."

"Yeah, we've met." Gino Bianco's words resurfaced in Kiley's mind. . . . *Consider how it looks . . . not there to back Nick up . . . comfortable around Nick's widow . . . stay away from Stella for a while . . .* Kiley could not help wondering if Gino wanted him out of the way so his son Frank could make a move on Stella. He wouldn't put it past the devious old bastard to try and take advantage of a grieving widow.

"Joe," Stella asked after a moment, "does the department know yet who killed Nick?"

"Not yet," Kiley replied, shaking his head. "There's a suspect, but nothing solid. I'll let you know as soon as something breaks."

Stella nodded, looked distraught for a moment, then said, "Joe, there is one thing I need done, and I wouldn't ask anybody but you. A man from the—the morgue—dropped off a box with Nick's things in it—his clothes and things. I—I haven't opened it yet—I couldn't—"

"Where is it?"

"On his workbench in the basement."

Kiley went down to the basement where Nick had one corner, nearest the furnace for heat, set up as a small workshop. It was where Nick repaired cupboard doors and broken toys, repainted the screens every spring, put new posts in sprinkler heads, whatever else needed doing by a husband and father. The work space on the counter was clear except for a plain gray carton made of shipping weight cardboard, sealed with filament tape. Printed on the top in felt tip marker was: BIANCO–1172307.

Kiley found a pocketknife in the drawer of the bench and slit the tape. Inside were two heavy-gauge, clear plastic bags: a large one containing Nick's clothing, some of it, Kiley could see, badly stained with ossified blood; and another, smaller bag containing Nick's personal effects: wallet, everyday watch, pocket comb, handkerchief, regulation revolver, ammunition, holster, handcuffs, backup pistol and holster, belt, tie clip, some loose change, keys, Nick's spiral pocket notebook, and a ballpoint pen. There wouldn't be a badge, Joe knew; Chief Cassidy had told him Nick's badge was missing from his body. Also no wedding band; Katie Muldoon, the public affairs lieutenant sent out to be with Stella the first day, had personally gone to the morgue and picked up Nick's wedding band so it could be buried with him.

Opening the smaller of the two bags, Kiley removed the things that had to do with the job: Nick's two guns, holsters, ammunition, the handcuffs, the spiral notebook. Those he put on top of the bagged clothing and closed the box. Using the outside basement door, he took the box out and put it in the trunk of his car. Returning to the basement, he replaced the remaining items in the smaller bag and put it in the workbench drawer.

Upstairs, he said to Stella, "I sorted his things out; there's a bag in the drawer down there. I'll take care of the rest of it. I thought I'd keep his guns and stuff for the time being—"

"Please do," Stella said, caught by an involuntary shiver. "I don't want them around in case the girls might see them. Tessie's such a little snoop lately: always into drawers, closets, whatever's closed. Nick had to threaten to spank her a couple weeks ago if she didn't stop prowling in Jen's dresser." Stella put the big bowl of sauce on the kitchen table. "We'll just eat out here, I think. It'll be cozier than the dining room. You don't mind, do you?"

"The kitchen's fine with me."

Stella patted his arm. "Get the girls while I dish up the spaghetti."

Later that night, when he got back to his apartment, Joe faced a dilemma about what to do with Nick's clothes. He put the morgue box on his coffee table and sat looking at it while he drank a glass of cold milk to help settle his stomach from Stella's spaghetti sauce. It did not seem exactly fitting to simply throw the clothes into a trash dumpster—yet what else was there to do with them? He could see without opening the bag that a great deal of Nick's blood had spread out on his shirt, one side of his coat, and the front waistband of his trousers. The clothes couldn't be donated to a thrift shop in that condition, and Joe guessed the suit—one of Nick's hijacked Valentinos, he supposed—would be impossible to dry clean. So the stuff *had* to be disposed of—but how, for Christ's sake? he wondered.

Joe knew he was procrastinating about the clothes because of the guilt he felt over Nick's death. For days he had been trying to neutralize that feeling by rationalizing that he and Nick had decided *together* on the course of action they took; that it was a *joint* decision, *equally* made, and that it had been the logical result of information connecting the dead dancer and Tony Touhy practically dropping on them out of nowhere. That and the fact that both he and Nick were buried in a GA slot they'd probably never get out of unless they attracted some attention. Not that he himself any longer coveted promotion; mostly all he did anymore was resent it when others got promoted, especially if they were black or Latino and had less seniority than he had. One of the things that had capped his and Nick's decision to take a run at Ronnie Lynn's killer themselves was when Dietrick and Meadows had shown up from Homicide. Both Joe and Nick knew about Dietrick; he was a dickhead who had made promotion by blowing away two punks in a liquor store heist while taking a slug in the thigh himself—pure fucking blind luck to go out for a bottle of Seagram's and walk in on a play like that. And Meadows, he made promotion by being a spade, plain and simple; he was part of the mayor's quota.

So Joe and Nick had decided—*together*—to go for a collar themselves. It was done all the time. But this time it had backfired. Backfired, big time.

Fuck it, Joe thought. All the justifying in the world wasn't going to wash it. He felt responsible for Nick's death—period.

Finishing the milk, he went into his little kitchen, rinsed the glass, and put it in the dishwasher. Always clean up after yourself right away, his mother had taught him early on. The secret to keeping a clean house is never to let it get ahead of you. Kiley's kitchen could have been on the cover of a hygiene magazine, it was that clean. Maddie Leary Kiley would have been proud of her boy.

From a cupboard, Kiley took another glass and a bottle of Beefeater's, and poured himself three ounces. Sitting back down in front of the morgue box, he sipped the gin straight, at shelf temperature. All right now, he began marshaling his thoughts. Deal with the accountability. If it's actually your fault that Nick's dead, then accept it; even if you just *think* it's your fault, it amounts to the same thing, so accept it. And if you're going to *make* yourself take the heat for it, then all you can do is look for atonement to go along with it, just like when you were a kid going to confession. Extricate yourself from sin by making amends. Fifty "Our Fathers" and a hundred "Hail Marys" would get you off the hook for just about anything back then, short of raping a Mother Superior.

But how, he asked himself as the gin bit his throat, could he do it now; how could he compensate for Nick's death? He couldn't bring him back. He had already decided to keep trying to nail Tony Touhy on his own time, even though it might cost him his badge if he got caught at it. And even though he didn't have the remotest idea how to proceed, he had nevertheless covered himself for unmonitored fieldwork by getting the bus bomber case, so he was pretty much free and clear to operate any way he pleased. But operate *how*? In what direction? Everybody had the Tony Touhy connection now: Homicide, OCB, IA, the Chief. The only way he was going to come up with something they *didn't* come up with, was to cross the line. Work dirty. Bend the rules. Break the law.

All of which Joe Kiley was perfectly willing to do. But again, how?

Assuming, he thought, that Nick's killer would be made, whether by Homicide, OCB, himself, or a combination thereof, what then? Arrest, arraignment, trial, conviction, and—what? The death penalty? A fucking joke. Illinois had one hundred fifty-three people on Death Row, and had only executed one—*one!*—in nearly thirty years. The implementation of capital punishment, in Illinois anyway, sucked.

Okay, so a life sentence. That put a killer up for parole in twelve, practically guaranteed release after no more than twenty, maybe twenty-two. Jennie and Tessie would probably be young marrieds with kids of their own, and the hood that murdered their father would be out walking the street.

Maybe, Joe thought with another sip of gin, his duty in the situation was to make sure justice wasn't served that palatably. Maybe it should be his function now to make sure Nick's killer paid in kind for what he did. Bullet for bullet.

And what *about* Jennie and Tessie? And Stella? He had to watch himself very carefully in whatever he did, because he had an obligation to them too. He had to make sure Stella's pension remained intact, no matter what. And, he nodded solemnly to himself on this one, he had to make sure she didn't get taken advantage of by Nick's pompous Uncle Gino and his flaky son Frank. Stella was too smart for that, Joe was almost positive, but in a time of loss, of grief, of uncertainty, she might be temporarily vulnerable. It galled him to think that Frank Bianco might have his eye on Stella, that he might be thinking of her in a personal way, a—sexual way; the dago son of a bitch.

Resting his head back against the couch, Joe forced the anger to pass by thinking back over the evening. Even though sad at times, tense here and there, on the whole it had been a nice evening. If he thought for a moment that at some time in the future Stella would even *consider*—

But he could not allow himself to start hoping in *that* direction. As far as he was concerned, Stella Bianco was still only a dream, a fantasy when he let her be, a woman unattainable; his partner's wife, who had looked upon him as a surrogate big brother to her husband, an "uncle" to her children, an unmarried friend whose bachelorhood she thought it was her divine destiny to undo. No, he was sure Stella would never think of him as he wished in the deepest part of him that she would.

Finally, with a heavy sigh, having accomplished nothing that made him feel one iota better, Joe set down the gin glass and opened the morgue box. The goddamn things *had* to be tended to. Putting aside Nick's guns and other things, he carried the box into the kitchen and put the morgue bag of bloodstained clothing into a green plastic trash bag. He broke down the sides of the box, flattening it, and put that in the trash bag too. Leaving the bag on the counter, he returned to the living room and the guns and other articles on the table. As he tried to decide where to put the things until—and if—Stella ever wanted them, his expression suddenly drew into a frown and, as if having an out-of-body experience, he watched his hand push everything else aside and pick up Nick's spiral notebook.

*Jesus Christ, how could he have been so fucking dense?*

Incredulous at himself, refusing to lean on any excuse—the shock of Nick's death, the funeral, the censure in the chief's office—he could only shake his head in total, abject disbelief. His exact words to Nick over the telephone now illuminated in his mind with dazzling brilliance, as if they had never lain dormant at all.

*"Get license numbers; if the Jag doesn't show, we can at least find out who has parking privileges."*

Then later, Nick's excited voice on the answering machine: *"The whole fucking parking lot behind the joint is full—"*

Slowly and deliberately, Joe fingered through the pages of the little dime-store notebook until he came to the last one that had anything written on it.

And there they were: seven license plate numbers printed in Nick's neat, precise hand.

Five minutes later, Kiley was in his car on the way downtown to the Shop.

B-and-A was deserted that time of night except for one duty cop who was keeping awake by doing the day's filing. "Help you?" he asked as Kiley came in. Kiley went over and extended his hand.

"Joe Kiley. I'm on TAD here, started today."

"Lee Tumac," the duty cop shook hands, then went to his desk and checked a squad roster. "Oh, yeah. You're the GA from Warren. Sorry about your partner. So what're you doing here this time of night?"

"Trying to clean up the last of my open GA stuff. I need to run a few plate numbers and I didn't want to go back to the division to do it. That's where my partner and I were together for eight years, know what I mean?"

"Absolutely," Tumac said. "Memories can be a bitch. No problem." He pointed to a row of three computer terminals against a back wall. "Help yourself."

"Thanks."

As Tumac went back to his time-passing work, Joe turned on a monitor and accessed motor vehicle records. Nick had taken down the plate numbers of three Cadillac Sevilles, two Lincoln Town Cars, a Lincoln Mark VIII, and a Corvette. Logging onto the data base host, Joe keyed in all seven numbers and waited. When the information began coming up, he saw at once that he was going to get nothing. But it was a *curious* nothing.

All three Sevilles, both Town Cars, and the Mark VIII showed:

ACCESS RESTRICTED
ORGANIZED CRIME BUREAU ONLY

But the Corvette showed:

ACCESS RESTRICTED
STREET GANGS BUREAU ONLY

Street Gangs only? How the hell does that fit? Joe wondered. The Street Gangs squad dealt with outfits like the El Rukns, the Latin Princes, the Disciples, the Cobras, and other street trash cliques which had staked out parts of the city as their turf, their 'hood; areas which they ran by intimidation and violence, while engaging in open warfare with other crews. But what did that have to do with organized crime, Kiley asked himself, with Phil Touhy and the mob? It was something he would have to find out.

Shutting down the terminal, he went back over to Lee Tumac and said, "I need to make a couple of calls but I don't have a desk yet—" He left the request hanging. There was an office full of unoccupied desks, but a cop did not just sit down at another cop's desk. That wasn't done. A cop's desk was as personal as his wallet.

"Use that desk over there," Tumac pointed, "the one with nothing on it; that's probably gonna be yours anyway."

"Okay, thanks."

The desk Tumac had indicated was the only one in the big office that was devoid of piles of paper and files, and missing as well individual items such as ashtrays, photographs, calendars. Kiley found a metro telephone directory in the bottom drawer and looked in the M section for Gloria Mendez, hoping almost against hope that she would not have an unlisted number. He found a Mendez, G., no address listed, in the 276 prefix, which was the Humboldt Park precinct where Nick said he and Gloria had worked together. The area was about eighty percent Puerto Rican. Joe dialed the number. On the third ring, a young-sounding female voice answered. "Yeah, hello—"

"Gloria Mendez, please."

"Who's calling?"

"Joe Kiley. I'm a police officer."

"Hold on," the voice said, unimpressed. Then Kiley heard in the background, "Some cop named Joe something."

A moment later, Gloria came on. "Hello—"

"Hello, Gloria. This is Joe Kiley. How come you don't have an unlisted number?"

"Why should I? Street cops make enemies, not Records cops. I don't have to conceal my phone number. Although right now I'm thinking maybe I should. What do you want, Joe?"

"I was just wondering: any flak yet?"

"No. And I don't want to discuss it any further on the telephone, understand?"

"Understand. But I do need to talk to you. Can I come by for a few minutes?"

"Look, Joe, that's not such a good idea. I'm out of the situation."

"So's Nick," said Kiley. "All the way out. I thought you might want to help with that. If I'm wrong, just tell me and I'll leave you alone."

There was a long moment of silence on the line. It told Kiley he was not wrong.

"Eighteen eighty-two Kimball," she finally said. "Three-B."

"Twenty minutes," Kiley told her.

The Humboldt Park section of the city didn't know whether it was a slum or a redevelopment area. Decaying, falling-down residential and commercial buildings stood next door to places that were being vigorously renovated and improved. In the former could be found the street trash of the district: the Latin Princes dressed in their red and green gang colors; the junkies and petty thieves; the winos who had given up trying; the ex-gang girls who had been dumped and now peddled pussy on the street. But in the latter, working at whatever their dream was, were the industrious, family-together *Latinos* who worked at honest jobs, usually for substandard wages, and at night nailed back together, cleaned up, began to paint and wallpaper some abandoned trap of a building or house that the city had taken over and sold to them for—to the city—pocket change. Somehow, the two diverse societies, perhaps because of their mutual culture, managed to coexist and survive.

The building at 1882 Kimball was a three-story six-flat that was only moderately well-kept on the outside and in the downstairs foyer, but looked better once Kiley had rung Gloria Mendez's bell and was past the buzzer-controlled door. Inside, it smelled heavy of salsa, and from more than one direction came the sound of mambo. Kiley took the stairs two at a time. Gloria, in jeans and sweatshirt, was waiting for him at the top with her apartment door open.

"Hi," Joe said.

"Come in," Gloria replied, without returning the greeting.

The living room was comfortably but not expensively furnished, clearly a female room with no sign of anything masculine. Lounging on the couch, chewing gum, wearing too much makeup, was a prime, pubescent body in tight toreador pants, a bare midriff halter top, and spike heels that should have come with a whip.

"This is my daughter Meralda, Joe. MeMe, this is Mr. Kiley."

"*Officer* Kiley?" the girl asked pointedly, rising.

"Detective Kiley," Joe said. "But you can call me 'Officer' if you want to. You can also call me Joe."

A very slight smile from Gloria seemed to say yes, that was the way to handle her. "Mr. Kiley and I have some business to discuss, MeMe," her mother said. "You may go into your bedroom and close the door, or you may go outside for a little while as long as you stay on the block."

"Is it police business or personal business you're going to discuss?" the teenager asked brashly.

"Your room or outside on the block—now," Gloria told her firmly.

As Meralda was walking out the door, she said over her shoulder, "I think you can do a lot better than another cop, Mama."

The door was closed before Gloria could respond, so all she did was roll her eyes in exasperation and say to Joe, "Sorry about that."

"Don't apologize to me," Kiley said. "I agree with her. You could do a lot better than a cop."

"I'll keep the opinions of both of you in mind next time I go shopping for a man," Gloria said dryly. "Sit down, Joe. What is it you want?"

Kiley handed her Nick's notebook, open to the last page the dead detective had used. "Nick wrote those down during the last few hours he was alive. All of those cars were parked behind the Shamrock Club during that time. Six of the plate numbers are access-restricted to OCB—"

"No, Joe, forget it," Gloria was already shaking her head.

"—but the Corvette is restricted access to the Street Gangs Bureau," Kiley continued talking. "It doesn't make sense."

"What doesn't make sense is for me to get involved in this any deeper than I already am," Gloria told him.

"I don't want any files here," Joe said, holding his palms up to reassure her. "Just names and addresses, motor vehicle stuff—"

"Restricted access is restricted access, Joe!" she said with an edge. "When I override it on a master terminal, a record is made!"

"Can't it be deleted?"

"Not by me, it can't, not for thirty days. Can you guarantee my cover for thirty days?"

Kiley shook his head. "You know I can't."

"All right then." Sitting in a club chair facing the couch, Gloria leaned forward, forearms on her knees, and Kiley became aware that her breasts shifted buoyantly with the movement. "Look, try to understand. I've got thirteen years invested in the department. I worked damned hard to get my sergeant stripes—in spite of what the Irish, Italian, and Polish cops think; Puerto Ricans and blacks *do* have to pass the exam. I've got a kid to finish raising, and hope to God I can get her to go to college instead of getting knocked up in some Latin Prince club room or in the backseat of some gas station attendant's sound-wired car. I've saving to buy a little house someplace so I won't have to pay rent forever." Her eyes hardened. "You're asking me to put a lot at risk, Joe. And for a dead man who wasn't even *my* man."

Joe stared at her for a long, steady moment, then slowly nodded his head. "You're right," he said quietly. "Right all the way. This isn't your fight. You weren't responsible for Nick being killed, I was."

"You are *not* responsible for Nick being killed," Gloria insisted. "You're crazy if you start punishing yourself for that."

"I'm responsible enough to want to nail whoever did it."

"Every cop in the department feels that way, Joe. Nick was a cop, one of us, part of us. Whoever killed him killed a little bit of all of us. But there's no personal *blame* involved."

"There's blame when you *feel* blame." Kiley rose and took the notebook from Gloria's hand. "I appreciate what you're saying. You may even be right, in theory. But I know how I feel—and how I feel is guilty. And I know in my heart and in my mind that the feeling will never go away unless I make things at least partly right by seeing to it that whoever pulled the trigger doesn't get away with it."

"Do you think it was Tony Touhy?" Gloria asked, rising to face him.

"I think he had to be involved," Joe reasoned. "It was him that Nick followed. And it stands to reason that Nick must have caught him with his knuckles bruised; I mean, Touhy had to have a *reason* to off Nick. Maybe Nick was afraid the punk would get away from us, so he tried to bust him for the Ronnie Lynn killing without waiting for me to get there. And maybe one of Touhy's friends interfered." He tapped Nick's notebook. "Maybe the driver of one of these cars interfered."

"You make it hard not to help," Gloria Mendez said.

"I don't mean to," Kiley told her, and meant it. "I realized something a minute ago, when you were talking about your job: I don't think Nick would want you involved either. Not any deeper than you already are."

"You're right," she agreed. "He was sorry he came to me in the first place. He told me so."

"When?" Kiley asked, surprised.

"The night he was killed. He called me about eight o'clock, from the stakeout. Same phone he was using to check with you. We talked for almost an hour. Even made plans to see each other again, just for lunch sometime. We were going to try to be friends, you know; just friends, without going to bed together. Anyway, Nick apologized for putting me in the position he had with the Tony Touhy file. And he took full blame for it: He said it was his idea, that he hadn't even told you about me until the day you two came down to the Shop. Was that true?"

Kiley nodded. "True."

"Well, see, then," she pointed out, "that right there should convince you that he was as eager to clear the killing of that girl as you were. He wasn't just following the lead of his senior team partner; if he had been, he never would've mentioned me as a way of helping the plan along. So you can stop blaming yourself so much."

"Maybe you're right," Kiley acknowledged. "But I still want to be in on taking down whoever killed him."

"Know something?" Gloria said, reaching out and taking back the notebook. "So do I."

When she offered her hand to Kiley, he hesitated. "You're sure?"

"I'm sure," she said, her tone unequivocal.

Joe Kiley took her hand. He felt like he had a partner again.

# NINE

The next morning, Kiley reported for work on the B-and-A squad and was taken around by Captain Madzak to meet the other day watch personnel. They all knew, without the details, about Joe having lost his partner, so their greetings were deferential, without the usual jiving and joking that would normally have been directed at a new man. "Nice to meet you, Kiley. Sorry about your partner," was about the extent of most of the introductions. Joe was given the desk that he had used briefly the night before, that Lee Tumac, the duty cop in B-and-A, had said would probably be his anyway.

"Draw your desk supplies from the squad secretary," Captain Madzak told him. "Spend an hour or so getting settled, then you can beat it for the day. But," he pointed an emphasizing finger, "I want something on my bus bomber, understood?"

"Understood, Captain," Kiley assured him. "You'll get it."

Kiley got his desk supplies from a heavyset black woman named Aldena, who brooked no nonsense about what he was receiving. "This stuff I'm giving you got to last ninety days," she warned. "This squad is on a tight supplies budget and I stick to it like glue. Don't go taking ballpoints and calendars and stuff home, then come expecting me to give you more, 'cause I won't do it. I made the *captain* go out and buy his own paper clips last week, that's how tight I am. You reading me, Detective?"

"Loud and clear," Kiley said. He had seen dozens of squad secretaries over the years; sooner or later, they *all* thought they ran the squad. Some of them, due in part to their civil service status, could be extremely difficult. But they were invaluable to most commanders, and for the cops in "their" squad, they would break almost any rule—except their own. "Here, take these back," Kiley handed her a box of six ballpoints. "These are medium points; I use fine points."

"I don't requisition no special items," she told him, shaking her head emphatically.

"No problem, I buy my own," Kiley said. Aldena smiled.

"You I like already," she told him.

Kiley returned to his new desk and was putting everything away when his phone rang. Gloria, he thought. She was going to trace the license plate numbers Nick had taken down behind the Shamrock Club and call him with the restricted information. But when he answered, it was Captain Madzak.

"Joe, step into my office, will you?"

Kiley went in and the captain had him sit.

"I just got a call from Deputy Chief Les Ward. The sister of some homicide vic is in the building from out of town somewhere; her name," he glanced at a scratch pad, "is Alma Lynn."

"Yeah, Bianco and I handled the GA workup on a Ronnie Lynn, two nights before Nick was killed. It was turned over to Homicide."

Madzak nodded. "The Homicide officers handling the case are both down at Stateville today interviewing a con involved in another case they're on. The chief's office wants you to handle the vic's sister, since you're the only one around with any firsthand details."

"Yeah, sure," Joe agreed at once. He sensed a possible source of information about Tony Touhy, but kept the interest out of his expression.

"Escort her to the morgue for the formal ID, then to Property for the vic's things. Answer whatever questions you can for her *except* those pertaining to the progress of the investigation; tell her that's classified. When you're finished, type up an FR for the chief and send it through me. Clear?"

"Yessir, clear." An FR was a Field Report that did not involve a crime.

"A secretary from the Public Affairs office is bringing the sister down right now. Check out a car from the motor pool."

Kiley returned to his desk and quickly dialed Gloria Mendez's extension upstairs. "Central Records, Sergeant Mendez," she answered.

"Gloria, Joe. Listen, I'm going to be out of the office for a few hours, so don't call me. I'll get back to you later, okay?"

"Sure. I haven't had a chance to do it anyway. They found three little kids hanged in a basement over around 92nd and Prairie this morning, and everything else is shut down while we run suspect parameters on that situation."

Kiley saw two women enter the B-and-A reception area and go up to Aldena's desk. "Okay, I've got to go. Call you later." Hanging up, he put on his coat, carried his hat, and walked toward the front of the squad room. As he got closer to the two women, his mouth dropped open in surprise. One of them had a trim figure, red hair, freckles——

"Detective Kiley?" said the woman with a police ID clipped to her dress. "This is Ms. Alma Lynn. Ms. Lynn, Detective Joseph Kiley. You've received Deputy Chief Ward's message, Detective?"

"Uh , yes—yes, I have—" Kiley was trying to overcome his surprise.

"My sister and I were identical twins," Alma Lynn said. "I'm sorry; I should have asked someone to alert you."

"It's all right," Kiley regained his composure. "I just wasn't prepared—"

"Of course not—"

"I'll leave Ms. Lynn in your care, Detective," said the woman from Public Affairs.

"Sure, fine. Ms. Lynn, if you'll come with me, I'll get a car and we can drive out to Steiner Center."

"Steiner Center?"

"The county pathology and forensics center, Ms. Lynn. The morgue."

"Oh. Yes, of course."


Driving up Roosevelt Road, Alma Lynn said from the passenger seat, "I really am sorry I shocked you like that."

"Forget it," said Kiley. He pulled a brief, reassuring smile for her. "Where are you from, Ms. Lynn?"

"Ripley, Indiana. It's about three hours south, just across the line." The line was a ruler-straight boundary that divided Illinois and Indiana for nearly two hundred miles. "A very small town," Alma Lynn added needlessly.

"If you don't mind my asking, how did your sister get from Ripley, Indiana, to the West Side of Chicago?"

Alma Lynn smiled bleakly. "She was bored. Ripley isn't a very exciting place. Some of the high school kids I teach refer to it as a 'one Coke machine' town."

"What do you teach?" Kiley purposely kept it conversational, working her slowly.

"Typing and girls' PE." She sighed almost inaudibly. Kiley wondered if it was for her sister, or because she too was bored with Ripley, Indiana. "Anyway," Alma continued, "Ronnie decided to try her luck up here. She wanted to get into broadcasting or advertising or—you know, something glamorous."

"I understand." Kiley understood, all right. Ronnie Lynn had been a pilgrim coming to Mecca. A young woman looking for the kind of life they show on television, then ending up dancing naked for a bunch of spades; later—or even before—maybe shooting dope; still later, maybe peddling pussy to pull the habit. Sure, Kiley understood; he'd seen dozens of them. "When was the last time you talked to your sister?" he asked, turning on Ashland Avenue and approaching the edge of the vast Cook County Hospital complex.

"Apparently just a few hours before she was killed," Alma said. "She called me about four-thirty—she knows I get home about four."

"Could you tell me what her frame of mind was? What kind of mood she was in? Whether she seemed worried?"

"Very good mood," the sister told him. "The first good mood she'd been in for a while. She'd broken up with a boyfriend a couple of weeks earlier, and a few phone calls before that one she had sounded depressed and all. But this time she seemed to have gotten used to the split and was dealing with it in a positive way. In fact, she was going to see her ex-boyfriend that night and return a ring he had given her."

"Yes, we knew about that," Kiley said. "What was the ex-boyfriend's name, do you know?"

"Tony something. I don't think Ronnie ever told me his last name."

Kiley silently cursed his luck at this latest dead end on Tony Touhy's last name. A connection through the dead woman's sister might have been enough for Dietrick and Meadows to get a warrant and pick the punk up on suspicion. Nail him for Ronnie Lynn, maybe nail him for Nick too. But no tie-in, no warrant.

Kiley pulled into a visitor space at the morgue and had Alma Lynn accompany him inside. Alma, he noticed as he held the door open, then followed her in, was slightly heavier than the dead Ronnie had appeared: upper arms a little rounder, a cup size larger in the bust, more defined buttocks. But her body was well toned, firm; from teaching PE, he supposed; Ronnie had probably been in equally as good shape from her go-go dancing, which was really nothing more than aerobics set to a jazzy beat, with some vulgar moves added. Odd, he thought, considering the divergent paths their lives apparently had taken, how they had remained so close in physical condition.

After checking in with an attendant and filling out the required form, Kiley and Alma Lynn were taken below street level by elevator and led into a large room with what looked like long, stacked rows of file drawers. The smell of formaldehyde wafted in the cool air; their footsteps were silent on the rubber-tiled floor.

"Let's see," the attendant said, scanning the rows as he walked, "Lynn, number three-two-nine—Lynn, three-twenty-nine—here we go—"

Kiley put a light grip on Alma Lynn's elbow, saying, "Just a quick look—"

The attendant pulled out drawer number 329 and turned back the light-gauge plastic cover, revealing Ronnie Lynn's battered face and breasts, her flesh an ugly black-and-blue cast created by her brutal death, compounded by the temperature of the morgue slab.

Alma Lynn's knees buckled slightly; she put one knuckle between her teeth to keep from crying out as she looked down on what was left of the sister with whom she had shared a womb. Kiley tightened his grip to steady her, saying, "Just nod that it's her, that's all you have to do."

But Alma said, "Yes—it's my—sister—"

"Okay." He put an arm around her shoulders and led her away, back out of the room of death, to the elevator in the hall.

Upstairs, Alma completed more forms that swore to her identification of the corpse, permitted the morgue to turn over to Alma the pathetic items— red bikini top and bottom with tassels, terry-cloth robe, scuffed terry-cloth sandals, ankle bracelet—taken from the dead woman, and made arrangements to have the body released to a funeral home in Ripley, Indiana.

When they got back out to the car, Alma opened the morgue box— much smaller than the one Nick Bianco's things had been delivered in— and delicately fingered the bikini bottom. "Not much to it, is there?" she asked, almost rhetorically. She looked at the morgue inventory list. "No ring. I guess she had given it back to that Tony, whoever he was."

"Ms. Lynn, do you have your sister's personal effects," Kiley asked, "from where she lived?"

"I'm picking those up this afternoon," Alma replied. "The police went through them but I understand they didn't take anything. Ronnie just had a room in a cheap little hotel; the management packed her things and is holding them. I think I have to pay some back rent—" Alma Lynn suddenly put a hand on Kiley's arm. "Detective Kiley, I have something I must confide in someone—it's something I have to find out about but it's not an easy subject to bring up—"

"The photographs?" Kiley asked.

"You have them?" Alma snatched her hand away from his arm as if it had been burned.

"No. I just know about them. Look, would you like to get a cup of coffee?"

"I'd really like to talk about those photographs—"

"So would I. But not in the car like this. Come on—"

They got out of the car and Kiley took her across the street to St. Luke's Hospital. There was a large cafeteria there, used mainly by medical staff, but open to visitors as well. Kiley had Alma go to a table for two in a near corner while he went through a counter line and got their coffee. At the table, Kiley leaned forward on his forearms and kept his voice low.

"Look, Ms. Lynn, I'm going to be honest with you about this case, even though I could get in a lot of trouble for doing it. The police department is very touchy about cops discussing evidence and the progress of a criminal investigation with civilians; but I have a personal interest in this case, and maybe we can help each other."

"May I ask what your personal interest is?" Alma Lynn stiffened perceptibly. "Did you know my sister?"

"No, it was nothing like that; the first time I ever laid eyes on your sister was in that alley. My interest is that I had a partner that I had worked with for eight years, who was like a kid brother to me, and he was shot dead two days after your sister was killed. He and I were looking for your sister's killer on our own time. I think it's possible that the same person either killed both of them, or is responsible for the killings."

"Oh. I see," Alma said, unstiffening, relaxing. "I'm sorry if I sounded curt. But I have very bitter feelings about the people in this city whom Ronnie knew. Everyone she ever spoke about since she came here sounded to me as if they were using her in some way, taking advantage of her. I can't tell you how many times I cried after talking to her on the phone—" From her purse, Alma took a tissue and dabbed at her eyes. "It's a bad place, this city—"

Kiley let the remark pass. He loved Chicago, every filthy gutter of it, every stinking alley, every spewing smokestack, every grating noise; it was in his blood, his city blood, and in his being. But he was not there to defend Chicago to this small-town Indiana schoolteacher who had just looked at her dead twin sister on a morgue slab. Before Kiley realized it, Alma Lynn was lightly touching his arm again, across the table.

"I'm sorry about your partner, Mr. Kiley; I didn't know. You must be feeling as miserable as I am right now. What can I do to help?"

"Let's talk about the photographs. What I know about them, I picked up from one of the other dancers at the 4-Star. I gather they were pornographic in nature, and that your sister wanted them back because of that. What do you know about them?"

"Only what Ronnie told me. She mentioned them to me one night on the phone; I think she was a little drunk at the time. The, uh—reason she told me—" Alma hesitated, uncertainty gripping her. "Look, is this going to go into a report of any kind; I mean, be written down later?"

"Absolutely not," Kiley assured. "I'm as much at risk in this conversation as you are, believe me."

"All right." She took a quick breath. "The reason that Ronnie told me about the photographs is that she and I used to do the same thing. Not sexually explicit, of course; just what we thought was titillating. When we were teenagers, after we had begun, uh, developing on top, we used to take Polaroid shots of each other in our underwear, posing like the pinups we'd see in magazines. We even removed the underwear sometimes and took close-up shots of—certain parts of our bodies without showing our faces. A couple of times before class we slipped a picture into a textbook of one of the male teachers, just to watch his reaction. Anyway, I think Ronnie told me about *her* photos because they reminded her of what she and I had done as adolescents. I asked her what *kind* of pictures she had taken with this guy, this Tony, but she just laughed and said, 'Pretty hot ones, Al, *very* hot ones.' I presume they were quite explicit." She hesitated a beat, then asked, "Do you know where the pictures are?"

"I know where they *might* be. In the apartment of her ex-boyfriend, Tony. But I can't get in there without a search warrant—and I can't get a warrant without having some definite connection between him and your sister; something that I can present to a judge to ask for a warrant. You're certain she never mentioned Tony's last name?"

"Sorry. I wish she had." Alma glanced down, then back up. "Are *you* going to tell me his last name?"

"Not right now," Kiley said. "I'd rather wait and see if you can learn it yourself; it would make better evidence that way. When you go to pick up your sister's personal belongings this afternoon, try to find out anything you can. Homicide detectives have already asked some questions, but on something like this people tend to dummy up. You being her sister, they might feel sorry for you, open up a little more. Ask about her friends, who she knew, who visited her there where she lived—"

"Yes, all right. I'll go through her things too," Alma volunteered. "Maybe she has letters, or an address book—"

"The Homicide detectives have already done that; they're looking for Tony too. But anything's worth a try." Kiley took out a card, one of his old GA cards, crossed off the Warren Boulevard precinct number, and wrote in the B-and-A number. "If you can call me in the morning, around nine, to let me know whether you came up with anything or not, I'd appreciate it."

"All right, I will." Lowering her glance, Alma toyed with her cup. "I want to thank you for—well, being interested. I realize that the death of—a person like Ronnie had become—probably isn't all that important in a place like Chicago. I appreciate you and your partner trying to find who did it on your own time. I'm just very sorry you had to suffer a personal loss too."

"It's nice of you to say that," Kiley replied. Rising, he said, "I'll drop you at your hotel, if you want."

"Yes. Thank you."

As soon as Kiley got back to his desk at B-and-A, he called Gloria Mendez.

"Anything yet?" he asked.

"Oh, yes," she said, her tone suggesting something noteworthy. She fell silent then, her way of telling Kiley it was not to be discussed over the phone.

"Want to meet somewhere?"

"I can't get out of here, Joe. That situation with those three kids they found hanged has got this place jumping; they're asking for files on sex offenders now: Two of the kids were sodomized."

"Jesus Christ—" Kiley shook his head, then was glad still again that he had used a sap on that degenerate who raped the six little girls a couple of years ago. He had broken the pervert's nose, all of his fingers, and was slugging away at his genitals when two uniforms pulled him off.

Shaking his head, Kiley threw the memory back down in his mind and refused to let himself think further of the three little kids just found. "How do you want to handle it?" he asked Gloria Mendez.

"Why don't you come over to my place again," she suggested. "I want to talk to you about this stuff anyway. Come over about six; I'm home and changed by then."

"See you at six," Kiley agreed.

Captain Madzak walked up to his desk. "Finished with that homicide vic's sister?" he asked.

"Yessir. Just about to type up the FR for you and the deputy chief."

"Then you'll be on the bus bomber, right?"

"Right, Captain."

When Madzak walked away, Kiley got out a Field Report triplicate set and put it into the typewriter next to his desk. The typewriter was on a

stand with wheels, so Kiley unplugged it and rolled it back to the computer bank. Parking it on an angle next to an unoccupied monitor, he plugged
it into another outlet, sat down, and turned both typewriter and terminal
on. With his notebook open, he first keyed into the terminal: WINSTON,
Harold Paul. Then he accessed DMV for automobile registration and drivers license. While he waited for the data base to be searched, he turned
to the typewriter and typed the date and subject matter on the FR form.
Presently the monitor showed:

> Winston, Harold Paul
> No Record

Kiley accessed central credit bureau records, and went back to his typing while he waited. When the credit bureau file came up, it showed Winston with a Visa card and accounts at two department store chains; all had
small balances, all showed prompt payment. Kiley moved the monitor's
cursor up to the file menu and asked for the subject's credit application
on the Visa account. It came up almost instantly. Dated four years earlier,
it showed that Harold Paul Winston was 46 years old, unmarried, no de-
pendents, residing at 3312 N. Kalvin Avenue for three years, employed as
a stock clerk for Food Services Restaurant Supplies for nine months.
Credit record clean, Visa card approved.

Kiley next accessed Commonwealth Edison records for 3312 N. Kalvin
Avenue, which was also the address on Winston's arrest sheet. It took a
couple of minutes for that, so Kiley managed to get a full paragraph typed
on the FR about taking Alma Lynn to the morgue. Then the monitor displayed a record:

> Winston, Harold Paul
> 3312 N. Kalvin Avenue Apt. D
> Service connected 4-10-90
> No previous service history
> Deposit required: $30

I wonder, Kiley thought, where this psycho lived before Kalvin Avenue?
He copied the information into his notebook, turned off the terminal, and
resumed typing the FR.

Twenty minutes later, Kiley had given the FR to Captain Madzak, had
it approved by him, and was on his way out of the Shop. He did not both-

er checking out another unmarked police pool car, preferring to use his own. That way he would not have to account for hours checked out or miles driven.

Kiley left the south edge of the Loop and headed for the Northwest Side on the Kennedy Expressway. As he cruised along in the fast lane, he tried to analyze what he had heard in Gloria Mendez's voice a little while earlier. "Oh, yes," she had said when he'd asked her if she had anything on the seven license plate numbers. There had been something in her tone that implied importance; then something in her immediate silence that added caution. He did not want to let his hopes get too high, did not want to speculate that some kind of major lead would come out of Gloria's information; yet the feeling was definitely there that her voice, her prudence, had to be indicators of something significant. That and the fact that he had decided at their first meeting that Gloria Mendez was a very solid cop.

Leaving the Expressway at Belmont, Kiley drove into the 3300-block of North Kedzie, then cut over to Kalvin Avenue and found number 3312. It was a six-flat, not unlike the building in which Kiley himself lived. Parking in the middle of the block, Kiley got out and locked his car. Walking back toward the beginning of the block, he gave the building closer scrutiny on foot than he had been able to from the car. It was a little newer than Mrs. Levine's eight-flat, but no better kept up. Apartment D, Kiley guessed, was on the second floor. At the corner, Kiley looked down two blocks to the cross street, Elston Avenue, where he knew there was a bus line that extended from the Loop out to the Northwest suburbs. Since Winston had no drivers license and owned no car, he probably used public transportation—unless, of course, he worked somewhere in the neighborhood, within walking distance. Kiley was certain the little man had lied when he said he was not currently employed; the frown, the shifting away of his eyes, were classic signs to Kiley: the former manifesting the subject's split-second indecisiveness about whether to tell the truth; the latter an evasiveness of eye contact after deciding on, and telling, a lie.

Crossing to the side of Kalvin on which Winston's building stood, Kiley retraced his route, walked directly past number 3312, and continued on to the corner in that direction. From there, looking south now, he saw, another two blocks down, an elevated track which he knew to be the Belmont Avenue El station. Another possible line of public transportation for Winston, since it, like the Elston Avenue bus, also ran between downtown and the bedroom communities.

Kiley bought a *Sun-Times* from a vending box and started back to his car to sit and wait. Once he knew from which direction Winston returned home, he would probably know which mode of public transportation Winston took; then, by getting on that bus or that El train himself at one end of the line, or both if necessary, Kiley would be able to "accidentally" run into Winston a couple of times—or, more accurately, let Winston run into *him*, because Kiley would already be a passenger when Winston boarded—and from there Kiley would begin to handle him, work him, maneuver him into tumbling some evidence. It should not be too difficult, Kiley though; he was convinced that Winston *wanted* to be caught, that he—

Suddenly Kiley had to interrupt his analytical thinking and put his mind into an emergency response mode—because walking toward him from the other end of the block was Harold Paul Winston. Quickly turning to the building nearest him, Kiley entered the ground-floor foyer. Had he been seen? he wondered urgently. If he had, at this early stage, it would effectively botch his whole plan. Through the glass of the foyer door, Kiley was able to watch until Winston came into view. The little man was ambling along seemingly unaware of Kiley's presence; he did not even glance over at the building from which he was now being watched. Lucky, Kiley thought, very fucking lucky; he told himself he'd better stay more alert if he wanted the freedom that fieldwork provided, and not get stuck shuffling papers at some desk job because he let Captain Madzak down.

Kiley watched, expecting Winston to go all the way into his building, after which Kiley planned to wait perhaps a full minute, then saunter casually up to where his car was parked, and split. But less than a minute after Winston had disappeared into his own foyer, just as Kiley reached for the doorknob to leave, back out came Winston, the day's mail in his hand, whistling, and continued on down the block. Where the hell was he going? Kiley wondered, stepping back from the door so Winston wouldn't see him. For a paper maybe, or to get something for supper? If he lived alone like Kiley did, he probably subsisted a lot like Kiley did: frozen dinners, take-out food, an occasional steak at one of the chain of Sizzler's. Maybe he read his mail while he ate.

As Winston proceeded down to the corner, crossed the intersection, and walked on toward Belmont Avenue, Kiley emerged from the foyer and at a discreet distance followed him. Winston sauntered along as if he hadn't a care in the world, never once looking back. Dressed in slacks and a light-colored windbreaker, carrying his mail, whistling, nobody observing him in this older Northwest Side neighborhood, Kiley thought, would possibly ever suspect that he might be a lunatic bus bomber. Criminals, Kiley had frequently, and fervently, wished in his younger, uniformed days, ought to *look* like criminals. So often they didn't; so often they looked like—sometimes *were*—the next-door neighbor, or somebody's seemingly harmless cousin, or a little old lady with six cats. A cop's job would be infinitely easier if people who looked nice always were nice.

When Winston turned the corner into the shadow of the Belmont Avenue El station, Kiley fell into a trot and double-timed toward the opposite corner in order not to lose him. He got to the corner just in time to see the little man enter a door under a sign that read: BEL-KED TAVERN.

Kiley's face took on a satisfied expression. This was far better than he had hoped; far, far better than "running into" Winston on a bus or an El. This was as sweet as it got.

Newspaper under his arm, Kiley walked back to his car, very pleased with his luck. When you found out where a man drinks, he knew, you had found out where the man *talked*.

It was six-thirty and still light outside when Kiley parked on Gloria Mendez's block and walked down to her building. Meralda was on the steps in front of the entry, talking with two young Puerto Ricans who both wore the red and green colors of the Latin Princes.

"Good evening, *Detective*," the teenager said elaborately, for the benefit of her friends.

"Hello, kid," Kiley replied, causing her sassy expression to become annoyed. The two Princes gave Kiley what he imagined they thought were hard-guy looks, which he ignored completely.

When Gloria, in jeans and sweatshirt again, opened the apartment door for him, Kiley said, "Your daughter is in fast company downstairs."

"I know," Gloria said wearily. "I'm going to get her out of this *barrio* as soon as I can afford to. Anyway," she became a little ethnically defensive, "some of the Princes aren't bad kids, not really."

Kiley wasn't going to argue the point. If Meralda was his kid, he would have left the two punks busted up in the alley, then laid a heavy belt across the girl's shapely little ass. But that was him.

"Come on in the kitchen," Gloria said, leading the way. Once there, she added, "Excuse the mess; Meralda was supposed to clean up in here today—"

Kiley noted a sink full of dirty dishes, garbage that needed taking out, and a basket of unironed clothes in the corner. In his mind he silently seconded his earlier thought: a belt, right across the ass.

"You like some coffee?" Gloria asked.

"Sure." What he really wanted was the information she had, but he knew he had to let her take her time. Women, he had learned over the years, break rules slower than men.

After pouring two cups of coffee at the kitchen table, Gloria took a single sheet of paper from atop the refrigerator and handed it to Kiley. "I think you'll find this interesting—"

Kiley's eyes scanned downward from the top of the sheet, along a single column of printed data that showed seven blocks of three items each: license plate number, make and model of vehicle, name of registered owner. The first five blocks were for three Cadillacs and two Lincoln Town Cars, with the names of the registered owners being Morelli, Dellafranco, Morowski, O'Shea, and Hennessey. All were known mob names: the two Italians from the South and West side mobs of the city; the two Irishmen from the North Side family of Phil Touhy; the Polack in the mob that controlled the O'Hare International Airport area. A sixth block of information, pertaining to a Lincoln Mark VIII, showed registration to Prestige Automobile Leasing Company, in upper-class suburban Lake Forest.

But it was the seventh and last block of information that Gloria Mendez had, correctly, believed would interest Joe Kiley the most. It read:

LICENSE: 67RY410
MAKE/MODEL: Chevrolet 93 Corvette Custom Eleven
REGISTERED OWNER: Lamont, Frazier Leroy

That had been the plate, Kiley remembered, on which information was restricted to the Street Gangs Squad. He had thought it odd at the time, but had no way to pursue it at that moment. Now he frowned as the name worked its way through his memory. "Frazier Leroy Lamont—" Suddenly his expression signaled surprise to Gloria. "*Fraz* Lamont?"

"Fraz Lamont," she confirmed. "Undisputed leader of the Disciples."

"That doesn't make sense," Kiley said. "The Disciples and the *mob*?"

"I know it doesn't make sense," Gloria shrugged. "But that was his car. The Disciples must be doing pretty good, too; do you know what a Custom Eleven 'Vette runs? Sixty-five and change." She shook her head wryly. "Maybe I ought to tell Meralda to go hang out with the Disciples instead of those Latin Princes."

Kiley took a long sip of coffee. His frown remained in place. The Disciples had been the premier and predominant black street gang in Chicago since a combined federal-state-county-city law enforcement effort had so diminished its predecessor, the El Rukns, that the latter no longer controlled much of anything. The primary turf of the Disciples was the Cabrini-Green housing project and its adjacent neighborhoods: a sprawling, inner-city, primarily black ghetto bounded on one side by a sooty, stinking, smokestacked industrial area that fed daily off the sweat of thousands of factory workers; and on the other side by trendy, upscale, in-vogue Yuppie City, a neat residential area where chic young moderns with university degrees had gathered to live and interact.

Where once it had been praised as a glowing solution to the expansion of tenement neighborhoods, "the Green" had, with surprising dispatch, itself become an urban bog of the first magnitude: a vast concrete maze of drug deals, gang shootings, fear, intimidation, and ongoing black-on-black terrorism. Rising to the scum level of this swamp had been a bottom-feeding but charismatic young ex-Muslim, ex-convict, and ex-*victim* named Frazier Leroy "Fraz" Lamont, who had wormed his way into the projects drug trade and, by various covert acts of violence, soon worked up to an executive position. At the time, there were perhaps half a dozen minor gangs in the Green, none seeming to have an edge over the others, all of them barely surviving by scrounging what share they could of the then wide-open drug-trade competition. Fraz Lamont saw at once what the problem was: too little control over too many distributors. Or in his own words, later preserved for posterity by a *Tribune* feature writer granted an interview, "Too many motherfucking chiefs, man, and not enough motherfucking Indians."

Donning black slacks and a purple silk shirt as his signature dress, Fraz began eliminating his rivals the only way he deemed both propitious and permanent—by killing them. It had been estimated by the Street Gangs Intelligence Unit that Fraz personally executed no fewer than seventeen individuals, probably more, on his way to the top. Along the way he recruited loyal followers whom he called "disciples," and whom he required to wear, in some combination, his "colors." After a period of selective bloodletting, a structured organization evolved with various levels of responsibility and power that spread out like a massive tent to cloak every facet of life in the Green. And on a throne in the center of that tent, ruling with homicidal charm, sat Fraz Lamont.

Kiley would not have been more surprised if the mayor's car had been on the list of those parked at the Shamrock Club. The other names could have been predicted; the city's mob hierarchy, oddly like the city's police department, had ultimately been forced to reach out and embrace new ethnic candidates. With the department, it had been the Irish letting in first Polish-Americans, then Italian-Americans. With the mob, it had been the Italians letting in the Irish, then both of them admitting the more recently corrupted Poles. But, as Joe Kiley acutely knew, *both* communities had held firm against the blacks with fierce tenacity. It was only in the wake of civil lawsuits, and the interest of obtaining federal funds, that the department had opened up to blacks, Latinos, and other minorities by establishing hiring quotas.

But that was the *department*, Kiley knew. That was *not* the mob.

"Do you think," Gloria asked, "that the Disciples could be involved in Nick's killing?"

"I don't see how," Joe replied. "I don't believe Tony Touhy or Phil Touhy or any of those hoods on that list would have anything to do with Fraz Lamont or *any* black punk. Blacks are like aliens to the mob: They're not trusted and not liked. And as far as the Disciples are concerned, they only kill their own people; I don't think they've ever been involved with a white vic."

"Do you think Fraz might have been there dropping a payoff?" Gloria wondered.

"Possibility, I guess—although it doesn't seem likely; the book on Fraz is that he delegates everything except counting the money and having sex. Those he does himself." Kiley finished his coffee and rose. Folding the sheet, he put it in his inside coat pocket. For a long moment he looked thoughtfully at Gloria Mendez, until she became self-conscious and asked, "What?"

"Nick said something about you the other day," Kiley recalled. "He said you'd help us because that was the kind of woman you were. I didn't understand at the time what he meant—but I think I do now. He meant you'd do what you thought was right. I want you to know that I appreciate your help. I owe you."

"You don't owe me." Gloria looked away.

"Yes, I do," Kiley insisted. "I owe you. And I want you to remember that I owe you. If I can ever help you in any way, with any*thing*, all you have to do is let me know. I mean it, Gloria."

She smiled—tentatively, still self-conscious—and nodded. "Okay."

She walked Kiley to the door and they said good night.

On his way out of the building, Joe had to pass Meralda and her Latin Princes again. "Good night, *Detective*," she singsonged.

Kiley paused and looked glacially at the teenager. "You've got a hell of a fine lady for a mother, kid," he said very quietly. "Someday you're probably going to wish you'd spent more time with *her* and less with people like this."

One of the Princes parted his lips to make a remark, but Kiley's icy light blue eyes turned on him, and whatever devil or demon the Prince saw in them, it suspended his words.

Turning then, Kiley walked away, down the sidewalk toward his car. For some reason, he felt that Gloria Mendez was watching him from her window.

But he would not allow himself to look back and see. He did not want to know for sure.

# TEN

**A**t eight the following morning, Joe Kiley was again at a computer terminal in the B-and-A squad room. And again he was fighting the battle of restricted access to information he needed. This time it was on Frazier Leroy Lamont aka Fraz Lamont. Every record Kiley tried to pull up on the leader of the Disciples displayed:

ACCESS RESTRICTED
STREET GANGS UNIT ONLY

It was clear that he was not going to get any help from official files in trying to determine what the connection was—if any—between the Touhy crime family and the city's leading black street gang. And why, he wondered, had he mentally qualified that question with an "if any" disclaimer? There *had* to be *some* connection; Fraz Lamont's car was seen by Nick parked behind the Shamrock.

Kiley turned his attention to the 1993 Continental Mark VIII, owned by Prestige Auto Leasing Company in the suburb of Lake Forest. Probably leased to some member of the Irish, Italian, or Polish mob families, Kiley thought, which would explain its plate being OCB restricted. Turning off the terminal, he went over to a library of telephone directories, with a sign above it that read: DO NOT TAKE DIRECTORIES TO YOUR DESK. REPLACE DIRECTORIES ON SHELF WHEN FINISHED. It was signed: ALDENA. Locating the book for the northern suburbs, Kiley opened it on a small worktable in front of the shelves. In the old days, he would simply have gone back to his desk and called Directory Assistance for a number he wanted; but now that information calls cost forty or fifty cents each, a memo had long since come down from the city treasurer forbidding it. Kiley found the number for Prestige Auto Leasing and jotted it down on the sheet Gloria had given him. Like a good little policeman, he then put the directory back in its

91

place on the shelf. And was glad he did, because on the way back to his desk he saw that Aldena, the squad secretary, had been watching him.

Pushing the button on his phone for an outside line, Kiley called Prestige Auto Leasing. A woman with a pleasant voice answered.

"Good morning," Kiley said, "my name is Arthur Davis, with Allstate Insurance. One of your leased cars has been involved in a little fender-bender with one of our insureds and I'd like to get the name of the person you lease the vehicle to." The woman asked for the make, model, and license number of the car, which Kiley gave her, then put him on hold to listen to canned classical music while she checked. Waiting, Kiley wondered why he was wasting his time; all he was going to get was another mob name to go with the five he already had—and what the hell good was that going to do him? The best he could hope to do was maybe locate some of their hangouts and cruise the places hoping to spot Tony Touhy's teal blue Jaguar. Tony—and everyone else connected with the mob—would be avoiding the Shamrock Club, that was certain. And Tony, if he *had* been there when Nick was killed, would be lying very low—

Presently, the woman at Prestige came back on the line. "Mr. Davis? I'm sorry, where did you say you were from?"

"Allstate. You know, the 'good hands' people."

"When did this accident occur, sir?"

"Just today. Early this morning. It probably hasn't even been reported to you yet."

"That's what I was about to say. And it isn't a leased car; it's an executive car driven by one of our officers—" There was a muted voice in the background, then she said, "Excuse me, would you hold again, please?"

Son of a bitch, Kiley thought. She was just about to give him a name when somebody stopped her. An officer of the leasing company drove the car, she said. If that was so, then Prestige Leasing was possibly a mob front—or one of the legitimate businesses the mob owned now that it was using corporate lawyers and accountants instead of hit men and strongarm thugs. Although Kiley doubted it had been a lawyer or an accountant who had conducted the last bit of business with Nick Bianco—

The woman came back again, and this time her voice sounded a little distant and not as easy to hear—as if someone might be listening on an extension. "I'm sorry, Mr. Davis, which Allstate office are you with, sir?"

"The main office."

"Well, if you'll let me have a number, our own insurance representative will give you a call back as soon as we have a report of the accident."

"I'll be happy to fax you a copy of the report," Kiley pressed. "Which one of your officers did you say drives the car?"

A man's voice cut in, saying, "Mr. Davis, this is Matthew Field, the general manager. I'm sorry but we can't give you any further information at the moment. Would you care to leave a number or not?"

"No, I'll call back," Kiley said. "Thank you." He broke the connection.

As soon as Kiley hung up, his phone rang, startling him slightly. It was Aldena. "There's some woman named Alma Lynn at the lobby information desk wants to see you."

"Tell them I'll be right down," Kiley said.

As Kiley walked past Aldena's desk to leave the squad room, she said, "'Member, you got to sign out on my log if you leave the building."

"Yes, dear," he replied, and kept going.

"Sweet talk going to get you nowhere; you still got to sign out."

Kiley rode down to the lobby and saw Alma Lynn waiting, suitcase at her side, out beyond the bank of metal detectors that separated the street doors from the elevators. She looked frightened. Kiley made his way over to her.

"Hi. I thought you were just going to call—"

"Hi. I was, but I had to come downtown to the bus depot anyway—" She looked around at the bedlam of traffic circulating in the lobby: a disorder of people that represented a cross section of Chicago's bowels. "Is it always so—chaotic?"

"Usually. Did you find anything in your sister's belongings?"

"Not exactly in her belongings. That place where she lived, it was a kind of semi-transient hotel, very small; she just had a room with a little kitchenette alcove. It was an older place, still had a switchboard at the desk; no direct dial, you know? Anyone wanting to dial out has to ask the switchboard operator to dial the number for them. They have a surcharge, so they have to keep a record of all outgoing calls—"

"You got a record of her telephone calls?" Kiley asked eagerly.

"Yes. I had to pay the back bill." Alma drew a folded sheet from her purse. "No names, of course, just numbers."

Kiley looked at the list of calls. Aside from two long-distance calls to Ripley, Indiana, all of Ronnie Lynn's calls had been local, and all to one of three numbers. Kiley knew the city's prefixes fairly well, so he was able to generalize the area where the called numbers were located. The calls to an 878 prefix, he thought, were probably to the Shamrock Club; the ones to 265 were, he guessed, the 4-Star Lounge, where she had danced and died.

The other, a 975 prefix, might have been Tony Touhy's apartment on Lake Shore Drive; that was a number Kiley couldn't check, because it had not been in the information Gloria Mendez had given Nick and him.

"I can probably verify two of these, if they're where I think they are," he told Alma. "You want to come up to my desk while I check them out?"

"I'd better not," Alma said, looking at her watch. "My bus leaves in an hour. If I give you my home number in Ripley, would you mind letting me know how things turn out. And, you know, if those pictures show up—" She was clearly embarrassed about the photographs. The way she kept glancing around, Kiley knew the noisy, turbulent lobby unsettled her.

"Listen," Kiley said, putting a hand on her arm, "I'll do everything I can to find those pictures and see that they don't get circulated or passed around—"

"We're from such a small town, Ronnie and me," Alma said. "If those pictures somehow ever were used as evidence against anyone and it got in the papers—"

"I'll do everything I can to see that it doesn't happen," Kiley assured her— actually, *promised* her, because that was what he felt like he was doing.

"I know you want to get the man who killed your partner," she said plaintively, suddenly on the verge of tears, "and I wouldn't ask you to do anything to hinder that—"

Moving his hand along her arm, Kiley laced his fingers in hers and let her squeeze. "I know," he said understandingly, "you don't have to explain—"

In his peripheral vision, Kiley saw Dietrick and Meadows, the two Homicide cops, come in the front door with a short, familiar-looking man walking between them. A quick glance at the man had just pulled an identification of him to the surface of Kiley's mind—when suddenly the man began to shriek.

"Aaaaaahhhhh! No—!" It was clearly a cry of terror.

"What the hell—?" said Dietrick, leaping away from him. Meadows moved away also, eyes widening, hand instinctively moving toward his gun.

It was Wally, the janitor at the 4-Star Lounge. He had looked across the lobby at Kiley and Alma Lynn, and without warning gone totally ballistic.

"No—! Aaaaahhhhh! Keep her away from me! She's a devil! She's a ghost! She can't be here, I killed her—!"

Wally was freaking out at the sight of Ronnie Lynn's twin sister, but only Kiley realized that. Kiley, Dietrick, and Meadows all stared in stunned silence as the little man ranted and raved like a maniac. Uniformed officers on duty in the lobby began forming a circle to move in and restrain him. Then Dietrick was walking toward Kiley and Alma, and Kiley, saying, "Stay where you are," to Alma, moved forward to meet the Homicide cop.

"What the fuck's going on, Kiley?" Dietrick demanded. He looked anxiously over at Alma. "Who the fuck is that?"

"Ronnie Lynn's twin sister," Kiley said. "What are you bringing the janitor in for?"

"Just to look at mug shot books. He said he thought he could recognize a customer the Lynn broad got chummy with. He told us he remembered the guy yesterday."

"He's remembering something else today. Did you or Meadows ever check his knuckles?"

"We *are* cops, Kiley. His knuckles were okay."

Wally was dancing around like a crazed simian, pointing at Alma Lynn, still shouting, "No—! Keep her away! She's dead! I killed her! She can't be here—!"

"Who *is* that man?" Alma, hurrying up, demanded of Kiley.

Assisted by the uniforms, Meadows got Wally under control and led him down a hall off the lobby. The little man kept looking back fearfully at Alma Lynn until he was out of sight.

"He's the guy who found your sister's body," Kiley answered Alma's question.

"But he just said that he—"

"I know," Kiley interrupted. "I know what he said."

Dietrick was now staring at Alma too. "Jesus, it kind of *is* like seeing a ghost." Turning his back to her, he whispered to Kiley, "Looks like you really fucked up on that Touhy lead, don't it? Maybe you should've gone ahead and gave everything to Homicide."

Meadows walked quickly up to him. "Come on, Deet," he said urgently. "I've got him in an interrogation room in Auto Theft. Steno's on the way. He's scared shitless and ready to cop."

As Dietrick and Meadows walked away, Kiley said to Alma Lynn, "Wait here for a minute," and hurried to catch up with the command cops. "Hold it, will you?" he said, getting in front of them to block their way. "Look, I know you're probably pissed at me, but stop and think for a minute anyway—"

"Move it, Kiley," Meadows warned. He, like many, knew Kiley's opinion of blacks in the department, and he clearly was not in the mood to be interfered with by some honky racist.

"Wait a minute, goddamn it," Kiley insisted. He pleaded his case to Dietrick, whom he knew to be senior. "What about the sister? You might be able to use her if Wally decides to stop talking."

Dietrick's eyes narrowed. "Not a bad thought," he said to Meadows.

"What the fuck do you want, Kiley? Part of the collar?" Meadows had one hand already balled into a fist. Kiley shook his head.

"Look, I lost my partner, okay? I'm not interested in anything but finding whoever did that."

"What do you want from us?" asked Dietrick.

"Let me listen to Wally's statement. To see if I can pick up anything that might tie Touhy to Nick's killing."

"We can't let you question him," Dietrick warned.

"Just listen," Kiley assured, holding his hands up as if in surrender.

Dietrick looked at Meadows, who finally gave a curt nod, and the senior detective said, "Okay. Stash the sister somewhere. Then come on down."

"Room C in Auto Theft," Meadows said. "And we ain't waiting for you, man."

Dietrick and Meadows continued on their way, and Kiley hurried back to do something with Alma Lynn.

"You guys can't imagine what it's like for somebody like me," Wally said. "I mean, look at me: I ain't exactly Tom Cruise. There's times I can't get no sex even *paying* for it. Then to have to work around all them women, most of 'em running around half naked or more—"

The little janitor was sitting at a plain, gray-topped interrogation table, nothing in front of him except a styrofoam cup of coffee heavily laced with powdered creamer. Dietrick sat across from him, hands folded on the table like a schoolboy. Meadows and Kiley stood back away from the table, using the wall for support. A black woman of about fifty, from the steno pool, sat several feet away from the table, legs crossed, steno pad on one knee, making little curlicues on the page as Wally talked.

"I always treated all them women very good," Wally said. "I never stared at them undressed if they could see me, an' I always knocked on their dressing room door when I needed to empty the wastebaskets or when one of them had a phone call. Laver, now, he just walked in, never knocked or nothing; half the time he didn't even have no reason to be going in, you know: just wanted to remind them that he was the boss an' could walk in if he wanted to. Thought he was a big deal, throwing his weight around. But, like one of the girls said, what else could you expect from a jig?"

"Wally, if you were bothered having all the undressed women around, why'd you work there?" Dietrick asked quietly, his question not a challenge or criticism of any kind.

"I had to work where Mr. Getman told me to work," Wally said. "I been working for him for a long time, five or six years. I clean his poolroom over on Pulaski Road, and his cigar store on Lake Street, an' I take care of the furnace in an apartment building he owns. I've always done the 4-Star for him, even back when there wasn't no dancers, when it was just a bar."

"I understand. Why don't you tell me about Ronnie Lynn now, Wally?" the Homicide detective suggested.

Wally shrugged. "What do you want to know?"

Kiley and Meadows exchanged quick glances, each wondering if the suspect was tightening up on Dietrick; if he was beginning to dummy up now that the scary "ghost" of his victim could no longer be seen.

"Well," Dietrick said, shrugging also, "for instance, did you like her; did you like any of the women who danced there?" Kiley was relieved to find that Dietrick, despite his wrestler-like appearance and dickhead reputation, had a conversational, almost gentle interrogation technique. Kiley also became aware that a heavy body odor was becoming evident in the close little room.

"Sure," Wally replied, "I liked all the girls. I would've taken any of them home with me, kept her, taken care of her, supported her. I liked the white girls best, naturally; then the black girls; the gook girls I didn't like very much: I didn't like to look at those funny eyes they had, an' most of them didn't have much in the tit department."

"A tit man, huh?" Dietrick said with a conspiratorial leer and a quick, buddy-buddy wink.

"You got me there, Mr. Dietrick," Wally replied with a wide smile that was eerily engaging considering the circumstances.

"George," the detective told him. "Call me George." Taking out a handkerchief, Dietrick brushed at his nose. The body odor was becoming very heavy.

"Sure, George," Wally replied, pleased.

"You have a favorite among the girls?" Dietrick asked.

"You bet. Ronnie. She was my favorite."

Dietrick tried not to seem surprised. "Oh, yeah?" he said calmly. "Why was she your favorite?"

"Well, George, first of all, I could tell right away she wasn't no city girl," Wally said analytically. "The city girls, you know, they're all smartasses, think they know it all, an' they always badmouth the customers. Ronnie wasn't like that. She was from a small town and it showed. She never said nothing mean or nasty about no one, not even Laver, who *nobody* liked. An' she didn't talk down the customers neither. Some of the girls call the customers names: you know, 'fucking animals' and 'pervert assholes' and things like that; but not Ronnie. She always seemed to like the customers, an' I guess they must have felt it 'cause Ronnie always knocked down twenty, thirty a shift in tips when the others was making ten or fifteen."

"So Ronnie was your favorite because she was such a nice person," said Dietrick.

"Yeah. That and her tits, George. She had the best tits of all the dancers." Wally seemed to stare off in space. "Nice and big around, but not hard like the ones with that Jell-o or whatever it is in them. An' she had nice big nipples that had a lot of neat little bumps on them an' stuck out hard but wasn't pointed like the gook girls' nipples are." Wally smiled. "I think she knew I liked her tits, because whenever I'd go and get snacks and stuff for the dancers, Ronnie would always let her robe hang open when she paid me, so's I could see them real good. I'm pretty sure she knew."

"Wally, tell us what happened to Ronnie in the alley," Dietrick soothingly eased the story along.

"Well, this guy Tony called her on the phone, see. He was some sharpie hood, had kind of a mean look; I'd see him sometime when he come to pick her up. Mr. Getman and Laver, they fell all over themselves trying to be nice to him, so I figured he was either somebody important or he was dangerous, you know? He wore real slick clothes, drove one of them foreign cars—"

Kiley practically had to bite his tongue to keep from asking what color the car was. Next to him, Meadows also had a handkerchief out now; body odor pervaded the little room like smoke.

"So anyways," Wally continued, "he called on the phone, I answered, he says go get Ronnie, tell her Tony's on the phone. No fucking please or nothing, you know? So I knock and holler for Ronnie to come to the phone. While she's out on the phone, there's no other girl in the dressing room; one was on stage and one was in the john. The door's open, so I went in to collect the trash an' I had my broom to maybe sweep up real quick. While I'm in there, this gook dancer, Amy, comes back in from the john, then Ronnie comes back from the phone and says to Amy, 'That was Tony on the phone. He's going to meet me out back in half an hour to get his ring and give me those pictures he took. I will be *so* glad,' she says, 'to be out of that relationship.' Then Amy says something like, 'Never suck a guy off for pictures unless you get paid, honey.' That's the way the gook girls are, you know: anything for money. Except with me. I offered a gook hooker money one time on the street an' the cunt walked away from me without a word. Can you believe a hoor like that, George?"

Dietrick shook his head in resignation. "Just goes to show you, Wally, you never can tell about people. This boyfriend—what was his name? Tony?—did he actually come over and meet Ronnie back in the alley?"

"Yeah, sure. I went downstairs in the basement. The furnace an' all my cleaning supplies an' stuff is down there. An' there's a door to the alley, at the bottom of some steps. So I left the light off and the door open a few inches." Wally grinned. "I'll be honest with you, George: I was hoping they'd do something out there an' I could watch."

"Did they do anything?"

"Nothing," Wally said, "not a damn thing." The disappointment seemed still to annoy him. "All he did was pull into the alley in that sports car of his, an' Ronnie was standing there waiting for him. He says, 'You got the ring?' and she says, 'You got the pictures?' Then he says, 'What, you don't trust me?' But he hands her an envelope and she glances inside it, then she takes a ring out of her robe pocket and hands it to him. He smiles and says, 'I got another finger waiting for this already.' 'I know you're a fast worker, Tony,' she says. 'You don't have to remind me.' He laughs, gets back in his little faggot car, and drives off."

Wally stopped talking and did not immediately resume. Dietrick waited, nodding as if he understood the silence, as if he knew that it was only a temporary pause. But Wally looked up at the ceiling, as if he were through talking for the day. Dietrick gave him a full ninety seconds, then asked, "Is that coffee okay, Wally? I notice you're not drinking it?"

"It's fine, George," the little janitor said. "I'm just not very thirsty."

"Wally, what made you come up out of the basement after Tony drove away? You weren't mad at Ronnie or anything, were you?"

Wally shook his head. His expression turned sad and he blinked several times as if to check tears. "I—I didn't come out to hurt her, George, I swear to God I didn't——"

"I know that, Wally," the detective said. "She was your favorite."

"Right. An' I didn't plan to hurt her, I want you to believe me——"

"I do believe you, Wally. But why *did* you come out of where you were hiding?"

"I wanted to help her, to comfort her. She started crying——"

"Crying about what?"

"The pictures Tony had given her. She went over by the back door of the club, where there was a light, and she took the pictures out of the envelope and looked at them. Then she started crying."

"Why do you think she was crying? Was she ashamed of being in pictures like those?"

"No, that wasn't it, George," the suspect said with more than a hint of impatience. "They were the *wrong* pictures."

"The wrong pictures?"

"Yeah! See, I came out of the basement and went over to her and said, 'Ronnie, what's the matter, why are you crying?' And she handed me the pictures and the envelope and said, 'These are the wrong pictures! They aren't pictures of me! The son of a bitch, he did it on purpose, I know he did!' I looked at the pictures, and sure enough it wasn't her in them. It was some naked broad had hair like hers, sucking this guy's cock and taking it in the ass doggie-style, but it wasn't Ronnie."

"What happened then, Wally?"

"She started crying harder," he said, again blinking back tears himself. "She was, like, sobbing, like, wailing, like she was in pain, really hurting. I felt so—so sorry for her; I wanted to take that guy Tony and kick him in the fucking balls. I started saying, 'Don't cry, Ronnie, everything will be all right, it's not so bad, don't cry, Ronnie'—you know, like you'd talk to a kid that was hurt. Well," Wally's expression changed now to indignation, "you know what she did? You know what the cunt did, George?"

"What did she do, Wally?"

"She slapped the pictures out of my hands and she says, 'What the hell do you know about it?' So I right away got down on one knee and started picking up the pictures, and I says, 'I just want to help you, Ronnie.' She's shaking her head and wailing, 'You can't help me! Nobody can help me!'" Wally leaned forward, arms on the table, as if to begin speaking confidentially to Dietrick. "Now, I'm down in a crouch in front of her, right? She's got on a robe but the belt has come loose some and it's open a little below the waist. I mean, George, I'm looking right at her pussy, man. She's wearing that bikini thing that she dances in, but it don't cover squat, you know. So I start thinking, hey, maybe ol' Wally's about to get lucky here. I get all the pictures stuffed back in the envelope and stand up, and I say, 'Come on, Ronnie, it'll be all right.' I say, 'Come on down in the basement, I got a little corner fixed up with a table and chairs, got a little bottle down there.' I did have, too: good stuff, 'cause I don't have to drink cheap booze,

I got a cough medicine bottle I fill up behind the bar when nobody else is here. Shit, I drink Chivis, Glenlivet, Cutty—only the best."

"What did Ronnie say when you invited her into the basement?" Dietrick asked.

"She said, 'Oh, just leave me alone, Wally.' And I says, 'Come on, Ronnie, a drink'll do you good.' And I, like, put my hand on her shoulder, you know, to comfort her and walk her over to the basement steps. And you know what the cunt does then?"

"What, Wally?"

"She slaps my hand away. Says, 'Don't you touch me! Who do you think you are touching me? Get away from me,' she says. 'You stink!' she says. So I look at her and I say, 'I stink?' 'Yeah,' she says, 'you stink, Wally. Hasn't anybody ever told you that before? You *stink*. You smell bad!' I couldn't believe it, George. Couldn't believe she would talk to me like that."

"Did it hurt your feelings, Wally?"

"Yeah," he swallowed dryly, "it did."

"Make you mad?"

"Goddamned right it did," he declared, nodding assertively.

"What did you do about it, Wally?"

"Slapped her across the fucking face, is what I did." He smiled slightly. "That made *her* mad. She tried to hit me back, but I just held up my arms and she hurt her hands on them. I've got arms like logs, George. Hell," he looked up at Kiley and Meadows for the first time, "I'm probably stronger than anybody in this room."

"I'll bet you are, Wally. What happened next?"

Wally shrugged. "She called me some names."

"What did she call you?" There was almost a sympathetic note in Dietrick's voice, Kiley thought.

"Well, you know," Wally shifted his eyes away from all contact, "she called me a stinking garbage man, an' an alley crawler, an' a pervert, stuff like that. And she kept on saying, 'You stink, Wally, you stink and smell bad.' Stuff like that."

"What did you do about it, Wally?" Dietrick asked, repeating exactly his earlier question.

"Slapped her across the fucking face again, the little cunt."

"Wally, when you say 'slapped,' do you mean hitting her with your hand open? With your palm?"

"Yeah."

"Did you start hitting her with your fist, after? Or with both your fists?"

"Yeah."

"When did you start hitting her with your fist, or both your fists?"

Wally shrugged. "I don't know. Couple of minutes, I guess. I slapped her a few times first. Then she got real sorry, you know, for all the names she called me. She started saying, 'Look, I'm sorry, okay?' Started kind of begging me, like, to quit pounding on her. 'I'm sorry, okay?' she kept saying. Well," he stared off at space again, remembering, "it *wasn't* okay. It was too late to take back what she said, because she *meant* it." He looked at Dietrick again. "I was really pissed by then, George. I was ready to really give it to her. I put on my lifting gloves; they're made of roughout boar skin, an' the knuckles is padded for protection. I wear 'em when I'm lifting those fifty-five-gallon drums of garbage; keep my hands from getting skinned up—"

"Where are your gloves right now, Wally?" asked Dietrick.

"My locker in the basement of the 4-Star. The pictures are there too."

"Okay. What happened after you put your gloves on?"

Wally began to mimic a pleading female's voice. "She started saying, 'Please, stop. No more, please, no more.' Know what I told her? I said, 'You fucking little slut, I haven't even started on you yet.' Then I proceeded to beat the holy shit out of her. I beat her fucking face in, an' then I ripped her bra off and beat her fucking tits until they felt like mush." Wally grunted softly. "Teach her to tell me I stink."

Joe Kiley quietly let himself out of the malodorous little room.

Two hours later, in a cocktail lounge across Randolph Street from the Greyhound Bus Terminal, Alma Lynn took a long, cold swallow of dry martini and said, "Well, I guess that's that, then."

"Looks like," Kiley said, lifting his own glass. They were in a back booth, away from the still bright day showing through the front window.

"You don't suppose Ronnie could have made a mistake about the pictures, do you? I mean, it *was* dark out, and—"

"I doubt it," Kiley said. "Wally saw them too, and he sounded pretty convinced that they were pictures of another woman." After a pause, he added, "I wouldn't worry about them."

Alma rolled her eyes. "You would if they were *your* identical twin. And if you taught high school in a little Indiana town."

"All right, I'll try to get a look at them," Kiley placated, "just to make sure. I'll call and let you know."

"Thanks. I really would appreciate it." Now it was she who paused, then said, "What does this do to your theory that the same person who killed Ronnie also killed your partner?"

"Blows the *theory* all to hell," Kiley told her, "but doesn't change the fact that I still believe your sister's ex-boyfriend killed Nick, or had him killed."

"You mean Tony whatever?"

"Yeah, Tony whatever."

"Are you still not going to tell me his last name?"

"I'll tell you his last name," Kiley said. "Why not? Everybody else knows it, and now we all know that he didn't kill your sister. His name is Tony Touhy. Anthony Francis Touhy. He's a two-bit punk with heavy connections."

"You said a moment ago you believed he either killed your partner or *had* him killed. Could he do that?" Alma asked almost in revulsion. "Have someone killed?"

Kiley nodded. "His older brother, Phil, is a big man in the mob; one of five or six men who control organized crime in the city and suburbs. I'm not sure Tony could order a hit without his brother's approval, but if my partner had caught Tony in some kind of criminal act, something serious, that night, and tried to arrest him, Phil might have said do it. Or if it was a situation where my partner had to be hit right *then* or else Tony would have gone down for something heavy, then Tony probably could have done it on his own." Kiley lifted his glass again, drained it, and sighed heavily. "It's all very vague right now, very mixed up in my mind. Tony didn't beat your sister to death, and he wouldn't have had bruised knuckles—so I have no idea what my partner would have braced him about. He *had* to have caught Tony at something; I just have to find out what."

Kiley held his glass up as a signal for the bartender to bring another round.

"I can't imagine," Alma said, shaking her head, "how Ronnie got mixed up with someone like this Tony Touhy. A hoodlum—"

"Yeah, but a real glitzy hoodlum," Kiley qualified. "Expensive sports car, fancy high-rise apartment with a view of the lake, tailor-made clothes, a tab everywhere in the city because of who his brother is. That kind of flash can turn a small-town girl's head, believe me. I've seen it happen before."

"Was she—was Ronnie on drugs, do you know?"

"I don't know," Kiley said. "I haven't seen her autopsy report. By the time it was sent over to Homicide, my partner was already dead and I was downtown being grilled about that." Kiley stared at nothing for a moment, lost in the unthinkable, improbable, totally unpredictable chain of events. "It's all happened so goddamned fast—"

Fresh drinks arrived but Alma kept her first one, not even half finished. When the bartender left, she said, "I wish you hadn't ordered another for me—"

"It won't go to waste," Kiley assured her. Taking a swallow of his new drink, he rested his head back and let his thoughts range. "Another thing that bothers me now is the time element involved," he said. "In the time it took me to drive home that night, my partner had already followed Tony to the Shamrock Club and called my apartment. I wasted about ten minutes before I finally listened to my answering machine. Couldn't have taken me more than twenty minutes to get to the club; added to the ten I lost in the apartment, that totals half an hour. What I can't figure is how something major could have gone down, my partner killed, and the place locked up tight and deserted—all in that short time. Somebody had to have made the decision to waste my partner awfully quick."

"I'm not sure I'm following everything you say," Alma admitted. "It's all a little foreign to me; I'm sorry."

"Don't worry about it," Kiley said. "I'm talking mainly for my own benefit anyway; to get my thoughts organized." It was true, in a way. What he was trying to do was crunch facts, then smooth them out and see if they made any sense. Brainstorm the case. He and Nick had done it together many times, and the two of them had done it with other cops on mutual cases. It was like participating in a cop think tank. But, Kiley realized, it wouldn't work with Alma Lynn, even though she was an intelligent, educated woman. The woman he *really* needed across the booth from him was Gloria Mendez. That fine female cop mind of hers would have been perfect for Kiley right then.

"May I ask you a question?" Alma's voice, Kiley noticed for the first time, was turning a little throaty; he wondered if it was from stress or the gin. "This person Wally," she wanted to know, "what will happen to him for what he did to my sister?"

Kiley bit his lower lip slightly before answering that one. Alma had not been in the interrogation room when Wally gave his statement; she had only observed him during the brief, turbulent incident in the lobby when Wally panicked. And, as she herself had stated only a moment earlier, these things—events, people, crimes—were foreign to her.

"I'll explain it to you the best I can," he said. "Only don't expect all of it to make sense, or be fair, or turn out the way you'd like it to turn out. It's a *system*, see, and systems don't always work like they're supposed to—" Kiley leaned forward and drank some martini. "Understand, I don't *know* that things will happen the way I'm going to tell you; it's just my best prediction, okay? First, Wally will be booked, charged with homicide. There'll be an arraignment at which he's taken before a judge and the charge formally made, and he'll be asked if he can afford an attorney, he'll probably say no, so his case will be assigned to the public defender. Then there'll be a preliminary hearing, kind of a mini-trial, at which an assistant state's attorney will present evidence to convince a different judge that Wally should be held to answer the charge that was made at the arraignment. The public defender will make a lot of motions and objections, which in this case will probably be overruled, and the judge will find that there is reasonable cause to believe that Wally committed the crime—"

Alma frowned deeply. "Reasonable cause? He *confessed!*"

"There are times when a person's confession can't be used as evidence against them," Kiley said. "For instance, if the arresting officers failed to advise Wally at once of his right to ask for a lawyer, or warn him about saying anything self-incriminating—"

"Did they?" Alma wanted to know.

"Probably not," Kiley replied. He had not personally witnessed Wally being read his rights, but Dietrick and Meadows were both experienced cops, and Kiley was sure—

Or was he sure? It had been a pretty hectic few minutes after Wally lost control. Sometimes in an earthquake, things fall into a crack.

"Go on, please," Alma said. "I didn't mean to interrupt."

"Yeah. Well, anyway, the judge will probably hold Wally to answer the charge or charges against him—"

"*Charges?*" Alma said. "Did that son of a bitch do anything to Ronnie before he killed her? Anything besides beat her, I mean?"

"No, I don't think so," Kiley told her. "Like I said, I haven't seen the autopsy report—"

"He didn't do anything—sexual to her, did he?"

"I don't believe so."

"All right," Alma said. "Go on." Kiley was beginning to feel like he was on a witness stand.

"The state's attorney will have to try and decide what degree of homicide to try and prove against him—"

"He'll be charged with murder, won't he?"

"Not necessarily. He might be charged with voluntary or involuntary manslaughter—"

"But it was *murder*," the dead woman's sister said in exasperation.

"If it was," Kiley pointed out, "it has to be decided whether it was murder in the first degree or murder in the second degree—"

"My God. That animal *beat* my sister to death!"

"But he may not have *murdered* her," Kiley said, as patiently and calmly as he could. "See, for it to have been murder, it has to have been planned by Wally; it has to have been premeditated." He sat back again. "I have to tell you, I don't think that's the case here. I think we're looking at voluntary manslaughter here."

"Who'll decide that?"

"A jury, most likely. Could be the judge will do it, if both sides agree to a bench trial: a trial without a jury. Or maybe there won't be a trial at all; maybe an agreement will be reached for Wally to plead guilty to a pre-specified crime in exchange for a predetermined sentence—"

"But," Alma asked, "you don't think there's any chance of him being executed, or at least being sent to prison for life?"

"None at all," Kiley leveled with her. "Whoever decides Wally's future, whether it's a judge or a jury, is going to have to consider a lot of things in his favor—"

"Such as?" Alma was close to being hostile now; an adversary.

"Such as one or more psychiatric reports that will be made on him, which will probably show very low intelligence as well as inability to make rational decisions under pressure; such as a background history that may contain no criminal record or violence of any kind; such as testimony from the other dancers at the 4-Star Lounge about what a hell of a sweet guy poor, stupid Wally is; such as a lot of things I probably haven't even thought of." Kiley finished his second drink and with one finger dragged Alma's untouched second martini over to his side of the table. "Like I said, it's a system."

"Bottom line," Alma said. "What's the end result of this—system?" She used the word as if it were obscene.

"Bottom line should be—" Kiley paused several beats, considering; then guessed, "ten years."

Alma Lynn stared at him in utter revulsion. "He beat my sister to death—broke every bone in her face—beat her breasts until they were completely flat, black and blue—and all he'll have to serve is ten years in prison?"

"That's not the worst of it," Kiley told her quietly. "If he's smart, keeps out of trouble in the joint—in prison—and cooperates with the psychiatric people in the therapy program they set up for him, he'll probably get out in about seven. Of course, he'll be on supervised parole; they won't just turn him loose on the public—"

"What makes you so sure?" Alma Lynn challenged.

"That's not how the system works," he answered, before realizing that it had been a sarcastic, disparaging question. Kiley then fell silent. There was nothing more he could say to this woman. She had finished her martini by now and Kiley had already drunk about half of her second one. But he pushed the glass back to her, saying, "You want to reconsider this? Or I can get you a fresh one—"

"What's left of this one is fine," she said, picking up the glass and drinking the rest of it down. For a long moment she stared at the empty glass in her hand, her expression as devastated as any Kiley had ever seen, her eyes sad, unbelieving, hurt. She was almost as much a victim as her sister was. Finally, Alma brought herself to look at her watch. "I guess I'd better get on across the street," she said listlessly. "Wouldn't want to miss another bus home."

"I'll carry your bag over," Kiley said, starting to rise, but Alma quickly protested.

"No, please, I'd rather you didn't. I'd—just like to sit in the bus station by myself for a few minutes—"

"You're sure? I'll be glad to—"

"No, thank you anyway," she insisted, rising, picking up her suitcase. Kiley stood and they clumsily shook hands. "You've been very kind, Detective Kiley. Very honest. You have my sincere appreciation. Good-bye."

"Good-bye, Ms. Lynn."

Kiley watched Alma Lynn walk out the door. Then he sat back down and held his glass up for the bartender again.

# ELEVEN

**A**t his desk the next morning, Kiley had the Harold Winston bus sabotage file open in front of him, but he was actually looking at something else—the restricted records information Gloria had given him on the cars Nick had seen parked at the Shamrock—and trying to decide on his next move. He doubted he could get anywhere with the mob names on the list: They were men who had spent a lifetime covering their trails and avoiding cooperation with the police. If they even suspected they were going to be questioned about *anything*, let alone a cop killing, they would drop out of circulation at once. The only leads, Kiley decided, that he might get someplace with were the two non-mob names: the Disciples leader Fraz Lamont, and the leased car belonging to Prestige Auto Leasing. He did not want to try working Lamont yet; *that* would take some careful thought, planning. And the sketchy information he had obtained so far from Prestige—that the Mark VIII was driven by one of its officers—tentatively seemed to indicate that the auto leasing firm probably was a mob front of some kind. Kiley began to wonder if Tony Touhy and the others at the meeting might be involved in Prestige, and that it was just a legitimate business meeting of some kind—

The phone rang and he picked it up. "Bomb-and-Arson, Kiley—"

"Hi, Joe, it's Stella."

"Hi. How are you doing?"

"Oh, I'm hanging in, Joey, but it's hard as hell, you know—" Her voice broke slightly. Then: "I was surprised when they gave me a new number for you at the station. What are you doing on the Bomb Squad?"

"TAD," Kiley told her. "They want me on the shelf for a while, until the situation settles down."

"Oh. Well, how do you like it?"

"It's all right," he said, but without enthusiasm. "I'm working on a bus sabotage case; not exactly thrilling. How are the girls?"

"Oh, I don't know," Stella admitted. "They've both really been in a funk: Jen is just kind of listless, moving from one thing to another without actually *doing* anything; and all Tessie wants to do is watch TV, mostly cartoons. Neither one of them wants to go back to school yet, and I haven't made them. I don't know if that's smart or not—"

"It won't hurt them to miss a little school," Kiley said.

"I guess not." Stella paused a beat, then asked, "Want to come over for dinner again? Maybe if the girls and I have some special company—you know, besides relatives all the time—we can work up some energy to get out of these doldrums."

"Shouldn't you be getting as much rest as you can?" Kiley asked.

"Hell, Joe, all I've *been* doing is resting," she complained. "I think one of the things that's wrong with all three of us is that we're getting too *much* rest. We're not doing anything. And it's because we don't have anything to look forward to like we did when Nick was coming home every day. He'd either be getting home late in the afternoon if you guys were working days, or getting up to eat breakfast with us if you were on nights. He was *around*, you know, and we all counted on seeing him. With just the three of us, there's nothing to look forward to."

There was an unexpected silence between them. Kiley could not help thinking about Gino Bianco's words, could not avoid the thought that in spite of the uncle's request, he had been over to see Stella and the girls again just a few days earlier, could not elude the worry that his secret feelings for Stella Bianco might be surfacing, showing, exposing a hidden part of him for others to see. He was trying to weigh that against his desire to be with her.

Presently Stella said, "Look, Joe, if you're busy—" she let the words hang.

"I'm not," Kiley said. "I *want* to come over, Stel; I *want* to be with you—you and the girls; but I've been thinking how it might look and all—"

"You sound like Uncle Gino," Stella said. "He told me the same thing: that it might not look right if you came around too often."

"What did you say?"

"I told him that I appreciated his concern and respected his advice, but that you were our closest family friend and that I did not intend to deprive either the girls or myself of your support and comfort. So he said he understood and would leave it to my best judgment, and he backed off."

I'll bet, Kiley thought. The old dago son of a bitch never backed off from anything in his life. Neither Stella or himself had heard the last of Gino Bianco, Kiley was certain of that.

"So," Stella asked, "will you come?"

"You know I will. When?"

"Tomorrow night." She sounded pleased. Over her shoulder Kiley heard her say loudly, "Girls! Uncle Joey's coming for dinner tomorrow night." Then to Joe, "Okay, make it about seven and we'll eat at eight."

"It's a date," Kiley said, and was immediately sorry for his choice of words. Because that's not what it was, he thought, a *date*; that's what Gino Bianco would probably think it was; but that's not *actually* what it was—

"Okay," Stella said. "See you tomorrow then. 'Bye."

As Kiley hung up, Aldena, the squad secretary, walked up to his desk and said, "You're wanted up in IA; they just called. I hope you're not in any trouble 'cause I don't have time to be fooling with a lot of extra paperwork."

"Your concern is touching," Kiley said. "If it's anything I think will add to your work load, I'll just submit an immediate resignation."

"I appreciate that," Aldena said, and kept on walking, the barest hint of a smile on her lips.

Truth be known, Kiley had to force the levity; the mere mention of IA had sent a spasm of nervousness through his stomach. What the hell was shaking now? he wondered. His first fear was that Gloria Mendez had somehow been made, and that he was being called in to rat her out. If that was the case, IA could go fuck itself.

Closing the Winston file, Kiley put it in a drawer and followed Aldena toward the front of the squad room. He noticed on the way that Captain Madzak was not in his office, and wondered briefly if *he* was on the carpet for releasing Kiley to unsupervised fieldwork. The department was beginning to feel like the goddamned KGB.

"Don't forget to come back here and sign out if you decide to leave the building," Aldena warned as he went through the door.

"Whatever you say, boss."

Upstairs, when Kiley entered IA, Vander and his deputy, Bill Somers, were just coming out of Vander's office. "Come along with us, Detective," said the IA commander.

"Where to?" Kiley asked, following them back into the hall.

"OCB."

"What's up?" Kiley asked.

Vander ignored the question, but Somers said, "You'll find out when we get there."

You pompous little prick, Kiley thought. Somers was the one Vander had sent to Joe's apartment to pick up the answering machine tape with Nick's last message on it. Joe had sarcastically given Somers permission to search the place if he wanted to, and suspected the bastard had done just that—although, to give him credit, if he *had*, he'd done a good job of covering his work, because Kiley had found not a piece of paper, not a cup, not a sock out of place. Actually, Kiley's main reasons for disliking Bill Somers were both general and specific. First, generally, Somers was IA, and all other cops loathed IA cops; second, specifically, Somers had a college degree, was younger than Kiley, had less time with the department, and was already a goddamned lieutenant.

Kiley rode the elevator in silence with the two IA officers, then followed them down another hall and into OCB.

"Go right in, Captain Vander," the OCB secretary said with a smile. "Captain Lovat is waiting for you."

Gordon Lovat's office was smaller and less richly decorated than Kiley had found Chief Cassidy's to be, but it nevertheless was smartly, stylishly impressive, particularly considering the building it was in. Like the chief, Lovat had a glass case of trophies and plaques, and a wall of photographs. There were two men already in the office with Lovat when Vander, Somers, and Kiley entered. Seated before Lovat's desk, they were not, Kiley thought, cops.

"Come in, Allan, Bill," said Lovat, rising. "Sit down, please. Kiley," he shot a curt glance at Joe, "take a chair." Sitting back down, the OCB commander said, "I'll dispense with any unnecessary cordiality in this matter so we can get it over with as quickly as possible. These gentlemen," indicating the two who were already in the office, "are Mr. Philip Touhy and his attorney, Mr. Edward R. Malcolm." Both men were expensively but conservatively dressed. If they had not been introduced, it would have been hard to tell which was the lawyer. "Mr. Touhy came downtown and voluntarily gave us a statement regarding the finding of Detective Bianco's body behind the Shamrock Club, a property which he owns. In the presence of Chief Cassidy, Deputy Chief Ward, Captain Fred Cleary of Homicide, four officers from Captain Cleary's command, myself, and with his attorney present, Mr. Touhy submitted to questions regarding Detective Bianco's killing." Lovat picked up a sheaf of typewritten pages. "Mr. Touhy himself has an airtight alibi for the night of the killing, and has provided a similar alibi for his brother, Anthony Touhy, who is also represented by Mr. Malcolm. Anthony

Touhy is unavailable to give his own statement due to being out of the country—"

"Out of the country since when?" Kiley interrupted, almost indignantly. Gordon Lovat gave him a scathing glare.

"Detective Kiley, I am conducting this meeting. You are ordered to remain silent unless asked a direct question." The OCB commander's eyes returned to Touhy's statement. "Mr. Anthony Touhy, whom their attorney, Mr. Malcolm, believes was under suspicion both in Detective Bianco's death and in an earlier homicide involving one Veronica Lynn, has made the following statements: He was acquainted with Ms. Lynn on an intimate social basis, did meet her in the alley behind the 4-Star Lounge on the night of her death, exchanged some personal photographs for a ring he had given her, and left her there, alive and unharmed, when he drove away." Lovat's eyes flicked to Kiley. "It is my understanding from Homicide that the Lynn case has been resolved, and that Mr. Anthony Touhy is no longer a suspect in that matter. With respect to Detective Bianco's death, Mr. Anthony Touhy states the following: At about midnight on the night Detective Bianco was shot, Mr. Touhy left his apartment building at 3333 Lake Shore Drive and in his car, a 1993 Jaguar, proceeded to his brother's place of business, the Shamrock Club, at 630 West Lawrence Avenue. He states that the club was closed when he arrived, it being a policy to close any time after eleven p.m. on weeknights unless there is sufficient business to warrant remaining open. Mr. Touhy states that he used his key to enter the premises in order to pick up his passport, which he kept in a personal file in the office there. He then drove to his brother Philip Touhy's home in suburban Wolf Ridge, spent the night there, and was driven by his brother to O'Hare Airport the following morning, where he boarded Aer Lingus flight 36 to Shannon, Ireland. Homicide has confirmed that Mr. Touhy was a first-class passenger on that flight, and it has been verified by the Royal Ulster Constabulary that the subject is presently visiting relatives in the city of Belfast." Lovat put down the typewritten pages and looked at the attorney, Edward Malcolm. "Do you have anything to add, counselor?"

"No, I think you've covered it adequately, Captain Lovat," the lawyer replied. He turned to his client. "Phil?"

The North Side mob boss nodded. Despite his expensive tailoring, Phil Touhy was, Kiley now saw on closer observation, as shanty Irish as Kiley himself. Touhy had the same mousy, thinning hair, the same pale skin that cut so easily under a razor, the same light blue eyes that every lower West Side mick kid had inherited since their great-grandfathers had brought them over from the Old Country following the potato famine. Touhy might be big time North Side now, but he was low-class Kedzie Avenue before—and Joe Kiley recognized it. He managed to pull his gaze off the racketeer only when Gordon Lovat spoke again.

"It is the official position of this department that unless significant new incriminating evidence to the contrary develops, that neither Philip Touhy nor his brother Anthony Touhy is to be considered a suspect in the death of Detective Nick Bianco. That position has been endorsed by Chief of Police John J. Cassidy. In light of that position, Mr. Malcolm has agreed not to file charges of harassment against the department with respect to an unauthorized surveillance of Anthony Touhy, and not to ask for a restraining order prohibiting further investigation, without probable cause, of either Philip Touhy or Anthony Touhy." Lovat drummed his fingertips silently on the desk top. "Satisfactory, Mr. Malcolm?"

"I believe so, yes," the attorney said. He touched Phil Touhy's arm and they both rose. "On behalf of my clients, we want the department to know that we sincerely hope the killer of Detective Bianco is brought to justice as rapidly and efficiently as the murderer of that young dancer. Thank you, gentlemen, and good day."

As the lawyer and his mobster client left the office, Kiley realized that Phil Touhy had not spoken a word; all he had done was nod once.

When the door closed and only policemen were left in the office, Lovat said, almost curtly, "That, I hope, is the end of the matter."

"Gordon, I think the chief and you did a damn fine job of getting the department out of what was becoming a very sticky situation," said Allan Vander of IA. "I hope we've *all*," he glanced at Kiley, "learned a lesson from this."

Kiley met Vander's eyes directly. "A lesson in what?" he asked. "How to let a cop killer get away?"

"You are out of fucking line, Detective!" stormed Bill Somers, Vander's deputy.

"And you—all of you—are out of your fucking minds," Kiley retorted, "if you think Tony Touhy had nothing to do with killing Nick!"

"Detective Kiley," said Gordon Lovat very evenly, "you were included in this meeting at the suggestion of Chief Cassidy. He thought perhaps it would help you better understand what the department concluded was the best compromise in this situation. Apparently the chief feels you are worth

saving as a police officer—something," he glanced at the others, "my col-
leagues and I don't agree with. If *I* were the chief of police—"

"But you're not," Kiley interjected, on the very cusp of outright insubordination.

"No, I'm not," Lovat agreed coldly, "but if I were, you wouldn't walk
out of this office with a badge in your pocket and a pistol on your belt. But,
that personal comment aside, let me make you aware of the fact that my
Organized Crime Bureau ran a complete and in-depth check on Tony
Touhy for the entire day that led up to Detective Bianco's killing. You see,
Kiley," the OCB head could not resist a slight smile here, "we *do* know not
only where he lives but also his hangouts, the addresses of his girlfriends,
where he drinks, where he gambles, even the location of the laundry that
does his underwear. We backtracked him from the time he got up that
morning, until the time he got on the plane for Ireland the *next* morning.
We found not a single thing—*nothing*—in his behavior or activities to indicate that anything at all was going down at the Shamrock Club that night.
Nothing in Phil Touhy's conduct either. No indication from any source in
the neighborhood that anything *did* go down. The club closed shortly after
eleven-thirty when the last customer left and no new customers came in.
The bartender called Tony Touhy at the time and asked for permission to
close. Tony said yes, but not to set the burglar alarm because he intended
to drive over later to get his passport. In other words, Kiley, there is no evidence of any kind to indicate that Detective Bianco interrupted Tony
Touhy in any illegal activity and tried to arrest him, as you suggested to the
chief. And there now *is* evidence that Touhy was *not* involved in the killing
of that dancer and did *not* have bruised knuckles, so Bianco wouldn't have
been trying to arrest him for that either, would he? In other words, Kiley,
there is absolutely no reason to suspect that there was any confrontation
at all between Bianco and Touhy. The only contact we might even remotely surmise is that Bianco could have approached Touhy when he parked at
the Shamrock Club, seen that the punk's knuckles were normal, and—if
he had any cop sense at all—backed off. Touhy apparently went into the
club, got his passport, and left. What happened to Detective Bianco afterward—well," Lovat spread his hands, "Homicide will have to determine
that."

"Sorry, but I don't buy it," Kiley said, shaking his head emphatically.
"On that theory, Nick just let Tony Touhy go on his way, then stood there
doing nothing in a dark alley until somebody entirely unconnected to the
case came along and blew him away. Bullshit."

"I'm sure it'll turn out to be a little more complex than that, Detective," said Lovat. "What we know is that Bianco *was* waiting there for you; that it *was* a dark, practically deserted commercial block; it *was* almost one o'clock in the morning. Perhaps Bianco was sitting in his car and saw someone he suspected was a burglar go into the alley, followed him, then lost control of the situation. Maybe he saw a drug deal going down. Hell, maybe we'll find out that some goddamned night watchman shot him by mistake when Bianco was prowling around—"

"Don't buy any of it," Kiley still shook his head. "And how the fuck did Phil Touhy and his shyster lawyer know that the stakeout on Tony was unauthorized, tell me that?"

"I can't tell you that," Gordon Lovat admitted crisply. "I wish I could. There are bound to be information leaks in a police department this size; somehow Touhy found out what we were dealing with as far as you and Bianco not being on the job that night. Right now it really doesn't matter *how* he found out—"

"This whole thing stinks like a Halsted Street sewer," Kiley said accusingly. "I don't buy one fucking word of it."

"I'm sure that doesn't surprise any of us, Kiley," said Vander of IA. "You can't seem to go along with anything that's *right*, can you? You only buy into what's *wrong*, don't you? You thought Tony Touhy beat that dancer to death, and you were wrong. You and Bianco withheld information from Homicide, and that was wrong. You went after the collar on your own, against the book, which was wrong. You set up two unauthorized stake-outs, which was wrong. Now, when the department is bending over backward to keep you clean in the situation, you refuse to accept the way the department has decided to partially clear the case, because you don't want to accept the fact that this punk you've been dogging, this Tony Touhy, might be innocent. Tell me something, Kiley: Don't you have the least little bit of concern that you might be wrong on this too?"

Kiley's head stopped shaking; his lips parted slightly as if to speak, to rebut, retort. But no words came. Staring at Allan Vander, the realization of all those wrongs suddenly compounded in his mind, came together like amoebas attaching themselves one on another to form a larger body—this one a body of self-doubt, stigma, guilt. He could refute what Gordon Lovat had said; disallow in his own mind the theories accepted and being advanced by the department with respect to Tony Touhy's culpability. But there was no answer to what Allan Vander had just said; there was no disputing his own responsibility for all the *wrongs* he had bought into. Bottom line, it was his mistake in arbitrarily accepting a shred of circumstantial evidence and believing from it that Tony Touhy had beaten Ronnie Lynn to death; that had been the foundation of all that later turned sour on him. That had been the mistake, ultimately, that killed Nick Bianco. At that moment, under the accusing stares of Lovat, Vander, and Somers, with his vulnerability compounding, his remorse multiplying, Kiley understood for the first time, really understood, how a *suspect* felt.

Oddly, it was Vander's deputy, Bill Somers, the lieutenant Kiley suspected of tossing his apartment, who now canceled the terrible quiet in the room and tried to show him a little mercy. "Look, Kiley," the IA deputy commander reasoned, "we all know how you feel about Tony Touhy. The guy is a scumbag punk, the kind that makes being a cop worthwhile when we're able to bust him for something and make it stick. Getting him for Bianco's killing would be a dream bust—but we couldn't take it all the way. In the end, he'd walk and we'd all look like chumps. Homicide will *get* Bianco's killer—one way or another, sooner or later. It just won't be Tony Touhy. The quicker you accept that fact, resign yourself to it, the quicker you can settle back into being a working cop again." Somers, who had been speaking very quietly, almost conversationally, now leaned forward, forearms on his knees, seeming to seek an intimacy with the man listening to him. "Don't you think that would be best for everyone involved, Joe?" He almost sounded friendly. "For everyone to just get on with their lives again?"

Kiley could do nothing for a moment but nod. He had heard every quiet word spoken by Bill Somers, but he was still wrestling with the impact of Allan Vander's bulls-eye accusation, still trying to control surges of profound regret, intense shame, and somewhere, rebounding off both, a driving need for revenge. That was the feeling his mind most recognized, most quickly accepted; that was the emotion Kiley used to reduce the damage of other emotions.

Revenge *on* somebody.

Retribution *from* somebody.

Reprisal *for* somebody.

Joe knew deep down that Vander and Somers had just run a good cop–bad cop number on him—but they were wasting their act. It wasn't within them to assuage any of his guilt, any more than they could, in the end, control his actions. But they had been in charge too long to understand that; they were accustomed to obedience, not defiance. Kiley knew what they wanted, and he was capable of performing too—just to get away from them.

"I guess I never thought of it in just that way before, Lieutenant," he told Somers. "Somehow it makes a lot of sense all of a sudden."

"Well," Somers said, more surprised than he wanted to display, "good, Joe. Very good. I'm glad you're seeing the situation in a different light." Somers threw a quick glance at each of the captains. "We're all on the same team here, and we've got to pull together, so to speak."

"Yes, sir," Kiley agreed. Saying 'sir' to a nutless little prick like Somers was not easy—but Kiley *had* to get out of that office, out of their presence, away from their stifling, self-righteous authority. No matter what he had to say—

"Do you think," Gordon Lovat asked, "that you can go along with the department on this and not make any waves?"

"I think so, yes, sir."

Lovat glanced at Vander. The IA man said, "If you felt you needed some time off, Kiley, we might arrange a departmental leave—"

"No, sir," Joe said, "I think I'm better off keeping busy. Captain Madzak has got me working on a pretty interesting bus vandalism case over at B-and-A. I think I'll be able to do him some good on it."

"Well, that's fine, Kiley," said Vander, a little reserved, nevertheless *wanting* to believe him. "You know, if you keep on the straight and narrow after all this, in a few years we can wipe the slate clean and maybe find you a nice desk job in one of the patrol districts, where you can just kick back and wait for your pension. How does that sound?"

"Sounds fine, sir."

It was the 'sir' that finally got them. Coming from Kiley, that was as good as genuflecting and kissing their police academy rings. Since it was Lovat's office, it was Lovat who dismissed him.

"All right, Detective, you may return to your duties at B-and-A. I hope for all our sakes that this matter, as far as it involves any of us, is closed. Let's leave it in Homicide, where it belongs."

"Yes, sir," Kiley said.

As he left, Kiley wondered if the men in the office really thought that he believed the bullshit about a clean slate. If there was one irrefutable thing he had learned as a Chicago cop, it was that *nobody* ever forgot *anything*.

Walking down the hall to return to B-and-A, Kiley saw that Phil Touhy and his lawyer were still on the floor, talking quietly outside the men's room. Ignoring them, Kiley went over the elevator bank, pushed the call button, and stood looking out a window. As he did so, he heard a voice behind him say, "Hey, Kiley—" Joe turned. Phil Touhy was gesturing to him. "I want to talk to you—"

Malcolm, the lawyer, said, "Phil, this isn't a good idea—"

"Relax," Touhy said, walking away from him, coming toward Kiley. "Come on, Kiley, give me a minute. Off the record—" Touhy pointed toward a stairwell next to the elevators.

"Phil, I don't advise this," Malcolm stressed.

"Just wait there," his client said. Then to Kiley, "Come on, one mick to another, what d'you say?"

Kiley followed the mobster over to the stairs and Touhy led him down to the landing between floors. They faced each other in a quiet vacuum of stale, trapped air.

"Listen," Touhy said, "I want you to know that I am genuinely sorry about your partner—no, I mean it, Kiley," he emphasized when Joe looked away in disgust. "Come on, be reasonable," Touhy appealed. "A cop killing does nobody any good; I'd be an idiot to have any part of something that stupid. And my brother feels the same way; all my people feel the same way. I'm in the fucking rackets, Kiley: I deal in gambling, prostitution, protection, and turning trucks of hijacked merchandise. Profits from that I put into legitimate businesses: linen supplies for restaurants, airport gift shops, vending machines for cigarettes, gum, candy, rubbers. I mean, think about it, Kiley: What the fuck would I or any of my people want to kill a cop for? Come on."

"Your brother's dirty, Touhy." Joe's voice was flat and even. "He was involved in my partner's killing."

Touhy shook his head tolerantly. "My brother is a little slow, but he's not dirty—not for this anyway. Look, Kiley, if Tony had anything to do with your partner's death, first thing he would've done is run to me for protection—"

"And first thing you would've done is get him out of the country, right?" asked Kiley. It was not really a question, and they both knew it.

"Okay, I know how it looks," Touhy admitted. "But think about this: If Tony was involved, I'd already be trying to find a fall guy to get him off the hook. The gun he used would already be on its way to get planted on some junkie nigger in the projects, and then he'd be set up to take a fall for something, so the gun could be found in his possession, so your ballistics people could match it with the slug that killed your partner. I mean, this would be going on right fucking *now*, Kiley. But it isn't. Because I don't have nothing to cover up here."

"Where'd you get the information about the stakeouts on your brother being unauthorized?" Kiley asked, knowing he would not be told. Touhy merely shrugged.

"Look, I've got a lot of friends, some of them on my side of the fence, some of them on yours. I do favors for people, they remember me. Let me tell you a story, Kiley. Few years back, there was a cop and his wife had a little boy, three years old, had some kind of disease, I don't know what, needed one of them bone marrow transplants. This guy's a straight and narrow cop, understand, not on nobody's pad, living on a patrolman's salary, a credit to your department. Only thing is, his kid had been sick since the day he was born and the guy had used up the maximum on his medical benefits and there was no money for the bone marrow thing. Not even no money to look for a *donor*. Fucking bank wouldn't loan the guy no money; he's got no collateral. Fucking hospitals won't do nothing on credit—shit, they'll let you die in the office filling out admittance forms. I mean, this poor guy is really up against it, Kiley. So somebody comes to me on his behalf, says to me, 'Philly, this guy and his kid need some help.' So I make arrangements for the kid and his mother to go to the Mayo Clinic over in Minnesota; I make arrangements for a donor to be found; I pay for everything, no strings attached. And these people aren't even Irish, Kiley; these people are *black*." Touhy paused for effect, stuck his chin out a little, adjusted the knot in his tie. "Today that kid is happy, healthy, and doing good in the third grade."

"And you've got a cop in your pocket," Kiley accused.

"Absolutely not!" Touhy disclaimed. "See, that's your problem, Kiley: You're too fucking cynical about everything. I never once asked this guy for nothing. Now, I admit, since we're off the record here, that every once in a while I get a phone call from him with a piece of information he thinks might interest me. Sometimes he's right and sometimes he's wrong. But he never asks nothing in return, and I never offer him anything; I wouldn't insult him like that. You understand?"

"Very touching," Kiley said. "But what does it have to do with my partner's murder?"

"You wanted to know how I found out about the unauthorized stakeouts," Touhy said, shrugging. "That's an example of how I *might* have found out."

"Cuts no ice with me," Joe told him. "I still think your brother is involved."

Touhy shook his head. "You're a fucking hardhead, Kiley."

The label reminded Kiley poignantly of Nick, because his late partner had called him that a hundred times over the years. Called him that for refusing to buy stylish suits at the Maxwell Street "discount" prices; for not playing along when Stella tried to fix him up with eligible women; for always going to the well first in a potentially dangerous situation. Nick used to always say, "You're a fucking hardheaded shanty mick and I'm giving up on you. I'm putting in for a new partner."

But he never did, Kiley thought. He stayed around right up to the time I got him killed.

"You're wasting your breath, Touhy," he told the mobster. "I think your brother either did it or had it done—and I'm going to get him for it."

"How?" Touhy asked, eyebrows raising inquiringly. "Working B-and-A?"

"Know everything, don't you?"

"Everything worth knowing." Touhy pondered for a moment. "Let's see: Kiley, Kiley, Kiley—Did I know your old man?"

"Not unless you were a bartender."

"Hey," Touhy smiled broadly, "I hear that. I had the same problem: the old man a lush, my mother a saint. You too?"

"Pretty close." Watch it, Kiley warned himself. This guy was good; he was *very* good. Charm the goddamned birds right out of the trees.

"Let me ask you something, Kiley," the mobster lowered his voice to another level of confidentiality. "What's a fucking snake-eater like you carrying a badge for, anyways? Come to work for me and I'll put you next to something really choice. You can have your pick: gambling, women, vending machines, whatever. I'll make a place for you. Give you three grand a week to start, in cash, no taxes."

"Now I know for sure your brother's dirty," Kiley replied with a tight smile. But Phil Touhy only smiled back, shaking his head again.

"Wrong. If Tony was dirty, I wouldn't have nothing to do with you; you'd be the enemy." He held his hands up in resignation. "Well, can't say I didn't try. Good luck in B-and-A, Kiley. Don't let nothing blow up in your face."

Touhy walked back up the stairs from the landing, still shaking his head.

At four o'clock that afternoon, Kiley parked near the Belmont Avenue elevated station and walked two blocks down to the Bel-Ked Tavern. Dressed now in old khaki trousers and a pullover shirt, the only weapon he carried was his backup piece, a Smith and Wesson model 60, in an ankle holster. The 60 was a little bulldog of a pistol: snub-nosed, small, round butt with rubber grips, internal hammer, and one of the few palm-size re-volvers capable of firing .38 Special power loads without warping the cylinder. Kiley carried nothing *but* power loads; what, he figured, was the point of anything less? If a man had to carry, he might as well carry right.

At the Bel-Ked, he went in and stood just inside the door for a moment while his eyes adjusted to the dimmer light. Then he went over and sat at one end of the bar. There were only two other drinkers in the place, and they were at a table. When the bartender walked up, Joe said, "Pabst, tap."

The place, Kiley saw as he looked around, was a generic small neigh-borhood tavern, standard issue all over the city. The bar ran the length of one wall immediately to the right of the entrance, with maybe twenty low-backed bar stools up against its front and two ends. On the left wall was a line of four-person booths, upholstered in maroon vinyl. Between the bar and the booths were a few tables with straight chairs in the same maroon vinyl to match the booths. Against the back wall was a Majestic jukebox with a cabinet of red, white, and green illuminated plastic. On the front wall, fac-ing into the tavern, were several arcade games and a shuffleboard table.

When the bartender brought his pilsner glass of draft beer, Kiley hand-ed him a ten and said, "Let me have some quarters in change, will you?"

"You bet." The bartender was a young guy, husky going to fat, with a droopy blond moustache. When he returned, he put down a small plastic tray holding eight quarters and the rest of Kiley's change. Kiley passed him a dollar tip.

"Harold been in today yet?" he asked.

"Harold?"

"Harold Winston. He's a regular. Don't you know him?"

"Maybe by sight," the bartender said. "Sometimes I can't remember the name until I see the face."

"Kind of like a schoolteacher, huh?"

"What do you mean?'

"When you're a schoolteacher, everybody knows *your* name—what is your name, by the way?"

"Nate."

"Nate, I'm Joe. That's an easy one to remember." Kiley extended a hand over the bar and Nate shook hands. "Like I was saying, Nate, every-body in a class in school only has to remember one name, the teacher's, but the teacher has to remember *everybody's* name. Pretty much the same for a bartender and the regular customers in a bar, I'll bet."

"Never thought of it just that way before," Nate said, "but you're right."

"Say, Nate," Kiley pointed, "let me have a bag of those mixed nuts, will you?"

After Nate gave him the nuts, the bartender went over to the table to check on his other two customers. Kiley took his glass of beer and the quarters and went over to the arcade games. He dropped one of the coins into a Pac Man machine and began playing. He was in his fourth game, half an hour later, when Harold Winston came in, carrying his mail.

Winston froze when he saw Kiley, stopping almost in mid-stride halfway between the entrance and the end of the bar. Kiley could see him in his peripheral vision without turning his head away from the Pac Man screen. While Winston was standing there, watching him, Kiley purposely ran Pac Man into one of its pursuers and let it be eaten, ending the game. "Damn," Kiley said to himself, but loud enough for Winston to hear. "I almost made it to the banana level that time." Still without turning in Winston's direction, he took a long swallow of beer, dropped in another coin, and pressed the button for a new game. As Kiley began to play again, he saw Winston put the mail in his jacket pocket and walk toward him.

"Detective Kiley, are you following me?" Winston asked sternly when he got to where Kiley stood.

"What?" Kiley asked, looking at him, frowning. Pausing in the game, he tilted his head as if trying to remember. Then he said, "Oh—uh, Mr. Winston, right?"

"That is correct."

"I'm sorry, what did you ask me?" Kiley shifted his eyes between Winston and Pac Man, and kept playing a little.

"I asked if you were following me."

Kiley pressed the game's pause button. "Mr. Winston, how could I be following you? I've been here an hour; you just came in. Are you following *me*?"

"Of course not. What are you doing here?"

Kiley sipped his beer and shrugged. "Playing Pac Man."

"No, I mean what are you doing *here*, in this bar? In this neighborhood?"

"I live in this neighborhood, Mr. Winston. I think I told you that when we met at the jail. Now look, I'm off duty, okay. I'm just playing a little Pac Man and having a few beers, see. I'm sorry if my being here makes you nervous—"

"You don't make me nervous at all," Winston declared. "You just surprised me, that's all."

Kiley made his voice very low. "Listen, I'm not going to say where we met, if that's what's worrying you. We can just pretend we know each other from the bar here. Hey, what do you drink?"

"Why, uh—I drink Miller's—Miller's Lite—"

"Hey, Nate," Kiley called over to the bartender, "can you bring my friend a Miller's Lite and me another Pabst tap?"

"Coming up," the bartender said.

"You play Pac Man, Mr. Winston?" Kiley asked, then said, "Hey, how about I call you by your first name so it doesn't sound so formal in case Nate hears?"

"I suppose that's all right."

"This is kind of embarrassing, though," Kiley said with a grimace. "I don't remember your first name."

"It's Harold."

"Thanks, Harold. Hal for short?"

"I don't know about *that*," Winston said. "No one has called me Hal since high school."

"So pretend you're back in high school. Call me Joe. Ah, here's the beer." Kiley took the two glasses off the bartender's tray and said, "Money's on the bar, Nate. Take another buck for yourself."

"Thanks, Joe," said Nate.

Kiley resumed playing Pac Man, but was careful not to let lull the dialogue he had established. "Speaking of high school, I went to Crane Tech, Hal. Where'd you go? Wait, let me guess. I'll bet you went to Austin."

"No, I, uh—I didn't go to high school in Chicago."

"Oh. So where you from originally?"

Winston's expression became sly. "You're not by any chance doing a little detective work now, are you—Joe?"

Kiley pushed pause again. "Look, pal, I told you I was off duty. I mean, I'm just making conversation, you know. You don't have to tell me anything you don't want to. As a matter if fact, just because I bought you a beer doesn't mean you have to talk to me at all. Go sit at the bar by yourself if you want to, and I'll just keep playing Pac Man."

"I didn't intend to be rude," Winston said. "It just sounded as if you were prying."

"Just being friendly, Hal. I really don't give a shit where you're from."

"Well, I'm from Detroit originally, if you want to know. But I went to high school in Dayton. Ohio."

"I don't know what you're so jumpy about anyway," Kiley said, seeming not to pay any attention to the background information. "You haven't done anything. You were turned loose, not charged." Kiley resumed his game.

"I'm not jumpy exactly," Winston interpreted the impression he was giving. "It's just that seeing you was such a surprise. It seems very curious that we've never run into each other before."

"Damn," Kiley said, after deliberately sacrificing Pac Man again. "I'm going to give up this game." He turned to face Winston directly. "Look, the reason we've never run into each other is that I've only just started back working the day shift. I was just transferred over to the Bomb-and-Arson squad. Before that, I was working nights on General Assignments out of the Warren Boulevard station. And," he sighed heavily, "the reason I was transferred is because my partner was shot and killed recently—"

"Oh. I didn't realize that—"

"Yeah. You may have seen it on the news or read about it in the papers: a detective found dead in an alley—?"

"Yes!" Winston said, suddenly cognizant. "I do recall that. He was your partner—?"

"For eight years," Kiley confirmed. "I'm godfather to his youngest daughter; she's seven. He left another daughter too; ten. And his wife, of course—" Shaking his head sadly, Kiley raised the glass of beer and drained it. "Want to sit down and have another?" he asked. When Winston did not accept immediately, Kiley shrugged and added, "You don't have to—"

"No, no," Winston said at once then, "let's have another. My turn to buy—"

"Nate!" Kiley called, holding up the empty. "Couple more, please."

Kiley and Winston sat in a booth, and Nate brought the fresh beers and what was left of Joe's money from the bar. Winston handed the bartender a five to pay for the new round. When the bartender brought his change, Winston promptly picked it up and put it in his pocket.

"Listen, I'm very sorry about your partner," Winston said, after the bartender left. "I'm not a big fan of the police after them keeping me down in that filthy jail for seventy-some hours, but I can certainly sympathize with someone who's lost a close friend."

"Thank you, Hal," Kiley said, making his voice sincere. "And I don't blame you for not being a fan of the police; I'm not too crazy about them myself right now. They've refused to let me work on finding my partner's killer, which I think is pretty low."

"Well, I should say," Winston agreed. "Why in the world won't they let you help?"

"They say I'm too close to it. They say I won't be objective."

"People in charge," Winston grunted softly, "always seem to have an answer, don't they?"

The two drank in silence for several minutes. A few more customers drifted in, singly and in pairs, and another bartender came on duty. A Slavic-looking woman with big arms went over to play Pac Man, causing Kiley to comment, "Hope she has better luck than I did." Winston smiled and nodded.

At one point, Kiley asked casually, "So what do you do for a living, Hal?" Then immediately held up a hand and retracted the question. "No, never mind. Forget I asked. Bad question. I don't want you to think that I'm being a detective."

"Oh, that's all right," Winston replied, seeming to be a little more relaxed now. "I didn't tell you at the jail because I was afraid the police might come around to where I work. Not that I have much of a job, really. I'm just an inventory control clerk. I work for Olson Rug Company, at their big warehouse over on Montrose."

"Nobody's going to bother you on your job, Hal, I guarantee it," Kiley assured. "Your file is closed; I sent it over to IF myself."

"What's IF?"

"Inactive Files."

"Oh. Well, that's good to hear." Winston took a long swallow of beer. "Uh, anything new on the bus case?"

"No, they're still looking."

"There doesn't seem to be anything on the news about it," Winston explored. Kiley merely shrugged.

"Like I said, I just got over to Bomb-and-Arson, so I haven't been following the case. And with what happened to my partner and all, well—"

"Yes, of course," Winston sympathized, "you've had other concerns."

After a while, Kiley signaled Nate for more beer, and when it came gave him a five and said, "Take a buck for yourself, Nate, and put the rest in the jukebox."

"Sure thing, Joe," the bartender said.

"None of that bullshit rap music," Kiley warned as Nate walked away. The bartender laughed.

"I'm not sure I can keep up with you on the beers," Winston said cautiously. "I usually only have a couple before I go home for supper."

"Quit any time you want, Hal. This will probably be my last one anyway. Got to try and get some sleep tonight. I'm having a hard time readjusting to the day shift, you know."

"I can imagine."

"So tell me, what's inventory control like?"

"*Bor*-ing," Winston said, rolling his eyes. "There's this huge warehouse, right? And these huge trucks drive up and unload these huge rolls of carpet. I log them all in by stock number, decide where they'll go, then have them taken away on these huge forklifts. It's eight hours a day of sheer tedium. Not exciting like I'm sure police work is."

"Police work isn't exciting, Hal. It's ninety-nine percent monotony."

"Yes, but what's the other one percent?" Winston asked, leaning forward on his elbows, eager for the answer.

"The other one percent is cold fear," Kiley said. "It's when you don't know what's going to happen next, but you *do* know it could be very bad."

"What made you become a policeman?" Winston wanted to know.

"My dad was a cop," Kiley replied with a straight face. He realized that it was the first actual lie he had told the thin, intense man; everything else Kiley had said to him, oddly, had been the truth. It occurred to Kiley that it was a peculiar way to be handling a suspect—telling him the truth. But then, he reminded himself, Harold Paul Winston was a peculiar suspect.

"Is your father still living?" Winston asked.

"Yeah. He and Mom are retired, down in Florida." Asshole, Kiley chastised himself. Now you've got to remember all this shit. "How about you? Any family?"

"My parents divorced when I was in high school," Winston said. He grunted wryly. "Both of them remarried within a year. My father married a woman he worked with, so I guess that's what caused the breakup. My mother later married a man *she* worked with, also. It's funny, but they live within half a mile of each other, buy groceries at the same store, shop at the same mall, but they never *speak*. Never say hello, never even look at each other." Winston shook his head. "Strange."

"I've got a sister the same way," Kiley sympathized. "She and her ex have two kids, and whenever there's a program or anything at school, they both go, sit on opposite sides of the room, never talk. Even when her ex comes to get the kids every other weekend, he never goes to the door;

blows his horn and waits for them out in the car. Only time my sister ever says a word to him is when the child support check is late."

Winston shook his head again. "It would be so easy for people to get along—if they'd just make the effort."

"Absolutely," Kiley agreed emphatically. "Take you and me. We met under the worst possible circumstances—and look at us now. Drinking beer, having a nice talk. You're right, Hal: All it takes is effort." Kiley had seen Nate take off his apron and leave, his shift over; he wouldn't be around for Winston to question about Joe, if Winston was so inclined—which Kiley really didn't think he was. But he had waited for Nate to leave anyway. Now he drained his glass and said, "Well, I'm going to call it a day—"

"It's early yet," Winston objected tentatively.

"I know, but I'm still fighting that change of hours." Standing, Kiley offered his hand. "Been a real pleasure, Hal. Enjoyed talking to you." As they shook hands, Kiley leaned down and whispered in mock seriousness, "Don't blow up any more buses, okay? I wouldn't want to have to arrest you."

Kiley laughed at the joke, then Winston laughed also, but not as quickly.

Giving Winston a wink, Kiley turned and walked out of the bar.

# TWELVE

**W**hen Kiley went to the Bianco home for dinner the second time, he saw at once that the evening was more planned, more organized. "Come see how nice the girls have fixed everything," Stella said at the door, taking his hand and practically dragging him to the dining room. There, Jennie and Tessie had set out what Joe knew to be the good china, the good silver, and the crystal.

"We're getting everything ready, Uncle Joey," Jennie said, pulling him down to kiss his cheek in passing.

"I'm helping," Tessie boasted. She came over to hug Joe while surreptitiously, she thought, patting his coat pocket for jelly beans.

"Tessie, stop that," Stella scolded. "You mustn't always expect something—"

"Actually, I brought a strawberry whipped cream cake," Kiley said. "If you already have dessert, I can give it to Mrs. Levine—"

"No, *we* want the cake!" the girls shouted in perfect unison.

"All I planned was spumoni," Stella said. "The cake sounds delicious."

"I'll bring it in," Joe said. "It's from Dominici's—"

On the way out to the car, he wondered if he should have mentioned that. Dominici's was an Italian bakery on Milwaukee Avenue that specialized in whipped cream fruit cakes. Nick had picked up something there at least once a week to take home to his family. Earlier, Joe had thought it was a good idea; now, suddenly, he felt self-conscious about it. But he took the cake in anyway.

"This all looks really nice, girls," he told the two sisters as he passed back through the dining room to the kitchen. Placing napkins, they smiled primly, then giggled at each other.

"Let's put that in the fridge," Stella said when he walked into the kitchen. She took the box from his hands. "They've been like this all day," she nodded toward the dining room. "So excited. It was really Jennie's idea; tacky me, I was going to make you eat in the kitchen again." She put a hand on his arm. "How is it on the job, Joe?"

"Not too bad," he said. "Things seem to have settled down a little. I don't think there'll be any problem with your pension; the department has decided to cover Nick and me being off duty." He did not mention that the department had to drop its investigation of Tony Touhy in order to do so. But she did not know about Tony Touhy anyway, not by name; all she knew was that there was a suspect in Nick's killing.

"What about your job, Joe? Is that okay too?"

"Looks like."

"I'm glad, Joey. We need to put this whole thing behind us and, like you said, go on living. That's what Nick would want." Turning, she opened the oven door, hot pads in hand. "The lasagna's ready. Girls——!" she yelled into the dining room. They hurried in. "Take the salads out of the fridge and put them on the table. Joe, you get out the wine——"

Stella Bianco was clearly functioning again.

Dinner reminded Joe of the first time he had ever come to the Bianco home, about a month after he and Nick became partners. Tessie had not been born yet, and Jennie was just a toddler, going back and forth between Nick and Stella for bites from their plates, until finally Stella gave her a bottle and put her down. But the table had been set the same way—smartly, elegantly, in a fashion Stella had copied from a magazine—and Nick had shown off the crystal he was so proud of; crystal he had paid retail for. "I would never, ever, put anything from Maxwell Street on my table, Joe," he had subsequently told his partner some months later. "Not even food. There's a guy down there moves USDA Prime for three bucks a pound, Joe. It goes for seven-something a pound in butcher shops—but I don't touch it. Nothing hijacked goes on my table."

The first visit, when Joe had met Stella, who was a young, first-time mother then, she had been wearing a Chinese-red dress in which she looked like a dream. Tonight she was in a dressy navy blue pantsuit, and both girls were wearing Sunday dresses.

"You ladies," Kiley said at the table, raising his glass to them, "look absolutely beautiful tonight. You have got to be the three prettiest girls in the whole world."

"Well, thank you, kind sir," Stella replied elaborately.

"Jennie and me made the salads all by ourselves," Tessie said.

"Jennie and *I*," Stella got in edgewise as Joe said, "And fine salads they

are. If I ever hear of a salad-making contest anywhere, I'm going to enter
you girls in it."

On thinking about the evening in retrospect, Kiley was not certain
whether there had already been an underlying tension among them that he
had simply failed to notice, or whether it was his own insensitivity that had
generated it. He knew that even though he was enjoying himself very
much, he was also acutely aware that it was Thursday night, when the bus
bomber usually struck. There had been four blasts on four consecutive
Thursdays; then a Thursday was skipped—one of the days Harold
Winston was in jail. Now another Thursday had arrived, Winston was
loose, and Kiley was restless to know whether, after their meeting in the
tavern, Winston would strike again. Kiley did not think he would; he felt
Winston was too crafty to risk placing another explosive when the possibility existed that he could be under surveillance. Kiley still felt Winston
*wanted* to be caught—but he didn't think Winston wanted it to be an in-
the-act apprehension. Winston probably wanted to be put on trial—but
he *didn't* want to be found guilty and put away.

The other thing on Kiley's mind was that he had come up with a plan
to try and connect Tony Touhy to Nick's murder. It was a scheme that was
still fermenting in his mind—he wasn't sure yet he could even carry it
out—but *that* was there during the evening in addition to the Winston
thing, and he supposed he had not been as alert to the atmosphere at the
dinner table as he should have been. It was he who ruined the dinner with
his loose mouth, trying to be understanding, considerate, empathetic—all
the traits that were naturally alien to his personality except in rare in-
stances, with the scant few special people in his life.

It happened innocently enough. Little Tessie said, "Jennifer didn't take
her singing lesson today, Uncle Joey. Her teacher called Mommy."

Joe saw Jennie stop eating and look down at her plate.

"It's the second one she's missed," Stella told Joe, a little self-consciously,
again pointing up the fact that without Nick, she did not have the Bianco
household functioning very well. "Her teacher said if she hasn't been
practicing and if she keeps missing her lessons, she'll have to start all over.
But she just didn't want to go," Stella shrugged, "so I didn't make her."

Now Jennie looked up, looked at Joe as if she had some need for reas-
surance from him.

"It won't hurt her to miss a few lessons," Joe said supportively. "And I'm
sure she won't have to start over. She's got a voice like an angel already."

As soon as the unfortunate words were out of his mouth, Joe regretted
them. *Jesus, just let them pass*, he silently implored.

But he knew it was too late when tears started to flow down Jennie's cheeks.

"My—my daddy—is with the angels—" she said in a pitiful little strained voice, the words directed at Joe.

"I know, sweetheart," Joe said softly. "I know he is."

"And he's—never coming back—"

Bursting into hysterical sobbing, she fled the table.

Stella stood and started to hurry after her, but stopped instead and looked at Kiley. "You go up to her, Joey."

"Me? Stella, I—"

"Please. She needs someone stronger than me right now. Go up to her."

Feeling he had caused the regrettable reaction himself, and not at all sure Stella was making a wise decision, Joe nevertheless left the table and followed Jennie upstairs.

It was more than an hour before Kiley came back downstairs again. The dining room table had been partially cleared off; Tessie's plate was gone, and clean plates and fresh napkins were set out where Stella and Joe had sat. Kiley found Stella and Tessie in the kitchen, tidying up.

"Is she okay?" Stella asked, worry shadowing her face.

Kiley nodded. "She's sleeping. I took off her shoes and put a blanket over her. I had to lie down with her for a long time before she stopped crying."

"Yeah, she always wants that when she's sick or when things aren't going just right for her. Usually it was Nick that did it. I'm glad you were here for her, Joe."

"I don't know what made me say what I did about angels," Joe shook his head, perplexed. "It was such a stupid comment—"

"It was a perfectly natural thing to say," Stella defended. "Listen, Tessie's finished her dinner and I'm keeping ours warm in the oven. You and I can sit back down to eat in a few minutes, but first your goddaughter has something to ask you."

Teresa came over to where Joe was standing and hooked an arm around his leg. "Uncle Joey, will you rock me in the rocker until my bedtime?"

"Sure, I will, beautiful," he said. "Right now?"

"Yes!" she screeched in delight. "Come on!"

Kiley let the child take his hand and lead him into the living room where there was a very old but still very solid mahogany rocking chair that had once belonged to Stella's grandmother. It had been given to them when Stella was three months pregnant with Jennie, along with the charge to "Rock'a the un'aborn baby one hour every night, makes'a baby form perfect, see?" Of course, Stella did; of course, Jennie was perfect; of course, the grandmother gleaned all the credit for that perfection. The sturdy old chair was now cushioned seat and back with pillows covered with material that matched Stella's drapes.

Kiley settled into the chair, into the depression he knew Nick had made and left. "I had to rock that godchild of yours for an hour last night to get her to go to sleep," he had occasionally grumbled good-naturedly. "I swear to God, between you and Stella, she's getting spoiled rotten."

As soon as Kiley sat, Tessie was on his lap, handing him a book. "What's this?" he asked.

"It's a *book*." She gave Joe a very impatient look. "For you to read to me."

"Oh. What's it about?"

"Read it and you'll see. It's about Sleeping Beauty."

"Well, if I read you this book and you fall asleep on my lap, then you'll be *my* sleeping beauty, won't you?"

"Yes, I will," she replied primly. Then added: "But I won't fall asleep."

She was asleep in twenty minutes.

Kiley carried the sleeping child and Stella led the way back upstairs to the bedroom where Jennie was already asleep. Kiley helped set Tessie up on the other bed and held her while Stella wrestled her out of everything but her panties, then pulled a nightgown over her head and got her into bed with a Barbie doll in one arm and a Panda bear in the other. Finished with the youngest, they did the same at Jennifer's bed with the oldest: to Joe, a distinctly more difficult job because Jennie was so much bigger.

"Jesus, that's a lot of work," he said to Stella as they went back downstairs.

"Tell me," Stella agreed. "Fortunately, it doesn't happen all that often." In the dining room, she said, "Pour us both some wine. I'll get the lasagna back out."

When they were finally settled down to eat again, Kiley felt the need to once more apologize for the comment he was certain had disrupted the evening. "Stel, I'm really sorry about what I said. I guess I didn't think—"

"Joe, it's okay," she assured. "I've been half expecting it from Jennie sooner or later. Tessie, you know, seems to go in and out of her periods of grief, but Jen, I don't know, is like moody *most* of the time. She doesn't want to do anything, go anywhere, she's not interested in seeing anybody; this dinner for you is the first thing she's shown any enthusiasm for since the funeral—"

"Great. And I had to be the one to spoil it."

"That is *not* so, Joe Kiley, and I don't want to hear it again out of you!" Stella scolded with all the authoritarianism she could marshal. Then her voice softened again. "I *am* worried about her, though. Maybe I expected us all to, I don't know—*regroup* faster than we have. We're not weaklings, any of us—"

"Jen is going to be all right," Kiley said confidently. "All of you will; you'll all be fine. It's just going to take time."

"Time," she said wearily. "I hate the goddamned word." She took a long swallow of wine between bites. "It's not just a word, you know, Joe: time. It's an *existence,* it's *real.* The hours of the day drag like a heavy weight on all of us; sometimes the girls and I just sit, not doing anything: We just *sit.* And the nights—well, sometimes I think the goddamned nights won't pass at all—"

"It'll *all* pass, Stel."

"I know. I know it will. But, God, when? *When*, Joey?" That last was a plea, clear and urgent.

"I can't tell you when," Kiley said quietly. "Nobody can tell you that. But you've got to keep working at it, Stel. For the sake of the girls as well as yourself. Don't let yourselves just sit. Make yourselves *do* something."

Kiley tried not to lecture; he wanted only to support, reinforce, bolster whatever *needed* bolstering in Stella's present shaky foundation. And he was aware that what he was offering her was limited by his own narrow view of life—life that was either good or bad, white or black, with no shades of gray; life jaded by fourteen years of the badge, the gun. He was aware that all he kept offering was a repeat litany of "Time heals everything"; aware that he was incapable of approaching subjects like the years of love Stella had enjoyed with Nick, the enormous physical pleasure they obviously had together, the beautiful little girls they had produced, the pride she could take in Nick's years as a police officer—because, the Valentino suits and a few other things aside, Nick Bianco had for the most part been a god-damned good cop. The drug peddlers, rapists, muggers, child molesters, purse snatchers, drunken wife beaters, brutal pimps, and all the other gross street trash that Nick had been involved in arresting for a dozen years, more than made up for a weakness he indulged in expensive suits—a weakness he knew helped support warehouse burglars and truck hijackers.

But Kiley could not speak of those things to Stella Bianco; they were, to his mind, subjects on the other side of an imaginary line that he felt he could not cross. It would have been like talking to Stella about Gloria Mendez. So Kiley kept to his own side of that line, the side he had always stayed on, the *familiar* side, and spoke to his late partner's widow in a series of clichés about strength, time, responsibility. She had probably already heard exactly the same things from her priest.

"Joe," Stella said after several moments of silent eating, "I feel so self-ish telling you about all *my* problems, when you've got so many of your own. I know you must miss Nick very much too—" She let her words hang, providing Kiley an opening to speak if he wanted one.

"I do, Stella," he told her earnestly. Up until then, he had not verbalized to anyone the depth of his own loss. "I know it'll sound like a line from some soap opera, but I really feel that I lost a part of myself; not like an arm or an eye, anything like that; like something *inside* of me has been taken away. Nick and I had reached the point where we worked so smoothly together, where we functioned like synchronized gears in a machine of some kind; we always seemed to know exactly what each of us was supposed to do, because we knew what the *other* one would be doing. And neither one of us even had to think about it; we just knew." Joe looked away from the table and seemed to stare off into space. "There are some old-timers in the department who believe they can actually read their partner's mind; I mean, seriously believe it. There are two cops in burglary who've been partners for thirty-one years. Their minds are supposed to be so attuned to each other that when one of them is having an argument with his wife, the phone will ring and it'll be the other one, and he'll say, 'What are you two fighting about now? You're keeping me awake.' And once one of them left a theater in the middle of a movie, saying, 'My partner needs me,' and sure enough, his partner had just been in a car accident and was on his way to the hospital. True stories, both of them. Really happened. I know they're extreme examples, but they show that between cops who are longtime partners, some kind of connection *does* exist. Nick and I were partners for eight years; not a long time by some standards—but long enough for us to bond, to link up. When two cops fuse like that, especially street cops, it's like something invisible between them is spliced together. After that happens, when one of them loses the other, the one left behind feels like he's had an organ removed. He feels like he's been through major surgery, only without being cut." Kiley looked back at Stella and smiled slightly, self-consciously. "Yeah, Stella, I miss him very much."

Stella rose and came around the table, and as if he had been waiting for her, desperately needing her, Joe also rose, and met her. Their arms went around each other and Stella pulled Joe's head down onto her shoulder, his face against her neck, and held him there as he began to sob.

He cried for a long time.

Driving home that night, Kiley's mind was in a turmoil.

Stella had comforted him that evening like he imagined she must comfort Jennie and Tessie; comforted him like he was a child; he the weak one, she the strong. The way he had cried had not been like the sporadic weeping he had experienced in the immediate wake of Nick's death: some brief tears as he had left Nick in the alley to get to a phone for help; again when the body bag was zipped up and the morgue van took Nick away; then in the men's room at the Shop, between interrogations; and since the funeral, every night, alone in his apartment, drinking.

But that had all been brief tearfulness, moments of grief intermingled with long hours of guilt. This, tonight, had been an emotional explosion, the proverbial dam giving way to a veritable flood of tears. This had been uncontrollable sobbing—the shaking, jerking, quivering kind, the kind one is certain will never end, will never remit its spasms, never absolve the grief that has generated it.

And all through it, as his tears wet Stella's neck and collar, she had held him close, one hand in the middle of his back, the other stroking the back of his head, her voice, as soft in its own hoarseness as it could be, whispering, "All right, Joey—it's all right—let it go—let it out, baby—it's all right—"

When the convulsion of it all finally ended, Stella had led him into the downstairs half-bath and let him have a few minutes of privacy to clean up. He felt like a fool, but at the same time experienced an enormous sense of relief, like waking up the first morning after a virus had been purged from one's body. Following the almost complete limpness, the awful slack, of the sobbing spell, he could now actually feel himself becoming physically stronger, muscles reforming; mentally stronger, endorphins expanding.

He had found Stella in the living room, idly thumbing through a magazine, and sat down next to her on the couch. "I feel like an idiot," he said.

"Don't be silly," she slapped his arm gently. "You're human, Joe, just like all the rest of us—even though you'd probably be the last one to admit it." She patted where she had slapped. "You needed a shoulder to cry on, that's all."

"I'm glad it was yours, Stel."

"So am I."

When he was about to leave, a little while later, Stella got a fully packed garment bag out of the foyer closet and gave it to him. "Some of Nick's things. Suits and stuff. You and Nick were about the same size, and I want you to have them."

Like the Movado watch she had given him the day of the funeral, there was no way he could refuse to accept the gift. Stella did not know that all of the suits were probably hot; Nick had only told her that a friend gave him a "discount" for sending other cops around as customers. Both he and Joe occasionally had to field questions from Stella about why Nick never sent Joe around to get nicer suits. Nick's usual answer was, "Because, Stella, face it, the godfather of your youngest daughter *wants* to dress like a hick."

When Joe had taken the garment bag, Stella had added jokingly, "Now, listen, this has nothing to do with the fact that I've hated your gray suits all these years. I just thought you might get some wear out of these things. And I can't give them to charity, Joe; to strangers."

Now, as he left the suburbs and drove into the night city, the garment bag lying flat on the backseat was not what had thrown Kiley's recently rejuvenated mind into its latest unrest. The disturbance this time was the memory of Stella's body pressed close up against his. Even in the throes of his sobbing, there had been flashing spears of thought that she was *against* him: her breasts, stomach, thighs— His crying jag had not been allayed by those flashes; he could not have caught them in his mind even if he'd wanted to. But their presence—their *purpose*, for all he knew—had left indelible impressions for him to remember later: her breasts, her stomach, her thighs, *against* his body—

He tried to berate himself for the thoughts, but failed. Whether they were decent thoughts or not, whether honorable, seemly, moral, ethical, whether *right*, they were honest, and they were *there*.

Joe Kiley *wanted* Stella Bianco, and there wasn't a goddamned thing in the world he could do about it.

But what he *could* do, he told himself firmly, was meet the problem head-on, as he usually met all problems; meet it squarely and directly— and overcome it. Not overcome the desire; he wasn't sure that was possible. But overcome the growing, gnawing nagging that the desire generated. Kiley could not stop wanting Stella, but he could damned sure force himself to stop *thinking* about wanting her. Thinking about her at length, anyway; stop himself from dwelling on her, from sliding so dangerously near to deliberate, habitual fantasies of her. He had overcome that weakness once before, years earlier, when he had first been brought home by Nick, first met Stella, first been so taken with her; when he had realized that his feelings were getting out of hand that first time, and he had done something about it.

He would do something about it again, he told himself, ordered himself, now.

The key to overcoming bothersome thoughts—the nuns had called them "provocative" thoughts, those that led to an "occasion of sin"— the key to overcoming them was to use *other* thoughts that were just as compelling, just as demanding. A priest had once told Kiley's eighth-grade boys class, bluntly, "Don't think of titties, think of sports: baseball, basketball, and the like." Joe and his hooligan friends had compromised. "She's got tits like basketballs," they would say, or something similar.

The theory, nevertheless, was sound. Substitute one pressing thought for another.

Deciding to begin right then, driving now well back into the city, Kiley started looking for an outdoor pay phone. He found a booth outside a closed cigar store and pulled over. The ceiling light of the booth was smashed out and an old wino, his bottle of Ripple on his lap, was sitting in it with his legs stretched out on the sidewalk. Kiley instinctively pulled out his badge and said, "Move it."

"Okay—okay, ossifer, sir—I'm going—" the wino said immediately.

But when the old man began a frustrating struggle to get to his feet, Kiley put the badge away and said, "Never mind, forget it. Stay where you are; just don't make any noise while I'm on the phone, understand?"

"Yes, sir, ossifer—"

Taking a slip of paper from his wallet, Kiley reached into the booth, dropped a quarter in the slot, and held the receiver in the same hand with which he dialed Captain Leo Madzak's home number. Then he pulled the receiver as far out of the booth as it would reach and warned the wino, "Don't you piss on my shoes."

After two rings, Madzak's number was answered by a machine. Kiley waited for the greeting—by a female voice, Mrs. Madzak, he guessed—to play, then after a beep, said, "Captain, this is Joe Kiley. I'm sorry to bother you this late, but I was wondering—"

The answering machine was cut off and Leo Madzak said, "Yeah, Joe, what is it?"

"Sorry it's so late, sir," Kiley said. "I was wondering if there's been any activity from our bus bomber tonight—it's Thursday—"

"Nothing, Joe," the B-and-A commander said. "I've spoken to the transit people twice and everything's quiet. What have you got?"

"I've made direct contact with the guy, Captain. We're practically buddies; had a few beers together last night. I think he may be gun-shy right now; he doesn't want to be busted in the act. There's some new background information I have to run tomorrow that might flesh the guy out a little."

"You still think he's the man?"

"Definitely do, yessir."

"What kind of time frame we looking at, Joe?"

"A week, max," Kiley said. "We won't have to worry about next Thursday."

"That's what I like to hear, Joe. You keep me up to date on it."

"Yessir, I will."

"Goodnight, Joe."

"Goodnight, Captain."

Kiley hung up, feeling momentarily elated. The scam he was running on Winston was working! Winston's pattern had been broken: he was on the street, he wasn't under surveillance, it was Thursday, and he hadn't planted a bomb. It made Joe feel good. This was the first thing that had gone right since he and Nick went into that alley where Ronnie Lynn lay dead.

Looking down at the wino, he asked, "You live anywhere? You got a place to stay?"

"Shurtenly, I do," the drunk replied.

"Where? Where do you live?"

"Right down the street there—shee that sign—?"

Kiley saw a sign half a block down that said HOTEL—NIGHTLY & WEEKLY. "You want me to walk you down there?"

"Definen'ly not," the old man said. "Sho happens I am waiting for a call—"

"Suit yourself," Kiley said, and left him there.

Now, he thought, back in the car, driving away, was the time to tentatively put into place his plan to nail Tony Touhy. Although it was not entirely laid out in his mind—he was not sure exactly where it would lead him, for one thing—he did have enough of a course plotted to at least begin.

So he began. He drove to 3333 Lake Shore Drive.

There was a half-circle driveway in front of the building for picking up and dropping off people, and two limited-time parking spaces along the driveway curb. Kiley parked in one of them and walked over to the buzzer-controlled foyer entrance. Beyond the double glass doors operated by the buzzer, an older man in a maroon doorman's uniform sat at a desk, idly directing his attention between a newspaper spread open before him, and three small TV monitors each with a different black-and-white picture. The lobby itself, smart and stylish without being opulent, was deserted except for the doorman.

Kiley used a knuckle to tap on one of the glass doors, and held up his badge for the doorman to see. The buzzer was sounded and he pushed on in as the doorman got up to meet him. Kiley let him take a close look at his detective's badge, but kept his photo ID folded under.

"Ed Monroe," Kiley said, extending his hand. "Robbery detail."

"Bernard Oznina, night doorman. Is something wrong?"

"Nothing for you to worry about, Mr. Oznina. We've had a rash of purse snatchings a few blocks from here—over on Broadway, around there. Some young jigs doing it. We've got stakeouts trying to catch them but the bastards have been too fast for us so far—"

"Yeah, them jigs can run—"

"We're trying to get a line on which way they go after they snatch a purse. Have you seen any black kids running past your building, say, last week, ten days?"

"No, not once," said Oznina. "You think they're running down here, to the Drive?"

"We think they may be running over into the park," Joe said. "Just thought they may have run past one of the buildings along here. What hours you work, Mr. Oznina?"

"Four to midnight."

"You're the one to see, then. All the incidents have occurred between nine-thirty and eleven-forty. Say, have you got a water fountain in here?"

"Water cooler. Follow me." The doorman led Joe to a small utility room off the lobby and pointed to a bottled water dispenser with a tube of paper cups on its side. "Help yourself."

Kiley drank two cups of water, tossed the cup in a wastebasket, and said, "That was good. Thanks a lot, Mr. Oznina—"

"Anytime, officer. Listen," he said as he walked Kiley to the door, "you'll let me know if these purse snatchings get any closer to the Drive, won't you?"

"We don't think they will," Kiley told him. "Most residents here on the Drive come and go in cars. These punks are hitting people on foot: leaving the all-night market, coming out of a movie, that kind of thing. But I'll let you know if anything happens closer. In the meantime, I wouldn't mention it to anyone. No sense alarming your tenants."

"Mum's the word for me," Oznina said.

Kiley gave him a wink and left.

Now, he thought as he got back into his car, all he had to do was find a way to get Bernard Oznina to let him into Tony Touhy's apartment.

# THIRTEEN

**E**arly the next morning, a full two hours before his shift was to begin, Kiley walked into the B-and-A squad room and hung his coat on the back of the chair at what was now his desk. Lee Tumac, who was still the night duty officer, looked up from his own desk where he was surviving the last two hours of his shift on steaming black coffee from the machine in the hall.

"Jesus, Kiley, what the fuck are you, an insomniac or something?" he asked, without rancor.

"My body clock's all fucked up," Kiley told him. "I guess I worked nights too long. I've been awake since three; finally I decided I might as well try to accomplish something."

"Well, don't log in until eight, okay? Otherwise you'll make the rest of us look bad."

"I've been on the force fourteen years, Tumac," Joe replied. "I don't need to be told something like that."

"No offense," Tumac said, waving a hand to dismiss the subject. "It's been a long night."

"Take off now if you want to," Joe said. "I'll cover for you."

"Seriously?" Tumac's face lit up.

"Why not, I'm here anyway. I'll log you out at eight when I log myself in. Go on, beat it."

"All right! Listen, Joe, I owe you one."

"Forget it."

As Lee Tumac was leaving, Joe was activating one of the terminals against the back wall and turning on its monitor. When the document window came up, he cursored across the menu bar to FORMS and keyed ENTER. The terminal asked: INTERNAL OR EXTERNAL? Kiley selected the latter. A cascade menu immediately dropped down the window listing the various forms developed by the department for communicating with external agencies. Kiley cursored down to REQUEST FOR INFORMATION and keyed ENTER again. Several seconds later, the form came onto the screen. Kiley began to fill in the blanks.

Directing the form to the Detroit Police Department in Detroit, Michigan, he requested a full record check run on Winston, Harold Paul, beginning with birth records, department of health records, board of education records, available juvenile offender records, plus any related or other informational records the Detroit Police Department considered appropriate. As the reason for the records request, Kiley stated that the subject was a suspect in the vandalism of Chicago city buses by use of minor explosive devices.

When he had completed the form, Kiley keyed in the Spell Check feature of the terminal and watched as it went through his typed input and found his errors. After he corrected his mistakes, he turned on the printer connected to the three terminals, initialized the proper terminal to the printer, and requested four copies of the filled-out form. The printer warmed up in thirty seconds, read the hard disc of the terminal in two, accessed the information on that disc in five, and began printing one second later. The four copies slid out one by one, smoothly and precisely, like playing cards being cast by an expert dealer.

When the printing function terminated, the terminal asked in its document window: ANOTHER FORM? or CLOSE? Kiley keyed for another form. This one he directed to the Dayton Police Department, in Dayton, Ohio. He asked for the same information, just in case, but added several new areas of search: adult police records; city, county, or state employment records; local credit bureau records; civil litigation records; city and county real estate records; and business license records. When he had the form completed, he went through the same procedure again and had four copies printed.

Back at his desk, Kiley put one copy of each request into his own file. Then he got out a B-and-A inter-squad memo form, rolled it into his typewriter, and typed:

To:        Captain Leo Madzak
           Commander, B&A
From:      Joseph F. Kiley, Det. 1st (TAD)
Subject:   Requests made for external agency information.

In the text section, he wrote:

Enclosed are copies of two requests for information on subject Winston, Harold Paul. Will advise upon receipt this information. Proceeding with second personal contact with subject as soon as possible, and will advise results. Transferring field surveillance to place of employment: Olson Rug Co., 4484 Montrose Avenue.

That last item was a cover. Kiley did not intend to conduct a surveillance of Winston at his job or anywhere else. *Watching* Winston would have been as useless as giving him the third degree. The only way to make Winston was to *handle* him—slowly, subtly, slyly. But Kiley needed a reason to be out of the office nearly all day, in order to keep Leo Madzak clean, and there wasn't a better way than a reasonable, logical surveillance excuse.

Stapling the Madzak memo to the information request forms, Kiley crossed the squad room to the commander's office and dropped the papers into the IN basket. Then he returned to his own desk and took out still another blank form, this one mimeographed instead of printed, and only one-third the size of a normal sheet. He filled it out in ballpoint:

To:      Aldena
From:    Kiley
FAX to:  Detroit PD Mich.
         Dayton PD Oh.

At the bottom, he printed in capital letters: ASAP PLEASE. He stapled it to two copies of each request.

As Kiley was going over to put it on Aldena's desk, in she walked, with her customary don't-fuck-with-me frown.

"You come in early just to think up more work for me to do?" she demanded.

"That's right," Kiley said "Captain told me to try and keep you busy. Said when you're not busy, you start messing with the male employees."

"*Shee*-it," Aldena scoffed. "Nobody in this building *worth* messing with. I be better off going over to the jail and messing around."

"I'll have to report that remark," Kiley told her solemnly.

"Don't make no difference to me what you report," she declared. "I'm black, female, a single mother, and handicapped. Can't *nobody* touch my job."

It reminded Kiley of what Gloria Mendez had said about her own job, except for the last part. "Handicapped? You don't look handicapped to me."

"That's because you're not as alert and perceptive as a trained police office supposed to be," she replied loftily. "Let me see what you got there," she jerked the papers from his hand, while dropping a huge, pastel green purse heavily onto her desk. "Next time," she said, scanning the pages, "make out one fax form for each city."

"I'll change it," Kiley said, reaching. She drew the papers out of his reach.

"Do it myself, then it'll be done right." Sitting down, she used a staple remover to neatly separate the pages.

"How are you handicapped?" Kiley asked. "Besides your personality, I mean."

"Just for that, I'm *never* going to tell you," Aldena swore. She looked at the bottom of the small, handwritten form. "'ASAP.' My, my, must *really* be important. Somebody planning to blow up the Wrigley Building?"

"Prudential Tower," Kiley said. "Seriously, Aldena, how are you handicapped?"

Aldena sighed dramatically. "Come around here," she ordered, standing. Kiley felt a fleeting trepidation that she was going to hit him. Aldena picked up on it at once. "Come *on*. I'm not going to hurt you."

When Kiley got around the desk, Aldena got right in his face. She began rolling her eyes: clockwise, counterclockwise, left, right, up, down. Then she stopped.

"Okay, Detective," she challenged, "which one is the real eye and which one is the glass eye?"

"You've got a glass eye?" he asked, incredulous.

"You are really dense, Kiley, you know that," she said. "You ought to be working night traffic court."

"I don't believe you, Aldena," he said, smiling what was at best an uncertain smile

"I don't care if you believe me or not, man. I'd take it out and show you, but it's been seamed to the socket muscles by laser surgery; that's why I can move it in conjunction with my real eye." She sat down at her desk. "If you'll excuse me now, Detective, I have some 'ASAP' work I got to get done."

Aldena began unlocking her desk and Kiley walked away, not sure at all whether she really had a glass eye or was just busting his balls. Whichever, he did not have time to dwell on it; he had to begin finding out everything he could about Bernard Oznina, the night doorman at 3333 Lake Shore Drive.

It was a pleasant change of pace for Kiley when he sat down at one of the computers this time and began to access information. Keying in Bernard Oznina's name brought him a virtual avalanche of facts from every data base he went into. Motor Vehicle records showed Oznina owning a 1987 Chevrolet Caprice two-door, color blue, license number B403Y21. During the last ten years he had been issued three overtime parking tickets; he had no moving violations. His date of birth was March 4, 1930; residence address was shown as 4406 W. Grainger Avenue. Real estate records showed that the property at that address was a single-family dwelling, constructed in 1946, containing twelve hundred and eighty square feet, with a detached garage. Mr. Oznina had owned it since 1960. Credit records showed that he had a valid Visa card, Standard and Texaco gasoline credit cards, charge accounts at Sears, Montgomery Ward, Western Auto, and ABC Sporting Goods. He had a credit rating of B-minus: frequently a slow pay, but never a collection account. His twenty-five-year mortgage had been paid off in 1985, leaving his home free and clear. All of his taxes were up to date. Vital statistics showed that he had married Vera Marie Boronski in 1953. A son, Bernard, Jr., was born in 1955; a daughter, Marie Agnes, born in 1958; and a second son, Laurence Stephen, born in 1962. His wife had died of cervical cancer in 1988. All three children were married, the oldest for the second time, and lived in nearby suburbs. Oznina had been employed by the Chicago Public Library system as a bookbinder from 1954 until 1984, when he had retired on a full thirty-year pension. Since 1984 he had been a night doorman for Blaisdell Property Management at its high-rise apartment building at 3333 Lake Shore Drive. A veteran of the U. S. Army, he had fulfilled a three-year enlistment from 1949 until 1952, serving overseas in a noncombatant supply corps assignment during the Korean War. His religion was Catholic.

Instead of printing a hard copy of all the information, or retaining it in the computer's memory, Kiley made notes of everything he deemed important, then closed all files and when asked SAVE DATA?, keyed in NO and exited.

As he was walking back to his desk, the phone rang.

"Bomb-and-Arson, Detective Kiley," he answered.

"It's me, Joe," said Gloria Mendez. Her voice was more tense than Kiley had ever heard it. "I just spent two hours in my captain's office. IA and OCB were both there. How soon can we meet?"

"Any time," Kiley said, feeling his stomach tightening. "I was just about to log out."

"I don't want to be too obvious by leaving right away," Gloria said quietly, "so here's what I plan to do. A lady friend of mine works at the Chavez Neighborhood Clinic over at Irving Park and Kedzie. I'm going to have her put me down for a two o'clock appointment. If anyone checks, it'll look legitimate. Then I'll log out of here at one-thirty. Meet me in the waiting room of the clinic around two."

"Got it," Kiley said.

Gloria hung up without further conversation.

Kiley stared at his receiver for a long moment, wondering what had gone wrong now.

When Kiley got there, he found the waiting room of the Chavez Neighborhood Clinic to be a very large area, with seating capacity for at least fifty patients. It was spartanly furnished, a little cluttered and noisy with numerous children, but nevertheless clean and antiseptic smelling. Most of the patients waiting to be seen were female, Puerto Rican, with a few blacks, only one white woman, she with a mulatto child. Kiley felt distinctly out of place as he took a seat in an uncrowded corner, but to his surprise no one seemed to pay much attention to him. If the women had all been men, he knew he would have been subjected to a wall of hateful stares and mean glares as the hot, *macho* blood of the Latinos challenged his presence. But Puerto Rican women, like black women—like white women, for that matter; like *any* women—seemed to have more sense than their men when it came to avoiding trouble and conflict. So Kiley sat there, bothered by no one.

Gloria came in at two on the dot. Stopping first at the counter to speak to her friend, she then came over and sat next to Kiley.

"Well, nobody called to see if my appointment was legitimate, so I guess I'm not being monitored too closely, if at all," she said.

"What happened?" Kiley asked, keeping his voice as low as hers was.

"Apparently OCB pulled up Tony Touhy's file for something; nobody said what. But the record of my master terminal override was seen. OCB came to my captain with it and I was called in as soon as I got to work this morning. IA was there too; I don't know if OCB brought them in, or if my captain did it for his own protection."

"Who was there for OCB and IA?" Kiley asked, hoping against hope that it was only a routine roust.

"The commanders," Gloria said. "Lovat and Vander. I think they've got us made, Joe."

"What did they ask you?"

"To explain why I had accessed Tony Touhy's file. I told them exactly what I told you and Nick I would say: that it was an erroneous access, and that I closed the file as soon as I realized the error."

"What was their reaction?"

"Skeptical. Suspicious. The captain wanted to know the name of the file I was *trying* to access when I made the error. All I could say was that I didn't recall; that it might have been another Touhy, like Andrew instead of Anthony; or a file I was trying to locate phonetically, like T-*w-o*-h-y. I explained to OCB and IA that we run thousands of names every shift. I figured it was better to say I didn't remember the circumstances; otherwise, it might look like I had a story ready in advance."

"That's good thinking," Kiley said. He felt a tinge of pride for Gloria, and even more admiration. "What else?"

"IA asked if I knew you. I said I had met you once, when an officer I used to work with stopped in to say hello and had introduced you. My original thinking had been to deny that you and Nick were ever in my office—but that had only been if it was a routine bitch from OCB. I couldn't stick to that because I didn't want to put any of my people in the position of having to lie to IA."

"I understand," Kiley said.

"IA asked who had introduced us and I said it was Nick. I'm sure they had already run a scan match of our names and found out about Nick and me both being assigned to Humboldt Park at the same time—"

"Sure, they did."

"—because then they started asking a lot of personal questions, like had I ever met his wife, had he ever met my daughter, had we ever socialized, things like that. I'm almost sure they couldn't have known that Nick and I had an affair, Joe; my God, we were always so careful—"

"They probably don't know," Kiley said, mainly to make her feel better. Whether they knew or not didn't matter one way or another as far as the present situation was concerned. All that mattered was how they intended to proceed regarding the restricted access override. "What's the status of the thing right now?" he asked.

"My captain finally told them that he accepted my explanation; he said for them to either put something in writing and send it through channels, or leave me alone. That was when OCB offered to make a deal—"

"OCB is good at that," Kiley interjected, thinking about the compromise with Phil Touhy and his shyster lawyer. "What was the deal?"

"Run an audit on the master terminal during my shift for the last thirty days and get a printout of every restricted file I've accessed. If there are no other unauthorized OCB files on the list, Lovat will drop the matter."

"And?" Kiley wanted to know at once. Gloria shrugged resignedly.

"The captain agreed."

"So they're going to audit you?"

"Right."

"When?"

"Some time next week; I'm not sure exactly when." She rested her head back against the wall. "All I'm sure of is that whenever they do it, they're going to find the seven other overrides for the license plate numbers Nick took down—six of which are OCB. And that, Detective Kiley, is going to finish me."

"Shit," Kiley said, more to himself than to Gloria, as he rested his own head back against the same wall. For a while they sat like that, side by side, faces tilted partly toward the ceiling, almost shoulder to shoulder but not touching, their expressions for the moment inert, as if their lives were on hold. Eventually, Kiley shook his head unguardedly. "I don't know what to say, Gloria—"

"There's nothing *to* say," she told him, her tone neutral. "I went into it with my eyes open. I knew what I was risking. I took a chance and lost— just like you and Nick did."

"Difference is," he pointed out, "we stood to gain something from it; you didn't."

Gloria grunted softly. "When you get caught, Joe, it doesn't matter *why* you did something. You've been a cop long enough to know that." She sighed quietly and rose. "I've got to go. I need to do some heavy thinking on this. I know they'll bring me up on charges; I've got to decide whether to hire a private lawyer or let the PPA handle it for me—" The PPA was the Police Protective Association, a quasi-union to which eighty percent of Chicago police officers belonged.

Kiley stood and faced her. "It's not over yet," he said, but without much conviction.

"I think it is," Gloria said. "I think three cops threw away the book and stepped over the line—and all three are going to end up paying the price for doing it—Nick most of all." She reached out and squeezed Kiley's arm. "So long, Joe. Good luck."

Kiley felt completely impotent as he watched Gloria Mendez walk away.

• • •

Kiley had been in the Bel-Ked Tavern for nearly two hours, sitting alone in a corner booth, engaged in solitary drinking and a program of ongoing self-upbraiding, self-denunciation, and self-revilement—when Harold Winston entered the bar and came over to him.

"Hello, again," the tense little man said, adding tentatively, "Joe."

Kiley frowned at him for a moment, then replied, "Oh, hello, Hal." Looking solemnly down at his gin for a moment, Kiley then said, "I don't mean to be impolite, Hal, but you'd be better off not drinking with me tonight. I got lots of problems and I'm not in a very good mood."

"Well, I don't want to intrude—"

"You're not intruding," Joe assured. "I just don't want to ruin your evening. Personally, I'd *like* to have your company—"

"All right, then," Winston said resolutely, "I'll join you. Maybe I can cheer you up." He turned toward the bar. "Nate—!"

"That's not Nate," Kiley told him. "Nate's off today. I don't know this guy's name—"

"I'll just get my own drink then," Winston said at once. He seemed to be in a very decisive mood.

As Winston went over to the bar, Kiley tried to remember why he had decided to come to this particular tavern in the first place. He had, of course, planned a second encounter with Harold Paul Winston at some point, and then a third, in the course of his strategy to make Winston for the bus bombings. But the second encounter had not been on his agenda for this particular day. What he'd planned for this particular day was to make a field investigation of Bernard Oznina in the neighborhood where the apartment building doorman had lived for the past thirty-three-plus years. He needed a hook with which to snag Oznina; something with which to apply leverage on him regarding Tony Touhy.

But Kiley's agenda for the day had been irreversibly disrupted by the unexpected call from Gloria Mendez and his subsequent meeting with her. Learning that Gloria was about to be made for her involvement in his and Nick's—really now only *his*—fiasco of department rule breaking, made him sick with shame. For two hours he had sat in his car after they had parted, and racked his brain for some way to take the fall for her; some way to relieve her of all, or nearly all, responsibility for the computer transgressions. But there was nothing he could imagine that would wash with IA; nothing that, given Gloria's time with the department, her rank and experience, would be believed. Every possible scenario he came up with seemed more ludicrous than the previous one.

His frustration was compounded by the fact that he knew—without any faint degree of mitigation such as he'd been applying to Nick's death—he *knew*, that this one was his fault and his alone. Gloria had bluffed her way through the accessing of Tony Touhy's file; her own captain had told OCB to either put it in writing or get lost. An audit of her terminal, with only the Tony Touhy access on it—what *Nick* had asked her to do— would have exonerated her of further suspicion, at least with her own superiors. But add what *he* had asked her to do, add the other seven "accidental" accesses of restricted information, and Sergeant Gloria Mendez was royally fucked. Courtesy of Joseph Patrick Kiley, who apparently now had the power to turn everything he touched into nothing but so much shit.

Winston returned with a draft beer and another drink for Kiley. Sliding into the booth, he said, "The bartender's name is Greg. He's new. He said you were drinking Beefeater martinis; I hope that's right—"

"Completely, totally, and absolutely right," Kiley said, drinking down what was left in the glass he already had and drawing the fresh one in front of him.

"I'm sorry things have got you down," Winston said. There was a tentativeness in his voice, as if he thought he might be prying.

"It's not 'things' at all," Kiley said. "It's my goddamned job, is what it is." He suddenly realized again, as he had the last time he had talked to Winston, that he was essentially being honest with the little man. How much of it, he wondered, was by design—and how much simply to have someone, now that Nick was gone, to talk to? Somehow, it did not seem to matter right then. "You see, Hal," he said, very evenly, "I'm beginning to question even *being* a cop."

"It's probably because of losing your partner, don't you think?" Winston offered.

"That's part of it, sure," Joe said. "But there are other things, too. Like, I'm afraid there's going to be some kind of cover-up about who killed him. And I think maybe there could be a problem with his family's pension. And now it looks like the department might be coming down real hard on another officer who was working with us, trying to help us on a case. It's like everything about being a cop is suddenly going sour, turning moldy all at once. I'm thinking about resigning—" Was *that* a lie? Kiley found himself wondering.

"Well, I can't say I'd really blame you, Joe. I always thought police work was kind of glamorous, but after listening to you now, and what you told me the other night—"

"Frankly," Kiley said wryly, "I don't remember *what* I told you the other night. Too many beers. And tonight, drinking these," he indicated the martini, "I probably won't even remember *you*."

Winston sat back, seemed to relax a little, and took a long swallow of beer. "Well, anything new on our bus bomber?" he asked. Kiley frowned again for a moment, then shook his head.

"I don't think so. If there is, I haven't heard it yet."

"Still nothing on the news or in the papers about it," Winston commented.

"I think they've got the whole case under wraps," Kiley said. "No media attention of any kind, in case that's what the guy is looking for. Personally," he took a sip of gin, "I hope they *don't* catch him."

"You're kidding me!" Winston reacted with surprise.

"No, I'm not," Kiley asserted. "I think the guy—if it *is* a guy; could be a woman, too—"

"A *woman*?"

"Why not? Crime is an equal opportunity employer, Hal. But let's just *say* it's a guy. I think he's got a *reason* for what he's doing. I think he's trying to make a point of some kind—"

"Like what?"

"Wait, let me finish, Hal. I think he's trying to make a point of some kind, and he's doing it in a very commendable way—"

"Commendable?" Winston was clearly surprised at that.

"Yes, commendable," Kiley insisted. "Look at the facts, Hal. You know why the department has been able to keep this story away from the media? Because nobody's been killed or injured, that's why. And you know why nobody's been killed or injured? Because the guy has been placing his bombs to go off *after* the bus has made its last run of the night and is parked in a transit authority garage. In other words, he's being extremely careful not to injure anyone, Hal. I'd say that was commendable, wouldn't you?"

"Well, yes, I'd say so. Certainly," Winston agreed.

"Another thing he's doing," Joe continued, "is placing his bomb in the back of the bus so that the only damage it does is to tear out a few seats and shatter a few windows. I'd say that was commendable too. I mean, he could stick the thing under a seat up front where it might blow up the steering wheel, drive shaft, door control, all kinds of things that might total the bus completely. Right?"

"Looking at it from that perspective," Winston said, "I'd have to agree with you, Joe." He finished his beer and held up the glass for the bartender to bring another round. "What really interests me is your theory that this person is trying to make a point of some kind. I mean, what could it be, for instance?"

"Hell, I don't know," Kiley admitted. "Maybe he's a disgruntled ex-employee who feels that he was unfairly fired. Or maybe he's a guy who was involved in some kind of accident with a bus and doesn't feel that the city gave him a big enough settlement—"

"Can't they check their records for people like that?" Winston asked.

"Sure. Doing that already. But it takes time, Hal. In a day or two, the captain will probably dump a bunch of names on my desk and I'll have to start wearing out shoe leather checking on them." Kiley finished his martini and smiled slyly at Winston. "Hope I don't find your name on any of those lists, Hal."

Winston smiled back, just as slyly. "You won't, Joe," he said confidently. "You won't."

Greg brought their fresh round of drinks and when Joe started to hand him some money, Winston pushed his hand back and said, "No, on me, Joe. I'm ahead of you from the other evening." He gave Greg a ten and said, "Take a buck for yourself and put the rest in the jukebox." Glancing at Joe, he added, "But no rap music."

When the bartender left, Kiley objected to Winston paying. "Should've been my round, Hal."

"No, no, I keep mental track of who's ahead, Joe. Inventory control, remember? Your turn to get the next one."

"Have to be some other time, then. I'm going to make this one my last."

"Quit any time you want to," Winston said. He took a swallow of beer. "Speaking of quitting, I'll bet you weren't serious when you mentioned a while ago about resigning from the police department. Especially since your father was a policeman before you—"

Kiley stared down at his drink, recalling his father, Sean Patrick Kiley, a pick-and-shovel day laborer who got paid in cash after each ten-hour day and who gave his wife part of the money to feed the kids and pay the rent only when she met him at the door of the bar and demanded it. Good old Pat Kiley, he'd always stand his cronies a round of Irish whiskey, but Maddie had to slave over the steaming, stinking tubs of a goddamned commercial laundry to buy milk. What a bastard Pat Kiley had been, and what a saint he'd been married to.

"Hal, I have a confession to make," Kiley said quietly. "I do remember some of the things I told you the other night, and one of them was a lie.

My old man wasn't a cop; he was an alcoholic construction laborer. And he isn't retired in Florida, he's dead; he strangled on his own vomit one night when he was too drunk to regurgitate." Kiley sighed, as quietly as he was speaking. "I apologize for lying to you, Hal."

"That's all right, Joe. I guess everybody tells lies about their parents once in a while. Most of the time we do it to make ourselves look better; you know, impress somebody about how hard we had it as a kid, and how well we turned out in spite of our parents. Those are the people who tell everything bad there is to tell, never any of the good. And on the other side of the coin are people like you, who are ashamed of a parent, but lie to make that parent look *better*. There aren't many people, Joe, who don't have *some* kind of animosity toward their parents."

Kiley stared at Harold Paul Winston, impressed, but sober enough to wonder how much of it was Winston and how much the numerous martinis soaking into his brain tissue. Winston, he was beginning to realize, was not your average ding—and was not, Kiley decided a little hazily, going to be as easily handled as Kiley had originally predicted. Get out of here right now, his instinct told him, before this guy starts handling *you*.

"Hal, I really have to go," Kiley said, finishing his drink. "Thanks for letting me bend your ear. I'm sorry I wasn't better company——"

"You were fine, Joe, cut it out," Winston chastised mildly. "Probably see you in here again, right?"

"Look forward to it, Hal. Take care now."

As Kiley left the booth, Winston rose and followed him, catching up with him at the door.

"Oh, Joe——"

"Yeah?" Kiley turned back.

"That point you said the bus bomber was trying to make? I wonder if it could be pollution?"

It did not register at once and Kiley frowned. "Pollution?"

"Yeah. Didn't you know, city buses are the biggest air polluters we have. Haven't you ever noticed all the putrid exhaust fumes from all that starting and stopping, all that standing in rush hour traffic? It just seems to me that this guy might be some kind of environmentalist trying to get the transit authority to clean up its act."

The two men locked eyes there at the front door of the Bel-Ked Tavern, and Kiley suddenly wondered if he had been mistaken in his conclusion just moments earlier that Harold Paul Winston was going to be harder to handle than he had expected. Maybe he was going to be *easier*.

"That's an interesting theory, Hal," he told Winston. "I'm going to give that some thought." He bobbed his chin at Winston. "See you."

"Sure, Joe. See you."

When Kiley got to his apartment, the message light on his answering machine was flashing. He immediately sat down to listen to it; not since the night he unknowingly ignored Nick's last message for ten minutes had he not attended to his messages at once. This, he guessed—even hoped— might be Stella, asking him over again. But after the tape rewound, he heard an entirely different female voice.

"Detective Kiley? Hello, this is Alma Lynn, calling from Ripley, Indiana. I just wanted to apologize to you for my behavior the other day. I know I said some things that were pretty naive, and I realized on the bus coming home that I probably wasn't fair in being so critical of everything you said, the way I did. I hope you'll understand that I was pretty stressed out at the time; I still don't think I'm over the shock of seeing that awful person who beat my sister to death." She paused, as if not certain what else to say. Kiley was staring at the machine, picturing her serious, freckled face as she spoke. "Anyhow," Alma continued, "I also wanted to let you know that Ronnie has now had a proper burial in our family plot here in Ripley. I had a small, private funeral for her—I'm not sure whether I told you our folks were dead or not—anyway, just a few close friends and neighbors were there, and the casket had to be kept closed because of how she looked, but it was a very nice service. I want to thank you again for all your help. I hope we can talk again some day. And I hope you are successful in catching whoever caused your own loss." Again a pause—very brief. Then: "Good-bye, Detective Kiley."

Turning off the machine, Kiley removed his hat and tossed it onto the coffee table, then slumped back on his couch and stared straight ahead at nothing. So much for Ronnie Lynn, the person who was the catalyst in everything that happened, he thought. Another small-town girl chewed up by the big city and spit out like so much phlegm. A virgin, an innocent, a child—perhaps not literally, but certainly figuratively when vying in the same arena of life as men like Tony Touhy, Max Getman, and Ed Laver: users and purveyors of young female flesh. And Wally, the janitor: unbalanced, unsettled, moving innocuously, insipidly, through life, toward one awful moment of madness.

Why, Kiley asked himself in the silence and safety of his apartment, didn't they stay home, these simple, inexperienced, gullible young women from the sticks, the hick towns; these uninitiated *country* girls; why didn't they, as Alma Lynn had done, stay home and become schoolteachers or librarians or young wives and mothers, or *something*? Why in Christ's name did they have to pack their suitcases, get on the Greyhound, and travel from a bright place where flowers grew, to a darker place where predators flourished—why?

Kiley didn't know. Kiley would *never* know. All he could do now was think, Rest in peace, pretty young Ronnie Lynn; the unfortunate misfit who killed you will be punished for it—after a fashion.

But Kiley could not yet think the same thought about Nick Bianco. That matter had yet to be resolved.

And now there was an even more urgent reason for making Nick's killer: to save Gloria Mendez's career. If Kiley could nail Tony Touhy, tie him up in some irrefutable evidence, and say that Gloria had worked with him to do it, the department would let her off the hook—there was no question in Kiley's mind about that. Help bring down a cop killer and an infraction of the restricted-access-to-information rule would be looked upon as something very minor.

So now Kiley was carrying three loads. Stella Bianco's pension. Gloria Mendez's career. And Joe Kiley's guilt.

With what he planned to do in the next thirty-six hours, he hoped to alleviate all three.

# FOURTEEN

**E**arly the next morning, Kiley drove past 4406 W. Grainger Avenue, on the Northwest Side. Bernard Oznina's little single-family residence, which he had owned for more than thirty-three years, appeared neat, well-maintained, and properly situated in a block of similar homes probably all built around the same time, just after World War Two. The neighborhood was predominantly Polish, which accounted for its cleanliness, the Polish districts of Chicago having traditionally been among the most fastidiously tidy in the city. It was an ethnic characteristic passed on to each succcessive generation. Bernard Oznina's three grown children, Kiley knew instinctively, lived in similarly groomed homes out in the suburbs.

After scouting the neighborhood for several blocks in each direction, Kiley parked on Lawrence Avenue, the nearest commercial street, and took a walk, scrutinizing the small business establishments that served the area. After several minutes of matching in his mind various stores with stories he had devised, he finally selected Wojic's Polish Bakery. Entering, he stayed back away from the counter until a big-boned, rawly attractive woman with bleached blond hair finished waiting on two older women and they left. Then he smiled and said "Good morning. My name is Arthur Davis. I'm with Blaisdell Property Management. Do you happen to know Bernie Oznina, lives over here on Grainger Avenue?"

"Yeah, I know him. Why?" she asked, just a touch reticent.

"I was hoping you would," Kiley said. "Bernie works for my company; we have the building at 3333 Lake Shore Drive, where he's the night doorman—" Kiley glanced anxiously out the front window. "I hope he doesn't walk in on me; it would ruin the whole surprise—"

"What surprise? What do you mean?" the woman asked.

"Well, I hope you'll keep this a secret now, but next month is going to be Bernie's tenth anniversary with us—it doesn't seem like it's been that long, but he started with us four years before Vera died—did you know Vera, his wife?"

"Yeah, sure. Everybody in the neighborhood knows the whole Oznina family."

"The one thing I regret about this party we're planning," Kiley did a good job of sounding sad, "is that Vera won't be there for it—"

"So you're having a party for Bernie, is that it?"

"That's it. Giving him his ten-year pin, and the other employees are chipping in to buy him a gift. Anyway, we want to order a big cake, see, but we don't have any idea what kind he likes: chocolate, strawberry—"

"Apricot," the woman said unequivocally.

"Apricot?"

"Apricot," she confirmed. "I've been selling Bernie *kalachkes* every Sunday morning after ten o'clock mass for must be twenty years now, and he always orders apricot."

"I'm sure glad I talked to you," Kiley said, shaking his head in amazement. "Nobody would ever have thought of apricot. Listen, do you bake cakes like for special occasions?"

"Sure, all the time. We could do you a real nice cake for Bernie with apricot icing. When's the party?"

"In a couple weeks. We don't have the exact day yet. Can I call you a few days ahead of time?"

"At least three. I need three."

"No problem. What's your name?"

"Doris."

"Write your phone number down for me, will you, Doris?" While she was doing that, Kiley said casually, "So Bernie goes to ten o'clock mass every Sunday. What parish is this, anyway?"

"St. Melvin's. It's over on Leland Avenue." She handed Kiley her telephone number.

"Doris, you've been a big help. You'll be hearing from me. Remember now, don't let on. We want this to be a surprise."

Outside the door, Kiley paused for her benefit, looked furtively up and down the street, then hurried to his car.

At his bank, Kiley pushed a withdrawal slip through the teller window and said, "Five hundred in tens and five hundred in twenties, please. And put it in an envelope for me, please."

Kiley watched while she counted out the money. Then he put the envelope into his inside coat pocket and returned to his car in the bank parking lot.

Twenty minutes later, he was driving down Flourney Street in the neighborhood where he had grown up. It had been a poor, shabby street in those days; it was a disaster now. Once shanty Irish, it had turned to mixed black and brown, with only a smattering of leftover whites too poor or too lazy to move on. The White Castle where he'd devoured ten-cent hamburgers was now a rib joint. Sweeney's Candy Store was a 7–11 convenience store. The little corner market where his mother sent him to buy bread from the day-old table was now a liquor store. Half the buildings on the block were deserted, boarded up. He saw a scrawny dog sniffing an old bag lady sprawled in a doorway. Four young blacks, none of them wearing gang colors, were jiving around a parked Mustang convertible with its rear end raised nine inches; a condom hung from the rearview mirror. Little brown and black preschoolers played unsupervised on the sidewalk. A white girl who looked no more than fourteen sat lethargically nursing a baby on one front stoop, while a few doors away an obvious drug transaction was taking place between two Hispanics in front of an abandoned building.

It was a gutter when I lived here, Kiley thought. Now it's a fucking sewer.

The only thing that was still the way it always had been was the church across the street on the next corner: St. Susan of Alexandria. It had aged, its gray cement walls changed in shade from parochial light to ghetto dirty, its entry doors no longer polished and shiny, now dry, cracked in places, even its name above the door now missing an N so that it read "St. Susa." Kiley grunted wryly at that; as kids, he and the other hoodlums had called it "St. Sue"—a name forbidden by the nuns as blasphemous.

Parking behind the church, where the rectory hall and living quarters, as well as the cathecism classrooms, were located, Kiley walked over to the rectory door, where a young priest was picking up beer cans, take-out food wrappers, and other litter, putting it into a plastic bag. As Kiley approached, he paused and wiped his brow on the sleeve of his black shirt.

"Look at this mess," he said to Kiley, anger and frustration mixing in his tone. "The young heathens park out here at night with their slut girlfriends, drinking and doing God only knows what else, with their radios so loud a person can't even concentrate to pray—it's a disgrace, a scandal, a—a—a defilement of Holy Mother the Church—" Stopping abruptly, he squinted slightly at Kiley as if trying to recognize him. "I'm sorry—can I help you?"

"Is Father Conley still at this parish?" Kiley asked.

"Yes," came a curt reply. "Yes, he is. You'll find him at his desk in the rectory office, no doubt having his morning Scotch."

"Thanks," Kiley said. As he started in, he heard the young priest mutter an added comment behind him.

"I hope you're early enough to catch him sober."

Kiley turned back. "What was that?"

"I think you probably heard me." The young priest's chin came up defiantly.

"A comment like that is considered disrespectful irreverence toward a holy brother, isn't it, Father?" Kiley smiled, but without warmth. "You'll have to confess that."

Inside, Kiley found the short hallway of cathecism classrooms to be dingy and uninviting, where once they had been cheerfully hung with religious cutouts and construction paper artwork done by the Tuesday and Thursday afternoon students from the nearby public schools. On impulse, Kiley stopped at one of the rooms and opened the door. The desks were exactly the same: old light brown wood with scarred lift-up tops and a hole in one corner for an inkwell. As Kiley's eyes scanned the rows, he had a flashback of faces in his mind: Willie, Dermid, Zach, Cueball, other boys he'd run the streets with; but only one girl's face manifested itself: Mary Ellen Daly—the sassy little Irish girl he had loved passionately, totally, helplessly—and secretly—for five entire semesters until her family had moved away. Jesus, Kiley thought, disregarding where he was, how sweet and simple life had been then—except for his misery over Mary Ellen Daly.

At the end of the hall was a door with OFFICE lettered on it. Kiley knocked once and waited. No one answered. Probably hoping whoever it is will go away, he thought knowingly. He knocked again, louder, and this time heard impatiently, "Yes, yes, come in—"

As Kiley entered, a gray-haired old priest looked up from a cluttered desk, squinting as the younger priest outside had. He wore no coat, no clerical collar on his black shirt, and had not shaved yet that day.

"Yes, what is it?" he asked. He tilted his head slightly. "Who's that?" Then his eyes widened slightly. "*Joseph?*"

"Hello, Father," said Kiley He stood in front of the grossly untidy desk, hat in hand.

"Joseph Patrick Kiley," the old priest said. "My, my, my. Well, sit, sit—"

"How are you, Father?" Kiley asked.

"Not well, I'm afraid, Joseph, not well at all." From a top desk drawer,

Father Conley retrieved a tumbler of whiskey and put it back in the one bare spot amongst all the disorder. "I've a number of ailments that God has seen fit to plague me with after a lifetime of service to His name. I've lumbago, arthritis, sciatica, glaucoma, tinnitus—do you know what that is?"

"Buzzing in the ears," Kiley said. Father Conley raised his eyebrows in surprise.

"You're absolutely right. You'd be surprised how many people never heard of it, Joseph." He frowned. "You don't suffer from it, I hope."

"No, Father."

The priest took a sip of whiskey, then said, "I won't offer you a drink, Joseph, because I don't approve of drinking this early in the day. I only do it for medicinal purposes, to lessen my constant pain." Sitting back, he laced his fingers over a protruding little belly that forced his belt down several inches. "Well, how long has it been, Joseph? Five years, about?"

"About," Kiley agreed. "I stopped around a few times," he lied, "but I missed you—"

"Did you, Joseph?" Father Conley nodded knowingly. "Well, it's the thought that counts. Still a policeman, are you?"

"Yes."

"Are you a sergeant by now? A lieutenant maybe?"

"No," Kiley said. He knew the question was a dig; Father Conley had never predicted anything for him but failure. "What about you?" Kiley asked. "You a monsignor yet?"

"Ah, you wouldn't believe the problems I have down here, Joey," the priest replied in a kindlier tone, ignoring the retort. "Membership in the parish is down by sixty percent—and those that *are* members contribute such a trifling amount to our support that it's all but impossible to maintain even a modicum of church activities. We don't have a car anymore to visit the sick and bereaved; there's no money for equipment to sponsor a youth athletics program; why, we don't even have Bingo anymore, Joseph, because most of the parishioners can't understand the letters and numbers in English! Can you imagine St. Susan's without *Bingo?*"

"Everything's changed, Father," Kiley said. "Nothing's the way it used to be."

"We're reduced here to nothing except masses, baptisms, and the cathecism lessons. Not even weddings any longer; people get married over at St. Hortense of the Angels because it has a gazebo out back with a bubbling fountain where they can take pictures after. Ah, I'll tell you, Joe—" His words dropped off, slowly and sadly, like dying leaves in the fall.

"Could you use a thousand dollars, Father?" Kiley asked.

"A thousand dol—?" The old priest was flabbergasted "We haven't had a donation that large in years—not even from our business supporters." His eyes flashed suspicion. "It's not dirty money, is it?"

"No. It's my own, money I've saved."

"This is amazing," the old priest said, barely louder than a whisper. "You, of all people—"

Kiley took out a checkbook and ballpoint. "I'll make this out to 'cash' so you can use it however you see fit—"

"Yes, that'll be fine, Joseph—"

Before he signed the check, Kiley said, "Father Conley, I wonder if you'd take a little ride with me? There's someone I need to convince of something, and I think you could help me do it. I'll be glad to wait while you shave and put your collar on. Better gargle, too—"

An hour later, Kiley and a very proper-looking Father Conley stood on the porch of Bernard Oznina's neat little house and rang the bell. Oznina, in his undershirt, a newspaper in his hand, opened the door.

"Hello, Mr. Oznina," said Kiley. "I'm the policeman who stopped by your job the other night about the purse snatching problem. You remember me?"

"Yeah, sure—"

"This is Father Andrew O'Brien, the Catholic chaplain for the Chicago Police Department. Can we come in and talk to you for a few minutes?"

"Yeah, come in—" Oznina, confused, held the door open, then led them into a modest, somewhat untidy living room. "Excuse the mess; I live alone—"

"Think nothing of it," said Father Conley. They sat down. "Mr. Oznina, I've come along on this visit because the police department has looked into your background, and knows that you're a good Catholic; we know you faithfully attend mass over at St. Melvin's, and that you had a good Catholic marriage and raised three fine children in the church. You're a credit to our religion, and because of that we believe we can come to you in confidence and ask your help."

"Well, thank you, Father O'Brien," a bewildered Bernard Oznina said. "I've always tried to be a good Catholic—"

"Mr. Oznina," Kiley cut in, "we want to be completely honest with you, so I'm going to tell you that my name is not Detective Ed Monroe, of the Robbery Detail, as I said it was the other night. I am actually Sergeant Dick

Mason of Homicide; I lied to you the other night because the department wasn't sure then that it could count on you."

"We didn't know then what a good Catholic you are," the priest interjected.

"What we're actually doing, Mr. Oznina—"

"May we call you 'Bernie'?" Father Conley asked.

"Sure, Father. And I'll do whatever I can to help you, whatever this is about."

Kiley and Father Conley exchanged solemn looks. "He's our man, all right," Father Conley said, reaching over to pat Bernard Oznina on the knee.

"What we're actually doing, Bernie," said Kiley, "is investigating the brutal murder of a police officer—"

"A Catholic officer, sad to say," Father Conley added.

"You may have seen it on the news, Bernie: a detective found shot to death in an alley—"

"Yeah, I think I did—"

"Well, Bernie, we have reason to believe that the officer was killed by a resident of your building."

Bernie's eyebrows went up. "*My* building? Why, I can't believe it—"

"Do you know the tenant in apartment 2201. Anthony Touhy?"

Bernie's eyebrows came back down. "Oh, yeah," he replied in sudden recognition, "him. There's been some rumors about him being a mobster, but nobody knew if they was true. The building management don't like us gossiping about the tenants—but there's been some talk."

"The man is a criminal," Kiley said, "part of the city's organized crime that's controlled by his older brother, Phil Touhy. You've heard of him, haven't you?"

"Oh, sure. The one they call the Irish Al Capone."

"That's him. Bernie, these people are involved in drugs, illegal gambling, prostitution, child pornography—"

"My God, child pornography?" Bernard Oznina, a grandfather of young children, was shocked.

Kiley nodded. "One of the biggest producers and distributors of the stuff in the whole country. They call it 'kiddie porn.' Bernie, have you ever noticed those pictures of missing children on grocery bags and milk cartons?"

"Sure—"

"Well, a lot of those kids—little boys as well as little girls—end up in kiddie porn movies made by your tenant in apartment 2201."

"The dirty son of a bitch," Bernard Oznina said softly. "Pardon my language, Father."

"Don't apologize, my son," said Father Conley. "The man is that and more."

"We've never been able to get enough evidence on him for pornography or drugs or any of that," said Kiley. "The guy is very good at covering his tracks and staying in the clear. But now, Bernie—now he's killed a cop, and we want very badly to get him for that. If we can get him for a cop killing, we may be able to put a stop to all the rest: the drugs, the kiddie porn—"

"And that," Father Conley intoned, "would be a gift from on high."

"What can I do to help?" Oznina asked.

"I want to get into his apartment, Bernie." Blunt and to the point. "I want to search it."

"Oh, Jesus Christ—excuse me, Father—are you serious?"

"Very serious."

"I couldn't do nothing like that," the doorman protested. "I thought you just wanted me, like, to keep an eye on him or something. I let you into his apartment, I'll lose my job. I'd like to help, but—"

"No one will ever know," Kiley said.

"*He* would. He'd be able to tell soon's he walked in; things messed up, things out of place—"

"No, Bernie, he wouldn't be able to tell," Kiley explained. "I would go through the place myself—very slowly, very carefully. Everything would be left exactly as I found it. There will not be one trace that I was ever in there."

"But if you found something, some kind of evidence, and used it against him, then it could come out—"

"Nothing I find can be used against him, Bernie. This is a search being done without a warrant. It falls within the illegal search and seizure statutes."

"I don't get it," Oznina said, puzzled. "What do you want to do it for then?"

"To try and find something that would lead us to some evidence we *could* use. It's been done before, Bernie. We get into somebody's house or office, carefully go through everything, maybe we find a diary or a bar receipt or a coded mark on a calendar—and maybe from that we are directed to some other evidence outside the house or office, or even to a witness; it's happened, Bernie. It could happen in this case."

"Oh, Jesus, I don't know," Bernie said, not bothering to apologize for his blasphemy this time. "What if he should walk in on you?"

Kiley shook his head. "He's in Ireland, Bernie. That's been verified."

Bernie got up and paced nervously about the room. Father Conley rose also and stepped over to a gold-framed painting of the Sacred Heart of Jesus. "Lovely," he said quietly, "lovely. Your late wife selected it, no doubt?"

"Uh—yeah, Vera got that on a trip we took to California. It's painted on real velvet."

"God rest her soul, she must have been a woman of rare taste."

"Look," Bernie stopped and turned to Kiley, "exactly what would I have to do?"

"It's simple," the detective said. "Give me a duplicate key to his apartment, and a duplicate key to some back door of the building that I can use to get in."

"You wouldn't do it on my shift?" Bernie asked, almost in horror.

"No, it'd be around three in the morning, when the place was the quietest. Is there a delivery door or something off the back alley?"

"Yeah. By the service elevator. But you can't use that elevator. After ten o'clock at night, it signals the doorman's desk if anybody uses it."

"I won't use it," Kiley said. "I'll walk up the fire stairs."

"Christ, that's *twenty-two* floors—"

"Don't worry about it. Is it all right to use the fire stairs; they're not monitored?"

"No, they're okay, if you want to use them—" Oznina was softening. "I really do want to help—I mean, that kiddie porn stuff makes me want to puke—"

"We all feel the same way, my son," said Father Conley.

"None of us likes to break the rules," Kiley added, "but sometimes it's the only way to catch scum like this Tony Touhy."

"He's an evil person," the priest said for emphasis. "An agent of the devil hisself." Going over to Bernie, he put a hand on the doorman's shoulder. "Do this, Bernard, and it'll be a service not only to Christ but to your fellow man, as well."

"And all those kids on the grocery bags and milk cartons," Kiley reminded.

Bernard Oznina stared for a moment across the room at the Sacred Heart of Jesus painted on real velvet, then nodded his head emphatically. "I'll do it."

Immediate praise was heaped on him by both priest and policeman, there was a round of hearty handshakes, and then Kiley took the bank envelope from his pocket.

"Bernie, I don't want you to take this the wrong way, but a lot of the murdered officer's fellow cops took up a collection to show their gratitude if you decided to help us. It's their way of saying thanks for your part in possibly catching a cop killer. There's a thousand dollars in this envelope; it's yours."

"A thousand dollars—?"

"Don't even try to refuse it," Kiley said. "It's from the Chicago police department to you, as a good citizen."

"Well, I—" Bernie took the envelope.

"If you'd care to donate some of that to the church—" Father Conley began a pitch.

"—you can do it in your own parish," Kiley finished it for him. He took the priest by the arm and guided him to the door. "Get the keys tonight if you can, Bernie," he said over his shoulder. "I'll call you in the morning." To Father Conley, he whispered, "Bless the house—"

"Of course. God bless this house and all in it," the priest said, making the sign of the cross.

Bernard Oznina followed them onto the porch and waved good-bye with the envelope of money as they got in Kiley's car and drove away.

"I didn't know you were going to give him money," Father Conley said, on the way back to his own parish.

"Insurance," Kiley explained. "Makes it almost impossible for him to reconsider and back out of the deal."

"Well, I'm not altogether sure," the priest groused, "that he should have received the same amount of money that I did. Or rather, my parish did."

"Why not?" Kiley said. "He's risking his job; you're not. Anyway, he has to take chances getting the duplicate keys; all you had to do was lie." He glanced over and saw that the priest was pouting. "If it'll make you feel any better, I'll send you a case of Scotch."

"What kind?" Father Conley asked with renewed affability.

"You name it."

"Cutty."

"Cutty it is."

They rode in silence for several minutes, then the priest asked, "Are the Touhys really involved in child pornography?"

"No," Kiley said. "Or drugs either, far as I know. There are only a couple of kiddie porn creeps in Chicago, and they're both just distributors.

Most of the actual production of the stuff is done up in Minneapolis. The feds know all about it; they just haven't been able to stop it. But the Touhys aren't involved."

"Well, thank God for that," Father Conley said. "It doesn't bother me all that much any more when Irish Catholics run gambling houses, and deal in stolen televisions and the like; even prostitution, if it's operated properly, isn't all that harmful. But narcotics and child pornography—those things are truly evil, Joseph."

Kiley did not comment. It would do no good to try and explain to this old man of the cloth that prostitution frequently went hand-in-hand with narcotics, or that narcotics frequently was responsible for kids as young as twelve being involved in child pornography. Priests, ministers, pastors, rabbis didn't understand the interlinks of crime any better than grocery clerks, housewives, business executives, or anyone else. Only a cop understood. A *street* cop, at that. Even police officers who moved up in rank—lieutenants, captains, administrative commanders, chiefs—more often than not forgot the basic credo that they learned on the street; the credo that others in the criminal justice system—the judges, prosecutors, defense lawyers—never understood at all. And it was so simple.

Crime bred crime.

Crime *was* crime.

To say that one form of it was all right but another wasn't, was, to Joe Kiley, insanity. Crime happened, just like shit, and it multiplied, just like lice, like cockroaches, like mosquitoes. Allowing it to go unchecked, un-dealt with, in *any* form, served only to abet the vermin in becoming as strong as the exterminators. Anyone who didn't believe that, was suffering from *cranium analitis*—their head was up their ass. All Kiley ever had to do to reinforce his total belief in that philosophy was to remember one very often forgotten and neglected category of society: the vics. Victims of crime. For every criminal, there was an average, directly or indirectly, of nineteen victims. The prison population in the United States, the last time Kiley had seen figures, was the largest in the world: more than nine hundred thousand. They were responsible for more than seventeen *million* victims. Staggering numbers. Frightening statistics. *Increasing*—all the time, every day, every hour.

And Joe Kiley knew, without ever consciously admitting it, that he was, peculiarly—and especially in his present situation—part of both the solution *and* the problem.

And apparently Father Conley was aware of that fact also, because when Kiley parked at the rectory of St. Susan's, the old priest quietly said,

"Well, Joseph, now that we've done this thing, where is it likely to take you? I ask because I must share in the responsibility for what you do from this point on."

"I can't answer that right now, Father," said Kiley. "A lot will depend on what, if anything, I find in Tony Touhy's apartment."

"If I understood correctly what you told Bernie, no evidence you find can be used against him in court, right?"

"In court, right."

"But you could find some evidence that would then lead to other evidence which *could* be used against him?"

"That's what I'm hoping for."

"But suppose you find evidence that you can't use against him, and it *doesn't* lead you to anything you *can* use against him? What then, Joseph?"

"I don't honestly know, Father, where I'd go from there."

"You'd be in quite an uncommon position, wouldn't you, lad? You could judge, sentence, and punish—by no one's standards or ethics or morals except your own." The priest tilted his head as if to study Kiley more closely. "Almost a God-like position, wouldn't it be? Omnipotent."

"I suppose so," Kiley admitted. He was staring out the windshield, not meeting Father Conley's eyes.

"Only a divine person should have power like that, Joseph. If it comes to that, I hope you won't do anything foolish."

Kiley looked at him now and shook his head. "I won't, Father. Don't worry about it." He smiled scantly. "One of these nights, I'll drop over and have a sip of that Cutty with you."

"I'll look forward to it," the priest replied enthusiastically.

They shook hands and Father Conley got out of the car. As Kiley backed up, the old priest was hurrying toward his young assistant, waving the check Kiley had given him.

"Father Theodore!" he shouted. "We've just been given a donation to have our school desks refinished!"

Kiley drove off, expression set, conscience clear. He didn't *like* lying to Father Conley, as he had just done. But what was he to do? Tell the old priest that if there was indisputable evidence against Tony Touhy but it couldn't legally be used, that Kiley really *did* know what he was going to do? That there was only one thing he *could* do—one way to expiate himself from guilt, just as the church had taught him to do, by penance? Kiley couldn't tell Father Conley that.

He couldn't tell the old priest that he intended to kill Tony Touhy.

# FIFTEEN

It was two nights later that Kiley prepared to illegally enter and search Tony Touhy's apartment.

Earlier that day, around noon, he had driven out to Bernard Oznina's house again, alone this time, to go over the plan and schedule with the night doorman, and pick up two master keys Oznina had brought home. They had a cup of coffee together at Bernie's kitchen table.

"I'm nervous as a son of a bitch about this," Oznina had admitted. "Look at this—" he held out a hand with trembling fingers.

"You've got nothing to worry about," Kiley, again posing as Sergeant Dick Mason of Homicide, assured him. "I'll be in and out of the place in one hour maximum tonight, some time between two and four a.m., while the morning shift doorman is on duty. The keys will be in your mailbox when you get up tomorrow morning. Nobody's ever going to know about this, believe me. You're completely safe, completely protected." Kiley took a sip from his cup. "This is good coffee, Bernie," he tried to shift the conversation to a lighter level.

"My sons say I make crappy coffee, but my daughter likes it."

"Fathers and sons are never happy with each other, Bernie. My mother pointed that out to me once."

"Yeah? Smart woman."

"Bernie, about that service door," Kiley came back to their main discussion, "there's no chance, is there, that the guy on the morning shift would double-lock it from the inside?"

"Can't be done," Bernie shook his head. "There's no dead-bolt lock on that door. That short key there will work, I promise."

Kiley had spent half an hour with Bernie, then driven down to 3333 Lake Shore Drive and walked around the area for a while, deciding where he ideally would like to park, the route he would walk to the service door off the alley, even strolling past that door to take a closer look at it. The entire plan, as far as Kiley could see, looked like an in-and-out job: no obstacles, no trouble spots, no problems. The very smoothness of it all was enough to make Kiley leery, however; such had been his luck lately that he was beginning to automatically expect the worst around every corner. At this stage, he did not think it would surprise him to find a boa constrictor slithering around Tony Touhy's high-rise apartment.

At seven o'clock that evening, Kiley had gone out to see Stella and the girls. He had taken them to a pizza restaurant called Chuck E. Cheese's, where there were arcade games for Jennie to play, and kiddie rides for Tessie, as well as a comfortable booth from which Joe and Stella could observe the girls, relax, and drink a second beer after the pizza. Stella, he was pleased to see, was beginning to look a little like her old self again; she was less drawn, seemed less frightened, and the dark hollows beneath her eyes had disappeared.

"There was a lady out from the pension board today," she told him. "I had to sign some forms and stuff. She didn't act like there was going to be any problem with my pension."

"You didn't say anything, did you?" Kiley asked.

"No, Joe, of course not." Stella sounded a little surprised at the question. "Nick taught me better than that."

They sat in silence for several minutes, watching the girls out in the game area with some other children. Both girls were back in school now, Stella had told Kiley earlier on the phone, and she felt that their lives were returning to some degree of normalcy. "It's strange being alone in the house as much as I am," she shared. "Never having Nick at home, you know. But I've found that time seems to go by faster if I find something to do—just like you said. One of the secrets, I think, is not to turn on the damned TV; that only encourages sitting around, lying around, dozing; best thing is to keep moving, just make yourself keep moving."

Tessie came up and said, "Jennie wants to know if we can have more tokens."

"You used up five dollars worth *already?*" Stella asked, shocked.

"Jennie used most of them—"

"I'll bet. Joey, don't—" she protested as Kiley gave Tessie another five.

"Last one," he promised.

They watched Tessie run and get Jennie, and the two of them skip to the counter for a bag of tokens.

"They're going to be spoiled rotten," Stella said, "between you and Frank—"

"Frank?"

"Nick's cousin. Uncle Gino's—"

"Uncle Gino's son. Yeah, I know."

"Don't you like him?" Stella had a slight frown.

"Don't like him or dislike him," Joe said with a shrug, trying to make the lie sound like indifference. "Nick wasn't crazy about him, was he?" Probing cautiously.

"Nick wasn't really crazy about any of his cousins. Except the females; he loved the females. But I think Frank's okay. He certainly has been nice to the girls and me since we lost Nick."

Don't let him be too nice to you, Joe wanted badly to say, or he'll have one hand on your checkbook and the other between your legs. But he held his tongue.

"Joe, have you tried on any of Nick's things that I gave you?" Stella asked presently. "You're still wearing the same old gray."

"I don't think I'd feel right with Nick's clothes on," Kiley said self-consciously. Especially the hijacked suits from Maxwell Street, he thought.

"Oh, that's so silly," Stella said. She put her hand on his across the table. "Do you have any idea how pleased Nick would be if he could see you in some of his clothes. He used to say, 'I swear to God, Stella, I'm gonna get that drab, nondescript'—honest to God, he said 'nondescript'—'that drab, nondescript mick into some decent clothes if it's the last thing I ever do.' It would really make him happy, Joe." She paused a beat, then: "Me too."

"I'll try some of them on," Kiley said.

"When?"

"Soon," Kiley promised

It had been a pleasant evening, Stella wearing a beige pantsuit that flattered without emphasizing her lithe, trim body, so unlike most Italian wives and mothers her age, Kiley thought. Joe had met the female cousins Stella said Nick had liked; the ones Stella's age, with children, were, without exception, all fleshing out where they shouldn't be, and clearly going to fat. And all their mothers, including Uncle Gino's wife, had the same problem but were farther along. Stella, now—Stella was built like Raquel Welch.

"I guess there's nothing new about Nick's case, huh?" she asked, interrupting Kiley's mental comparison of her to the others.

"No, nothing, Stel," he had said. Kiley had yearned to tell her what he was going to do that night, longed for her to know what unlawful lengths he was going to, what illegal steps he was taking, to nail the person he was so certain killed her husband, his partner. He wanted her to know that just because the department had tried to isolate him in B-and-A, just because he was supposed to be quarantined away from the Bianco homicide case, just because he was being treated like a leper or something by the brass, did *not* mean that he was abandoning Nick. He would get his partner's killer if it took him the rest of his life, breaking the rules all the way.

Later, after Joe had taken his little surrogate family home and was on his way back into the city, he wondered *why* he hadn't told Stella anything. He trusted her; at least, he *thought* he trusted her. Now that he thought about it, the occasion had never really presented itself for him *to* trust her. Of course, he had made her aware early on that Nick and he had not been on duty the night Nick was killed; as far as he knew, she had kept that confidence—but it had been in her financial interest to do so.

What about something like this, he wondered? Something that probably wouldn't affect her one way or the other? Kiley knew Stella would never intentionally inform on him—but suppose she were to slip and mention something to Frank Bianco? That son of a bitch, or his snake of a father, would probably be on the phone with an anonymous call to IA before Stella finished talking. No, it was best kept to himself, and it had nothing to do with a lack of confidence in Stella. Not very much, anyway.

It was eleven o'clock when Kiley got back to his apartment. He showered and put on fresh underwear and two pairs of dark socks. Then he dressed in dark jeans, a navy blue crew-neck pullover, and an old pair of black crepe-soled loafers. He laid out a black windbreaker, both his guns and ammunition, his badge and ID case, wristwatch, a few dollars in currency, a fresh handkerchief, a pair of black pigskin gloves—little Tessie had given them to him one Christmas—and two pairs of clear surgical gloves that he had picked up at a medical supplies store earlier in the day. And the two keys he had obtained from Bernard Oznina.

At midnight, Kiley drank a glass of milk, set his alarm clock for two a.m., and stretched out on the bed for a nap.

He had slept, but only fitfully, and had been wide awake to shut off the alarm fifteen minutes before it was scheduled to buzz. Since his time frame was not an exact one—his only requirement was to be in the building during the dead hours of the morning—he collected the articles he had laid out, put on the windbreaker, and left a few minutes early.

Driving over to the high rise, through night streets now quiet and mostly deserted, reminded Kiley of the morning shifts he and Nick had worked together: shifts on which they did a lot of talking, drank too much coffee, usually took turns dozing off and on. There had been times, of course, when there was police work to be done, especially before two a.m. when liquor stores were still open, and in neighborhoods where there were all-night businesses; but after two-thirty or so a kind of calm settled in—except on Friday and Saturday nights, naturally—and their patrols became lulls of inactivity, hushed hours as close to tranquility as two armed men can get while on duty deep in an inner city.

It was during those periods, Kiley remembered, that they became closest, that their most personal feelings were shared. There is no relationship on earth like that of two police officers who last as longtime partners. It is, when successful, like two men each finding a strange clone that neither looked like the other, spoke, acted, felt like the other, dressed or had the same presence, bearing, attitude, demeanor of the other, in fact was in no discernible way *anything* like the other—yet *was* the other. Just as Joe Kiley, as a Catholic, believed irrefutably in the Holy Trinity of the Father, the Son, and the Holy Ghost, so too did he, and many of his peers, believe in the Triad of the Partner, the Other Partner, and the Bond Between Them. The Trinity promised life after death; the Triad was concerned with life *before* death—specifically, keeping it going in the face of all the SAMs in the world: SAMs being Savages, Assholes, and Maniacs.

Everything he and Nick knew about each, Kiley realized as he drove, had been learned in the night cocoon of their worn, weary, unmarked police unit, when there were no SAMs about to distract them. Kiley had told Nick things about his father, brother, sisters, and especially his mother, whom he had worshipped, that he had never told anyone, not even Peg, the woman with whom he had shared an apartment and bed for two years, until both decided that it wasn't quite right so why go on wasting time with it? And Nick, of course, had shared with Kiley his most intimate feelings about the extended Bianco family, Stella, the kids, and how his own parental veneration had been directed at his father rather than his mother. Comparisons between the Irish family and the Italian family had been ongoing in their patrol car for years; the similarities they discovered were as startling as the differences. The honesty that linked them, the frankness between them, the candor they shared, had been consummate and absolute—

Except for the part that concerned Gloria Mendez, Kiley reminded himself. That had been a flaw in the fabric of their relationship; but one which Nick, almost but not quite too late, had rectified. And in retrospect,

Kiley was not even too sure anymore that Nick *should* have told him earlier about Gloria; perhaps to have done so would, because of Joe's deep feeling for Stella and the girls, have ruined the partnership they had.

Nick, Nick, Nick, he thought as he parked on a side street two blocks from Lake Shore Drive, whatever was right, whatever was wrong, whoever was at fault in what now had become the past, one thing was still certain: Kiley was going to get the scum cocksucker who killed his partner. No matter what.

Like some other cautious, career policemen, Kiley had no interior lights in his personal car, they being disconnected on purchase; so that now when he opened the car door at night he was not illuminated getting in or out. He left the car unlocked, in case he needed to get into it in a hurry; closed the door by pushing, not slamming; walked at a normal pace along the dark two and a half blocks to the alley that ran behind 3333. The building had no security lights in the rear because there were no windows in that wall of the building, and only one door, the service door, on a small loading dock three steps up from the alley.

Standing with his back to the wall, Kiley removed the pigskin gloves he was wearing and put them in a back pocket. He stretched and pulled on one pair of the surgical gloves, then removed from his right trousers pocket one of the keys Bernard Oznina had given him. Easily feeling the contours of the service door lock through the skintight rubber of the gloves, he inserted the key, slowly turned it, at the same time gripping the doorknob, turning it, and pushing in just enough to assure himself that the door would open. Before actually entering, he replaced the key in the same pocket and put the pigskin gloves back on, this time over the surgical gloves.

Stepping inside, Kiley closed the door as quietly as he had opened it, and stood still as a post with his back against it until his eyes adjusted to a subdued light being thrown from an overhead sign above an inside door off to his left, which read: STAIRS. After assuring himself that there was no sound, no movement, anywhere around him, Kiley, staying as close to the wall as he could, moved silently over to the inner door, and in the same slow, soundless manner, let himself into the ground level of the building's steep stairwell. He found better illumination there because these were fire stairs, sealable by metal doors, windowless, their condition dictated by public safety regulations. It was while on these stairs, in this high vertical tunnel, that Kiley knew he could be most easily seen and most quickly trapped. Even so, he was also still confident that it was highly unlikely at that dead hour of the morning: It was now, he looked at his watch, three o'clock straight up.

And straight up was where he had to go. After first testing the crepe soles of his loafers on the bottom step to assure himself that no sound would be generated against the texture of the cement stairs, Kiley began his climb. He moved slowly, gripping the handrail on the wall for both support and leverage. On his first effort, he made it to seven before feeling his chest constricting for breath. At that landing, he sat, turning partway to lean against the wall. Looking at the second hand on his watch, he rested exactly two minutes, listening intently as he did.

Resuming, Kiley reached twelve, rested again, resumed again, reached sixteen, rested, climbed to nineteen, then sat, chest heaving now, for four full minutes. Going up the last three floors to twenty-two, he made himself rest still again, even though he was very eager now, wanted urgently to be inside Tony Touhy's apartment, to begin the search, his journey toward vindication, toward justice, toward—he desperately hoped—some relief from the terrible guilt he felt about Nick.

When he was breathing normally again, Kiley quietly opened the fire door and stepped onto well-padded carpet lining the hall of the twenty-second floor. He was, he saw at once, standing equidistant between apartments 2206 and 2207. Moving quickly, he padded past 2206 and down to the end of the hall where, as he and Nick had surmised the first time they studied the high rise, 2201 was a corner apartment, which on a clear day, Nick had said, must have had a view into the next time zone.

At the door, which was large, formidable looking, dark blue in color, Kiley once again removed the leather gloves and put them in his back pocket. He took the second key Bernard Oznina had given him, this one from his left trousers pocket, and with only a suggestion of metal-against-metal noise, unlocked the door and was inside the apartment.

In the foyer, Kiley turned on the lights and looked the length of a long, sunken living room that stretched to a front picture window facing Lake Michigan. It was a rich, plushly decorated room done in two shades of blue intermixed with a single gray: blue leather sofas and chairs, blue tile-and-smoked-glass tables, silver gray metal lamps with blue shades, enameled blue bookcases and cabinetry, containing stereo equipment, speakers, a fifty-inch television screen, all behind smoked-glass doors, everything standing on luxurious thick gray carpet, surrounded by sumptuous blue-and-gray relief wall covering that elegantly embraced a series of seascapes done in oil, identically framed in blue lacquer.

Jesus Christ, Kiley thought, his eyes slowly sweeping the place, it looked like something out of *Lifestyles of the Rich and Famous*. He shook his head in slight disbelief. All this belonged to a cheap little punk who would have been a complete and total *nothing*, a nobody, a nonentity, except for one tiny detail: He got shot from the same dick that also ejaculated Philip Touhy. They were formed in the same womb. Came from the same genetic sperm. Except that part of Tony must have run down his mother's leg.

Removing his windbreaker and shoes, Kiley began with the living room, working clockwise from the foyer. The first and most obvious place to look, in which he expected to find nothing, he eliminated at once: a small desk just off the foyer. It contained virtually nothing: automobile registration, a few travel folders, apartment lease—the punk paid forty-five hundred dollars a month for the place—and some miscellaneous writing materials. The bottoms and backs of the drawers had nothing taped to them. The sterility of the desk did not surprise Joe; the most common place for ordinary people to keep personal records was the last place a hoodlum would use.

Next he turned to the bookcases: each book, tilting it out, squeezing it to see if it had pages or was hollow, cutout to conceal a hiding place. Then the bar: looking for replica bottles, secret compartments. The paintings: plastic-gloved fingers along the underside of each plane, each angle of the frame, along its sealed seams, from each side an arm reaching under it to the middle—seeking holes, slits, pockets, indentations in the wall upon which it hung. The sofas and chairs: tilted back on rear legs, undersides visually examined, cushions removed, unzipped, inner foam felt, squeezed, probed. The stereo center: between and behind the records, tapes, discs. The video center: behind and beneath the double-track cassette recorder, inside each videotape box—

Here Kiley stopped. Among the commercially prerecorded and packaged movies was a shelf of tapes labeled with female names: Amy, Cynthia, Madeline, Fran, Tina, a score of others. Kiley's eyes eagerly searched for a label reading Ronnie or Veronica, but there was none. Turning on the VCR and the monitor, muting the sound, he inserted a tape picked at random—Jean—and started it playing. An image came on of a young woman, nude, on her knees at the side of a bed, performing fellatio on a handsome though somewhat vacuous-looking young man who might have been a decade-earlier version of Phil Touhy, except that the hardness of the eyes and the solidity of the expression were not there. Kiley realized that he was looking at the features of Tony Touhy for the first time; he had never even seen a photograph of him before. Now here he was, naked on videotape, his hard-on in the mouth of a young woman who may or may not even have known her performance was being preserved for—whatever. Kiley could easily imagine slime like Tony Touhy entertaining his scum friends with these tapes. He did not even bother checking any of the others; they would be variations of the same. How many naive, confused, wanting young women like Ronnie Lynn had this animal taken advantage of over the years? he wondered.

Replacing the tape, turning off the equipment, Kiley got down on his hands and knees to check along the corner baseboards where the carpet met the wall, looking for any edge that might not be tacked down, that might lift up to reveal a sunken repository of some kind other than a floor safe. Then he checked lamp bases, undersides of tables, stands holding two exotic potted plants: nothing. The last thing he checked was an oval-shaped, mirror-paneled bar in one corner. It was filled with crystal glasses and the best Scotch, bourbon, gin, vodka, and fancy liqueurs that money could buy—but nothing else.

The living room, Kiley felt, was clean. As he explored a hallway off to the right, looking for the bedroom, he noticed that his socks were generating static electricity as his feet brushed the thick carpet. Pausing, he checked for footprint depressions in the fibers, but there were none; the carpet was too expensive, too tightly woven to accept tracks.

The bedroom, decorated in the same motif as the living room, had its own television and video cabinet, a selection of still more personally labeled tapes—Lois, Annette, Rachel, others; but again no Ronnie or Veronica—and a remote control panel next to the bed. Inside the cabinet was another dual tape system. On an enclosed top shelf was a video camera, concealed except for a single half-dollar size hole through which the camera lens focused on the entire bed. Cute, Kiley thought. With one VCR, Touhy could show a porno movie for them to watch during foreplay; with the other VCR, probably unknown to the girl, he could be taping *them* for his own movie.

After thoroughly checking the unit for anything hidden, Kiley turned to a bookcase the lower half of which had a set of doors enclosing the lower three shelves. The doors could have been locked; there was a desk-type lock on them; but Kiley found they were not. Opening them, he saw a matched set of eight blue leather photograph albums. Removing the first one in order, he opened it to page after page of explicit photographs of various females engaged in sexual activity with a man whose face was never seen; either it was out of the picture because the figure was standing up during fellatio, the figure's back was to the camera during intercourse, or the face was turned away or buried between the woman's legs during cunnilingus. Kiley went through every page of the first three albums—the other five had nothing in them yet, although Tony Touhy apparently had definite expectations, having bought a set of eight; but Kiley found no photographs of Ronnie Lynn, and he now had, from close contact with her twin Alma, a better image of her in life than he had seen in death. Kiley did find, however, two double-page spreads, each in a different place, where photographs had obviously been removed. He did not even have to pause in his search to figure that one out: one removed set was the pictures Touhy had, intentionally or accidentally, given to Ronnie Lynn; the set that Dietrick and Meadows by now probably had taken into evidence along with Wally the janitor's padded gloves. The other set—those *had* to be the pictures of Ronnie Lynn, which Tony Touhy must have done something with after learning of her death. Phil probably told Tony, before he got him off to Ireland, to get rid of anything he had connecting him with the dead dancer. There was always the chance that Tony had destroyed them, but Kiley did not think so. More likely, Tony had transferred them to a hiding place somewhere in the apartment. Tony Touhy was a trophy collector, that much was clear: the videotapes, the photographs; he was a hunter of women, and those were the heads he had mounted in his den. Joe Kiley was now more certain than ever that somewhere in this luxury high-rise apartment he was tossing, would be found what was now Tony Touhy's ultimate trophy.

Moving farther into the bedroom, still in a clockwise pattern so as not to overlook anything, Kiley came to the bathroom door and went in, beginning a clockwise path in there also. Opening the medicine cabinet, he saw that Touhy had an array of pills: uppers, downers, opiates, hypnotics, painkillers of varying strengths—all legally prescribed and in pharmacy-labeled containers. Kiley quickly took everything out, removed the glass shelves, and with Touhy's own fingernail clippers removed the two screws that held the cabinet into the wall. Lifting it out, he set it on the closed toilet seat, and with one hand felt all around the inside of the opening into which it fit. Nothing. He replaced everything, wiped some plaster residue off the wall with a tissue, and put the tissue in his pocket. Under the sink, he checked two drawers—inside, outside, underside—and a small cabinet of bath supplies. He felt under, around, and in several stacks of thick, monogrammed towels. Removing the lid of the toilet tank, he checked for a waterproof container commonly marketed underground for use by drug dealers; but the tank was clean. As was the light fixture, the mirror attachments, the hair dryer, the shower head—a popular place to hide a single key; although Kiley had yet to come across anything that Tony kept locked.

Out of the bathroom, Kiley's path took him immediately to another door: entry to a walk-in closet. To Joe Kiley, with the sense of cleanliness, neatness, orderliness instilled in him by his mother, it was a thing of consummate beauty, impeccable, flawless, everything arranged as a haberdashery might have it displayed for sale. To Kiley's left, suits: two dozen or more; sport coats and slacks, another dozen; all hung by color, and within each color by style; all in custom suit bags, a clear panel in front for viewing. Kiley unzipped every bag, checked every pocket, sleeve, trouser leg, waistband. Nothing.

Shoes next: again arranged by color, on racks, fitted with cedar shoe trees. Kiley checked every shoe, every tree, behind and under the racks.

A built-in bureau with glass-doored shelves and a dozen drawers held fifty shirts, every color of the spectrum, laundered, folded, stacked; underwear, socks, handkerchiefs, belts, jewelry. Kiley was not surprised that there were scant few empty spaces, did not even bother to ask himself what Tony Touhy had taken to Ireland with him. A six-piece set of matching Hartmann belting leather luggage was on a shelf near the ceiling, with no room for missing pieces. Tony had probably gotten on that plane to Shannon with a suitcase full of big brother Phil's clothes, to hasten his timely departure.

Kiley was beginning to tire; although he was relatively free from nervousness, he was nevertheless tense, his stomach was becoming nettled at the effrontery of denied rest, and his feet were cold, Still, he worked efficiently, almost by rote, his rubber-gloved fingers—still the first pair, no snags yet—worming inside all the folded shirts, shorts, undershirts, socks, lifting up drawer liners, feeling along drawer sides, bottoms, backs—

It was on a top drawer used for cuff links, tie tacks, and watches, that, when he bent his fingers over to feel the rear of the back, Kiley encountered a surface softer than the wood he should have felt; a surface that was as smooth as the enameled built-in, but one which nevertheless caused his covered fingertips to drag. Like rubber against rubber, or plastic against plastic.

Swallowing, wetting his lips, Kiley felt more carefully, his mind polarized on detecting what his fingers were feeling. It was, he decided, a plastic bag of some kind, like a sandwich bag, a freezer bag, the zip-loc kind. And it was not taped or mounted to the back of the drawer in any way; it was *hanging*, from two small screw-in hooks that he could feel. Kiley half smiled. Tony Touhy, the son of a bitch, had gone to a little trouble to do this: to put the bag in what he determined to be a secret, safe place—and yet be able to remove it and replace it very conveniently, without the nuisance of using tape. All Kiley had to do was use thumb and forefinger to unhook the bag in both places and it lifted right out—

Joe did not even have to open the clear, plastic bag. It contained a set of probably eight Polaroid photos, the top one being of a nude Ronnie Lynn, so clear that her freckles were distinguishable, lying on her back on Tony Touhy's bed—on sheets that matched a comforter Kiley could see, through the open closet door, on the bed at that moment; her head propped up against several pillows, her plentiful breasts, which should have spread over her chest evenly, instead cupped up by her with each hand, pushed up to globular shape to make a nest for Tony Touhy's scrotum which lay partly between them, the *glans* of his erect penis hidden by the circle of her lips.

Under the pictures, in the palm of his hand, Joe felt something else: heavier, harder. Even as he turned the bag over to look at it, he knew what it would be.

He was right.

It was Tony Touhy's ultimate trophy.

Nick Bianco's detective badge.

# SIXTEEN

At noon on Saturday, Kiley got in his car, drove to the far South Side, and turned onto the Indiana Expressway. When he got to Gary, Indiana, he found a state highway, Route 41, that followed pretty closely the "Line"—that ruler-straight boundary between Illinois and Indiana—and started downstate, through a series of busy little town-square type towns with names like Lowell, Morocco, Boswell, and New Market. There was an interstate he could have taken, but he was in no particular hurry, and having to slow down going through the small towns was a pleasant respite for his overworked mind.

He had only decided to even go just two hours before starting, after sleeping until nine o'clock. The previous day, Friday, he had gone through the motions of the day like a zombie, walking around with Nick's badge in his pocket—he didn't know why, only that he had not wanted to leave it behind when he went to work that day, as if he had some inexplicable reason to fear it would not be safe in his apartment. He thought maybe it was something subconscious; after all, it hadn't been safe in Tony Touhy's apartment. Without mentally debating it, he had simply put the badge in his pocket.

There had been no hesitation on Kiley's part to *take* the badge from Tony Touhy's closet. Even if Touhy were never brought to justice for Nick's killing, Kiley was not going to let the scum-sucking son of a bitch keep his trophy of cop-killing to take out and admire when his twisted pleasure desired it. Kiley had taken the entire plastic bag, Polaroid photos included, and had even unscrewed the two hooks that were fastened to the back of the drawer. Then he had switched the drawer with another one from down at the bottom, very carefully transferring their respective contents, so that there would not even be any screw holes on the back of the top drawer now. Let the asshole figure *that* out. Maybe it would drive him crazy, trying to figure out what happened.

Drive him crazy if he lived long enough, that is. Kiley still intended to see him dead.

Joe had not slept at all after getting back to his apartment just at sunrise Friday morning, following a drive out to the Northwest Side to drop the two keys into Bernard Oznina's mailbox. He was physically tired, his eyes burning with strain, and his stomach by then churning up acid like a geyser; but his mind had kicked into such an uncontrollable overdrive that he could not even sit still, much less lie down and sleep. Now that he knew—really *knew*—that Tony Touhy had done it, or ordered it done, or *been* there when it was done, there were dozens of new questions that now began to plague him: questions he had not bothered addressing until he had his proof. Such as: Did Touhy actually pull the trigger? Did he personally take Nick's badge? Did he somehow know Kiley was on his way to back Nick up; is that why Nick's body was left there instead of being taken away and dumped somewhere else less conspicuously connected to the Touhy family? Who among the names Kiley now had from license plate registrations was actually present at the killing? Who—and what—and why—and—? It seemed that each question generated another, each speculation on his part bore the fruit of an additional, "Yeah, but what if—?"

As the sun rose, Kiley had paced his little apartment first with a double shot of gin to slow down the mental rush he was experiencing, then paced it some more with a glass of icy milk, and finally paced it with a mug of hot, black coffee to jolt his coming-in-second body back to pace with his brain. Finally, at seven, he had headed downtown to the Shop.

Friday he had spent on the telephone and at a computer terminal expanding the information he had received on Harold Paul Winston from the police departments in Detroit, Michigan, and Dayton, Ohio. Winston had said he was "from" Detroit originally, but had "gone to high school" in Dayton. Kiley had a dozen reports from both cities: There was nothing to indicate that Winston had ever even *been* in either of them. He's working me, Kiley thought, just like I'm working him. Sneaky little son of a bitch. Except—Kiley knew he was now one up on old Hal. Because Kiley had only told Winston one insignificant lie, about his father being a retired cop living in Florida; and he had subsequently recanted that lie and told Winston the truth. So that Winston was probably thinking that while Kiley had leveled with him now, Winston himself still had lies to Kiley in the hopper—and that, Kiley suspected, was going to wear on him. Kiley could not, of course, confront Winston with the information from Detroit and Dayton, because then Winston would know Kiley was still checking on him—after Kiley had assured him that his file was inactive. It was a cat-and-mouse game in which the roles continually changed.

Kiley had spent as much time at a computer terminal as he could on Friday afternoon, hoping that the long period of staring at the screen—long, *monotonous* period, actually, because he developed nothing of any significant use regarding either Nick's killing or the bus bombings of Winston—but he hoped the time spent at it would tire his eyes, mind, and back muscles sufficiently to dictate an early-to-bed night. It did. Along with the lack of sleep the previous night when he'd tossed Touhy's apartment, Kiley's Friday activities left him wiped out and dozing on his couch, after a TV dinner, by eight-thirty. Just before falling asleep, he had roused himself enough to call Gloria Mendez.

"I just wanted to let you know: I've got proof now that Tony Touhy was involved in Nick's killing. I found Nick's badge in his apartment."

"The son of a bitch," Gloria said quietly. Then: "How'd you get a warrant?"

"I didn't."

"Oh." She sighed quietly. "So he's still in the clear."

"As far as prosecution, yeah. But not as far as the department—or you and me. I'm going to take the badge to the chief Monday morning, tell him the whole story. I think it'll take you off the hook with OCB. You can admit to the chief that you were working with Nick and me. I think the fact that we were right will carry a lot of weight with Cassidy. He's a good cop. I think he'll be a Chinaman to both of us, and let IA and OCB know it." Gloria knew what Joe meant. In the department, a "Chinaman" was someone in a position of high authority who looked after the interests of a cop on a lower rung of the ladder.

"Are you sure you want to put yourself on the line, Joe?" Gloria asked. "Right now your job and pension aren't at risk. I think Cassidy's a good chief too, but he *could* go the other way and put both of us out on the street."

"If that's the way it turns out, fine," Kiley told her. "Either we both stay or we both go. I'm going to shoot the works with Cassidy. I just wanted to let you know so you wouldn't sweat it over the weekend. Listen, I've got to go—I was up all night last night—I'm falling asleep holding the phone—"

Sometime around midnight, he woke up, turned off the television, undressed, and went to bed, *in* bed. In all, he slept once around the clock, not waking up again until nine Saturday morning.

After a luxuriously hot shower and a slow, close shave—for which he got out his father's old shaving brush, soap cup, and straight razor, something he did once in a while, he didn't know why—but after the shower and shave, he felt good enough to prepare what he called a "killer breakfast"—eggs, bacon, buttered white bread with sugar sprinkled on it, and strong, black coffee: everything medical science preached would shorten one's life. But it was delicious, and he sat in his underwear eating it while he watched the morning sports news.

It was when a weather report came on, predicting a clear, balmy spring day for northern to central Illinois and Indiana, that Kiley got the notion to drive down and see Alma Lynn. She was, he thought, probably giving herself an ulcer over the photographs of Ronnie that Touhy had taken. Kiley knew her kind: Once she got her mental teeth into something, she never let go; she wouldn't draw a peaceful breath until the matter of Ronnie's pornographic photos was resolved. Calling her would have been the simplest way of doing it, but not the most satisfactory. Merely telling Alma that he had found and destroyed the photos would forever leave a spark of doubt in her mind, a nagging hint of suspicion that he was only *telling* her that to relieve her mind. He knew too that he could have mailed them to her: probably the best plan; but for some reason he was inclined to drive down and hand them to her in person.

It had been the prospect of the drive, as much as anything, that had decided him. A nice, long, leisurely drive, away from everything and everybody, to give his mind a few hours of R-and-R. There was no way he would not think about the case, of course; *cases*, really, because Harold Paul Winston was in his thoughts also. No way he could avoid reflecting on everything he knew so far, both about Nick's killing and Winston's lies and crimes, but at least he could contemplate in a new, more neutral environment than his apartment or the Shop.

He had dressed in a fairly new pair of khaki trousers and one of the plain white polo shirts he usually selected when shopping, and then he had done an odd thing: He had unzipped the garment bag Stella had given him and picked out one of Nick's expensive sport coats. It was a muted plaid number in subtle earth tones, single-breasted, American cut although it had an Italian designer label on the inside pocket. The fit was not perfect but it was good enough, and Kiley decided to wear it.

And, as he had done the previous day, he put Nick's badge in his pocket again too.

• • •

When Kiley arrived in Ripley, Indiana, shortly after three that afternoon, he found, instead of the sleepy little place he had originally pictured, a town square bustling with men, women, kids, cars, pickup trucks, and traffic moving so slowly that it took him fifteen minutes of circumnavigating the courthouse before he found a place to park. The other little towns he had gone through on the way down had been crowded the same way, but going through them had not been as bad as stopping in one. It took another ten minutes of walking around to locate a pay phone. The directory showed Alma Lynn living at 420 Elm Street. When Kiley dialed her number, it rang long enough to make him wonder if she too were up at the town square, until finally she answered.

"Hello—"

"Ms. Lynn?"

"Yes—"

"This is Joe Kiley—"

"Oh, *hello.* Sorry I took so long to answer; I was doing my yard work. How are you?"

"Okay. You?"

"Well—you know—" It was like there was a shrug in her voice.

"I'm here in town," Kiley said. "Would it be okay if I dropped by?"

"You're in town? Here in Ripley?"

"Yeah. I just drove in. This little town is really jumping."

"Saturday," Alma explained. "All the farm families come to town to shop. Believe me, it doesn't jump any other time. Well, this is a surprise— where are you?"

"At a pay phone in some drugstore; I don't know the name of it—"

"Brown's," she told him. "City Drug doesn't have a public phone." She seemed to hesitate. "I wish you'd called before you got here; I'm really a mess—the yard work—"

"I really don't have to stay but a minute," Kiley told her. "I have something to give you."

"Oh." It took her a moment. "Oh! Really? Is it what I hope it is?"

"Yes."

"Okay, listen, drive around the square until you get to the corner where the bank is, then turn right. That's Elm Street. It's four blocks down, number four-twenty. I'll be outside waiting."

"Okay," Kiley said.

When he got away from the anthill of the town square, Kiley found Elm Street to be a wide, straight thoroughfare with sidewalks fronting deep, maturely landscaped front yards shaded by enormous old oak trees with only a sprinkling of elms after which the street was named. The lawns were backed by large, brick-foundationed, wooden-sided, shingle-roofed, dormered, shuttered, and porched, two-story, 1940s vintage homes, all of them looking solid and stately. Flower-edged walks led from the streets to the porches, and no-nonsense driveways ran in a straight line back to rear detached garages, connected to the houses by covered breezeways. To Kiley, it was like a street Norman Rockwell might paint, missing only a little boy playing with a ball and his dog.

Alma Lynn, a red bandanna on her head emphasizing her own red hair and freckles—another Rockwell image, small-town picture-of-America woman—was waiting as she said, standing by the drive in shorts and a worn man's shirt not tucked in, her feet in deck shoes without socks, a pair of gardening gloves holding the shirt up in back where they stuck out of a hip pocket. Kiley pulled into the drive, saw a blue Chevrolet two-door parked back near the garage, and stopped where Alma was standing.

"Well, hello," she said as he got out. She pulled a mock pose. "I told you I was a mess—"

"Hello," Kiley said, feeling a little embarrassed. "I'm sorry I didn't think to call ahead before I got to town—"

"Oh, that's all right," she waved away his apology. She tilted her head slightly. "You look different somehow; maybe it's the sport coat—I've only seen you in gray suits and ties; it's a very nice coat."

"Thanks. I don't wear it much—" He had no idea why he said that.

"Come on in," Alma invited. "Have something cold to drink—do you like limeade? This is *real* limeade, homemade."

"I've never tried it, but it sounds good."

She led him onto the porch and inside to a large, comfortable living room furnished with older but substantial pieces arranged around a floor-to-ceiling used-brick fireplace and hearth. "Make yourself comfortable," she said. "I'll get the limeade."

Instead of sitting, Kiley ranged: moving, pausing, studying things in the room. There were three club chairs and a couch, lamps at all of them, no television in the room; a reading family, Kiley thought. Magazines on a coffee table: *National Geographic, American Heritage,* something called *Persimmon Hill.* No ashtrays anywhere. Open drapes on the windows, sheers closed under them. A game table against one wall; a shelf above it holding boxed games: Parcheesi, Monopoly, Chinese Checkers, others. A grand piano, its top laden with family pictures: a lot of them with freckle-faced twin girls in various stages of growth—the twins in leotards and ballet shoes, the twins in Brownie uniforms, the twins on a parade float, the twins in graduation gowns. And there were pictures of a man with a pleasant face but weary shoulders; a woman with tight lips, trying to look pretty. One picture of a sad-faced dog—

"Here we go," Alma said behind him, and Kiley turned to see her brushing aside the magazines and placing on the coffee table a tray with two glasses, a pitcher of limeade with ice cubes and fresh lime peel floating in it, spoons, sugar, napkins. "Those are my parents," she said of the photographs. "And the family dog, Oscar. My father named him that because he said the dog looked like somebody named Oscar Levant, whoever that was. Did you ever hear of him?"

"No," Kiley said.

"He used to be in movies, Daddy said. He said they both had sad faces." She paused briefly, looking over at the photographs. "Those others are Ronnie and me—" She shook her head at the pointlessness of the remark. "I'm sure you'd figured that out." Holding out a glass, she said, "Here, try this for taste; then sweeten it if you like."

Kiley sat and sipped the limeade, then reached for a spoon. "Is this all the sugar you have?"

"Is it that bad?" She looked genuinely pained.

"Just kidding," Kiley said. "Actually, it only needs a little—" Not easy to joke with, he thought. Although it could be the recent circumstances. "You live here with your parents?" he tried to move away from his lame humor.

"No, my parents are—I thought I mentioned to you on the phone that they were dead. I left a message on your machine—"

"Yes, you did. I'm sorry, I forgot."

Alma glanced at the piano. "I'm the only one over there still alive. Even Oscar is gone."

Stirring two spoonfuls of sugar into his glass, Kiley moved away from the subject of death. "This looks like quite a house."

"It is." Alma rose. "Come on, I'll show you the rest of it. Bring your glass."

She led Kiley first into a formal dining room with deHavilland china and Waterford crystal displayed behind the glass doors of a mahogany cabinet that matched a gleamingly polished table and eight chairs; then to a smaller room with a television and some easy chairs in it—"This was originally a sun room when Dad first had the place built," she said. They went on into a large country-style kitchen, light and airy, its appliances not new, their age made all the more obvious by a modern microwave in their midst. From there to a wide, screened-in back porch with wicker rockers, a swing, a portable TV, and bamboo sun shades that unrolled down. The backyard, Kiley could see, was as deep as the front, with wooden lawn furniture under two mammoth oaks the foliage of which reached out to each other, forming a natural canopy. There was a brick barbecue nearby. Old automobile tires hung from each tree. Twins.

"Why don't we sit out here," Alma said when they were on the screened porch. "I'll get the limeade."

When she returned, Kiley was in one of the rockers but not rocking; he saw no point to it. As Alma sat in the swing, he said again, "Quite a house."

Alma smiled a melancholy smile. "Ronnie and I were born in this house—literally: in the front bedroom. Mother's water broke one morning while she was fixing breakfast in her nightgown and robe. She went upstairs to change clothes while Daddy called the doctor. But before Mother could even change, she went into shock labor and Ronnie started coming. Dad called the doctor again and the doctor called for a nurse, and they came over here. By the time they got here, Ronnie was out and I was coming right behind her." Her smile brightened. "We made such a mess, Daddy had to throw the mattress out and get a new one. An ambulance took Mother and us to the hospital for a couple of days, mainly so Mother could rest." Now she sighed quietly. "Daddy wanted to try for a son, but Mother refused to have any more children. Her two 'little missies'—that's what she called us—were plenty, she said."

"How long have your folks been gone?" Kiley asked, trying to keep the question conversational rather than inquisitive.

"Let's see," Alma said, turning in the swing, working out of her shoes and putting her feet up, leaning back against a big pillow. Her legs, Kiley noticed, were tanned, firm, the thighs slightly too large in proportion to the calves. "Daddy's been gone almost five years now. He was a two-pack-a-day man: Camels, no filter, no menthol, just cancer. It got him in the lungs first, then threw a clot into his brain. It took him a long, rough year to go. And Mother—" Alma took a quick swallow of her limeade "—Mother went a few years before Dad. She was a closet drinker in her later years; used to stretch out on a chaise in her sitting room upstairs and while away the afternoons sipping Jack Daniels and looking at photo albums of her pictures when she was young and pretty. By the time Ronnie and I got home from school, she'd be swacked and we'd have to put her to bed and fix Daddy's supper. Cirrhosis finally got her. Our family doctor put kidney failure on the death certificate so nobody would know."

Alma stared into space for several moments, and Kiley, not wishing to intrude on whatever private memories had seized her, maintained a silence, himself staring also, out at the big backyard, trying to imagine how it would have been growing up in a place like this. Probably dull as hell, he decided. How could growing up be any fun without alleys to duck through, rooftops to run across, outdoor ballparks and indoor stadiums and big downtown movie houses to find ways to sneak into, El trains to ride— there was probably no place in a little town to *prowl.*

Alma abruptly sat back up on the swing and asked directly, "Did you find those pictures of Ronnie?"

Kiley nodded. From his inside coat pocket, he took an envelope and handed it over to her. Putting aside her glass, Alma took out the Polaroids and looked at them one by one. There were eight. Two fellatio, two cunnilingus, two doggie-style, and two tit-fucking. Alma's expression did not change as she went through them. When she was finished, she put the pictures back in the envelope and reached over to place it on a wicker table that also held the portable TV.

"Well," she spoke resignedly, "Ronnie said they were really hot." She sighed quietly. "Where did you find them?"

"Where I thought I would," Kiley told her. "The ex-boyfriend's apartment."

Alma's eyebrows rose. "Oh, you got your search warrant then?"

Kiley shook his head. "No."

"But how did you—I mean—?"

"You don't want to know any details," he said. "If you know details and I give you the pictures, you become an accessory after the fact to a felony."

"Oh. I see. All right."

Alma rose, collected the tray and limeade glasses, and walked to the kitchen door.

"I'll be right back—"

Kiley heard her in the kitchen—rinsing glasses, opening a dishwasher, opening the refrigerator. Keeps a clean kitchen, he thought. The clink of more glasses. A cabinet door closing. Then the screen door to the kitchen opening and Alma was back, standing in front of him with the same tray, but now it held a bottle of Tanqueray, two glasses, a small pewter bucket of ice, and a dish of olives.

"Gin, right?" she asked. "I also have vodka, bourbon—"

Kiley shook his head. "It's a long drive back to Chicago."

"Detective," Alma said, putting the tray on a wicker table, "you look to me like a man who enjoys a good steak. Am I right?"

"Who doesn't?" Kiley admitted.

"I buy New York cuts, USDA Prime, sixteen dollars a pound. I barbecue them on that grill out there with mesquite chips in the coals. You never tasted steak so good." She put her hands on her hips. "How about salad—you like salad?" Before he could answer, she pointed to a back corner of the yard and said, "See that string running between those four poles? That's my garden. Tomatoes, lettuce, cucumbers, celery. No pesticides, no packing, no boxed ice, no exposure to exhaust fumes being transported. Just exquisitely good fresh vegetables lovingly washed in pure Indiana well water—"

"Are you inviting me to dinner, Ms. Lynn?" he interrupted.

"How quick!" she marveled. "No wonder you're a detective!" She sat down on her heels in front of him, expression turning very serious. "How about it? I could really use some company that I don't have to put on a front for."

Kiley pursed his lips, as if in deep contemplation. "Did you say no pesticides?"

Alma stood back up, slapping his knee on the way. "Pour yourself a drink while I go shower off my yard work smell. Then I'll have one with you."

When twilight came, Kiley and Alma were sitting on the lawn furniture, feet up on individual little tables, with a table between them for the gin and ice. In the barbecue, coals had lost their leaping blue flames, and the intense, invisible heat over which Alma had cooked the steaks was now turning to gray ash around the edges. On a brick ledge next to the pit were dishes, bowls, utensils that Alma and Joe had used to eat their steaks and salads. Alma had been right: Kiley had never tasted steak so good; a far cry from Sizzler's, even from the steaks Nick had cooked on the Bianco barbecue. "You've got to buy USDA Prime," Alma insisted. "That's the only way you get that flavor. My dad taught me that."

"Sounds like your dad knew his steaks," Kiley said.

"Sometimes I think my father was the smartest man I ever knew. He was a teacher also; taught history for more than thirty years at the same school where I teach. But it wasn't just that he was intelligent—you know, book smart; he had common sense too. You'd be surprised how few intellectuals really have that."

Kiley didn't know if it was the gin, the food, the ambience, or what—but he was feeling very good, very relaxed, and thoroughly enjoying the company and conversation of Alma Lynn. After she had earlier left him on the screened porch and gone upstairs, he had taken off Nick's sport coat, draped it over the back of another rocker, and poured himself a drink. Presently he had heard the sound of Alma's shower, seeming like it was right above him. He imagined her under that spray of water: naked, suntanned, freckled, body toned, firm. The photographs of Ronnie were still on the TV table where she had put them; Kiley went over, looked at them again. Now that he knew Alma better, and had not known Ronnie at all, it was strangely like looking at pictures of Alma. He found himself studying Ronnie's—Alma's—breasts, buttocks, mouth—

Then he heard the shower stop. Putting the pictures back in their envelope, he returned to his chair and drink.

When Alma came down, she was wearing a kind of muumuu: loose, flowing, mid-calf length, scooped neckline, multicolored in what looked like Aztec patterns. A panty line showed in back when she turned around, but no bra showed when she bent over.

"First thing I have to do," she said, "is put out the smudge pots; then I'll join you for a drink."

"Smudge pots?"

"For the mosquitoes. The pots are actually dried-up eucalyptus plants; it smells very nice, but its natural content, which protects the plant from mosquitoes nesting in them, also drives the little bastards away when you burn it." She had smiled. "Daddy again."

Kiley had walked out into the yard with her and watched as she placed the pots, which were about the size of a grapefruit, on four hardwood blocks placed in strategic locations around the outdoor furniture. A moment after she lighted them, their wispy black smoke wafted the fragrance of eucalyptus over the yard.

The two had returned to the porch then and Alma had poured a drink for herself. Barefoot, she seemed very much at ease with Kiley, as if he were an old friend. He did not want the conversation between them to go back to her murdered sister, so he tried to keep on more untroubled ground. But it was difficult, and Kiley began to understand for the first time that being a twin did not simply mean looking like someone else; it meant being *part* of someone else. So no matter what the subject, Ronnie Lynn was somewhere in or around it.

"This is really a great old house," Kiley had commented at one point, restating earlier praise. "Being from the city, I've never seen one like it."

"It's actually way too big for just me," Alma replied. "I have three of the rooms upstairs closed off. But I couldn't give it up; there are so many memories here. It was half Ronnie's, you know, until—well—"

Even impersonal, neutral comments were not immune. "I don't think I've ever been any place so quiet, so peaceful," he tried.

"Maybe you should try small-town living," Alma suggested. "In a place like Ripley, you could probably be chief of police. Or get elected sheriff of the county."

Kiley had shaken his head. "I couldn't live in a small town. I've got city blood. People with city blood have to live in the city."

Alma tilted her head curiously. "Why?"

"We just do," Kiley had shrugged. "City blood gives you a kind of pace. Everything else about you adjusts to that pace: the way your heart beats, your pulse; the way you move, see, smell, sleep—everything you do. With city blood in them, people don't fit anywhere but a city."

"That's almost poetic," Alma had said softly. Then: "It reminds me a little of something Ronnie said just before she left home. She said, 'If I don't get out of this town, I think my blood is going to stop circulating.' Maybe she had country blood that didn't work in the city."

Kiley had thrown in the towel then and stopped trying to avoid the subject of Ronnie Lynn. "For twins," he said unguardedly, "you two seem to have turned out very differently."

"We always *were* different," Alma told him. "Even the way we were named. Mother and Dad made a deal that she would name one baby and he would name the other. He named my sister Veronica, after some 1940s movie star he liked named Veronica Lake. He was a great movie fan, as you've probably gathered: the dog, my sister—he even gave his old Plymouth the nickname 'Bogart' because Humphrey Bogart had driven a Plymouth in some gangster picture." She took a swallow of her icy gin. "Anyway, I was named by Mother, after a favorite aunt of hers. Alma, she said, was a good, solid, middle-America name. She didn't approve of Veronica for a name, said it was too pretentious. She even went to the library and researched the name. She found out that the original Veronica had been a Catholic saint: the woman who offered Jesus a handkerchief on the road to Calvary—you know, the cloth that supposedly kept an image of Jesus's face on it? Well, Mother was *upset*. I mean, her daughter with a *Catholic* name—" Alma suddenly interrupted herself, looking greatly chagrined. "I'm sorry, Joe, are you Catholic?" They both realized that it was the first time she had called him Joe.

"I'm Catholic," he said, "but don't worry about it. My relationship with the church is only occasional." He thought of old Father Conley. "Go on," he urged when Alma still hesitated. "I'm not going to be offended."

"There's not much more to tell," she said, obviously now wanting to close the subject. "Mother tried to get Daddy to legally change Ronnie's name to something more suitable for a Presbyterian family, but Dad couldn't be budged. Veronica it was, and Veronica it stayed."

"Good for him," Kiley said. "Sounds like he was a good man."

"Yes, he was."

"Besides the name, how else were you and your sister different?" he asked, casting all caution aside.

"Oh, lots of ways. Come on," she had said then, picking up the tray and shouldering her way out the screen door and down three steps to the yard. Kiley followed her out to the now fragrance-filled, mosquito-free barbecue area, where she turned on a string of Chinese lanterns with yellow bug bulbs in them. "In high school, for instance," Alma continued as she then got a bag of charcoal from under the grill, "Ronnie went steady with the president of the thespian club. I mean, this guy was so drop-dead handsome that every girl in school, myself included, lusted after him. But he wasn't interested in anybody but my sister—my *twin* sister. Me, I dated a skinny kid who worked after school at a soda fountain—when I dated at all, that is. Of course, I *did* get free sundaes from him. But Ronnie just seemed to naturally gravitate toward what was perceived by everyone that age as glamorous: movie dates, dances, school plays, that sort of thing. Ronnie had a kind of glow, a spark for life, that I didn't have. Ronnie participated; I *watched*."

Alma had doused the spread charcoal with starter fluid and tossed a match on it. Eerie blue flames shot up twelve inches, burning off any residue left on the grill, then diminishing to settle into the charcoal and begin turning it from crispy black to glowing yellow. Moving back from the heat, Alma and Kiley stood with their drinks and watched the slow change of color.

"I guess a perfect example of the difference between Ronnie and me," she said, "is this barbecue. Dad built it and taught Mother and me how to use it: spread the charcoal evenly, wet each piece with starter fluid, toss the match in from at least three feet away, so on. But Ronnie wasn't interested; Ronnie never learned. She said she wanted nothing to do with steaks until *after* they were cooked." Alma chuckled. "Ronnie always said I'd end up married to someone very masculine: a forest ranger, or a fireman." She paused a beat, then added, "Or a policeman."

She and Kiley had locked eyes for a moment in the glow of the Chinese lanterns. Then, a little embarrassed, Alma said, "I'll fix the salad and bring the steaks," and had gone indoors.

Now the meal was over, the glow fading in the well of the barbecue pit, and an opalescent full moon made the light in the backyard on Elm Street a shadowy, indistinct place that in a Chicago alley would have been shrouded in fear, but here was only cloaked in contentment. They sat side by side on an old wooden glider, shoulders and thighs only an inch from touching, their heads back against the padded cushions that were tied in place, eyes on the stars, the unseen heavens.

"Joe?' she said. Tentative.

"Yeah?"

"When you looked at the pictures of Ronnie, did you think of me?"

Kiley did not answer. He did not want to tell the truth, but he did not want to lie to her either.

"Did you?"

She waited for what seemed like a long time without asking again. Kiley finally answered.

"Yes."

"You told yourself that's how I would look doing it, didn't you?" Her voice had become throaty again, as it had in the bar across from the bus station in Chicago. So it was gin, not stress, that did it, Kiley decided. "Didn't you?" she prompted.

"Yes."

Rising, Alma lifted her flowing skirt and in a fluid movement slipped her panties down her legs and off. Without dropping the skirt back down, she straddled him, gripping his shoulders with each hand, pressing her face to his neck.

"I want it, Joe—" Barely a whisper.

Kiley put a gentle hand on the back of her head. "Nothing will come of it," he said quietly. "It won't be the start of anything."

"I don't care. I want it."

"Then take it."

She backed off of him enough to unbuckle his belt, unhook his waistband, unzip his trousers, and work the elastic of his briefs down just far enough. His freed erection bounded into her hand and she moved forward again, raising her hips, and covered it, engulfed it inside herself.

"God almighty—" Her words were bursts of warm breath on his neck; then her lips kissed and sucked on the softness of his earlobe, as her hips slowly moved what was inside her in a tight circle: two, three, no more than four revolutions before she stopped, remained very still, curbing the flood of feeling that was on the brim of release. Over and over she did it, the warm wetness of her working its rigid ally to perfect pitch, perfect concert, to the closest, most minute margin of climax—then stopping again, halting ecstasy at the edge, delaying the rapture, basking in what she knew was now hers to take when she could no longer stand not to.

For Kiley it was much like fellatio: He was required to do nothing, had no responsibility other than erection, could not have thrust anyway with her weight on him. His only participation, except to provide a tool for her work, was to slip his hands under the tent-like dress and find her breasts, swollen; nipples, extrusive; armpits, wet, just the barest bristle of shaved hair. It would not have been difficult to imagine, with her lips sucking, sucking, sucking on his neck now, that it was *them* working on him, instead of the grand part that actually was. But to have imagined that would have required Kiley to think about it, to transfer his thoughts, and he could not do that—because his thoughts were not of the woman astraddle him but instead were of the woman he wanted. His thoughts, insuppressible, were of Stella Bianco.

Even at the supreme moment, when Alma could no longer hold in harness the implosion of her climax, no longer cunningly check by stillness what her body was impelling her to let happen, when she had to abandon the little revolutions of her hips and begin a jackhammer movement of her pelvis, when she *came*, made Kiley *come*, brought them both off with exquisite precision, wet against wet, wet *into* wet—even then, Joe Kiley was thinking of his dead partner's wife.

And detesting himself because of it.

# SEVENTEEN

**K**iley got back to the Chicago city limits just after four on Sunday afternoon.

He had ended up staying with Alma all night, sharing the big antique four-poster bed on which she and her twin had probably been conceived, and had been born. Kiley had not wanted to stay, because of what he had perceived to be impropriety in that small Indiana town where Alma lived and taught school.

"It won't look good if I stay," he had protested first her invitation, then her plea. "Your neighbors will see my car—"

"I don't *care* what my neighbors see." Alma had been adamant about it. "Anyway," she said, when they were back in the house, she carrying her panties as if they were a towel, "you can't leave here like that. Look at your trousers, for God's sake—"

She was right. The front of his trousers where she had straddled him, grooving out the juices of her body with such abandon, were stained in a very obvious pattern.

"Come upstairs to bed," she said, taking his hand to lead. "I'll put them in the washer and iron them for you in the morning."

Joe had thought briefly of lying his way out, saying he was scheduled to work the next day, insisting that no one would see his trousers on the way home anyway; but the gin, the food, the sex, the prospect of a long drive back to the city, all compounded to make him finally, docilely, follow her. After he undressed, Alma put all of his clothes in the washer, then they showered together, she getting out first because nothing would do but that she put clean sheets on the bed for him. After she stayed up, in her robe, to put his clothes in the dryer, she climbed into bed, with him already sound asleep, and lay contentedly naked next to him, not sleeping as he was, merely dozing along the fringe.

At some point during the night, they made love again, virtually the same

194

way, her on top, except now Kiley was stretched out prone and they were both naked, in the dark. And it was easier for Kiley to imagine that Stella Bianco was on top of him.

At three in the morning, they both woke up hungry. Alma went down to the kitchen and brought up a tray of cheese, pumpernickel bread, apple slices, grapes, and the rest of the limeade. They ate in bed, one small lamp on across the room, and Alma verbalized the sexual hunger she had already twice demonstrated.

"You can't imagine what living in a town like this is like for an unmarried woman. There's not an eligible man in Ripley that I would even consider going steady with, much less marrying. And in the area of having an affair, something just to satisfy one's physical needs, I've got a selection of beer-guzzling poolroom loafers, prissy store clerks, or married men who are eager to cheat on their wives." She popped a grape into her mouth. "I know you must have thought down in the yard that I was some kind of nymphomaniac barracuda, but honest to God, Joe, I was just *starving* for it. I can't even remember the last time I slept with a man. It's been two, three years, at least—"

"Why don't you move somewhere else?" he asked. "Wouldn't have to be Chicago; some smaller city like Evansville or Springfield. They must need teachers everywhere."

"I don't *want* to move away, Joe. I love this house. I love my job. And, really, the town itself is a very nice little community to live and work in. It's just that the prospects for a personal relationship are so limited." She sighed rather dramatically. "I'm sure I'll end up an old maid. 'There goes poor Miss Alma: ninety years old and still living alone. Bless her heart.' God, I hate it."

"Somebody will come along for you," Kiley said quietly, with no conviction at all. At one time, he had felt pretty much like her: his own prospects so limited because he considered the availabilities unacceptable; he had resigned himself to a similar fate—that of lifelong bachelorhood; come to actually *like* it after a few years, and gave no further thought to marriage and a family. Then his partner had been killed and left a widow—

As Kiley was preparing to leave late the next morning, after a *real* killer breakfast of fried farm eggs, country sausage, biscuits and gravy, and freshly ground coffee, Alma had said, tentatively, "You know, Joe, I'd love to have you come back any weekend you want—or," glancing away, "if you liked, I could even run up to Chicago—" She paused, sighed, laced her fingers in front of herself. Then she said, making a feeble attempt at levity, "I don't know whether I'm being brazen or just shameless—"

"You're not being either," Joe said, taking her clasped hands in both of his own. "You're just being honest, which is very nice—particularly to me, because in my line of work I don't hear a lot of it. So," he took a deeper than usual breath, "I'm going to be honest back. I'm not what you'd call completely involved yet, but there is a woman back in Chicago—"

"Oh." Spoken like a surprise she hoped would not occur.

"—someone I've known a long time, who—"

"No, please, I'd rather you didn't give me any details," Alma objected.

"I did tell you last night that nothing would come of it—"

"I know you did. I'm not upset with you, Joe, really I'm not. Disappointed, sure; people always hope, don't they?" Alma bit her lower lip. "I wouldn't change last night for anything in the world, I want you to know that. It was beautiful, it was—incredible, and the memory of it will probably sustain me through many, many lonely nights."

"I can't believe that the right guy won't come along for you, Alma," he said. "You are a hell of a special woman. Any man would be lucky to find you."

She had forced a smile. "Well, not any man."

Now, cruising back into Chicago on the expressway, Kiley almost wished he had not gone to visit her in the first place. One of the things he hated worst about his work was seeing blameless, unprepared, unsuspecting people get hurt by the crimes of others—as, himself aside, Alma's life had now been emptied by the death of her sister. It bothered Kiley not a fleck when mob guys killed mob guys, street gang punks killed other street gang punks, wives killed abusing husbands, daughters killed molesting fathers, convicts killed convicts; but he sometimes had difficulty dealing with residual victims: those outside the immediate circle of the criminal act itself. Like Alma. Ronnie had been the primary level victim; Alma was a secondary level victim. She had lost her twin sister, been exposed for the first time to violent crime, introduced to an imperfect criminal justice system—and now, because of him, suffered a disappointment in her personal life that he might have prevented. *Might* have, but probably not been able to, even if he had tried—because his own hunger had been as compelling as hers; he had needed a release from his own burden of pressure, his own stress, his own guilt.

But he was very, very sorry that what they had done for each other had soured in its aftermath.

It should not have surprised him, he knew. Almost everything else in his life had soured since the night he and Nick had looked down on Ronnie Lynn's poor, battered, dead body.

When Kiley drove up to his apartment building, he saw two familiar faces in a black Cadillac parked out front. Uncle Gino Bianco and his flaky son Frank. As Joe got out of his own car, they also got out and walked over to him, Gino Bianco smiling.

"Joey," the elder man greeted him with a show of warmth, "how's my favorite cop doing?"

"Doing okay, Gino." Joe shook hands with both of them as they offered. "How's everything with you?"

"Ups and downs, Joe, ups and downs. You know how the car business is. But I don't complain; life has been good to me. Listen, Joe, Frank and me would like to buy you a drink. We got something we want to talk to you about."

"Can't do it right now, Gino. I'm tired; just drove," he exaggerated it a bit, "three hundred miles."

"Hey, that's a sharp sport coat," Frank Bianco said, studying Joe. "Didn't Nicky have one just like it?"

"We're not here to talk wardrobe, Frank," his father said, apparently not getting his son's point. Then, to Kiley, "Joe, please, one drink. A nice little talk. Believe me, I'm trying to save everybody a lot of unnecessary trouble. And I'm including Stella in that."

At the mention of Stella's name, Kiley relented. "Place on the corner," he bobbed his chin.

They walked half a block to the neighborhood bar where Kiley did most of his social drinking. It was fairly crowded with customers watching a Cubs game on a fifty-two-inch Sony wall-mounted above the far end of the bar. The bartender and half the customers they walked by greeted Joe by name.

"Okay to use Connie's booth for a few minutes?" Kiley asked the bartender.

"Help yourself, Joe."

Kiley led the way to a separate rear booth with stained glass partitions that was the private domain of Connie, the owner. She allowed it to be used by certain select individuals, Kiley among them, when she was not on the premises.

Sitting, Kiley and the Biancos ordered and casually watched the ball game, waiting for their drinks to be served before talking. Then, after a toast by Gino—"Good health to everyone we love"—the elder Bianco made his pitch.

"I'm gonna put all my cards on the table, Joe," he said, "in the hope that with honesty and sincerity on both sides, we can all reach an agreement. My boy Frank here is interested in Nick's widow, Stella. When I say interested, I mean in a proper, respectful way. He wants to wait until an appropriate period of mourning has passed, then have an appropriate period of courtship, an engagement, have the banns of marriage announced, and have a formal wedding in the church. At a later time, perhaps, with Stella's consent, a legal adoption of the girls can be considered." Gino patted his son's arm. "Everyone in our family thinks this is a good match, Joe. Frank and his cousin Nick were pretty close; they thought a lot of each other—"

"Bullshit," Kiley cut in bluntly. "Nick thought Frank was an asshole. He told me so a dozen times."

"Why, you fucking mick bastard—" Frank, face turning an angry red, started to rise.

"You come at me, you guinea prick," Joe warned coldly, "and I'll take your fucking face off."

"Frank, you calm down!" his father ordered, the hand on his arm becoming a grip. To Kiley he said, "There's no need for name-calling here. Can't we be civil, Joe?"

"Maybe we can, maybe we can't," Kiley clipped his words out. "You said you were putting all your cards on the table; then you try to handle me with some cheap shit about Nick and Frank being buddies. I was Nick's *partner*, remember? He and I were as tight as two guys can get. I know how he felt about everybody—even you, Gino."

"Okay, okay," Gino concluded, "so you're an expert on my dead nephew's personal opinions." His voice now took on the hint of an edge. "We're not here to talk about Nick. This is about Stella. Frank wants to marry her. And there are many reasons why such a match would be a good idea—"

"Is that so?" Joe cut in again. "What reasons, Gino? A nice house in the suburbs, maybe—that's now paid off by the mortgage insurance? The lifetime widow's pension that Stella gets? The lump-sum insurance settlement?" Kiley pulled a cold smile. "Those are nice incentives for a used-car salesman who probably doesn't even have a checking account—"

"Go fuck yourself, you shanty mick bastard!" Frank snarled.

"I'd rather fuck you, Frank. Everybody says you take it in the ass—"

"Enough!" Gino snapped. He leaned forward a little, eyes hardening. "Those are also nice incentives for a city cop who ain't got much either. What, are you that much better than my Frank?"

"I'm a *lot* better than *your* Frank," Joe replied flatly. He pointed a finger at Gino. "You haven't once said that he *loves* Stella."

"Love is something that grows—"

"So does a pile of shit if you keep adding to it, and that's all you're doing. Give me one good reason why Frank should marry Stella that doesn't have a dollar sign attached to it."

"All right, I will." Now the edge disappeared from Gino Bianco's voice and its tone reverted to reasonableness. "Stella is Italian. Her kids are Italian. A minute ago you called Frank a guinea. Is that what you think of Italians, Joe? You call us guineas? Maybe dagos too, huh?"

"One of your problems, Gino, is that you only hear what you want to hear," Kiley said. "I called Frank a guinea prick just like he called me a mick bastard. But to answer your question honestly, since we're putting all our cards on the table, I only call *some* Italians guineas and dagos." He looked squarely at Frank. "The ones who *are* guineas and dagos."

"You motherfucker," Frank growled, almost gutturally.

"My mother is dead, Frank, I can't fuck her," Kiley replied easily. "But I understand yours is still alive. Maybe I can fuck her instead."

Frank looked pleadingly at his father, who still had a grip on his arm— and now, for the first time, Gino Bianco's own face darkened with anger. His eyes, on Kiley, looked like bullet holes. "You're talking about my wife," he said coldly.

"Your son brought the subject up, not me. If you don't want his mother talked about, tell him to watch his fucking mouth."

"It don't seem to me," Gino said, same frozen tone, "that you want to be reasonable here, Kiley. It don't seem to me that you care much about the welfare of your dead partner's widow and kids, because you refuse to cooperate in what her family thinks is best—"

"My not 'cooperating' with you, as you call it," Kiley said, "doesn't have a goddamned thing to do with how I feel about Stella and the girls."

"We think it does."

"Then 'we' is wrong." Kiley drummed his fingers on the table. "This discussion is starting to bore me, Bianco. If you've got a line to draw, do it."

"Fine," Gino nodded curtly. "The Bianco family wants you to stay away from Stella. Completely."

Kiley shook his head emphatically. "Not unless Stella tells me to."

"If she remarries, it should be to an Italian."

"If she remarries, it should be to whoever she wants it to be."

Gino's bullet-hole eyes were locked onto Kiley's own. "We don't want to have to get nasty about this matter, Kiley."

"Oh, shit," Kiley said, half in amusement, half in disgust. Rising, he stood looking down at the father and son. "You've been reading too much Mario Puzo, Gino. I'll go on seeing Stella Bianco as long as she'll let me. And I'll tell you something else—something I haven't even told her: I'll marry her in a minute if she'll have me. Now take a little sincere advice: Stay the fuck out of my personal life. And," he pointed a threatening finger at Frank, "keep Sonny Corleone here away from me or I'll pull his pants down in public and kick his ass all over the street. *Capice?*"

Turning, Joe walked out.

When he got into his apartment, Kiley found that his hands were trembling. Not from any nervousness or fear of the two Biancos; Kiley had learned long ago, even before becoming a cop, that Italian hoods were mostly talk and threat, very little action. They beat up their wives and girlfriends, intimidated their underlings, occasionally killed one of their own to purge the Italian mob bowel, but they seldom pressed a matter with an outsider beyond what they perceived to be the menacing stage. There were few things, they felt, worth endangering themselves for.

Kiley's hands were trembling because of the obvious belief on the part of Gino Bianco that Kiley was serious competition for his son Frank in the matter of Stella Bianco's future. To Kiley, that could mean only one thing: Stella must have *said* something, to *someone*, that led them to believe that she thought of Joe as more than just a friend. And now Joe Kiley trembled at the thought—incredible as it seemed to him—that he might, in spite of everything, have a viable chance to win Stella's affection. He had never imagined that it could really happen—

Neatly hanging his clothes away, putting his old robe on over his underwear, Kiley went into the bathroom and washed up. It was still daylight but he was tired from the drive, still tense from the Bianco confrontation, so decided to stay in. There were frozen dinners in the freezer, gin in the cabinet, and he had plenty to do in the way of planning for tomorrow—when he would put Nick's badge on Chief Cassidy's desk and tell him the whole story, from beginning to end. In a little while, he thought—because he could not get her out of his mind now—he might call Stella just to talk.

Pouring himself a couple ounces of gin, Kiley sat on the couch, put his feet up on an ottoman, and used the remote control to turn on the television. As he took his first sip of gin, the local news came on, muted. His mind still dwelling on Stella, he did not immediately deactivate the mute signal. It was not until he saw a familiar face on the television screen that surprise registered in his mind and a finger automatically pressed the correct button on the control. The newscaster's words came crisply across the room.

". . . apparently committed suicide around ten o'clock Friday night. The cause of death, according to the Cook County coroner's office, was an overdose of sleeping pills combined with an undetermined quantity of alcohol. The deceased had been a Chicago police officer for twelve years, and a sergeant for four . . ."

On the screen was a police identification photograph of Gloria Mendez.

# EIGHTEEN

**K**iley was sitting at Aldena's desk, a file in one hand, when she got to work the next morning, a few minutes before the day watch began.

"I don't need nobody to warm my chair for me, Detective," she said when she found him there. Then she took a closer look at him. "You better take a sick day, Kiley. You look like hell."

Joe did. There were dark circles under his eyes and his usually ruddy complexion was much lighter, as if he had paled from some illness. His expression, normally implacable, was slack: the look of a loser, someone who had given up. Only his light blue eyes showed that there was any mettle left in him.

"I need a big favor, Aldena," he said, rising to vacate her chair. "I've got some deep background digging to do on a suspect named Winston—"

"That bus bomber man? The one we got replies back from Dayton and Detroit with no record?"

"That's him. I think he may have been lying about living there—"

"A suspect lying? Mercy me!" She dropped her big purse, a pink one this time, onto the desk with a thud. It sounded to Kiley as if she might have a gun in it. A large gun.

"I have a suspicion I might have been thrown off his real background trail—which is here in Chicago," Kiley admitted. "So I need some digging done in all vital stat areas. I promised the captain I'd have this guy made before Thursday—"

"Better work fast, Detective." She began unlocking her desk.

"Aldena, I've got to go out to a mortuary this morning to see a dead policewoman's daughter. It's very important that I talk to her."

Aldena stopped and looked at him. "You mean Mendez? The suicide? You know her?"

"I knew her, yeah."

"The word's coming down that she was a righteous cop. Why'd she OD like that?"

"I don't know, Aldena. She had problems, but I thought she could handle them—"

The feisty secretary studied Kiley for a moment as he let his words hang. "What I been hearing, you got some problems of your own. I hope *you* not planning to OD."

"I'm not."

"Good, 'cause it just make extra paperwork for me. 'Sides, you the only one around here dumb enough to believe I only got one eye."

"I don't think I really believed that." Kiley smiled wanly.

"You don't *think*," she scoffed—but gently. She snatched the file from his hand. "This everything you got on your suspect?"

"Yeah."

"All right, get on out of here before anybody else sees you looking so sorry. Call me this afternoon."

"Thanks, Aldena."

"Don't forget to sign out."

Fuentes Mortuary was only a block down from Chavez Neighborhood Clinic, where Kiley had last met with Gloria. As he drove past the clinic, he felt a heaviness in his chest that caused him to suck in two deep breaths. Gloria, Gloria, Gloria, his mind recited her name. Why? Jesus Christ, *why?* It wasn't the end of the world. Even if Chief Cassidy had refused to side with them, even if OCB had pushed its charge all the way, even if IA went to the wall with it, and it meant the end of the department, her career, her pension, it still wasn't the end of the goddamned world. Especially since she still had Meralda to look after for a couple of years—

Kiley admitted to himself that Gloria had seemed—if not despondent, certainly depressed—at their last meeting. They both knew that the audit of her master terminal would turn up seven additional unauthorized accesses besides the one for Tony Touhy—and that would then mean official charges against her; but she also knew that Kiley had planned to go to the chief today, give him Nick's badge, try to gain Cassidy's support. Gloria *knew* there was hope.

Why in *hell*, Kiley castigated himself, hadn't he kept her out of it? Why in hell, if he *had* to go after Tony Touhy so badly, hadn't he done it on his own, without dragging her into it more deeply than the superficial, and explainable, involvement initiated by Nick? Christ, he silently bemoaned, she was such a good cop, a good woman, so straight, upright, so *solid*—

Then *he* had to come back to her, waving those goddamned license plate numbers in her face like a red flag; reminding her that Nick had bought it in a dark alley, and that whoever did it was still walking around; playing her, using her—

Just like he used everybody, he admitted to himself. Gloria, Alma, Father Conley, the doorman Oznina—

He didn't really care who got walked on along the way—as long as he got whoever killed Nick.

And bodies by the wayside didn't matter to him—

Like hell.

Gloria Mendez mattered. She mattered a lot.

Kiley pulled in next to the mortuary and parked. Even though it was still early, there were several cars already there. When Kiley walked in the front door, he saw a black felt announcement board with removable white letters that read:

GLORIA ARENAS MENDEZ
Slumber Room Three

Going back there, Kiley stood in the doorway of the small viewing room and looked past the half dozen people already there, to the casket on its bier, and the still, embalmed body of Gloria Mendez, not in uniform but in a silky white dress, hands together at the waist, fingernails nicely buffed as usual without polish.

A Hispanic woman came over to Kiley. "Are you here for Gloria?"

"Yes." Dryly, his throat constricting slightly.

"Would you sign the visitor book, please—"

"Sure—"

Kiley wrote his name under about a dozen others on the first page. Then the woman gestured for him to approach the casket. Kiley saw that Meralda was sitting with several other people on folding chairs just off from the bier. She stared at him as he stepped up to the casket.

The first thing Kiley thought in looking at the body was that Gloria Mendez was actually a very beautiful woman. He had never seen her dressed in anything but her police uniform, down at the Shop, and the jeans and sweatshirt she had worn at home. Here, upper body cloaked in silky white, a single strand of pearls around her neck, small pearl earrings on those flawless ears, she looked as elegant, as lovely, as exquisite as any woman Kiley had ever seen on the television screen, or in a magazine, or anywhere. Looking at her, he began to again feel as devastated by her death as he had when he first heard about it on the news. Turning away from the casket, he felt his eyes fill with tears, which he blinked to hold back.

"Crying, Detective?"

It was Meralda, standing now, very close to him. Her face was a mask of hurt and hostility.

"Crying, MeMe," Kiley confirmed.

"Don't call me that," she said. "Only my mother called me that."

"I'm sorry."

Now she stepped very close to him, so near that he could see tiny white flecks in her dark green eyes. Dark green *angry* eyes.

"My mother did not commit suicide," she said in a clear, firm voice. "You police are lying."

"It isn't the police who determine that," Kiley self-consciously tried to explain. "It's the medical examiner, the coroner—"

"It is a lie," the girl said. "Whoever told it, it is a lie."

A tiny spark of something ignited deep in Kiley's mind, something minuscule, not yet demanding, just there; a barely discernible warning light.

"What makes you so certain, Meralda?"

"Because she had the Scrabble board set up."

"I don't understand."

"We always stayed up very late on Friday nights and played Scrabble. It was the way we started our weekend. Mama always bought fancy pastry for us to eat, and we drank Cokes; it was our weekly party, 'just the two of us girls,' Mama used to say—"

"Excuse me, but who are you?" A Hispanic man, ill-fitting suit, necktie, smelling like a heavy smoker, had come up to them.

"Papa, he's a policeman friend of Mama's," Meralda said.

"Oh? Well, I am George Mendez," the man announced somewhat pompously. "I am Meralda's father. I do not wish her to be further upset by this suicide talk."

"Papa, please, I want him to know—"

"I will not have any more of this talk, Meralda. I am in charge here—"

"Who put you in charge?" Kiley asked quietly. The man did not look clean; his moustache was untrimmed and he needed a haircut. The thought of him even touching Gloria made Kiley's skin crawl.

"I am in charge," George Mendez repeated affectedly. "I am her husband—"

"Husband or ex-husband?" Kiley asked. His voice grew softer but somehow threatening. Gloria had never mentioned Meralda's father to him, but it didn't take much for Kiley to put the picture together. A *macho* phony who had probably looked pretty slick seventeen years earlier when he got the young Gloria pregnant; then, like a lot of the homeboys, had turned out to be worthless as shit, and left mother and child to get out of the *barrio* on their own—if they could. Gloria had been one of the smart ones: she had taken a civil service exam; she *would* have gotten out—in spite of *macho* George.

Would have gotten out if Kiley hadn't come along.

"We," Mendez stated with forced authority, pointing at Gloria again, "are still married in the eyes of the church. You are out of place here."

"We're both out of place here," Kiley said evenly. "But I'll be leaving as soon as I finish talking to Meralda." Gently he took the girl's arm. "Come outside."

"Please, Papa," Meralda said, holding back. Gloria had raised her properly. This man, regardless of his noninvolvement in Meralda's life, was nevertheless her father, and she had learned that he was entitled to her respect.

George Mendez, like the young Latin Prince on the porch with Meralda that night when Kiley visited, must have seen something in Kiley's eyes that gave him pause for thought, and generated in him a sudden caution, because he finally waved a hand, as if in dismissal and, saving face, said, "All right, go. I permit it. But only briefly."

Meralda walked out to the parking lot with Kiley, where they had all the privacy they needed. "Go on with what you were saying," he told the girl.

"I went on a movie date Friday night," Meralda said. "With a Latin Prince named Hector—only Mama didn't know he was a Prince; he didn't come to get me, I met him there. But I had to be home by eleven-thirty, that was my curfew. I would have come home anyway, because it was our party night, Mama's and mine. And I even came home a little earlier on that night, about eleven-fifteen, because Hector is just a friend, you know, not really a *boy*friend; I mean, Hector and me, we don't make out, you understand?"

"I understand. What kind of mood was your mother in when you left?"

"Kind of, like, real tired. I think she had something on her mind, something she was worried about—" Meralda fixed her eyes on Kiley. "I thought maybe you and her were getting involved, and had a fight or something—"

"We weren't and we didn't," Kiley said. "She never told you what she was worried about?"

"No."

She wouldn't have, Kiley thought. Wouldn't have shared her burden of concern, her dread of the future, with her daughter, because it probably would have upset Meralda very much, even though undoubtedly being of some comfort to Gloria in the sharing.

"Was your mother dead when you got home at eleven-fifteen?" Kiley asked.

"Yes. But I didn't know it right away. The bathroom door was closed, so I just yelled, 'Mama, your baby girl is home safe and sound, underwear intact.' That was our little joke, you know. Anyway, I saw the Scrabble game set up on the middle cushion of the couch, and I went into the kitchen and looked in the fridge to see what Mama had bought for our party. It was chocolate eclairs, four of them. So then I went into the bedroom and got undressed and put on my nightgown and robe; that's what we always wore for our parties. And I got out some polish remover and stuff, because we usually do our nails between turns, see." Meralda sighed heavily. "I guess I was home for about fifteen minutes before I went back to the bathroom door, and I yelled—" At this point she began to weep. "Oh, my God, I just remembered—sweet Jesus, forgive me—I yelled, 'Hey, Mama, did you die in there?'" The girl's weeping turned to sobbing, and Kiley awkwardly put an arm around her shoulders and let her cry up against him. He did not say anything to her, did not try to comfort her with words; they would have been the same platitudes about time healing everything that he had been exhausting with Stella. They had not worked that well with her, and probably, Kiley thought, wouldn't work at all with this sixteen-year-old. So he just held her until she got through it.

When Meralda's crying began to subside, Kiley asked, "Did you finally open the bathroom door and find your mother?"

"Y—yes— She—she was slumped down against the side of the tub, with—with one arm draped into the tub—and her head was back and her—her mouth open. There was a small empty whiskey bottle on the floor next to her. She had on her—her nightgown and robe for our party—" Now Meralda suddenly regained much of her composure and quickly began to dry her tears. "That's why I know Mama didn't kill herself," she said firmly. "If she was going to do that, she wouldn't have had everything ready for our party like she did. I'm sure of that. Plus she never ever had a little bottle of whiskey around like that. She had one big bottle of whiskey that she kept on hand for visitors, but never a little bottle like that—"

"The Valium was hers, right?" Gloria had once given him one.

"Yeah," Meralda shrugged, "she's been taking that for years. She had a regular prescription for it." The girl shook her head emphatically. "I know she didn't kill herself, Mr. Kiley—"

"Do you think it could have been an accident? That she could have taken too many pills by mistake—"

"Mama? Come on, you must know better."

She was right; he did know better. "Meralda, you got home at eleven-fifteen. What time had you left?"

"Just a little after eight, maybe five minutes."

Kiley's mind was racing. A little after eight until a quarter after eleven. Three hours plus. Plenty of time for anything to have happened. It could have been an impulsive thing, a moment when full-blown desperation came crashing down on her and she needed an urgent, immediate release from the pressure. Or it could have been a lengthier scenario: a couple of hours of intense brooding, pill-popping, a whiskey chaser each time, until the cumulative effect totaled her. As for the unfamiliar small whiskey bottle, Gloria may have been sipping a little on the side, picking up an occasional pint so that she didn't have to tap the guest bottle, which Meralda probably would have noticed. There was a reasonable explanation for everything Meralda was denying.

But none of it took into consideration Kiley's telephone call to Gloria around eight-thirty; a call that *had* to have made Gloria Mendez feel better, *had* to have given her fresh hope for the future.

And the business of the Scrabble game and the eclairs was too compelling to discount. Meralda's instinct on that could not be refuted—at least not without solid evidence to the contrary. A depressed, suicidal woman probably wouldn't have prepared their party. Except—Kiley had already decided that Gloria had been concealing her problems from Meralda, so wouldn't it have been natural to have the party as usual?

Kiley had to have some answers—quickly.

"Listen to me," he said, taking Meralda by her upper arms, capturing her full attention. "I'm going to look into this, see what I can find out. I'm not promising anything—but I'll work on it." Kiley lowered his head a little. "I liked your mother, Meralda. She's one of the best people I ever met. I'm sorry you've lost her."

"If you liked her that much, then prove that she didn't do it to herself," Meralda said grimly. "Please prove that."

"I will if I can," Kiley told her.

At Steiner Center, Kiley skipped the elevator and walked up two flights of stairs to a hallway that housed the offices of half a dozen deputy examiners who made up the medical support staff of the county coroner. Stepping into the first unoccupied office he saw, he used the telephone to call B-and-A. When the secretary answered, he said, "Aldena, it's Kiley. Got anything for me yet?"

"Have I!" she said almost gleefully. "I may just have the key that unlocks your whole case, Detective. Vital stats didn't show no birth certificate, but civil litigation records *did*."

"Civil litigation—?"

"You heard me. See, your suspect's original name was not Winston; he was born Harold Paul Codman. His mother, Bernice Codman, divorced his father, Aaron Codman, and married Jerome Winston a year later. The birth father, Mr. Codman, went over to Saudi Arabia to work for a couple of years—his employment records show that—and apparently while he was gone, Jerome Winston adopted little Harold Paul, and in the absence of the birth father, the adoption court granted a motion changing the kid's name from Codman to Winston. Reason you didn't find no previous utility service is that he lived at home with his mother and stepfather until he was almost forty. School records and voter's registration both show him living in the Winston home in Elk Grove until April 1990 when he went out on his own. *But*—and this is interesting—he has also lived from time to time with his birth father since Mr. Codman returned from Saudi Arabia. Codman also remarried, *also* lives in Elk Grove, and sometimes when Harold Paul stayed with him, he used the name Harold Paul Codman. In fact, he's got a driver's license under that name, listed at the father's address. And he took some city college courses at Wright Junior College registered under that name. How you like them apples?"

"I'll be goddamned," Kiley said quietly. "Aldena, you're wonderful."

" 'Bout time you noticed," she said.

"You have time to keep playing with this a little?"

"In among and between my other important responsibilities, I might have a few minutes. Where do you want to take it?"

"Let's see if he ever had a job under the name Codman—transit authority, in particular. And find out what his records show out at Wright College."

"Got it." Aldena paused a beat, then asked softly, concerned, "You do-ing okay?"

"Yeah," his voice became quieter, "I think so."

"Well, hang in," she told him bluntly, and broke the connection.

Kiley stood for a moment with his hand still on the replaced receiver. Aldena, he thought, you are a gem. And Hal, *you* are a lying little son of a bitch. Born in Detroit, grew up in Dayton, my ass. The little bastard had laid a totally false story on Kiley, and Kiley had fallen for it. Maybe it wasn't *to-tally* false: the part about his parents divorcing but still living in the same area, shopping at the same stores, was apparently true; but the background cities—and that little scam he'd run on Kiley as they were parting company the last time: "What about pollution?"—all of that was pure bullshit. Ki-ley's instinct in the bar that night had been dead on target: Get out of there before Winston began handling *him*. Kiley just hadn't left soon enough.

But the good thing about it was that Winston was probably overconfi-dent now, smug in the belief that Kiley, sour on the department, was real-ly his drinking buddy; Kiley had confessed to and apologized for the lie he had told Winston, so now Winston would probably believe that Kiley spoke only the truth to him—while he, Winston, was free to fabricate at will, and good old honest Joe Kiley would believe him.

You are mine, Hal, you son of a bitch, Kiley thought, finally letting go of the receiver.

Going down the hall, Kiley found the office of the deputy coroner who had handled the Ronnie Lynn homicide call, and whom Kiley and Nick had prompted for a little advance information on what the autopsy report would probably reveal. Tapping on the open door, Kiley said, "Hello, Doc."

"Oh, hello, Joe," the deputy coroner said, looking up from a selection of grisly photographs on his desk. He took a toothpick from his lips. "Come on in, pull up a chair—" After Kiley sat, he said, "I sure was sor-ry to hear about Nick, Joe—"

"Thanks, Doc—"

"He was a damn fine officer—"

"Yeah, he was."

Reaching across the photographs, the deputy coroner retrieved several stapled pages and rifled through them. "I saw on the stat report some-where that Homicide closed the case on that dancer—"

"Yeah. It was the club's janitor did it. He was standing with those oth-er guys over by the back door when you and Nick and I were talking."

"I'll be damned. We do lead interesting lives, don't we, Joe?"

"Can't argue that one, Doc."

The deputy coroner returned the toothpick to his mouth and with a forefinger scratched what might have been an imaginary itch where his hairline was receding. "What's on your mind, Joe?"

Kiley leaned closer to the desk. "Autopsy report on a case that's not supposed to be any of my business."

"On?"

"Gloria Mendez."

Eyebrows raised. "The policewoman—?"

"She was a friend, Doc. Of Nick's too."

"You have a problem with the statement given to the media?"

"Not exactly. Gloria has—had—*has* a sixteen-year-old daughter who's naturally pretty shaken up by the death. She doesn't believe her mother would pull the plug like that."

"Well, I didn't handle the call, Joe, but I'm familiar enough with it to know that it couldn't have been accidental because everything was ingested at once. So if it wasn't suicide, there's only one other alternative. Does the kid think somebody *forced* the pills and booze into her?"

"I haven't gotten that far with her yet," Kiley said honestly. "I thought if I could get a copy of the autopsy—" He let his words hang.

The deputy coroner shook his head. "I won't give you a copy of it, Joe. That's too risky on my part if something should develop. But I'll pull it up on the monitor and go down the hall to the john for a few minutes."

"Fair enough, Doc."

Swiveling, the deputy coroner switched on a terminal and monitor next to his desk and keyed input for several seconds until a printed page filled the document window. Then he rose and without further comment left the office.

Kiley immediately stepped behind the desk and scanned the report, skipping past the preliminary information regarding the brain, heart, lungs, liver, and other organs—mention of which made Joe feel queasy and uncomfortable, because he knew that for the autopsy Gloria's body had been surgically invaded so that every part of her could be examined, weighed, analyzed, and put on record before her body was finally turned over to Fuentes Mortuary for cosmetic work and dressing to conceal that invasiveness; Kiley skipped past that disturbing part of it, realizing that in all his years as a cop, this was the first autopsy report he had ever read on anyone he had known while they were alive; it made a lot of difference.

212 •••• CLARK HOWARD

But he skimmed through the beginning of the report and got to the part he wanted to see: the contents of her stomach and the chemical analysis of her blood.

There was no doubt *what* had killed Gloria. A massive quantity of diazepam, combined with a lesser quantity of chloral hydrate, both of them washed down with enough alcohol to raise her blood alcohol content to four times the legal limit for driving a car.

Chewing agitatedly on the inside of his mouth, Kiley moved the pages back to the beginning of the report. He was not well versed in the medical technicalities of autopsy reports, his experience with them limited primarily to the cause of death of a given victim. In fact, it now dawned on him that he had never actually read an entire autopsy report before; so now he began to read this one, from the beginning, starting with the preliminary remarks dictated by the person who had performed the procedure. It read:

> Case number CCM 10482, identified as Gloria Arenas Mendez, is a normal appearing female with light brown skin, black scalp and pubic hair, and brown eyes. Subject is 64" in length and has total body weight of 132 pounds, appearing to be well formed physically, bearing an old incision scar which appears to be from a caesarian section. She has a small black mole on the underside of her left breast—

Kiley had read about half the report when the deputy coroner returned to his office. Joe got up and gave him his chair back.

"Satisfied as to the cause of death?" the deputy coroner asked.

"I guess I'll have to be," Kiley replied.

Neither man spoke for nearly a minute. The deputy coroner seemed to study Kiley during that time, his lips pursed, again scratching at the spot where his hair had receded. Finally he said, "You haven't had much experience analyzing medical exam reports, have you?"

"No," Joe admitted. "Homicide always handles the real details. The GA report just needs the cause of death."

"Well, as I said, this isn't my case, and I don't know how your department is handling it, but as I recall when I read the report—no matter whose case it is, we usually all read the report if it's on a cop, a public official, a celebrity; gives us something to chat about at coffee—but when I read this one, it was pretty clear, as I told you before, that the subject's ingestion of both the drugs and the alcohol had been very rapid; in other words, she probably took all of the pills as quickly as she could swallow them, and drank nearly a pint of whiskey immediately thereafter. The alcohol was absorbed directly into the bloodstream almost like an intravenous infusion, and the pills began to metabolize at the same time. She was unconscious in probably ten minutes, dead in thirty." He turned off the terminal and sat back in his swivel chair. "Pretty cut-and-dried report, Joe—" he paused a beat, "except for those bruises."

"Bruises?"

"Yeah. You might have missed it in the report because it wasn't related to the cause of death. But the subject had a quarter-inch-wide bruise about three inches long, across the back of each hand between the top knuckles and the wrist. One of them could have been made when she fell and her hand hit the side of the tub; but the other one—well, let's say it's unusual for there to be similar bruises on *both* hands—unless, well—" He stared at Kiley. Kiley stared back. Until the words registered meaning.

"Unless she had been restrained in some way," Kiley said grimly. His expression was like it was set in stone: gray, immutable, foreboding. Rising, he extended his hand across the desk, and the deputy coroner stood to take it.

"Thanks, Doc," Kiley said as they shook hands. "Thanks very much."

"Nothing to thank me for, Joe. I haven't said anything."

Kiley went home and started changing into the casual clothes he wore to the Bel-Ked to drink with his old buddy, Hal. While doing so, he called Aldena.

"Anything new on the Liar of the Year?" he asked.

"Could be I got a link for you," the secretary said. "Transit Authority fired an employee named Codman in August 1982—but it wasn't Harold Paul, it was his birth father, Aaron Codman. Reason for the termination was for political soliciting among city co-workers, which is prohibited by the city charter." Aldena paused just enough to tease. "I'll bet you're going to want to know what kind of political soliciting, aren't you?"

"Come on, Aldena, play nice—"

"En-vi-ron-men-tal, that's what kind," she emphasized each vowel. "Man was circulating a petition to try and make the Transit Authority convert the engines of their buses to use cleaner fuel so they wouldn't mess up the air with all those nasty exhaust fumes—"

I'll be goddamned, Kiley thought. So the hint Winston had dropped—
"What about pollution?"—*hadn't* been bullshit, after all. Kiley had been
wrong in his analysis of Winston *again*. The little bastard was smart, give
him that. More than smart: he was clever, cunning, crafty. He was fucking
*shrewd*.

"Did you get his city college records?" Kiley asked Aldena.

"Oh, yeah. You want me to tell you what he studied, or you want to tell
me, Detective?"

"Chemistry," Kiley ventured.

"You got it, baby."

"Okay," Kiley said, relieved. *Very* relieved. "Okay, I think I can nail him
now. Aldena, when I make this guy, I want your name on the report. You've
got major credit coming here."

"We'll see," Aldena hedged. "Sometimes in civil service, Joe, too much
credit can hurt instead of help. You been around long enough to know
that. Let's talk about it first."

"Got you. The report aside, though, *I* owe you—big time."

"I'll remember that next time I want a new car. I got work to do now.
'Bye."

She hung up.

Kiley finished changing, then left for the Bel-Ked Tavern and what he
hoped would be his last buddy session with Harold Paul Winston.

# NINETEEN

**K**iley was alone in the back booth, drinking beer, when Winston came over carrying his own glass.

"Hello there, Joe." He slid in across from Kiley. "What's the matter? You look terrible."

"I *feel* terrible, Hal," said Kiley. "My whole fucking life is coming apart at the seams."

"I'm sorry, Joe. Is it the job thing still?"

Kiley looked across at Winston with a drawn, almost ill expression. "You remember I told you about a police officer who might be in some trouble because of helping my late partner and me on a case? Well, she's dead. She killed herself Friday night."

"Jesus, Joe, I *am* sorry," said Winston, surprised. "I remember you mentioning that officer, but I don't think you said it was a woman—"

"Yeah. Her name was Gloria. Good cop. Left a sixteen-year-old daughter—"

"Christ." Winston shook his head sadly. "Suicide is such a terrible solution to a person's problems. Was her situation that serious?"

Joe shrugged. "Depends on your point of view, I guess. I didn't think her problem was all that bad—but then maybe she didn't think *my* problems were bad either." Kiley drank a long swallow of beer. "I'm not so sure she made a bad choice, Hal. One thing about it: she doesn't have to worry anymore."

"Look, Joe," said Winston, "I don't like to hear you talk like that—"

"It's how I feel—"

"I know, I know. I just hope you're not thinking along those lines yourself." Winston paused, staring, waiting, but got no response. "Are you?" he finally asked.

"I don't know, Hal," replied Kiley, shaking his head slowly. "I don't know what I'm thinking anymore." He smiled wryly. "One thing I do know: I may not have to make up my mind about resigning from the department. I think the brass is getting ready to bring me up on charges."

"Bring you up on charges? What does that mean?" Winston was frowning deeply.

"Fire me," Joe explained. "See, if you're civil service, your boss can't just fire you outright. He has to file charges against you with the civil service commission, saying that you're not performing the duties of your job, or you've been insubordinate, or you're misusing your position in some way for personal gain, whatever—there are a lot of standard reasons. Then you get to file an answer to those charges. Both of you then appear before a civil service review board and they decide who's right. Needless to say, most of the time the employee loses."

"Of course," Winston agreed at once. "The little guy *always* loses. The big shots, the bosses, the 'brass,' as you call them, they all stick together. God forbid they let some common person like you or me come out ahead on anything." Winston held his glass up for the bartender to bring another round. "But, listen, Joe, I don't understand how they can do that in your case. I mean, what the hell could they have on you?"

"Well," Kiley seemed to reluctantly admit, "I haven't exactly been a model cop since my partner was killed, Hal. I've done a lot of bitching about not being assigned to my partner's homicide case; I've said some pretty strong things to a few captains about how the investigation was being handled; and since I was moved over to the Bomb Squad, I haven't been productive at all—which, frankly, may be what they had in mind. I mean, I don't know anything about bombs or arson, shit like that; maybe they just set me up to fail. Tell the truth, Hal, I really don't care; I'm almost ready to turn in my badge anyway— you know that. I just hate it being done *their* way."

Fresh glasses of beer came and Winston let Joe pay for it. Winston, who had begun taking his lead from Joe in such matters, waited until the bartender left before resuming the conversation. "What will you do if they bring you up on charges?" he finally asked.

"Give them what they want, I guess," Kiley shrugged. "Resign." He made a fist and seemed to restrain himself from pounding it on the table. "I just wish I could do it *my* way, you know. Go out on my own terms so I could get a job with the county or the state. I hate for my record to have a civil service termination hearing on it."

"What would it take," Winston asked with forced casualness, "for you to go out on your own terms? I mean, what would you have to do?"

"Get something significant on my record, then resign voluntarily."

"Give me an example of something significant."

Again Kiley shrugged. "Make a major bust of some kind, or perform an act of valor, or come up with some important evidence in a big case the department's not getting anywhere with——"

"Like the bus bombings?"

"Well—yeah, I guess so." Kiley now frowned, then smiled. "Hey, Hal, you're not going to tell me it's you, after all, are you?"

"No, of course not——"

"Well, I hope to hell not. I mean, *I* closed your file, Hal. Talk about me looking bad."

"No, no, Joe. But suppose I could help you come up with some kind of evidence that wouldn't necessarily result in you *catching* the bomber—but would make you *look* good."

"What kind of evidence are you talking about?" Kiley tried to look interested but puzzled at the same time.

"Hell, Joe, I don't know. Let me think about it for a minute——" There was a slight edge of irritation in Winston's voice, as if he had suddenly become aware that he wasn't quite sure where all this was leading him. But he forged ahead somewhat rashly nevertheless. "Suppose," he said, "someone leaked to one of the news stations that these bus bombings had been occurring, and the police department and transit authority had to admit that they'd concealed them from the public. Then suppose you were to find one of the bombs in a bus *before* it went off—not a parked bus but one still on a route: with passengers aboard. Wouldn't that make you kind of a hero, Joe?"

"Well, sure it would, Hal," replied Kiley, impatience seeming to grow. "But how the hell could that ever happen? Ever since the second blast, transit authority people have been searching every single bus after its last run of the day, and twice *they've* missed finding the bomb. How could I search a bus full of passengers, Hal? And how the hell would I know which bus to search?"

"I'd tell you which bus to search, Joe," the little man said evenly. "You'd search the one I put the explosive in."

"*You* put the——?" Kiley kept a steeled grip on himself to look perplexed. "Hal you're not telling me that you *are*——?"

"No, of course I'm not," Winston maintained. "What I'm saying is that I could prepare an explosive similar to the one being used by the bus bomber, put it on a particular bus myself, and let you find it."

Kiley shook his head. "I don't understand, Hal. How could *you* make a bomb?"

"Joe, anybody can make a bomb," Winston said easily. He leaned closer, forearms on the table, and spoke in an almost tutorial tone. "All it takes is a knowledge of basic chemistry and the ability to obtain and put together certain elements, certain materials. Fertilizer, for instance. Buy it at any plant nursery. If it contains fifty percent or more nitrogen, it has explosive properties. But it needs to be combined with something: kerosene, for instance. Most gift shops sell little bottles of it now, to fill those silly little fragrance lamps that weirdos use instead of incense. And you can get mercury from those large outdoor thermometers that people buy to hang on their patios and porches; just saw off the top of the glass tube with a Ginsu knife and pour the mercury out. Dissolve it in ordinary denatured alcohol that drugstores sell. Drain the mixture through one of those Mr. Coffee filters. The residue that you get is fulminate of mercury. You use that for a primer, see. Then you go to a gun shop and buy a pound of shotgun powder—"

"Wait, wait, wait," Kiley said, raising a hand and shaking his head. "You've lost me, Hal. I told you, I don't know anything about this kind of shit—" He pulled a white paper napkin from a dispenser on the table and unfolded it between them. Then he handed Winston his ballpoint pen. "Here. Now show me, step by step. And go slow, Hal, so I can keep up. Where'd you learn all this shit anyway?" he asked, as if astonished.

"I've got a little college," Winston shrugged humbly. "I went to Northwestern, the School of Science. But like I said, this is real basic stuff, Joe. High school chemistry students can figure this out if they're sharp enough. Look, I'll start all over," he drew the unfolded napkin closer. "First, ingredients," he began to print neatly on the napkin. "Two pounds of fertilizer with at least fifty percent nitrogen content. Large bottle of fragrance kerosene. Pound of shotgun powder. Small cheap alarm clock. Patio thermometer. Bottle of rubbing alcohol. Mr. Coffee filters. Ballpoint pen refill—"

"What the hell's *that* for?"

"Something to put the primer in. You wash the ink out with hot water, let the refill dry, and you've got a perfect little tube for the residue you get out of the Mr. Coffee filter—"

Slowly, quietly, almost proudly, Harold Paul Winston went step-by-step through the procedure for making a small explosive device: how to mix half a cup of hydrogen-content fertilizer with half a cup of shotgun powder; how to soak the mixture thoroughly in kerosene; how to dissolve the mercury in the rubbing alcohol; how to filter the mercury-alcohol mixture to produce a pulpy residue; how to press the residue into a clean ballpoint pen refill tube; how to run one end of a short piece of crimped alternating-current electrical wiring into the refill, attach the other end with the AC wires separated to the hour hand of a cheap clock and, with electrical tape, to the face of the clock at a particular hour; how to pack the now pulpous fertilizer-shotgun powder-kerosene mixture around the shell of the clock, stick the ballpoint refill into it, slip it into a plastic sandwich bag, and zip-lock it closed.

*Voila*, a bomb.

"All you need then," Winston said, "is a couple of strips of filament tape to attach it to the bottom of a bus seat. You do that from the seat *behind* where you're putting it, so anyone searching from the front of the seats won't find it—"

"Jesus Christ," Kiley whispered, as much to himself as to Winston. He turned the napkin around and perused, in genuine amazement now, what this little man had done. It was a draftsman-like diagram with neat little arrows running here, there, everywhere, connecting the neatly printed ingredients with each other to form new compounds which were then taken by other little arrows to various places around a precisely drawn clock face. Kiley shook his head in wonder. "This is incredible, Hal—"

Winston sat back, pleased with himself, pleased with the fact that he *knew* he had impressed Joe, pleased by what he thought was admiration in the detective's voice. "It's nothing, Joe, really—"

"You're wrong, Hal," said Joe. "It's *something*. It's definitely something—" Kiley folded the napkin back to its original size, then in half again, and leaned sideways in the booth to carefully put it into his pocket. "It's evidence, Hal."

"Don't be funny, Joe, give it here," Winston said, pleased expression vanishing. Reaching across the booth, he tried to stop Kiley's right hand. As he did so, Kiley's left hand came up, from reaching to his back pocket, and in a quick, smooth motion, he closed, with a muted clicking, one bracelet of a pair of handcuffs around Harold Paul Winston's right wrist.

"No, Joe—!" Winston yelled.

"Yes, Hal!" Kiley replied. He slid out of his side of the booth, pulled Winston out by the other bracelet, and spun him around to twist his arm up behind him, bending Winston over at the waist. A bartender and several patrons came hurrying over, and Kiley quickly shouted, "Police business! I'm a cop!" To the bartender, "You, call nine-one-one, give the operator this address, and say that a police officer needs help. Go on, move! The rest of you people just back off—"

"I can't believe you're doing this," the bent-over handcuffed man looked almost pleadingly up over his shoulder.

"Believe it, Winston," Joe Kiley said flatly.

There was hurt in Winston's expression when he realized that Joe wasn't calling him "Hal" anymore.

# TWENTY

**W**hen Kiley entered the front door of Sacred Holy Cross church for the funeral of Gloria Mendez, he was surprised at how few people there were in attendance. Walking down the aisle, he saw that only about a dozen pews were occupied—unlike Nick Bianco's funeral, at which there had been standing room only. Genuflecting, Kiley made the sign of the cross and turned to kneel in the first unoccupied pew. As he did so, he saw, off to the side near the confessionals, the IA captain, Allan Vander, with another man who was probably a member of his squad. Kiley looked across to the other side of the church and saw, as he expected, Vander's deputy commander, Bill Somers, with another detective. Sometimes a lead could be found among those in attendance at the funeral. Like Joe Kiley.

Ignoring the IA surveillance, Kiley pondered the scarcity of mourners. He knew, as most cops do, that friendship in one's own neighborhood, with one's close neighbors, is often, if not strained, then certainly forced, cordial but distant. There are always a few who will, usually for the benefit of others, go out of their way to give the impression of a real buddy-buddy rapport, but it was mostly show. Everyone else was congenial on the surface, guarded within. After all, a cop was a cop; they could, probably *would*, arrest anyone, for any violation—even something petty, like garbage overflowing in an outdoor can, an unleashed dog creating a nuisance, someone driving a little fast on the block.

Gloria had been a Hispanic cop, still living in a Hispanic neighborhood that carried a high crime rate, considerable drug traffic, and inherent suspicion of the police. It could not have been easy for her living there among her own, yet, because of her badge, her gun, not being one of them. She had been trying to get out of the *barrio*, saving to move herself and Meralda out to the farthest reaches of the Northwest Side where they could make a better life for themselves. But until she had enough money to do that, she lived where a single *Latina* mother with a teenage daughter *could* live—in the Hispanic community. But, because of the social standards of that community, she lived with a stigma—even more so than white cops in white neighborhoods, or even black cops in black neighborhoods, for it was felt that white cops and black cops still retained their ethnic ties despite the badge; but *Latinos* were deemed to have abandoned their own when they put on the uniform. Thus, Gloria Mendez had only a scant portion of the neighborhood mourners she would otherwise have had.

Some of the mourners, Kiley assumed, were cops who had known or worked with the dead woman, but none of them were in uniform. Word was probably out that IA had some interest in Gloria, which would have made gun-shy all but the most devoted. And there was no official contingent there from the department. Cops who committed suicide projected a bad image. The same as with Catholics. Until recently, Gloria could not even have been buried in the sacred ground of her own religion. Now the church, if not the department, embraced suicides.

In the front pew Kiley could see Meralda in partial profile, her pretty face looking older under the black lace mantilla that covered her head. Next to her was her father, George Mendez, looking much neater, cleaner, today than he had in the funeral home. The rest of the pew was filled mostly with women, a couple of men, who were all around Gloria's age, and whom Kiley presumed to be sisters possibly, brothers, cousins, whomever the family extended to. Nearby sat some younger mourners, kids around Meralda's age, probably her friends from the neighborhood. A few of the young men wore Latin Princes colors.

Meralda, Kiley saw, was sitting very straight, shoulders squared, looking directly at her mother's now closed casket, controlling her tears as best she could by occasionally dabbing at her eyes with a tissue. Her father was equally as board-still next to her, apparently maintaining what he considered appropriate *macho* decorum in the wake of losing someone he had years ago abandoned. Kiley longed to be able to go to Meralda, sit by her, put an arm around those aligned young shoulders, comfort her in any way he could. But he realized that his presence might not be a comfort; it might be an affront.

The funeral mass seemed to last interminably, and Kiley did not even try to follow it. Before Nick's funeral, he had not been to mass since Tessie's baptism, then Jennie's First Holy Communion; this was only his fourth mass in many years, and he rose, sat, knelt, and responded to prayers by rote rather than with any sense of participation. He was sorry down to the bone that Gloria Mendez was dead, but his sorrow had nothing to do with Catholicism, or heaven and hell, or repentance, or invocations for the dead, or supplications by the living. In the church of his parents and grandparents and all who had come before him, in the presence of Jesus on the cross and Mary, the Blessed Virgin, with holy water dried on his forefinger and his forehead, Joe Kiley sat with malevolence in his heart.

Gloria Mendez had been murdered.

Kiley knew that as certainly as he had known that Tony Touhy was responsible for Nick Bianco's death. Knew it in the face of the same kind of contradictory so-called evidence that was supposed to have deterred him from his pursuit of Tony Touhy. Knew it in spite of the same kind of official report that had tried to put the blame for Nick's death on an unknown person or persons. Knew it deep in his ulcerated gut, in his gin-tainted brain, and in his black Irish soul.

Knew it—and intended to act on it.

When the mass finally did end, Gloria's casket was rolled up the aisle on a bier by its pallbearers, and Meralda, her father, and the other family members, whoever they were, all followed along solemnly behind it. Kiley stood with the other mourners as the procession passed. Meralda glanced at him, his presence registered in her eyes, but her grief-drawn expression did not change. Kiley did not know whether George Mendez saw him or not; the dark, mustachioed man kept his eyes, which to Kiley's surprise were now teary, straight ahead.

As the casket was lifted and carried out to a waiting hearse, Meralda and her father stood at the head of the church aisle and accepted condolences from the mourners now moving up the aisle in a line. Kiley fell in at the very end of the column. Glancing around, he saw that Captain Vander and his men were no longer anywhere to be seen. But they no doubt had the name of every identifiable police officer in attendance—particularly his own.

Presently, Kiley came to Meralda and her father. She reached out to him and Kiley, taking her hands, leaned forward and kissed her on the cheek. Her skin tasted salty to his lips, and she smelled lightly of bath soap and some other subtle fragrance, perhaps the combined scent of the funeral flowers captured in her hair and clothes. After kissing her, Kiley whispered in her ear.

"You were right, Meralda. Your mother did not kill herself. When I find out what really happened, I'll come and tell you. Please don't do anything or say anything until you hear from me."

As he stepped back, Meralda's eyes, and the bullet-hole eyes of her father, were fixed on him unblinkingly.

"Will you swear to me," Meralda asked, "that I can trust you? Swear to me that you will not forget my mother?"

"I will never forget your mother," Kiley replied, a catch coming suddenly to his throat. "And I give you my word that I will make whoever is responsible for her death pay for it."

"Then I believe you," the girl said. "And I thank you, for myself and for my mother."

Kiley took a step past her and extended his hand to George Mendez. "I am very sorry for your loss, Mr. Mendez," he said.

"Thank you," George Menzez replied, swallowing. He shook Kiley's hand. "I appreciate your condolences." Glancing at his daughter, he then added, "Please accept my apology for my conduct at the funeral home. It was inappropriate behavior and I regret it."

"No apology is necessary," Kiley said, prolonging the handshake. "You were under great stress. And I was a stranger to you."

"I appreciate your understanding."

As Kiley was turning to walk away, he caught a glimpse of Meralda slipping an arm around her father's waist. For some reason, it made him feel good. He hoped father and daughter would heal together, helping each other.

Kiley's good feeling lasted only until he reached the back of the church, where cars were parked that were not driving in the procession to the cemetery. Standing next to Kiley's car, obviously waiting for him, were Allan Vander and his IA deputy, Bill Somers. When Kiley walked up to his car, Vander said, "We'd like to talk to you, Detective."

"See me tomorrow," Kiley replied, without even a pretense of respect now. "I'm off duty. I took a vacation day to attend the funeral."

"Off duty or on duty, we still want to talk to you," Vander said firmly.

"I don't have to talk to you when I'm off duty, Vander."

"Look, Kiley," the IA commander snapped, "I can bring you up on charges of gross insubordination any time I want to—and you know it. I can also suspend you—on the spot, right now, and walk away with your badge in my pocket. Do you *want* to be suspended?"

"I don't give a fuck whether you suspend me or not," Kiley faced the IA man directly. "Take my badge and I don't have to talk to you at all. You can talk to my lawyer."

"Joe, calm down," said Bill Somers, who apparently now considered himself the team peacemaker between Kiley and the brass. "Be reasonable, for Christ's sake. All we're asking for is a little cooperation here—"

"Cooperation in what?" Kiley asked.

"We're trying to get a line on why this officer killed herself. We need to know what she was involved in that caused her to take such an extreme measure—"

"What makes you think she was *involved* in anything?" Kiley's voice was demanding now.

"If she was mixed up with you, Kiley, she had to be involved in something," Vander said cuttingly.

"Go fuck yourself, Captain."

Kiley started to get into his car. Vander grabbed his arm and spun him around.

"That's it, Detective! You're suspended!"

Knocking Vander's hand away, Kiley stiff-armed him in the chest, shoving him back. "You cocksucker, don't you put your fucking hands on me!"

"Back off, Joe!" Bill Somers quickly stepped between them—but had the good judgment not to touch Kiley.

"You are fucking suspended, Detective Kiley!" a red-faced Vander stormed. "Turn over your badge or Lieutenant Somers and I will place you under arrest!"

"Captain, we can work this out," Somers said urgently, and for the first time Joe had a fleeting thought that perhaps the deputy IA commander was sincere in his conciliatory efforts.

"No, it *can't* be worked out!" Vander raged at his lieutenant. "I've had enough of this—this—goddamned *renegade*! He's not a police officer, he's a fucking outlaw!" Vander's eyes fastened on Kiley and his lips stretched to thin lines. "Your badge, Detective. *Now*."

Without disengaging from the cold staredown between them, Kiley got out his badge case, unpinned his detective's badge from the leather flap, and without warning tossed it to Vander. He hoped Vander would fumble the unexpected throw, drop the badge on the ground, and have to bend and pick it up. But Vander was quicker, more alert, than Kiley supposed; he snatched the badge out of the air with one hand.

"Now disarm yourself," Vander ordered He could not confiscate Joe's weapon because it was the officer's own personal property, but he could require him to stop carrying it concealed on his person for the duration of Kiley's suspension.

Opening the trunk of his car, Kiley removed the holstered .38 revolver from his belt and placed it inside.

"The backup too," Vander said smugly.

Putting his foot up on the bumper, Kiley raised his trouser leg far enough to unpeel the Velcro of his ankle holster and put it in the trunk also.

"You'll receive formal suspension papers from the department by registered mail," Vander said, his voice beginning to return to normal. "You'll also receive a notice from the civil service commission giving you fifteen days to respond to the charges against you. You may secure private legal counsel if you—"

"I know the drill," Kiley cut in. "Save your breath."

Turning stiffly, Vander walked away, toward an unmarked captain's car parked nearby. Kiley and Bill Somers looked at each other.

"I'm sorry, Kiley," the deputy commander said.

To Kiley, it sounded almost as if he meant it.

An hour later, Kiley guided his Buick around a circular off-ramp from the Edens Expressway at the edge of Skokie, one of the far northern suburbs of Chicago. As soon as he was in light enough traffic, he pulled to the side of the road, opened the trunk, and retrieved both of his guns. Back in the car, he snapped his main service revolver onto his belt, and attached the back-up with its Velcro straps just above his ankle again. He took Nick's badge from his pocket and pinned it in the badge case where his own had been.

Driving down Dempster Street to a small corner shopping center, Kiley parked and walked over to a narrow storefront business that had a single-word sign above the door: GUNS. As he entered, a one-eyed man wearing a black patch looked up from a workbench behind a rear showcase. The man's good eye fluttered briefly until he recognized his customer. Then he rose and came forward, behind another glass showcase that ran the length of the store.

"Kiley, right?" he asked.

"Yeah. Joe Kiley. How are you, Claude?"

"Still punching," said the man with the patch. His name was Claude Emer and he was an ex-cop who had been working the narcotics unit of the Tenth police district seven years earlier when a drug dealer had shot him in the face. The slug had taken out Emer's left eye and destroyed eighty percent of the hearing in his left ear, but miraculously had not damaged his brain before exiting the side of his skull. Pensioned off as disabled, Emer had later opened the little gun shop. His specialty was providing backup weapons and illegal power-loaded ammunition for police officers who didn't give a fuck about rules when it came to defending their lives.

"I seen on the news where the department lost another cop recently," Emer said conversationally.

"Yeah. Nick Bianco. You know him?"

"Not personally. I checked my files and seen where I sold him a piece back in '89. You know him?"

"Yeah," Kiley said. "He was a good cop."

"We're all good cops until some scumbag motherfucker shoots us," Emer replied

Kiley did not bother to tell Emer that Nick had been his partner; there was no reason to. And Emer did not mention the department's more recent loss: Gloria Mendez. There was a difference between being shot to death in an alley, and falling over a bathtub after a meal of booze and pills. The latter was not worth discussing.

"What can I do for you?" Emer asked. When he spoke, he tilted his head to the left to bring his good ear around for better hearing.

"I want a backup piece," Kiley told him. "I want it to be small, *very* small. But I want it to be potent, *very* potent."

Emer studied Kiley for a moment. "You want it strictly for backup, or you want it to kill somebody with? Don't bullshit me now; if you do, I can't help you."

"Probably to kill somebody with," Kiley said.

"Wait a minute—"

The one-eyed man went through a curtained doorway in the back of the store. He was gone only a minute, then returned carrying a black box slightly larger than a VHS videotape. Placing it on the showcase, he opened the box to reveal a small automatic pistol.

"This model is brand new," Emer said. "It's not even on the market yet; only samples have been sold to registered dealers. The manufacturer is Tutweilder Arms down in Florida." He pushed the box toward Kiley. "Go ahead—"

Kiley removed the automatic from its box. It fit comfortably in the palm of his hand without extending beyond it. The metal finish was satin nickel, the grips rubber. It looked almost like a toy.

"Weighs fifteen-point-four ounces," Emer said. "Overall length is six-and-three-quarter inches. Trigger is dot-three-one-one inches. Hammer is completely concealed. All metal parts are highest grade stainless steel. Fires three-eighties. Carries five in the magazine, one in the chamber."

"Power?" Kiley asked. Emer smiled confidently.

"Factory tested with pressure-loaded hydra shock ammunition. Hit a man in the end knuckle of his little finger and you'll knock him on his ass six feet back. Put a single head or chest shot into him and he's an obit."

"You fire it yourself?"

"Same day I got it. Ran half a box through it." Emer took the pistol from Kiley's hand and fingered it like a man might caress a woman's nipple: feather-lightly, lovingly. "Take my word for it, Kiley," he said. "This baby was made to use on your worst enemy."

"Right now," Kiley grunted softly, "I'm not exactly sure who that is." He took the gun back from Emer. "How much?"

"I paid six-fifty for it. Let you have it for eight."

Kiley pulled out his wallet and fished eight hundred-dollar bills from the currency compartment.

# TWENTY-ONE

**W**hen Stella came down from putting the girls to bed—they had gone under duress, more than an hour after their regular bedtime, because they were having so much fun playing "Go Fish" with Joe at the kitchen table; Stella finally had to get firm with them, threatening punishment if they did not take their baths at once—but she got them settled in at last, and when she came back into the kitchen, Joe was still at the table, idly playing Solitaire and, although Stella did not know it, trying to keep his mind off the very dangerous plan he intended to put into motion the next day.

"Christ, they are obstinate at times," Stella complained mildly as she came back in.

"I could have been a little more help, I guess," Joe said. He smiled. "But I was having fun too."

"Big kid," she scolded. She raised both arms to correct a thick strand of hair that had fallen over her cheek. Kiley could not help glancing at the way her breasts lifted under a white cardigan sweater she wore. When he shifted his eyes back to her face, he saw that *her* eyes were on *his* face, and he knew she had caught him looking. He thought he saw a tiny flicker of smile on her lips as he turned back to the cards.

"Enough of these," Stella said, taking the deck from his hand. "Come on—"

She led him through the living room into a smaller room that Nick had called the den: In it was an older couch, a small-screen TV, the stereo unit from which Nick had run speakers to various other rooms, a rack for magazines, shelves for Nick's collection of long-play records, and a cabinet where all the liquor in the house except table wine was kept.

"Pour us a brandy," Stella said. "I'll put on some music. *We* are going to relax, Officer."

"Yes, ma'am," he said obediently.

The record she put on was an old Ahmed Jamal set recorded live at the Pershing Room there in Chicago; it wasn't romantic music by any means, more like light contemporary jazz of the '60s, but the artist's delicate style on his keyboard made the numbers *feel* as if they were being played for couples rather than audiences. Kiley, who had virtually no ear for music, paid no attention to it. He poured brandy into two crystal snifters and handed one to Stella. As he sat on the couch, she dragged over a big cushion and sat cross-legged on it on the floor, leaning back next to his legs. The peasant skirt she wore spread out around her, reminding Kiley of the muumuu Alma Lynn had worn in her backyard.

"You really are so good with the girls, Joe; I shouldn't get too strict with them when they're with you," Stella said, almost apologetically. "But they have to get proper rest; they'd play cards with you until they fell over if I let them."

"I know. You're right, Stel."

"But you are good with kids; I've seen you with Nick's nieces and nephews on the holidays: you *listen* to them when they talk to you, like what they're saying is important. Kids pick up on that." She sipped a little brandy. "I've been telling you for years you should have a family of your own."

"*Telling* me," he scoffed gently. "You've been trying to *arrange* it."

"Oh, I haven't been that bad; you know I haven't." But she would not meet his eyes when she said it, because they both knew that over the years, she *had* been that bad. At times, it seemed that Stella had thought it was a divine mission, getting him married off. "Nick just wanted to see you settled down," she added as an afterthought.

"Don't blame it on Nick," he took light exception. "I know better."

"You just *think* you know," Stella rebutted. "Nick gave a lot of thought to improving your home life, improving your wardrobe—did you ever try on any of those clothes?"

"Yeah, I did. They fit okay. But, Stella, I'm not so sure it's a good idea to wear any of that stuff around the girls. Especially Jennie. I've been thinking that maybe it might upset them."

Stella shrugged. "I told them I planned to give the things to you. They didn't seem to mind. But maybe I should ask them—"

"Ask them?"

"Yeah, because we've been talking about a lot of things, the girls and me, that we never discussed when Nick was here. Like meals, for instance. We plan what *we'd* like for dinner. Before it was always me fixing what Nick wanted. Also, we discuss what to watch on TV. We've been watching lots of nature programs, wildlife, stuff like that—"

"Nick watched wildlife shows: the Cubs, the Bears —"

"Yeah, very funny. You guys and your sports. We girls," she said with mock loftiness, "prefer educational programming."

"If you three turn into intellectuals on me, I'm not coming around any-more," Joe threatened. "And I'll tell Tessie that it's your fault for watching animal shows."

"Please don't do *that*. You know Tessie would defend you with her life. I promise we'll go back to watching trash." Stella leaned her head against his knee. "Seriously, Joe, are you ever going to settle down?"

"I think I'm about ready to right now," he said. "As soon as I clear up a couple of matters."

"About Nick?"

"Yeah."

"Joe," she turned, facing him, "I hope you're not thinking of doing anything—that might get you in more trouble—or put you in danger of any kind. I want to see whoever killed Nick get punished for it, but not at the expense of—well, another loss. Do you understand what I'm saying?"

"I understand." He sipped some brandy. Her hand was on his knee now, and he reached out with his own to cover it. "But there's something you have to understand too—"

"Don't try to make me understand anything, Joe," she cut off his words. "I had enough of that when Nick was alive; he was always trying to get me to see something his way. There are times, you know, when a woman, like a kid, just wants to be listened to, just wants to talk without being convinced of something—"

"I listen to you, Stel. And I wasn't going to try and convince you of any-thing," he said quietly.

"I lost so much when I lost Nick," she said, staring into space. "I lost a husband, a father for my children, a friend—" she paused a bare beat, "and my lover." She reached past him to set her glass on the end table, and put both hands on his thigh now, leaning her cheek on his knee. "I don't want to lose anything else, Joe. I don't want to do *without* anything else. I'm not used to doing without—"

Kiley put a hand on her head and gently stroked her thickly layered hair—hair that he had almost venerated over the years, he thought it was so lovely; now, for the first time, he was actually touching it.

"If I had my way, Stel, you'd never do without anything," he said softly to her, the words not coming easy.

"Joe, can I tell you a secret?"

"Sure."

"It's a personal secret. You have to promise you won't laugh at me."

"You know I wouldn't laugh at you."

"And you have to promise you won't think less of me for it—"

"Nothing would make me think less of you."

"All right." She swallowed, getting ready for what she would say. "You know all those times I tried to fix you up with women? Well, they naturally used to ask me things about you, and I used to talk about you a lot. Sometimes, Joe, when I was talking about you to those other women, I used to think about you myself. I mean, *for* myself." She looked down, embarrassed. "I used to wonder how it would be to—well, you know, be *with* you." Now she looked back up, mortified. "My God, I can't believe I said that." Quickly she reached for her glass and drank a swallow of brandy. "I guess you must think I'm awful—"

"You know I don't think that." Kiley leaned forward a little, and when he did it seemed to move the hand that was still on his thigh slightly higher. "I'll tell you the same thing you told me last week when I broke down and cried over Nick: You're just human, Stella, like the rest of us. Don't you think I've had thoughts about you over the years?"

"I wondered about it—"

"Well, stop wondering. I did have. So often that right now I couldn't even guess how many times." He sat back, drinking some brandy; the hand on his thigh did not shift downward.

"Tell me what you thought, Joe," she asked, barely above a whisper. "Tell me what your thoughts about me were."

"You know what they were."

"I want you to tell me," she said. There was something in her voice that made him decide that it was important to her. "I want to hear you say it, Joey—"

Resting his head back, closing his eyes, Kiley said, "I used to think about you in a black slip with nothing on under it. I used to think about your lips, about kissing you, about you kissing me. And picture you wiggling out of the slip, pulling it up over your head. I used to wonder how much hair you had between your legs, whether it was a little or a lot—"

He got an erection, very quickly, and knew Stella could see it happening, just inches from where her hands rested. Then he felt her hand leave his thigh, felt her body shift away from him, and opened his eyes to see her go over and lock the den door. When she came back, she sat next to him on the couch. He put his arm around her and she casually rested one hand on the swelling inside his trousers.

"You aren't going to think I'm a slut, are you, Joey?"

"Don't be ridiculous—"

Kiley drew her gently to him and experienced with her subtly curved, slightly parted lips what he had been doing in his mind for so long: kissed Stella very lightly, very tenderly, as if to do it more passionately might somehow eradicate the reality of the moment and reduce it to fantasy again. It was finally Stella who began to press her lips to his with more intensity, more energy. Kiley moved a hand to the buttons of her cardigan and opened it partway down the front, enough to reach one of her breasts, which was not hampered by a bra; the size and roundness of it surprised him, because in his hand it felt much larger than it seemed in the scores of surreptitious glances he had recorded. The breast, her left, felt buoyant, strong, tightening eagerly to his touch, its nipple swelling out as if vacuum pumped.

"Don't think bad of me, Joey," she said, drawing her lips back just far enough to speak.

"I couldn't—"

"I'm not used to doing without—"

"I know. It's all right—"

Abruptly, Stella stood and removed the cardigan all the way, leaving herself magnificently erotic in black slacks and light olive flesh. Taking Joe's hands, she urged him to his feet and unbuttoned his shirt, enlisting his help to remove it and pull his undershirt over his head. Both naked from the waist up then, they embraced and kissed with passion now unbound, unrepressed by anything past or present: there was no unresolved murder of Nick, no mourning, no girls sleeping innocently upstairs, no job suspension, no family pressures from the Biancos—none of it mattered: not to Stella, because her need was too demanding; not to Joe because all of his long repressed hunger for this woman was driving him now like a powerful amphetamine injected directly into his bloodstream, engulfing his mind as that blood further engorged his manhood.

In another abrupt move, Stella uncoupled from him and stepped back far enough to continue undressing, and without hesitation Kiley did the same. Stella had only to kick off her loafers, step out of her slacks, and peel off the black panties she wore. Kiley watched her look at his erection as he dropped his briefs and raised first one foot, then the other, to remove his socks. And Stella watched Joe as his eyes followed her hand down to what was a mere shadow of hair.

"I have a lot," she said, "but I keep it trimmed close—"

Taking Joe's hands, she backed onto the couch and guided him to his knees between her spread legs.

"Kiss me, Joey—down there—"

They did not make love long. Stella's emotions were so pent-up that the pressure for release could not be contained. She was not practiced at prolonging anything; once she got going, it was unrepressed feeling, unimpeded motion—she was raw, unrefined, totally uninhibited, not a wife, a widow, a mother, nothing except a woman: functioning as such, thriving on her femaleness, not making love or anything like it. Stella was copulating, and that was all.

For Joe, it was not a question of holding back, trying to prolong; whether he wanted to draw out the length of their act did not matter. So fierce and frenetic was this woman he had secretly loved all those years, he could not have checked the natural progress of his excitement even if he had wanted to. Stella was like a savage who could not stop or even slow down until she had been seized by orgasm as many times as possible before leaving Joe drained and slack.

Afterward, dressed, they sat shoulder to shoulder on the couch and finished the brandy they had interrupted. Stella was as limp after the act as Joe was, and they felt softly tired, warmly relieved.

"I think I'd have gone crazy tonight if we hadn't done it," Stella said.

"Me too," Joe told her.

"I kept telling myself Nick hasn't been gone all that long—"

"I know. That's been on my mind too. But I couldn't help thinking about you—" Kiley turned sideways to face her, pulling one knee up on the couch. "Stella, what I was trying to tell you earlier, about having a couple of matters about Nick to clear up: I want you to understand that they're very important to me. I know there's been some talk from Nick's relatives, especially Gino, about me not being there when Nick was killed—and then some remarks about how much attention I've been paying to you since. Like maybe I didn't care that Nick was gone—"

"Joe," she turned and touched his lips with her fingers, "you don't have to go into all that—"

"I want to go into it, Stel," he insisted. "It's important to me that no matter what anyone else thinks or says, that *you* know how things really are.

Even the way I feel about you right now, I'd still do anything in the world to bring Nick back, give him back to you and the girls, make everything like it was before. I can't do that, but what I *can* do is get the bastard that killed him—and I intend to do that, no matter what. I couldn't bring my-self to ask you to make a life with me unless I had set that matter straight."

Stella frowned. "Make a life with you?"

"Sure. You and me and the girls. That's what this is all about." Now it was Kiley who frowned, sensing something between them of which he was not aware. "*Isn't* that what it's all about?" he asked. There was the barest note of plaintiveness in his voice.

"Are you talking about you and me getting married?" Stella asked. No uncertainty at all in her tone.

"Yeah. Sure. I thought—"

"Joe, I'm going to marry Nick's cousin, Frank."

"You're w-what?"

"I already decided that. I haven't told him, of course, and won't for a while, until I think it's the right time. But that's what I'm going to do."

Stella could see that Joe was stunned by the news. He had turned sickly pale and his lips were parted in numbed surprise. She took one of his hands.

"It's for the best, Joe. He's Italian, I'm Italian, the girls are Italian. The family name will stay the same. It'll be better all around, believe me. And I think Nick would approve. Oh, I know he thought Frank was an asshole, but you know as well as I do that Nick felt that way about *most* people— just like you do. When I say I think Nick would approve, I mean approve in general: you know, we're the same blood, we've got the same family name, we're all Catholic—"

"I'm Catholic too," Joe said lamely.

"Jo-*ey*," she derided mildly, "you have to be dragged to church—and even then it has to be some special occasion, like a First Holy Communion or something for the girls. Frank goes to mass every Sunday with his par-ents, and he'll continue to do that with us, as a family, after he and I are married. I need somebody to set a good example for the girls—"

"And you think *Frank* is the person to do it?" Joe asked, pulling his hand away from hers. There was incredulity in his voice as some of the concus-sion of her announcement began to dissolve into less jarring dismay.

"Yes, I do, Joe." Slightly defensive now. "I know Frank is considered pretty much of a flake—I mean, I'm not stupid and I'm not blind. But Uncle Gino says it's because Frank never had the *chance* to be anything else. Uncle Gino feels that with a wife, kids, a home, family responsibilities, that Frank will become much more of a man than he is now. And Uncle Gino has promised to give him all the help he needs; he says he'll make Frank a partner in his used-car business, and that he'll include Jennie and Tessie equally in his will with his own grandchildren—"

"Have you told Gino that you've made up your mind?" Joe asked. He was fairly certain that she hadn't, otherwise Gino and Frank would not have tried to lean on him the day he got back from Indiana.

"I haven't told anyone," Stella confirmed, "except you." Reverting back to her more sensitive self, Stella took his hand again. "Joe, the last thing in the world I'd ever do is intentionally hurt you, I hope you believe that. You know I care for you, my girls care for you, Nick loved you like a brother—"

"Is that how you love me, Stella? Like a brother?"

She stared piteously at him for a brief moment, then nodded her head. "Yes, Joey, it is."

The revelation of her intent to marry Frank had been like a kick in the balls to him; this admission of her real feeling toward him, a *brotherly* feeling, was almost like being felt sorry for, being consoled, as if Stella were trying to treat him kindly. None of it made any sense to him.

"What we just did together," he said, imploring for some understanding of what was happening, "didn't that mean anything?"

"It was just—just physical—" she struggled for words, the confusion of their communication now settling upon her also.

"But didn't it *mean* something?" Kiley persisted. Once again he removed his hand from hers. "Wasn't there any *feeling* there? Jesus Christ, Stella, that wasn't Frank inside you! You were fucking *me!*"

"Please keep your voice down," Stella said evenly, glancing upward where her daughters slept. "I know who I was fucking, Joe. I also know *why.* I thought I made it clear to you that I just—*needed* it—"

"You mean it didn't make any difference *who?* All you needed was a stiff dick?"

"Joe, please," she said, rising, moving a few steps away. "That's not true. I needed more than a cock. I needed somebody that I cared for, somebody that cared for me—and I don't mean somebody who was in love with me—it never occurred to me that you felt that deeply, Joe, I swear to God it didn't. I just wanted somebody that I could feel *close* to, with every part of me; somebody that I didn't have to hold anything back from; I wanted it to be like it had been with Nicky and me—"

"Do you expect to have that with Frank?"

"No, not at all. With Frank it'll be more like it used to be in the Old Country, for convenience, for the family's sake—"

"But you intend to fuck him, right?"

"Of course, I do. I'll do for Frank everything a wife is supposed to do. But I don't expect it to be like it was with Nick." She glanced down. "Or tonight with you."

"Then *why*?" Kiley sat forward pleadingly. "Why are you going to marry him?"

"Because that's not all there is to it, Joe!" she snapped. "Married people don't just *fuck*. They live together! They eat meals together, go to mass together, have family holidays together, raise kids together. I need somebody who fits into that picture, Joe. Not someone who's tough and cynical and ruthless and—*different*."

"If that's the way you feel about me," Kiley asked in confusion, "why were you always trying to get me involved with women to marry, talking about how I should have a family of my own, saying how wonderful I am with kids—?"

"Because I think you *are*. Because you might make a very good husband and father in the right circumstances," Stella explained, "married to the right woman."

"But you're not that woman?"

"No, Joey, I'm not—"

"Quit calling me 'Joey,' for Christ's sake, will you?" he suddenly railed. "That's what my mother called me." A thought of Meralda Mendez telling him that same thing flashed through his mind.

"I'm sorry—" Stella apologized. "I've been calling you that for so long—"

Kiley rose and paced the room like a nervous jungle animal sensing danger but not knowing what to do about it. He was caught up in an evening that was at once the most wonderful and the most terrible of his life. The lovemaking with Stella—and that was how he thought of it, as *lovemaking*—had been incredible, the most marvelous moments he had ever experienced, even in his fantasies about her. But the announcement of Stella's intention with respect to Frank Bianco had plunged him into the blackest pit of disbelief and despair that he could imagine. It was that pit that he was trying desperately to get out of. After pacing the length of the room several times, he abruptly stopped and faced Stella.

"I think," he told her quietly, "that I'd better go. I've got some heavy rethinking to do, and I can't do it when I'm with you."

He started for the door. Stella hurried after him.

"Joe, wait, listen—please—"

Kiley kept walking, out of the den, through the living room to the foyer, the front door.

"Joe, *please*," Stella implored, "don't walk out feeling like that—"

"I feel the way I feel," he said.

"Joe, I'm sorry—maybe what we did tonight was wrong, but I thought it would be good for both of us—I didn't mean to hurt you—"

Kiley stopped and faced her at the front door.

"I'm not *blaming* you for anything, Stella. I'm not saying anything's your *fault.* But you can't expect me to *like* it. You can't expect me not to feel like shit about it. We've been talking about both of us just being human like everybody else; well, I *am.* Sure, I'm cynical and ruthless and whatever else you said, but I'm human too. I can't help feeling like shit when life turns out to *be* shit. And that's what happened tonight."

"You're not just going to drop out of our lives, are you, the girls and mine?" Stella asked, beginning to weep. "Please don't do that—"

"Do you think Frank will allow it to be any other way?" Kiley asked bluntly.

"Frank's a reasonable man. He knows you've been a friend—"

"You're kidding yourself, Stella," he cut in, using without being aware of it the same tone he used with suspects. "Frank is a lowlife prick who's going to make your life miserable. And there's no way I'll be able to be your friend or help you in any way after you marry him. He'll be your *husband*, Stella. He'll be in *charge* of you, the girls, this house, your insurance money—everything." Kiley stared at her for a moment, and now it was he who had pity in his expression for her. "I feel sorry for you, Stella," he said in a much softer tone, "because you don't realize what you're doing."

Turning from her, he left the house and strode rapidly out to his car.

As he drove back into the city, Kiley could not help thinking that his miserable luck was running true to form. Of all the times for something like this to take place, it had to happen on a night that he badly needed to be stress-free and untroubled.

The night before he might have to kill Fraz Lamont.

# TWENTY-TWO

The next day, just at noon, Kiley guided his car to the curb on Division Street in the heart of one of the city's most heavily populated, most crime-ridden, and most dangerous black communities. He knew as he parked that a dozen pairs of eyes were already watching him from fixed, unfriendly black faces. It was extremely rare to see a lone white person of any age or sex in this area. Policemen, of any color but especially white or Hispanic, usually traveled along D-Street, as it was called, in teams of three rather than the normal two. Even the lowest white hookers did not venture onto D-Street. It was the tightest members-only street in Chicago—and the membership card was color.

Getting out of the car, Kiley locked it as three black adolescents, one of them wearing purple-and-black Disciple colors, watched him from in front of a take-out chicken wings shop where they were loitering. Before walking away from his car, Kiley went over to them and spoke to the one wearing colors.

"I'm on my way in to see Fraz Lamont," he said matter-of-factly. "When I come out, if I find my car fucked up, I'm going back in and tell Fraz that one of his Disciples is responsible for it. And I'm going to give him a description of you. I'm very good at descriptions because I'm a cop. So if my car gets fucked up, you get fucked up." He gave them a tight smile. "Have a nice day."

When traffic along Division thinned enough, Kiley walked across it to what had once been an area movie theater of the long defunct Balaban-and-Katz chain. With their flagship *Chicago Theater*, an ornate Loop palace offering films and top stage shows, and its sister giant across the street, the *State-Lake*, the chain had upper-class movie houses all over the city, and before the advent of television was considered the prime source of reasonably priced family entertainment in Chicago. As television expanded and

**239**

moviegoing decreased, B&K had gradually shifted its concentration to its larger first-run theaters, and closed its smaller houses. One of those closed was the *Cortez Theater*. It was now owned by, and the main headquarters of, Fraz Lamont and the feared Disciples street gang.

The old theater's box office was still in place, a cell-like structure, shaded by the marquee, standing back off the sidewalk on a chipped and faded tile foyer. An unsmiling young black man, wearing Disciple colors, sat in the booth, eyeing Kiley cautiously through the surrounding glass window as he approached. Kiley held Nick's badge up for him to see.

"Tell Fraz Lamont that Detective Joseph Kiley is here to see him."

The young man looked incredulous. "Yo, man, are you serious?" he asked disdainfully. "President Fraz don't talk to no motherfucking white *po*-lice."

"That's not for you to decide," Kiley said. "All you are is a fucking lookout." Kiley bobbed his chin at a telephone in the ticket booth. "Stop trying to be important, and don't pretend you're smart enough to make decisions. Just pick up the fucking phone and tell somebody I'm on my way in."

Kiley walked past the booth toward the door to the lobby.

"Hey, sucker, you can't go in there—!" the young man in the booth shouted. But he did not come out of the booth and try to stop Kiley, and when Kiley glanced back he saw the lookout quickly grab up the phone.

There were three sets of four doors leading into the lobby, glass doors that were now painted black, with brass handles corroded green from the grip of many hands. Kiley tried six doors before finding one unlocked. As he stepped through it onto badly worn carpet with a barely discernible Aztec design, he found the wide lobby deserted and dead looking, its poster windows empty, an old candy counter dusty and deserted, an outdated water fountain rusted over. A happy place that had died, Kiley thought. Then become occupied by snakes.

Four of those snakes were suddenly rushing toward him, as if he might be a substantial and immediate threat to them. They were a blur of purple and black as they rushed him. Kiley froze and held up both hands, palms out, the badge in one of them.

"I've got business with Fraz!" he announced loudly. "Better tell him I'm here—!"

In an instant the four Disciples had surrounded him, one on each side, holding him by his upper arms, one behind him with fingers gripping the back of his neck, the fourth man, flat-nosed with a block forehead, right in Kiley's face. Kiley had to steel himself not to knee the latter hard in the balls to back him off.

"Motherfucker, who the fuck *are* you?" the man in his face asked angrily. Saliva hit Kiley's chin when the man spoke, and Kiley had to steel himself even more.

"I'm a cop and I've got important business with Fraz—"

"*President* Fraz, motherfucker!" the man said angrily. He snatched the badge case from Kiley's hand and cursorily examined it. "Doughboy, what the fuck is the matter with you?" he demanded. "You can't just walk in here like this is the public fucking library! You askin' to disappear off the face of the fucking earth!"

"I'm *asking*," Kiley replied, "to see Fraz Lamont—"

"*President* Fraz Lamont, motherfucker!"

"President Fraz Lamont," Kiley complied. Anything to get past this retarded cocksucker, he thought.

"President Fraz don't talk to no fucking cops, man—"

"Why don't you just *ask* President Fraz if he's not a little curious why one white cop would walk in here all alone?" Kiley said. "See if he thinks maybe I've got something important to say."

"What kind of shit you talking, motherfucker?" the man in Kiley's face demanded.

"I'll tell President Fraz all about it. Nobody else."

"President Fraz ain't talking to you, man!"

"Okay," Kiley said, "then I'll leave. Whatever happens to him can be your responsibility. Tell these assholes to let go of me—"

"They are *Disciples!*"

"Whatever," Kiley said with an edge, the patience he girded himself with now ebbing, instinctive anger beginning to ooze through him. He did not like to be touched, and he certainly did not like the black man's breath and saliva in his face. A thought flashed through his mind: when they released him, drawing both his guns and opening up on them, killing all four, then wasting the guy in the ticket booth as he ran to his car, maybe even throwing a few rounds at the dudes on the street; then getting the hell out of the neighborhood as fast as he could. Going right to the Shop and making a report. Saying he went there investigating Nick's killing—wouldn't the brass fucking love *that*—and the Disciples tried to hold him against his will, kidnap him. Even if he went to trial, he'd be acquitted. No jury would send him over for killing street scum like the Disciples, not even an all-black jury.

"Tell your Disciples to let me go and I'll leave," Kiley acquiesced. "Whatever happens to President Fraz will be on your head," he emphasized.

"What the fuck's all the racket out here?" a new voice entered the fray. A black man of medium height but with a weightlifter's upper body, came across the lobby, walking very erect, expression stern, hair roped in dreadlocks. He wore sharply creased black slacks and a purple silk shirt, the sleeves rolled up over melon-sized biceps. "Who the fuck is this honky?" he demanded.

"He a cop, Regent Lennox," Kiley's interrogator told him. "He say he got to see President Fraz. The motherfucker crazy."

The newcomer nudged Kiley's interrogator aside. "Let me handle this, Otis." He did not get as close to Kiley, and his manner was far less aggressive. "My name is Lennox; I am one of President Fraz's administrative regents. Why do you want to see President Fraz?"

"I have something to tell President Fraz," Kiley replied. "Something he will definitely want to know."

"Something that is in his interest?" Regent Lennox asked. "Something that might help him in some way?"

"Yes."

Regent Lennox smiled slyly. "Then why do you want to tell him? Why would a white policeman want to help the president of the Disciples?"

"In exchange for something," Kiley replied "Something I want President Fraz to tell *me*."

"Which is?"

Kiley shook his head. "This has to be between President Fraz and me. If he wants to tell you, that's his business."

Regent Lennox pursed his lips and thought about it for a moment. Then he nodded at the three men restraining Kiley. "Turn him loose." To Kiley, "Sit over there and wait," he indicated an old velvet couch left over from the lobby's better days. To Otis, Regent Lennox said, "You and your men stay with him."

"I want my badge back," Kiley said. At a nod from Lennox, Otis handed Kiley the badge case. Kiley stepped over to sit where he had been told, and Regent Lennox left the lobby.

"Jive-ass honky motherfucker," Otis muttered to his men.

As Kiley waited, he reflected on why he was there. It was no longer to pave the way toward any kind of relationship with Stella Bianco, that much seemed obvious to him. Stella had totaled him on that plan the previous evening. He still could not get over the absurdity of her decision to marry

Frank Bianco. Apparently—and this was the *only* thing that made any sense to him—she had no idea of what a total, complete, absolute, and utter world-class *nothing* the son of a bitch was. Frank Bianco was consummately different from the way Nick had been; he was low-class, crude, uncouth, vulgar. Kiley had never been in a poolroom, hung out on a street corner, participated in a back-room card or dice game, or done anything else of that nature before he became a policeman, that there hadn't been some guy exactly like Frank Bianco somewhere on the fringes.

Even though things seemed to be over as far as a future with Stella, however, Kiley was still going ahead with his plan for extracting revenge for Nick's killing. Stella aside, the department aside, his own entire future aside, he was going to *get* Nick's killer—to that he was committed. And now, he had even greater motivation for doing it, because now there was the death of Gloria Mendez to add to his reasoning. Gloria *had* been murdered, of that he had no doubt; he just didn't know why, or how it was connected to Nick's killing. There were so many loose ends, Fraz Lamont being one of them—

Kiley looked up as Regent Lennox strode back into the lobby.

"President Fraz will see you—what did you say your name was?"

"Detective Joseph Kiley."

"All right, Detective Kiley. Are you strapped?"

"Yes."

"Give your gun to Otis—"

Otis stepped forward, scowling, hateful. Kiley handed over his service revolver, then without being told bent down and got his backup revolver.

"Two-gun honky motherfucker," Otis muttered.

"Pat him down," Regent Lennox said.

Otis gave the guns to another Disciple and Kiley raised his arms for the search. As Otis ran his hands over Kiley's back and sides, Kiley said, "Don't forget to feel my dick and balls. I want you to enjoy yourself—"

"You motherfucker—!" Otis growled, grabbing Kiley's coat lapels.

"Just pat him down, goddamn it!" Regent Lennox ordered. "President Fraz is waiting on him!"

Surlily, Otis resumed his search, stooping to run his hands up and down Kiley's legs, making sure he stayed well away from the genital area. Finally he said to Lennox, "The motherfucker's clean."

"All right, come with me," Lennox said, gesturing to Kiley.

Regent Lennox led Kiley from the lobby into what had once been the seating area of the old movie house. The floor, Kiley saw, which had originally been inclined to accommodate theater seats, had been overlaid with a new wooden surface which was level all the way to the front. Along both walls were desks, chairs, cabinets, cots, with perhaps two dozen purple-and-black-clad young men, and even a sprinkling of young black women, working at some task or loitering about. Although the movie screen was no longer there, the stage was still in place, with several steps leading up to it on each side. On the stage, a wall had been constructed to separate the auditorium from the backstage area. On that wall were photographs of Disciple members, headlines cut from *Sun-Times* and *Tribune* stories about the gang, and posters of printed slogans pertaining to other gangs: **VICE LORDS SUCK!** *LATIN PRINCES BEWARE!* Cobras Kiss *Whitey's Ass!*—and some praising their own: **FRAZ is the MAN!** *Disciples Rule!* **BIG-D IS IT!**

A door led behind the wall and when Kiley stepped through it he realized at once that he was no longer on wooden flooring but now on plush carpeting. He was in a reception room of sorts: there were two plush brocaded couches of African design, as well as several matching club chairs, all arranged around three walls which faced an inner set of double doors. On each side of those doors stood an oversize Disciple wearing an oversize handgun in a black shoulder holster strapped over the purple silk shirt. Besides the door sentries, there were half a dozen other Disciples in the room, all dressed in some combination of the colors, all apparently waiting for an audience with President Frazier Leroy Lamont, founder and undisputed leader of the organization, and—if the Street Gangs Intelligence Unit was to be believed—cold-blooded killer of at least seventeen people.

As Regent Lennox strode toward the doors, each of the sentries reached out to open them for him, and he led Kiley past the guards' threatening looks and the surprised scowls of the waiting Disciples, into an inner room that was as wide as the old theater and half as deep: a room decorated in purple and black but somehow not as dark as one might imagine because interspersed in those colors were African tribal patterns in white, yellow, orange, ocher, and lime. One end of the room was furnished as an office, the other as a bedroom; between them was a conference area with seating for a dozen, and in back of that a gleaming kitchen alcove with a bar. On a part of one wall were framed enlargements of Malcolm X, Angela Davis, Muhammad Ali, and others that Kiley recognized, as well as photographs of George Jackson, Paul Robeson, Jack Johnson, and many more whose faces he did not know. Directly in front of the photograph wall, at a conference table on which was stacked several ledgers, sat the thirty-year-old black man who ruled more than two thousand dedicated followers, and through them tens of thousands of others in the Cabrini Green housing project and its surrounding area.

Fraz Lamont was a color that had once been called "high yellow," later referred to as *café au lait*. In his facial makeup were none of the Negroid features once characteristically attributed to his race: no wide, flat nose, no big lips, no nappy hair. Fraz was an exemplar of the upscale late twentieth-century black man who wished he were white: straight nose, thin line of lip, processed hair; he was black, but not really that *color*. A precise enunciator of words, Fraz did not feel it necessary to lace his language with "motherfucker" when addressing males, "bitch" when talking to women. Unknown to most of his followers, as well as the public, he had spent some thirty thousand dollars having his teeth straightened, replaced where necessary, and porcelain covered by a white orthodontist, which accounted for a brilliant smile responsible for the recruitment of most of the young female Disciples. A man who could, had he so chosen, have had a harem of women at his disposal, Fraz Lamont was faithful to and kept only one, who lived on a suburban country estate with the couple's three daughters and infant son. The woman was white, the children mulatto.

When Fraz Lamont looked up from one of the ledgers which was open on the table before him, he did not display for Joe Kiley his trademark smile. Instead, he studied him briefly as Regent Lennox said, "His name is Joseph Kiley, President."

"What's your assignment?" Fraz asked without preliminary.

"Bomb-and-Arson Squad," Kiley said.

Amused eyes looked at Lennox. "We haven't bombed or burned anything lately, have we, Regent?"

"Not lately, President," replied Lennox.

"I don't see where we really have anything to talk about, Mr. Kiley."

"I think we do," said Kiley. "I think we can talk about the murder of Detective Nick Bianco behind the Shamrock Club down on Lawrence Avenue."

The expression of the Disciples leader did not recast in any way, but his eyes shifted to Lennox. "Did you check our visitor for a wire, Regent?"

"He was, uh—patted down—"

"But was he checked for a *wire*?" An edge of irritation surfaced.

"I'm not wired," Kiley said. He removed his suit coat and draped it over a chair, then held his arms up. "Go on, check it out," he said to both of them. "I'll strip down for you if you want me to."

A quick examination of Kiley's upper body under his shirt by Lennox revealed no wires above the waist, where a mini-microphone would have had to be for clear voice reception.

"I'm here to talk business with you, to make a deal, not to burn you," Kiley said. He left his coat over the back of the chair, and without being asked sat down around the corner of the table from Fraz. "What do you say we stop the bullshit?"

A moment of contemplation by the Disciples leader, then he motioned Regent Lennox into a chair around the other corner of the table, and said, "All right, what is it you have to offer?"

"Information that you are going to be framed for Detective Bianco's killing."

"That's absurd," Fraz said. "I didn't even know the man, had nothing to do with him."

"You were there when he was killed," Kiley asserted. "You drove there," he took a slip of paper from his shirt pocket, "in your Corvette Custom Eleven, license number 67RY410. I can tell you what time you got there, what time you left, and what they're going to say happened in order to nail you for the killing."

"*You*," Fraz pointed, "are a crazy man." After a pause, he added, "But you're a crazy man with some interesting information. And I would like to know how you got that information. On my car, for instance. Everything on record about me is supposed to be—" He stopped mid-sentence, apparently realizing that he was saying the wrong thing.

"Accessible to the Street Gangs Unit only," Kiley finished the statement for him. "But how do you know that?"

Fraz smiled. "Friends in high places. I can find out five minutes after you leave how you got the information on my car, Mr. Detective."

"Maybe so. But you won't find out how you're going to be framed for murder unless you deal with me."

Fraz sat back in his chair and seemed to silently appraise Kiley. "If I 'deal' with you, as you put it, what will you ask in return?"

"I want to know exactly how Nick Bianco came to be killed. I want to know why. And I want to know who had a hand in it."

"Tall order," Fraz said.

"Small price," Kiley countered, "considering the fact that it could keep you from being charged with Nick's murder."

"I'd never be convicted," Fraz said confidently.

"I don't think you would either," Kiley candidly agreed. "But you'd be arrested, locked up, held in jail without bail, and you'd have to stand trial. You'd be out of commission for at least a year, probably more. What would happen to the Disciples during that time?"

"I would still run it, with the help of my regents, from jail. It's been done before. Gabriel Morales ran *La Familia* from Stateville for six years."

"Gabe Morales was killed by his own lieutenants a year after he was released, too. Of course, he only had lieutenants; you have 'regents.' They're probably more trustworthy."

Fraz's expression hardened a little. "Don't try to handle me, Detective. It won't work."

"I'm not trying to handle you. You brought up Morales, not me. Maybe your people are a hundred percent loyal: I don't know and I don't care. All I'm saying to you is that the department is going to eventually have to nail somebody for Bianco's killing—and it's not going to be Tony Touhy."

Fraz's face remained stoic, but a quick fluttering of his eyelids registered the surprise of Kiley's statement. "Well," he said, after a quiet sigh, "you do seem to know what you're talking about."

"I know just about everything I need to know," Kiley said. "All I want from you are some specific details to flesh out the picture."

"And if I give you those details, you'll give me information on certain people who are planning to frame me for the crime?"

"Exactly."

"You'll give me names?"

"Yes."

"And tell me how they plan to do it?"

"Yes."

Indecisive fingers drummed on the tabletop. "Even if I should listen to your story," Fraz asked, "why should I believe it?"

"Because you're too smart not to," Kiley told him. "Just like I'm too smart not to believe that *you* had nothing to do with Bianco's murder— which I'm sure you're going to tell me. I *have* to believe that if I'm going to believe the rest of what you say."

Fraz exchanged quick glances with Regent Lennox before smiling slightly at Kiley. "I've got to admit, Detective, I am impressed by your analysis of everything. But the one thing you haven't told me is why all the concern on your part about Bianco? Was he a relative or something?"

"We were partners for eight years."

"Oh," Fraz said knowingly, a quick, cynical look passing over his face, "one of those white cop partnership things. I've heard they run pretty deep sometimes."

"You heard right," Kiley said, a slight ripple of anger again rising. "And not just with white cops, with black cops too. And Latinos. And Asians."

"The brotherhood of the badge," Fraz said, his tone implying that he thought it was irrational, even trivial, to feel a sense of fidelity that strongly. "Is that really what this is all about, Detective?"

"That's it," Kiley assured. "It might not seem like much to you, but it's important to me—because if the department doesn't get my partner's killer, I intend to."

Fraz stared solemnly at him for a moment. "You know something, Detective: I believe you. I truly believe you." Sitting forward, folding his hands on the table, he said, "You have a deal. Ask your questions."

Kiley shifted in the chair and reached to his coat hanging behind him for his spiral notebook. Opening it, he poised with his ballpoint pen to write.

"Who was at the Shamrock when Nick was killed?"

"Augie Dellafranco," Fraz said, as he began ticking off names on his fingers. "Al Morelli. Larry Morowski. Mickey O'Shea, Jocko Hennessey. Tony Touhy and Phil Touhy." He paused a beat, then added, "And me."

So, Kiley thought, big brother Phil was there too. All that charming Irish song-and-dance Phil had given him in their private discussion in the stairwell at the Shop, that had been just so much blarney bullshit, one shanty Irishman trying to fool another shanty Irishman. Fast on his feet, that was Phil Touhy. But not fast enough. Not this time.

"Who killed Nick?" Kiley asked.

"Tony. But it was Phil's idea." Fraz smiled. "Tony had never killed anybody before; Phil wanted him to make his bones. You know how those mob types are: Reputation is a way of life."

"But the others were there when it happened—Dellafranco, Morelli, the rest?"

"Right."

"Anybody else?"

"Just me—like I said."

"Where was Nick killed?"

"In the club. An office in the back, just off the alley. He walked in right after Tony got there; the back door was usually left unlocked until everybody arrived, then somebody would go lock it. We didn't have time that night." Fraz looked away from Kiley for a moment, contemplating. Then he said, "I want you to understand something, Detective: I wasn't there when your partner was killed because I *wanted* to be. This thing went down as we were getting ready to have a business meeting. I was there for the meeting. Been up to me alone, the cop would never have been wasted. I don't believe in unnecessary killing—and I definitely don't advocate killing policemen. Been my call, I would have had him roughed up and thrown out into the alley, that's all. I mean, he didn't *have* anything on us: None of us were even strapped that night, so he couldn't even get us for carrying. Wasn't no reason to kill the man."

"If none of you were strapped," Kiley asked, "where'd Tony get the piece to shoot Nick?"

Frowning, pursing his lips, Fraz said, "Let me see now—I'm not sure of that; maybe somebody went down to the bar and got one—"

"Did Phil and Tony come to the meeting together?"

"No. I think Phil came in with Hennessey. I know Tony came alone, in his Jag. He was the last one to get there. Phil was a little pissed that he was late. He was trying to groom Tony to take on more responsibility, but Tony just didn't have it. When it came to business, he never had both oars in the water at the same time. All he thought about was gash. Some of the people at the meeting didn't even think he ought to be there."

"Why were *you* there?" Kiley asked bluntly. Fraz's eyes narrowed.

"You're getting a little off the subject, aren't you, Detective? The reason for the meeting had nothing to do with why your partner was offed."

"Oh?" Kiley challenged. "If there was nothing he could arrest you for, and you yourself said there was no *reason* to kill him, then why was he killed?"

"Maybe," Fraz replied carefully, measuring his words now, "he *thought* he could arrest us for something—I don't know, maybe he overheard something before he came into the room—"

"Something to do with the meeting?"

"Could have been, I suppose—"

"Then I want to know what the meeting was about."

Fraz Lamont's expression contracted slightly, seeming to draw tighter defensively. "This will be your last answer, is that understood?"

"Understood," Kiley said.

"The meeting was about vending machine profits in the districts that belong to the Disciples. In the past, Disciples have provided protection to the mob guys who collect the money from the vending machines, and we

also put the word out that the machines themselves were under our protection too and were not to be fucked with. For our services, we were paid
a flat fee. As time went on, however, because the white mob had our security, they started putting more and more machines on our turf. They
were installing condom machines in every bar up and down D-Street; cig-
arette machines in every store that didn't already sell cigarettes; candy machines, gum machines, trading card machines, every kind of machine you
could think of. They even started putting in machines that dispensed prod-
ucts made specifically for black people: styling gel, hair straightener, skin
bleach, things like that. So I decided to ask for a piece of the action instead
of a flat fee. We negotiated the matter for a few months, then on that night
we were all sitting down to conclude an agreement under which the
Disciples would be co-collectors and take a percentage of the gross. That
was the reason we were all there." Fraz sat back, unfolding his hands. "End
of questions," he said flatly. "Your turn."

Kiley flipped his notebook closed, put it back in the pocket of his coat
hanging on the back of the chair, and removed the single sheet of paper
that Gloria Mendez had given him containing the information she had obtained on the cars Nick Bianco had seen at the Shamrock. Beside the
make, model, and license number of each car, was the name of the registered owner that the motor vehicle department data base, pathed to the
police department computer, had matched with it.

"I'm going to show you a police department computer printout," Kiley
said to Fraz, "so you'll know that I'm being straight with you. I already had
the names you just gave me. The only things I didn't know were that Phil
Touhy was there, and who actually killed Nick Bianco." Handing the sheet
to Fraz, Kiley at the same time fished a small, gray Tagamet tablet from his
shirt pocket. "I have to take an ulcer pill," he said. "Can I get something
to drink out of that refrigerator over there?"

"Help yourself," Fraz said. He motioned Regent Lennox around to his
end of the table to peruse the printout with him.

Kiley went over and opened the refrigerator. It was fully stocked with
soft drinks, mineral water, beer, bottles of champagne, plastic containers
of fruit juice, and other beverages. Kiley selected a medium-size green
bottle of some brand of mineral water. As he bent over to take it with his
right hand, his left hand went deep under his waistband, all the way to a
jockstrap he wore, and withdrew the powerful little automatic pistol he
had purchased from Claude Emer. As he walked back toward the table at
which Fraz Lamont sat and at which Regent Lennox now stood bent over

next to him, Kiley kept the automatic close to his left thigh, the bottle of mineral water held up near his waist.

"There's more on the back of that sheet," he said to distract them.

Fraz turned it over. He and Lennox found the reverse side to be blank. Both of them looked up inquiringly. By that time it was too late.

Moving quickly, Kiley used his right hand to smash the bottle of mineral water across the bridge of Lennox's nose, at the same time using his left hand to ram the muzzle of the automatic hard against Fraz Lamont's neck.

"You move, I'll blow your fucking throat out," he warned grimly.

Fraz Lamont froze shock-still. Regent Lennox had plunged back against the nearest wall, both hands to his face, blood gushing from his broken nose. The bottle had fallen intact to the floor; Kiley quickly kicked it away. Bending close to Fraz Lamont's face, he spoke in a quiet, murderous tone.

"I've got six three-eighty hollow point power loads in this piece, working off a hair trigger. There's no way I can miss getting at least two of them off. Tell your fuck-up regent to sit down on the floor and keep quiet."

"You honky son of a bitch," Fraz whispered, every word moving the muscles of his neck against the muzzle of the gun. "We are supposed to have a deal."

"You blew the deal when you lied about who was at the Shamrock." He glanced over at the bleeding regent. "If Lennox moves, I'm going to shoot you, Fraz—"

"Sit down, Lennox," the Disciples leader said crisply. His eyes fixed unblinkingly on Kiley. "No way you can make it out of here, cop."

"I die, you die," Kiley said. He pressed the gun a shade harder. "There was somebody else at the Shamrock that night. He came in a Lincoln Mark VIII. Who was it?"

Fraz did not answer. Kiley jerked the seated man's knees from under the table, knelt, and quickly moved the gun from his neck to his crotch. The black man stiffened and sucked in his breath.

"You want to piss through a tube the rest of your life," Kiley said. "You're covering for somebody: who is it?"

There was still no response, but sweat broke out along Fraz's hairline.

"Okay, nigger, it's your call," Kiley told him evenly. "Say good-bye to your dick and balls—"

"The arbitrator!" Fraz said quickly. "The other person there was the arbitrator."

"The what?" Kiley asked. "Arbitrator?"

"The man who made the deal. The man who worked out what percentage of the vending machine action the Disciples would get."

"Who is he? What's his name?"

"I don't know. Everybody calls him Mr. O. He's some kind of big shot—"

"*What* kind of big shot?"

"Just somebody important—"

"*What* kind of big shot?" Kiley snarled. Fraz lowered his eyes and stared at the gun pushed up against his manhood. He sucked in his breath before blurting an answer.

"Man, I don't fucking *know!*"

Kiley took the small automatic away from Fraz's crotch and placed it at his throat again.

"What does he look like, this Mr. O?"

"Man, I don't know—he's just a honky—"

Kiley pressed the gun harder again. "You can do better than that."

"He's, like, average height, average weight; he's got a little gray in his hair—the dude is like *medium*. That's all I can tell you."

"You say he was there as an arbitrator?"

"Not *just* as an arbitrator," Fraz corrected. "He was like the main big shot, you know. I mean, it was him put the mob and the Disciples together in the first place. He set up the original meet."

The white mob and the black street gang. Who the fuck could possibly have brought them together? It made absolutely no sense. But Kiley did not think he was going to get the answer here. It was time to see if he could work himself out of the Disciples headquarters in one piece.

"You want to go on living?" he calmly asked Fraz Lamont.

"What the fuck do you think?" Fraz countered.

"I think you do," Kiley theorized. "I think that you want to go on living so bad that you'll walk me right out of this fucking place. Right out to my car. Everybody being nice and polite all the way. Then we can part company with no hard feelings. And—your people never have to know what happened."

"What about me being set up to fall for the cop's killing?" Fraz asked.

"I was blowing smoke up your ass, Fraz. I just said that so I could get close to you. The only danger you're in is from this hair trigger." Kiley took a step back. "Get on your feet."

As Fraz rose, Kiley got his coat off the chair and draped it over his arm far enough so that it concealed the gun. Then he bobbed his chin at one of the photographs on the wall.

"You see the movie they made about him?"

"About Malcolm X? Yeah, I saw it."

"So did I. I watched it on HBO one night." He motioned with the gun for Fraz to move toward the double doors that led from the office. "As we walk out, we're going to talk about that movie. Anyone hearing us as we pass by will think it's just a nice, casual conversation. You understand the drill?"

"Loud and clear."

"Good. Tell Lennox to stay put."

"Regent Lennox, remain where you are," Fraz ordered.

"Okay, let's go," Kiley said. "And remember, it's a hair trigger. You don't want anybody even nudging me. When we get out of the office, close the door behind us. Move."

Fraz opened one of the double doors and he and Kiley stepped with a deliberate casualness into the reception room, Fraz pulling the door shut behind them. They moved past the two big sentries and the waiting black faces.

"I thought the guy who played Malcolm did a very good job," Kiley improvised. "What was his name?"

"Denzel Washington," Fraz replied.

"Yeah, that was him. Do you think he did a good job playing Malcolm?"

"Yes, I think he did a good job playing Malcolm."

From the reception room they walked into the much larger room that had once been the auditorium. People paused in what they were doing to watch them pass. Surprised faces followed every step they took. On out to the lobby they went, where Otis and his three men were still waiting.

"Tell Otis to give me my guns back," Kiley said quietly.

"Return Detective Kiley's guns," Fraz obeyed.

Kiley accepted the guns one at a time with his left hand, putting the service revolver in his belt holster, the backup revolver in his trousers pocket, all the time keeping the concealed automatic firmly against Fraz's kidney area.

"Otis here is the one who searched me when I came in," Kiley told the Disciples leader, smiling. "I thought you'd appreciate knowing how thorough he is."

"Yes," Fraz replied through compressed lips, "I do."

On out to the street they went, closely side by side, appearing to be in casual conversation, no indication of anything being amiss. A small contingent of curious Disciples followed them as far as the box office but no farther. And no one even considered *doing* anything; it was such a bizarre scene, and President Fraz seemed to be completely at ease with the honky cop. This was the first time many of them had ever seen him with a white man.

The young Disciple and his two loitering friends were still in front of the chicken wings joint, all with mouths agape as Kiley and Fraz crossed the street to Kiley's car. Kiley had to transfer his coat and the concealed gun to his left hand because his car keys were in his right pocket. When he got the car door open and rolled down the window, he held his right hand out and said, "Let's shake hands so everybody will see that we're friends. Then you turn and walk back across the street, nice and easy. And remember what I said about this gun having power loads in it. I can put one in your spine all the way to that box office."

Fraz raised his hand and they shook.

"Start walking," Kiley said.

As Fraz Lamont found a break in traffic and went back across Division Street, Kiley got in his car and started the engine. Finding his own opening in the flow of traffic, he pulled away from the curb. Fraz Lamont did not look back as he reached the opposite sidewalk. In the rearview mirror, Kiley saw him stride resolutely into the old theater.

Going to be a bad afternoon for Otis, he thought.

# TWENTY-THREE

I n the newspaper archives of the Chicago Public Library's main branch, Kiley spoke to a tall woman with eyeglasses hanging around her neck by a black cord.

"About fourteen or fifteen years ago," he said, "there was a big state crime investigation hearing held down in Springfield. It was similar to the Kefauver Hearings conducted by the federal government. Can you tell me how I can find the exact dates so I can read about it in the newspaper files?"

"Surely," she said. She came around the counter. "This way, please—"

Kiley was led to a collection of reference volumes kept in a center stack with several worktables around it.

"The blue set of books indexes all Illinois state news since 1950. You can select specific years and try them, or you can go to the master index, here," she touched an extremely thick book, "and find what you want under more general categories. When you have your dates, bring them over to the counter and someone will get the microfilm for you."

Thanking her, Kiley opted for the master index and began searching. Beginning with the general category of "Crime," he moved his finger down several long columns of primary subcategories until he came to "Illinois State Senate Investigation of." There was an additional long column of secondary sub-categories, which Kiley perused slowly and carefully. A short way down that column was an article headlined: CRIME HEARINGS END; WHAT WAS ACCOMPLISHED? AN OVERVIEW OF THE NEARLY YEAR-LONG STATE SENATE INVESTIGATION INTO ORGANIZED CRIME IN ILLINOIS. It was a Sunday *Sun-Times* article with an October 1980 dateline.

Scribbling down the date, Kiley took it back to the counter and this time was helped by a young Hispanic man in shirt and tie. Kiley waited while the young man went to a deep section of low, block-like filing drawers, scanned them, and pulled open one that contained several dozen microfilm boxes roughly half the size of a cigar box. Returning to the counter, he asked, "You know how to use the viewers?"

"No," Kiley said. He had never even *been* in the main library before.

"Okay, come on, I teach you—"

The young man selected an unoccupied viewer for Kiley and instructed him in loading and threading the microfilm through the lens bracket. Then he turned on the viewer.

"This strip is from July through December. You just turn this handle here to move the film forward to the date you want."

Kiley thanked him and started turning the handle that moved the film strip forward chronologically. In a couple of minutes he had reached the date he wanted and began slowly browsing that edition for the article he sought. He found it in the Sunday Magazine section.

CRIME HEARINGS END, subheaded, WHAT WAS ACCOMPLISHED, was a double-page spread, the narrative of which began:

> After eleven months and twelve days of hearings that cost taxpayers in excess of $17 million, the State Senate Sub-Committee for the Investigation of Organized Crime in Illinois, adjourned two months ago and has to date not made a single viable recommendation to the full Senate body for a plan to help city, county, and state law enforcement agencies begin to eradicate organized crime from our society ...

A box in the lower corner of one page broke down the expense of the hearings into numerous categories covering everything from heating and cooling the hearing rooms to living expenses for out-of-town subpoenaed witnesses. Another box showed a graph detailing the increase in the number of known members of known organized crime gangs in Illinois decade-by-decade since the days of Al Capone back in the 1920s.

The narrative of the article was, in addition to an overview of the Senate hearings themselves, a history of organized crime in Illinois, generally, and Chicago, specifically. There were, the text stated, tentacles of organized crime in such communities as Kankakee, East St. Louis, Quincy, Decatur, Rock Island, Peoria, and the state capitol, Springfield—but it was all controlled, according to the writer, by the three major crime families that were known to rule in Chicago. Those three were the crime families of Philip Algernon Touhy, Augustus Dellafranco, and Laurence Morowski. The three individuals had come into power in the late 1970s when the last undisputed crime lord of the state, Frederico Scarpelli, aka Fred Scarp, had gone into semi-retirement as a counselor and adviser to the three men he personally selected to succeed him. Scarp had close personal ties to each of the men he picked. Phil Touhy had been his longtime bodyguard and protégé, and Scarp had personally sponsored younger brother Tony for membership in the organization. Augie Dellafranco was Scarp's favorite nephew, the son of his favorite older sister. And Larry Morowski's father had been Scarp's closest friend during a seven-year stay on Alcatraz following a federal conviction for interstate transportation of stolen property in the mid-1950s. Al Morelli, Dellafranco's chief lieutenant, was an in-law of the Scarpelli family. Jocko Hennessey, Touhy's second-in-command, was married to a sister of Phil and Tony. Mick O'Shea, another top player in the Touhy family, was married to a niece. There were personal ties and blood ties in all directions. And every tie ran, directly or indirectly, to Fred Scarp.

When Kiley finished the article, he rewound the strip as instructed, re-boxed the film, and returned it to the counter. Then he went back to the reference books, found the volumes pertaining to the city of Chicago, and looked in the index under "Scarp." There were numerous articles listed for all of the Chicago daily newspapers during the 1950s and 1960s. They started to become sparser during the 1970s, when Scarp began to phase out his own leadership in favor of the younger men. During the 1980s, there were fewer and fewer mentions of his name, and by the early 1990s he was seldom mentioned at all. The last item under his name read: PHO-TO—WHERE ARE THEY NOW? CHICAGO SUN-TIMES. Kiley copied the infor-mation and returned to the microfilm counter where he was helped again by the young Hispanic man. When he was finally seated at a viewer again, the strip of film in place, he found the photo on a page that contained the newspaper's crossword puzzle and horoscope listings. The two-column photo had a heading identical to the reference listing: "Where Are They Now?" The picture itself showed a smallish, somewhat stooped man in plaid cap, sport coat, and open-collar shirt, binoculars hanging around his neck, long cigar clenched in his teeth, studying a racing form. The caption read: FORMER REPUTED MOB BOSS, FRED SCARP, IS SEEN HERE AT CHICAGO'S HAWTHORNE RACE TRACK. NOW IN HIS LATE SEVENTIES AND A WIDOWER, SCARP RESIDES WITH A LIVE-IN CHAUFFEUR-COMPANION-BODYGUARD ON A SMALL ESTATE IN MADISON ACRES, WEST OF CHICAGO. HE FREQUENTLY AT-TENDS THE RACES.

Sitting back in his chair at the microfilm viewer, Kiley studied the pho-tograph. Everything about Fred Scarp fit what Kiley was looking for: the background, the mob stature, the connections, the blood ties. To midwestern organized crime, he was like a retired head of state. And that's how he could expect to be treated.

Slowly Kiley nodded his head.

Fred Scarp was perfect.

When he left the library, Kiley got on the Dan Ryan Expressway and drove out to 59th Street, then turned east and cut around Washington Park to Drexel Boulevard. Near the University of Chicago School of Law, he pulled into a NO PARKING zone, turned the car's sun visor down to display a police department parking permit, and left his car. He walked down to a little barbecue restaurant just off Drexel, with a sign above the door reading: REGGIE'S RIBS. It was past the lunch hour and Kiley saw upon entering that the place was not crowded, although because of its proximity to the school of law and other university buildings, it still had about half of its two dozen tables occupied. Several older women in starched white dresses were waiting tables, serving wooden trays of barbecued pork and beef ribs buried almost completely in what the menu called, "Reggie's Own Secret, Savory, Southern Sauce."

At a cash register counter near the front door sat Reggie himself, a whip-thin black man with a razor scar down the left cheek of an otherwise pleasant-featured face that had a casual, easy, very genuine smile. When he saw Joe Kiley that smile widened to almost dazzling proportions.

"Hey, my man Joseph!"

"Hello, Reggie," said Kiley. "How's things?"

"Right as rain, brother," Reggie replied as the two men shook hands. Then his smile disappeared. "I ought to be good and pissed at you, though. Ain't been around to see me for three months—"

"Yeah, I know. I planned to a couple of times—"

"I don't want to hear no lame excuses," Reggie preempted. "You discriminating against me jus' 'cause I'm honest now."

Kiley shrugged. "Can't waste my time on people who don't break the law. Listen, you got a couple minutes?"

"Always got time for you, man, you know that." Reggie turned to the nearest waitress. "Tonisha, take care of the register for a spell. Come on, Joseph—"

Reggie led Kiley through swinging doors into the kitchen, where he had two white-outfitted barbecue chefs sizzling meat and stirring sauce; then on into a long, narrow pantry, the shelves of which were stocked with restaurant-sized containers of condiments, stacks of crisp white table-cloths and napkins, and large bags of flour, dried red beans, and raw brown sugar. At the far end of the pantry was a rickety card table and several fold-ing chairs under a single unshaded light bulb hanging from the ceiling. Reaching behind a sack of beans, Reggie retrieved a bottle of Jack Daniels and pulled two five-ounce paper cups from a dispenser mounted on the wall.

"You'll have a snort with me, won't you?"

"Short one," Kiley replied. He was normally not a drinker of whiskey in any form; Scotch, bourbon, or rye—to Kiley it all tasted like it should be poured into an engine of some kind. But he had not seen Reggie for a while and wanted him to know they were still friends. And—he had a ma-jor favor to ask.

Reggie handed Kiley a cup and raised his own in a toast. "To your very good health, my friend."

"And yours," Kiley said. They sat at the shaky little table. "Business all right?" Kiley asked.

"Never better," Reggie boasted. "There's a whole new generation of lawyers coming up who've been prime-fed my secret, savory, Southern sauce all the way to their bar exams. Someday I fully expect to have my ribs praised on the U-nited States Su-preme Court." He winked. "Not bad for a reformed burglar, say what?"

"You deserve it, Reg," said Kiley. "You've worked hard." He sipped a lit-tle of the Jack Daniels, then said, "I need a big favor from you."

"You got it, brother. Just ask."

"I'm going to need to get through a door a few nights from now."

"Oh?" Reggie was clearly surprised.

"It's very important."

Reggie laced his fingers around the paper cup of Jack Daniels. "Joe, you know I'll do damn near anything you want me to. Wasn't for you, no telling where I'd be today: back in the joint, fucked up on dope, maybe even dead. So I know I owe you, big time—"

Kiley didn't disagree. He had arrested Reggie years earlier, back when he was riding a squad car in uniform; caught Reggie, then a heroin addict, coming out of an Outdoorsman Sporting Goods store with eight hundred dollars in cash-drawer starter money, and a duffel bag filled with target pis-tols, hunting rifles, expensive fishing reels, designer jogging suits, and a va-riety of other marketable merchandise with a stolen goods street value of six thousand dollars. Kiley had testified against Reggie at his preliminary hearing, then seen him go down for four-to-six on a plea bargain arrangement prior to his trial date. Reggie had been sent to Pontiac Correctional Center and about six months later had done an unusual thing: He had written Kiley a letter in care of the department, explaining that he had no family to write to, and asking permission to send Kiley, as part of the prison program, reports on his rehabilitation efforts. He thanked Kiley for arresting him and said that he was cleaning up his act in prison and intended to return to society a new person.

Typically, Kiley had ignored the letter. Then he began receiving one every month, with details about educational classes Reggie was taking, drug therapy he was undergoing, and self-improvement programs he was participating in. After several letters, which were being forwarded to Kiley out in the district he was assigned to—and for which he was taking more than a little heckling—Kiley had finally answered the young convict, reluctantly and awkwardly wished him well in his efforts, and asked him to kindly stop sending letters in care of the department. Reggie immediately replied to the return address on Kiley's envelope, and before long the correspondence had become mutually friendly. In a rare instance of benefaction toward his fellow man, Joe Kiley had begun encouraging Reggie along the rehabilitative path the young drug-addicted burglar had already taken. Several times during Reggie's incarceration, Kiley had even driven down to visit him and put a little money in Reggie's commissary account. And when Reggie was cut loose on parole, Kiley had vouched for him to get a busboy job in a Thompson's Cafeteria. Kiley subsequently loaned Reggie money to buy his first car; vouched for him again when Reggie applied somewhere else for a short order cook's job; helped him pay his way through culinary school after Reggie decided he wanted to become a chef; and finally, nearly a dozen years after the original arrest, co-signed on a small business bank loan for the ex-criminal to finance the opening of Reggie's Ribs.

Kiley had never told Nick Bianco about his friendship with Reggie, just as Nick for years had not told Kiley about Gloria Mendez. But his relationship with Reggie, and the knowledge that he had helped someone turn around an unfortunate life, had been a gratifying experience for Joe Kiley—particularly so since Reggie was black and Kiley was generally predisposed toward prejudice, intolerance, and narrow-minded bigotry. Kiley's genuine fondness for Reggie was the one reservation he had about involving Reggie in his plan to avenge Nick. He was only doing so now because the possibility of Reggie being caught was, in Kiley's judgment, close to nonexistent.

"I wouldn't ask," he told Reggie as they sat in the pantry, "if I thought there was any chance of you taking a fall—"

"It's not that," Reggie assured him. "Even if there *was* a chance of taking a fall, I'd still do it for you, Joe, you know that. The thing that concerns me is that I might blow it. It's been a lot of years, you know; I imagine new locks have been developed, new tumbler systems; I know some doors open now with card keys, some with dial pads—"

"This won't be anything like that," Kiley assured. "This will be an ordinary door, an ordinary lock, probably in place for twenty or thirty years. There's no need for extra security where I'm talking about; it's a place nobody would break into."

"*You're* going to break into it," Reggie pointed out.

"Not to steal anything," Joe said, shaking his head. He shrugged. "There's really nothing to steal."

Reggie sat back for a moment, evaluating. Finally he tossed down the last of his Jack Daniels and snapped the fingers of both hands simultaneously. "Okay, bro. When do we do it?"

"I'll call you in a few days," Kiley said. He was feeling a little guilty. "I really appreciate this, Reg."

"My pleasure."

"Can you get a set of lock-pick tools?" Kiley asked, rising.

"I've already got a set," Reggie told him. He immediately looked away, aware of his slip. Hoping to cover it, he rose and went about putting the Jack Daniels bottle back in its hiding place.

"You've got lock-pick tools?" Kiley asked, surprised. Reggie kept his eyes averted and did not answer; his expression in profile told Kiley that he was desperately trying to conjure up an answer. "What for?" Kiley wanted to know. Still no answer. Kiley pulled Reggie around to face him. "Reggie, you are a fucking restaurant owner!" he snapped. "What the fuck are you doing with lock-pick tools?"

Reggie's thin shoulders slumped. "I had a couple of problems, Joe—"

"You on shit again?"

"No, man, nothing like that; I wouldn't never shoot dope again." He glanced down. "I been doing a little gambling, that's all: basketball games, fights—"

"And you've been working with tools again to cover yourself?" Kiley shook his head. "I don't fucking believe this, Reggie."

"Just happened twice, Joe," his friend mitigated. "I got in over my head a couple times on the fucking point spread in the Bulls games. I had to pay off," he shrugged, "an' I couldn't take it out of my place here 'cause it would've fucked up my cash flow." Reggie reverted to his businessman image. "You see, Joe, when you run a small business, cash flow is the primary element of a successful operation—"

"Spare me the fucking song-and-dance, Reggie," Kiley cut in irritably. "What did you hit?"

"Liquor store on 63rd, electronics store on Garfield Boulevard."

"Any hassles?"

"No, man. Clean jobs, both of 'em. I don't get caught, Joe, you know that. I only ever got caught once an' that was by you—"

"What was all that bullshit you were handing me about it being a long time since you worked?"

"I was jus' trying to let you know that I'm not up to any of the new locks and stuff." Reggie looked down at his shoes and shifted them around like a little kid would do. "You pissed at me, Joe?"

"More surprised than pissed. You realize what you stand to lose, don't you, you get caught in some store?"

"Yeah, I do, man, an' I ain't letting myself get in that position again, believe me. No more big bets for me, I swear. Hunnerd bucks is my limit now."

"Okay," Kiley nodded. He sighed quietly, no longer feeling guilty. "Listen, I've got to split now. I'll call you on that other thing."

"I'll be here for you, brother. Most definitely."

"I know you will," Kiley acknowledged quietly.

Kiley left the barbecue restaurant and walked back to his car, shaking his head at this newest revelation in his life. When was he going to learn? he wondered. Nobody ever changed. It was that simple.

Nobody ever *fucking* changed.

When Kiley drove up to his apartment building late that afternoon, he noticed two men sitting in the front seat of a car parked across the street and down a few doors. The first thing he thought was that Vander had set up an IA surveillance on him to try and develop additional information to support the suspension charges against him. But that premise quickly seemed unlikely to him because the car was a late-model Cadillac, which was not standard issue for police department stakeout cars. Besides that, he then noticed, the car was carrying dealer plates.

Uncle fucking Gino, he thought tiredly. He found himself wishing that Stella would hurry the hell up and tell the Bianco family that she had decided to marry dickhead Frank, so Gino and Frank would get off his case. If they kept fucking with him, he was going to lose patience and see to it that Frank had to get married in a body cast.

Locking his car, Kiley walked over to the Cadillac. As he got close to it, he saw that Gino and Frank were not in it after all; the two men were Ray Rinni and Michael Russo, Gino's two sons-in-law. That immediately incensed Kiley: not Gino and Frank come to try and talk to him again; now two punk used-car salesmen married to Gino's fat daughters, sent to watch Kiley, to spy on him, to log his comings and goings. Guinea prick bastards, he thought.

At the car, he used a knuckle to tap on the driver's side window. Ray Rinni, behind the wheel, rolled it down.

"Waiting for me?" Kiley asked, with forced affability.

"We're not waiting for nobody," Rinni said innocently. "We're just sitting in a car minding our own business." He smirked—a mistake. "Any law against that?"

"You bet your ass there is," Kiley said calmly, his irritation waning, a sense of enjoyment kicking in. "It's a violation of city ordinance number seven-eleven, which reads, 'No assholes shall sit in a parked car on Joe Kiley's block without a permit issued by Joe Kiley.' You got a permit?"

"Very funny," Ray Rinni said dryly.

"You're not going to think so very long," Kiley told him. He opened the car door. "Get out of the vehicle."

"What for? We ain't breaking no law—"

"*Get—the—fuck—out—!*" Kiley suddenly raged, mood swinging back to anger again.

He grabbed Ray Rinni by the coat with both hands and dragged him out onto the street. Rinni tried to resist, but Kiley had fourteen years' experience with people who tried to resist; he easily avoided Rinni's clumsy attempts to pull away and fight back. When Kiley had him all the way out, he dug a hard right fist solidly into Rinni's stomach, well below the belt. A burst of breath expelled from Rinni's suddenly wide-open mouth and he bent over double, clutching himself with both arms. Kiley then grabbed him by the hair and slammed his face against the Cadillac's rear door. Rinni groaned and slumped to the pavement.

"You mick cocksucker—!"

It was Michael Russo, out of the car and rushing around from the passenger side. Kiley saw him slip a pair of dull gray brass knuckles onto his right hand and close it into a fist.

"You dumb fucking jackoff," Kiley said scornfully to Russo. Methodically he drew his service revolver, leveled it at Russo, and cocked the hammer.

Russo froze at the front of the car, mouth dropping open in surprise. "You—you can't draw no fucking gun on me for this," he said indignantly.

"Fuck I can't," Kiley disputed. "Brass knuckles are classified as a deadly weapon, greaseball. You are about to be shot in your pasta gut—"

"Kiley, don't do it!" Russo yelled, throwing his hands up, face draining white.

"Take off the knucks," Kiley ordered. Russo quickly obeyed. "Toss them over by the curb." Russo did, the brass knuckles clanging and bouncing in the gutter when they hit.

Kiley uncocked his gun and holstered it. Then he moved deliberately over to Michael Russo and kicked him brutally in one shin. Groaning in pain, Russo leaned back against the front fender of the Cadillac and drew his knee up to clutch the point of impact. When he did that, Kiley kicked him in his other shin, and Russo collapsed onto the street. Kneeling next to him, Kiley spoke in a menacingly calm, ominously quiet voice.

"Tell your no-balls dago father-in-law that if he pulls this shit again, I'm going to permanently cripple whoever he sends. I mean it, punk. No more games—or they get serious. And *I* get serious." Kiley bobbed his chin at Ray Rinni, who was struggling to his feet at the rear fender, face smeared with blood from a broken nose—exactly as Regent Lennox's had been the previous day. Two for two, Kiley thought. "Take that asshole and beat it," he told Russo.

The two men negotiated themselves back into the car, Russo behind the wheel now, Rinni slumped in the passenger seat holding a handkerchief to his nose. Both shins shooting streaks of pain to his brain, tears streaking his cheeks, Russo started the car and drove slowly away.

Reaching down, Kiley picked up the brass knuckles and slipped them into his coat pocket as he walked over to his building.

# TWENTY-FOUR

**A**t ten o'clock two evenings later, Kiley drove at a moderate speed along a dark, two-lane suburban road. On one side of the road was a forest preserve; on the other, spaced well apart, were driveway entrances leading through high privacy shrubs into a community of estates, some small, some large, known collectively as Madison Acres. Once beyond the privacy shrub, which grew six to eight feet in uneven height, each entrance drive extended in a slight curved arc back to the individual house, which was set out of sight of the entrance itself. Each estate was on at least a two-acre lot, moderately wooded on each side, with a deep manicured lawn in front of it and a portion of the splendid Madison Acres Country Club golf course rambling around behind it.

Kiley had spent the better part of the previous afternoon, as well as the morning of the current day, reconnoitering the area. He had located Fred Scarp's estate through the DuPage County property records, Madison Acres being just across the Cook County line, a few miles west of the Tri-State Tollway. Scarp had the property in his own name; he even had, to Kiley's surprise, a listed telephone number. On reflection, Kiley had realized that there was really no reason for the retired crime lord to conceal where he lived. He had been out of active participation in the rackets for more than two decades; if he had left any enemies behind—alive—he would have heard from them long ago. The old man's only protection, as far as Kiley had been able to determine, was the live-in chauffeur-companion-bodyguard who accompanied Scarp out to dinner at suburban restaurants several nights a week, took him to the track during racing season at Sportsman's Park, Hawthorne, and Aurora Downs, and helped him in the cultivation of a large rose garden along one side of the house.

Driving down the country road now, Kiley had to make five passes by the Scarp driveway before he found himself with no other cars in view in either direction, enabling him to turn off his headlights unobserved before pulling into the drive. Keeping as far right as he could, he eased his dark car along until he came barely around a stand of American pines, just far enough to see the front of the Scarp house. Taking care not to go off the asphalt, into dirt where he would leave tire tracks, Kiley stopped, turned off the engine, and rolled down the window on his side. He listened intently. Nothing reached his ears except night sounds from the woods around him. From the passenger seat, he picked up his binoculars and focused on the house.

Fred Scarp lived in one of the smaller Madison Acres homes: a two-story Tudor-style house which, according to the property records, had thirty-one hundred square feet of living space and an attached three-car garage. As Kiley studied its night face now, he saw lights in two downstairs front windows, and a third light coming from a single window toward the rear of the house. Lowering the binoculars, he settled back to wait, window still rolled down so that he could hear any unusual noise that might occur.

As he sat there in the dark, it occurred to Kiley that this was the first time he had used his binoculars since the night he and Nick were trying to find Tony Touhy, when Kiley was watching the Lake Shore Drive garage for the teal blue Jaguar to leave. That had been the night Nick was killed. So much had happened since then; so many things he couldn't even have imagined: Nick dead; Gloria, whom he hadn't even known then, dead also; he and Stella entwined in sexual activity, something he'd only previously fantasized about; finally, his suspension from the police department. Before the night he and Nick had answered the radio call about Ronnie Lynn's body being in the alley behind the 4-Star Lounge, he could not have predicted a single significant change that would have been likely to alter his existence anytime in the foreseeable future. As far as he had been concerned, he was probably scheduled to go on living a comparatively inconsequential life of acceptable bachelorhood, a mostly boring job but with a decent pension at the end of it, a good partner whom he sincerely cared for, that partner's family of which he had been made a kind of honorary member, a secret passion for the partner's wife, which he had been able to accept and adjust to—

So common, so ordinary, so *regular* his life had been. Then he had come up with the great idea of Nick and him bringing in the girl's killer themselves—because he thought that killer was the kid brother of a rackets boss. From that point on, the reality, the very essence, of who he was, what he was, *why* he was, had turned into a nightmare steeped in darkness and doom.

He had fucked up everything about his life. There seemed to be no more reason for living—except to get Nick's killer. That was all that was left. When that was done, he really didn't give a fuck what happened to him. Tonight he was going to prove that.

Kiley had been sitting in the dark car for about an hour when he saw a light go on in one of the upstairs windows. Putting the binoculars to his eyes, he watched closeup as the two downstairs lights in the front of the house went out. Then a second upstairs light went on. The downstairs rear light on the side became dimmer but did not go out entirely.

Rolling up the car window, Kiley got out and stood silently listening for a moment. There were only night sounds, forest sounds. Kiley was dressed tonight much as he had been the night he tossed Tony Touhy's apartment: in dark-colored garments made for easy movement. His shoes were different; instead of his old crepe-sole shoes, he had on a pair of new Sperry Top-Sider deck shoes, navy blue canvas, with a sole made to resist wet, slick surfaces. Kiley did not know whether he would be able to avoid walking on dewy or water-sprinklered grass, but he did not want to take any chances. He had one additional article of clothing tonight: a dark blue lightweight wool muffler that he now put around his neck and tied securely in back with a double knot. In one jacket pocket he carried a five-inch leather-covered lead sap; in the other, an empty Cherry 7-Up can.

Leaving the car, Kiley walked briskly along the edge of the driveway, careful to keep away from the ground area beyond the asphalt where he, like his tires, might leave tracks. There was a half moon in the sky, throwing a bare, eerie light over the grounds of Fred Scarp's small estate, lending definition to the outline of the manicured lawn, the low, box-like shrubbery around it, and the facade of the ivory-colored house that loomed up in the background. Except for a night-light above the front door—and possibly one in the rear—there was no outside illumination except for the moon. Kiley's figure, as he moved stealthily along, was like something dark and unearthly being carried by a night wind.

Where the driveway curved up to the nearest corner of the house, Kiley paused and stood very still in its immediate foreground, eyes searching the shadows, ears heeding the night sounds. He was more relaxed than he had expected to be; possibly, he supposed, because at last he was *doing* something, making a move in the direction he was committed to. Everything up until now had, it seemed on reflection, been preliminary: the search of Tony Touhy's apartment, the talk with the deputy coroner about Gloria Mendez's death, the shakedown of Fraz Lamont for information, even the visit to Reggie to get that phase of the plan set up. All of it had been preparatory, all of it done to chart the course.

Tonight was the first actual step of that course.

When he had stood there at the corner of the house long enough to assure himself that he was the only thing moving about, Kiley stepped forward and moved quietly up to the triangle of light thrown from the
night-light above the front door. There was an entry stoop in the front, a
large slab of cement with a tall potted tree on each side of it. Along two
edges of the stoop were flower boxes lush with a variety of mixed violets.
Their fragrance in the thin night air was sweet and immediate, like a surprise kiss.

Kiley removed the empty Cherry 7-Up can from his jacket pocket and
set it near the center front of the stoop, about six inches inside the
perimeter of dim light from above the door. Then he stepped behind one
of the potted trees, worked the muffler up to cover the lower part of his
face, and slipped the sap from his other pocket. Reaching a gloved hand
behind the tree, he tapped twice on the side door panel—not loudly, not
hard enough to startle; just *thud-thud*: a what-the-hell-was-that sound.

Twisting his wrist toward the light, he waited as the second hand on his
watch made one complete revolution. Then he reached out and tapped the
door again. *Thud-thud*.

He waited.

Another full minute passed. He reached to the door a third time.

*Thud-thud.*

Twenty seconds later, Kiley heard a muted voice inside the door. He was
able to understand only part of what was said: ". . . out in front, I
think—"

Then there was the sound of locks disengaging and the front door
opened. In a long, narrow slit of space between the potted tree and the
frame of the door, Kiley saw a big-necked, big-shouldered man in a
skintight white T-shirt, pause and then take one step onto the stoop. There
he stopped, looking with a puzzled frown at the bright red Cherry 7-Up
can standing so innocuously at the edge of the stoop.

"What the hell—?" the man said to himself.

From somewhere well inside the house, a hoarse voice called, "What is
it, Lenny?"

"I'm not sure," Lenny called back, over his shoulder. "Just a minute—"

Lenny took a step toward the Cherry 7-Up can. When he did, Kiley piv-
oted from behind the potted tree and swung the lead sap hard against the
side of the big man's head. With a faint groan, Lenny staggered two steps
away from the direction of the blow and dropped heavily to his knees.

Jesus Christ, Kiley thought, anxiety rising. From a blow like that, Lenny should have been stretched out unconscious. Instead, incredibly, he was raising one hand to feel the place where he had been hit. Turning his head, he looked curiously at Kiley.

Wetting his lips, Kiley stepped over behind him and swung the sap in a horizontal arc to strike Lenny in the back of the head, just down from the crown of his skull. With the second blow, Lenny pitched forward on his face and lay still.

Putting the sap in his jacket pocket, Kiley looked inside the open door, found a panel of light switches, and turned off both the outside and foyer lights. Then he grabbed the big man by his ankles and started dragging him inside. It was laborious work; Lenny felt like he weighed two hundred and fifty pounds, at least. Kiley had to drag him in separate tugs of a couple of feet at a time; he had to get him through the door by pulling his feet and legs in, then taking him by the back of his belt and working him the rest of the way in. By the time he had the big man far enough in to close the front door, Kiley was laced with sweat. Taking a moment to lean back against the wall, Kiley pulled the muffler off his face, sucked in some deep breaths, and wiped perspiration from his face with one sleeve of his jacket.

"Lenny," came the hoarse voice from upstairs, "what was it? What was the noise?"

Across the foyer, Kiley saw a wide, lighted staircase leading to the second floor. A stooped old man with almost no hair, wearing only his underwear and felt house slippers, was coming down. In one hand he carried a portable oxygen tank; in the other he held a plastic breathing cup which he put to his mouth every few steps. When the cup was away from his face, Kiley recognized him from newspaper photographs as Fred Scarp. Pausing on the landing, the old man squinted down at the unlighted foyer.

"Lenny—?"

Kiley removed the muffler from around his neck, drew the Tutweilder .380 from his belt, and quickly wrapped the muffler around both his hand and the gun. Then he stepped over to the stairs and started walking up. "Lenny can't help you right now," he said to Fred Scarp.

"Who the fuck are you?" Scarp asked. Kiley saw no fear in his face, detected none in the hoarse voice. Without answering, Kiley kept moving up the stairs. "Do you know who I am, you asshole?" Scarp asked.

"Yeah, I know who you are," Kiley replied.

"Then you know what you're doing isn't very smart—"

"Nothing I do anymore seems very smart," Kiley said.

Reaching the landing, Kiley raised his right hand and Scarp could see in the folds of the muffler a stainless steel pistol muzzle. The old man's already pale face went even whiter, emphasizing half a dozen ugly liver spots that dotted it.

"Who—who sent you—?" he managed to ask, then quickly held the breathing cup to his mouth and sucked in air.

"The Touhy brothers," Kiley told him. Let him die thinking his own had betrayed him.

A wave of disbelief, followed at once by hurt, passed over Scarp's eyes. Then his racketeer mentality kicked in. "How—much—they paying you?"

Kiley shook his head. "I'm a volunteer." He brought the gun all the way up, aiming it at the old man's face.

"You—bastard—" Scarp hissed. Dropping both the oxygen tank and the breathing cup, the old man began to flail out at Kiley. He stumbled forward, feeble fists hitting Kiley's raised arm, his chest. Kiley brought the gun around to the side of Scarp's head and was about to squeeze the trigger when suddenly Scarp drew in a loud, vibrating breath and immediately started choking on the air. His tongue folded out and he staggered backwards. One hand clutched at his chest and his eyes bulged grotesquely. A gasping, sucking sound came from deep in his lungs.

Kiley watched in astonishment as Scarp lurched to the edge of the landing and went tumbling and bouncing down the half flight of stairs to the foyer.

"I'll be damned," Kiley said softly to himself. He walked quickly down the stairs and knelt next to the twisted old body, putting his fingers on Scarp's throat for a pulse. There was none. "I'll be damned," he said again, in a whisper.

Rising, Kiley crossed the foyer to the front door, putting the muffler back around his neck, tucking the gun away. He had bought that gun possibly to kill Fraz Lamont with, but that had been avoided. Now he had been saved from using it on Fred Scarp.

But gun or not, Kiley knew he had still murdered Scarp; he had no delusions about that. Maybe it was Scarp's payback for all the crime he had been responsible for during all the years he had been the undisputed mob czar of Chicago and the rest of the state. But that, Kiley knew, was only superfluous to the real reason Scarp had died. He had been killed because he was essential to Kiley's plan to avenge the killing of Nick.

Not for a moment did Kiley consider Fred Scarp a criminal finally brought to a just end. He did not even consider him a victim. To Joe Kiley, the dead old mobster was merely a tool.

Walking out of the house, Kiley picked up the empty Cherry 7-Up can, put it in his pocket, and started back toward his car.

# TWENTY-FIVE

**T**wo mornings later, Kiley woke to loud, persistent pounding on his apartment door. Struggling to come out of the haze of a deep, drunken sleep, he became aware as soon as he moved of a brutal hangover headache that seemed to be oscillating inside his skull like it was machine driven. He wanted to ignore the heavy hammering on his door, but every pounding rap was an individual jolt to his senses that was too painful to disregard.

"All right, all right, goddamn it!" he shouted. "I'm coming! Stop the goddamn pounding!" Somewhere in the pit of his agonized mind was the hope that his landlady, Mrs. Levine, had not heard him. He did not like for her to hear him use profanity.

In his underwear, Kiley walked unevenly into the living room and looked through the peephole in the door. Recognizing the two faces in the hall, he said, "Shit," under his breath, and opened the door. Dan Parmetter, his old General Assignments captain, and Leo Madzak, the B-and-A commander, came in and closed the door behind them.

"Jesus Christ," Madzak said, heading for a window to open, "it smells like a jig locker room in here."

"Nobody invited you," Kiley said grumpily, slumping down on the couch so they wouldn't see him reel as he stood.

"You mind your lip, lad," snapped Parmetter, pointing a warning finger at him. "Leo happens to be your captain at the moment, and you'll show him the proper respect. You want him to think you never learned nothing under me?"

"Where do you keep the coffee?" Madzak asked, as if he had not even heard Kiley's remark.

"Bottom shelf next to the stove," Kiley said.

Parmetter sat on the arm of the couch, facing Kiley. "How long have you been drunk?"

"I don't know," Kiley leaned forward, forearms on knees. "Three days, I guess."

Actually it was less than two; some thirty or so hours. He had begun drinking as soon as he got home from killing Fred Scarp, as soon as the reality of the death he had caused settled in his conscience. He told Parmetter it was longer in case he needed an alibi. "Jesus," he said, pressing each temple with his fingers, "this fucking headache is a killer—"

"I don't doubt that," Dan Parmetter replied. "You look like shit."

The GA captain got up and walked through Kiley's bedroom, grimacing and pausing to open a window in there also, then went into the bathroom and got four Excedrin tablets from a bottle in the medicine cabinet. Moving on to the kitchen, he opened the refrigerator, checked the date on a carton of milk, and poured a glassful. "He's got an ulcer," Parmetter said to Leo Madzak by way of explaining the milk.

"Who hasn't these days?" Madzak, who was making the coffee, asked rhetorically.

Back in the living room, Parmetter said, "Here," and handed Joe the headache tablets and milk.

A few minutes later, as Kiley shakily took sips from a cup of hot, strong, black coffee, with the two police captains now sitting in front of him, Parmetter said to Madzak, "Think he can shave himself without bleeding to death?"

"Maybe one of us ought to shave him," Madzak suggested.

"Shave me for what?" Kiley asked.

"For court, Joe," said Madzak. "Winston's preliminary hearing on the bus bombings is this afternoon. I need you to testify."

Kiley grunted softly. "What do you want me to say when the defense lawyer asks what my current assignment is? Suspended and facing charges?"

"We've got that covered, Joe," said Parmetter. "Leo and I went to Allan Vander and cut a deal with him. He'll drop the suspension if you'll agree to be interviewed about Sergeant Mendez's death. He thinks there might have been more to it than a suicide. He wants your cooperation, Joe, that's all." Parmetter drew a folded sheet of paper from his inside pocket. "This rescinds your suspension as of ten a.m. today. All you've got to do is cooperate."

"I need you at Winston's prelim, Joe," said Madzak. "Without you, he'll walk. And if you testify as a cop suspended such a short time after you busted him, he'll probably walk then too."

"Vander agreed to give me my badge back?" Kiley asked incredulously. "After I called him a cocksucker?"

"Grow up, Joe," said Parmetter. "He's been called a lot worse than that." The GA captain leaned forward a little. "Look, Leo and I don't have a high opinion of Vander either, but we think he's a straight cop, everything considered. It's his job that's so fucking despicable. But Leo told him what an A-one job you did on the bus bomber case, and I think Vander was impressed."

"That deputy of his, Bill Somers, he put in some good words for you too," said Madzak.

"Nobody wants to see you fuck up a fourteen-year career, Joe," said Dan Parmetter.

"You're a good cop," Madzak emphasized. "You proved that by the way you handled Harold Winston. I'd like to talk to you about staying in B-and-A, maybe going to school, getting some formal bomb training. I think you'd be an asset to the squad."

Beginning to feel the first hint of relief from his titanic headache, Kiley steadied his hands enough to get a good swallow of coffee down. His expression was drawn, his mood extremely depressed. He knew that Dan Parmetter was a decent man and an irreproachable cop, as straight as an officer could be; he assumed that Leo Madzak was straight also, or Parmetter would not be partnering with him in this situation. And he knew that if the two captains were made aware of the murder he had committed—regardless of Kiley's reason or who the victim was—they would turn their backs on him and have nothing further to do with him. And they would be justified in doing so. He knew he had never been as righteous a cop as either of them were, but he *had* been on the fringes of that rank. At times he was a maverick, at times he bent the rules, at times he lost his temper—usually at the expense of some scumbag he was arresting; so there were reprimands on his sheet, there had been promotion opportunities missed, there were reservations in some quarters about his prejudices and his personality. But there had never been any question about his reputation for honesty, for dedicated police work, and for loyalty to his partner and to his commander. Those traits had always reinforced his umbilical cord to men of the caliber of Dan Parmetter and Leo Madzak.

Now that was gone—although only Kiley knew it at present. He could no longer count himself even marginally on their perimeter. He was a murderer now, and that wiped out all ties.

Kiley was aware that he could break it off right then, very easily, simply by rejecting Vander's offer to rescind the suspension. That might, over the long haul, be the smarter thing to do—particularly in light of what he himself still had planned; but Kiley could not bring himself to give such a step more than cursory consideration. There was, still, deep down, some of the good cop left in him—and even though he knew his life was now spiraling downward toward some dreaded, dark doom, he could not turn his back completely on the job that had been his whole being for so many years.

"When's Winston's preliminary?" he asked.

"Two o'clock," Madzak told him. "Department Twenty-three."

Kiley nodded. "I'll be there, Captain."

Madzak reached in his coat pocket and handed Kiley a small envelope. Kiley opened it.

It was his badge.

That afternoon, as he waited outside Department Twenty-three of Superior Court, Kiley tensely read the updated *Sun-Times* story of Fred Scarp's death. It was follow-up coverage from the previous day's account of Scarp's body having been discovered by a housekeeper-cook who reported for work at seven a.m. two days previously to find Scarp dead at the foot of the stairs, and his live-in companion, an ex-wrestler named Lenny "Mountain" Pastrano, unconscious on the floor of the foyer. Scarp had died from a heart attack, the DuPage County coroner determined, probably caused by fright; Lenny Pastrano had been bludgeoned twice with a blunt object. Pastrano was hospitalized in serious but stable condition with two separate skull fractures; he was expected to eventually recover.

The DuPage County sheriff's office, under whose jurisdiction the case fell, had made a preliminary statement that Scarp's death may have resulted from a bungled robbery attempt, with the burglars fleeing without any loot. There did not seem to be much of a motive in any other direction. It was certainly not, everyone in law enforcement agreed, a mob hit; there was no reason for one, and the facts were not indicative of a gangland killing. There were no apparent clues at the scene, and investigators had no suspects at the moment.

As Kiley was reading the paper, an assistant state's attorney, whom Kiley knew slightly, came over to where he sat. "Detective Kiley, Robert Faber," he said, extending his hand. "I think we've worked together before."

"Yeah, about a year ago," Kiley said, rising to shake Faber's hand. "Child molestation case, I think."

"Right. Well, this one," he indicated his file, "looks pretty cut and dried. We're going to establish the background of Winston's father being fired by the transit authority, Winston's own knowledge of chemistry, the previous purchases of the types of small alarm clocks used for timers, and the diagram he drew in his own hand showing how to make an explosive device. I'm pretty certain the court will hold him to answer; I'm just not sure exactly what the charge will be. Incidentally, Winston has asked to speak to you. He's back in the holding cell. You can talk to him or not; it's up to you." Faber started on down the hall. "See you in a few minutes when court convenes."

After the prosecutor left, Kiley thought about it for several minutes, then decided to see what was on Harold Paul Winston's mind. He walked down the hall in the opposite direction from Faber, to a buzzer-controlled door operated by a jail guard. Showing his badge, he was passed into a corridor that led behind the courtrooms to a series of holding cells for incarcerated persons awaiting appearances in court that day. Winston, in a suit and tie, sat on a bench in the third holding cell down the corridor. He looked surpassingly glum. Kiley went over and stood in front of the bars. He waited for Winston to look up. It took a moment for Winston to realize that someone was there, but he finally noticed Kiley.

"Oh. Hello, Joe—"

"Mr. Winston," Kiley said. The little man smiled bleakly.

"No more 'Hal,' huh, Joe?" When Kiley did not respond, Winston blinked rapidly several times, as if he might be counteracting tears. "I want you to know," he said, a slight tremor in his voice, "that I think what you did to me was very deceitful, very unscrupulous, and very underhanded. You didn't play fair with me, Joe."

"It's not my job to play fair with people like you," Kiley told him flatly. "It's my job to stop you as quickly as possible, before you hurt innocent people—"

"That's nonsense and you know it," Winston cut in. "It was never my intention to hurt anybody. You said yourself—in one of our buddy-buddy conversations," he interjected sarcastically—"that you thought it was— 'commendable,' I think was the word you used—commendable that I had taken such obvious precautions to make certain that no one was hurt. I went to great lengths to make sure those buses would be in the garage, parked, at two or three o'clock in the morning, before my explosive detonated—"

"You're incriminating yourself, Mr. Winston," Kiley told him.

"I don't care!" Winston snapped in reply. "I intend to admit everything at my trial anyway. I just want it made clear that I wasn't trying to *hurt* anyone. I was disabling buses in order to make a statement against the transit authority for what it did to my father." It became necessary for Winston to again hold himself in check to keep from crying. "My father," he said emotionally, "was a heroic man. He was trying to combat a municipal department that year after year contributed to the pollution of this city's air by operating hundreds of outmoded buses with engines that had no catalytic converters on them to reduce fumes; engines that were not properly serviced and maintained to keep their carburetors and oil filters clean; engines that were run on the cheapest, lowest-octane fuel available, which produced the maximum volume of pollutants. My father was trying to help every man, woman, and child breathing air in this city—and for his efforts he was made out to be some kind of radical lunatic, and he was dismissed from his job for it—"

"Mr. Winston, that was twelve years ago," Kiley reminded him.

"I don't care!" Winston snapped again. "How long ago it was doesn't matter! It *happened*!" Swallowing tightly, Winston looked downward. "It happened," he repeated in a quieter, almost melancholy tone. "And it ruined my father's life. It actually *took* his life."

Kiley frowned deeply. "What do you mean?"

"You know what I mean," Winston replied with a soft, cynical grunt.

"If I knew, I wouldn't ask you," Kiley said. "What do you mean?"

"My father," Winston said, raising his eyes to meet Kiley's again, "committed suicide."

"Because he lost his job?" Kiley asked incredulously.

"Not just because he *lost* his job; because he couldn't ever get another one." Winston's voice became quietly bitter. "The bus authority blackballed him. Every time a prospective employer checked his references, the transit people would report that he was a troublemaker: an agitator, a rabble-rouser. So he wouldn't get hired. My father tried omitting the transit authority on his job applications, but that didn't work; he was always asked to explain where he was and what he was doing during those years. Somehow, the transit authority always came back to haunt him." Winston sighed heavily, wearily. "Anyway, he never worked again. Not one day. Eventually his unemployment benefits ran out, then he used up all of his savings, and finally he ended up on state welfare. His second wife left him. His car was repossessed. Even his television was repossessed.

"I tried to help him, but he wouldn't let me. He kept insisting that everything would work out for him, that it was only a matter of time. I finally convinced him that it wasn't going to happen; I finally got him to agree to come live with me. I was still living with my mother and stepfather at the time, but I was working and I had some money saved; I was going to get a place of my own where my father could live too. It took a lot of persuading on my part, but he finally said okay, that's what we'd do. But the very next day he took a handful of sleeping pills, put a plastic bag over his head and buttoned his shirt collar around the opening of it, and went to sleep for the last time.

"He left a note," Winston concluded his story, "saying that he was sorry, but that he loved me and didn't want to be a burden to me. He asked me to be sure and have him cremated at a crematorium that complied with federal environmental guidelines; he didn't want his cremation to pollute the air."

When Winston finished talking, the two men stood silently, bars between them, for an awkward, and what seemed to Kiley a very long, moment. Kiley was acutely aware that none of this should have been a surprise to him. Once learning of Aaron Codman's existence, collateral investigation should have been made of him at the same time that continuing investigation was being made of Winston himself. But Kiley had enlisted Aldena's help at that time, and had told her explicitly what he wanted checked after she had uncovered Winston's real father. That had been at the time of Gloria Mendez's death, wake, and funeral, when Kiley had been dealing with Meralda's insistence that her mother had not killed herself. Although working under a self-imposed deadline to deliver the bus bomber to Captain Madzak, Kiley nevertheless had given priority to looking into the details of Gloria's death—and left the bus bomber work to Aldena. The final objective had been accomplished, on time, and Winston was in custody as promised. And even if Kiley *had* done the background work himself, *had* made an in-depth check of Aaron Codman and learned ahead of time everything that Harold Winston had just told him, it would not have changed anything as far as Kiley's actions were concerned. Kiley probably would have felt sympathy for Winston, just as he was feeling it now, but it would not have interfered with his plan to develop some hard evidence against Winston, or deterred his objective of taking Winston into custody.

"I'm sorry about your father," Kiley told Winston now. "I didn't know about anything that took place after he was fired. You led me to believe he was still alive; you even told me that he and his second wife were shopping at the same stores your mother and her second husband shopped at. Maybe if you hadn't told me so many lies—"

"I told you what I had to tell you," Winston declared. "Anyway, you were lying to me just as much. All that stuff about the police department getting ready to bring you up on charges—"

"That was *true*, Hal," Kiley asserted, unawarely slipping back into the more casual version of Winston's name.

"Do you expect me to believe that?" Winston asked piquedly, ignoring Kiley's familiarly.

"Believe it or don't believe it," Kiley retorted. "It's still true."

Winston sat back down heavily on the bench again, shaking his head confoundedly. "I don't know what to believe anymore." He looked up at Kiley. "What do you think I'll be charged with?"

Kiley shrugged. "Could be anything from destruction of municipal property, to reckless public endangerment, even to attempted second-degree murder. It's basically up to the judge."

"Are you going to be the main witness against me?"

"Yes."

"You know," Winston sat back, head against the cement wall, staring straight ahead, "I'll bet you and I could have been real friends under different circumstances. I mean, I'll bet we could have even gotten to like each other."

"Maybe we could have," Kiley allowed. He recalled briefly how there had been a moment in the Bel-Ked Tavern when he had realized that he was confiding in Harold Winston much in the same way he had entrusted personal thoughts to Nick Bianco in the past. It had been an odd reflection, totally without precedent in Kiley's consciousness. It was almost as if there had been some seed of companionship struggling for recognition within him. Apparently Harold Paul Winston had felt it too. "Maybe we still can be friends someday, Hal," he said tentatively.

"I'm afraid it's too late for 'Hal' anymore, *Detective Kiley*," the jailed man replied. His head did not move, but his eyes, now hard and unforgiving, shifted to glare at Kiley. "We're back on opposite sides again."

Kiley endured the hateful glare for a long moment; he guessed Harold Winston had that much satisfaction coming to him. Then he nodded resignedly and said, "Good luck, Mr. Winston."

Kiley walked away, back toward the courtroom where he would testify.

# TWENTY-SIX

**W**hen Kiley reported back to work at B-and-A the next morning Aldena glanced up at him and said curtly, "Don't forget to sign in," as if she had not noticed his nearly week-long absence, and knew nothing of his short-lived suspension—which of course he knew she did, because nothing got past her.

"And don't forget," she added as he wrote his name on the squad shift roster, "to let me know as soon as the state's attorney's office gives you a disposition in the Winston case."

"You'll be the first to know," he assured her. "Decide yet whether you want your name included in the final case write-up?"

"In light of your recent difficulties with IA," she said dryly, "as well as the personal reputation you seem to be developing, I think I'll pass. I'd be better off having my name on something written by the Zodiac killer."

"Aldena," he said, as plaintively as he could manage, "I thought we were going to be friends."

"We are, Detective," she assured him. "We're just going to keep it a deep, dark secret."

"Who from?"

"The entire world. Plus," she added, "any planets that might be colonized in the future." She looked at her calendar for the day. "The captain's got you penciled in to meet with him the first thing this morning, so don't plan on going anywhere."

Kiley found his desk exactly as he had left it, and the other members of the squad who were on shift and sitting nearby took note of his return merely by exchanging neutral greetings with him. Only Lee Tumac got up and came over personally.

"How'd the bus bomber prelim go?" he asked.

"Don't know yet," Kiley said. "The judge continued it until today." He frowned at Tumac. "How come you're here in the daylight?"

"I finished my period on nights," Tumac said. A "period" was a four-week cycle of duty that was standard throughout the Chicago Police Department.

"Maybe it's going to be my turn next," Kiley ventured. Tumac shook his head.

"Not while you're on TAD. Can't work a night period unless you've been to bomb school and arson school, and only permanent members of the squad get sent to school. Think you'll be permanent?"

"Don't know yet," Kiley said. The two detectives looked over as Captain Leo Madzak came through the squad room on the way to his office. Seeing Kiley, he motioned him toward the office. "Maybe I'm going to find out," Kiley said to Tumac.

Tumac winked at him. "Good luck, Joe."

Madzak was hanging up his coat as Kiley came in. "Take a chair," he said. "Any news on Winston yet?"

"No, sir, not yet." Kiley cleared his throat. "Captain, I want to apologize for that crack I made in my apartment yesterday about you not being invited—"

"Forget it," Madzak said.

"I know I was way out of line; I know you and Captain Parmetter were trying to help me—"

"I said forget it, Joe," the captain repeated. "So forget it. What kind of coffee do you drink?"

"Uh—black, no sugar—"

Madzak dropped into a squeaky chair behind his desk and flipped on an old intercom, the kind Kiley had not seen around the department for years. "Aldena, my coffee, please, and a black, no sugar, for Detective Kiley."

"Coming up, sir," Aldena's static voice replied.

"Okay, let's discuss your future," Madzak said to Kiley. "We can go two ways here. As I told you in your apartment, I'd like to consider you for permanent assignment to my squad. I can keep you on, expend money from my budget to give you the proper training, and if I see that you have the aptitude and the right attitude, keep you on as a permanent member of the squad. Our work in this unit is not the most exciting in the department; it's primarily investigative in nature, and frankly involves mostly very low-profile offenses, with an occasional big-time case, but not often. We don't get much glory here, there's not a lot of room for promotion, but there's also not a lot of personal exposure to gunshots, knife wounds, AIDS infections from suspect bites, high-speed chases, and that sort of

thing. But, in my biased opinion, I think I have the best, most professional and efficient group of detectives in the department—"

Aldena came in and put the coffee on the desk as Madzak was talking.
"Don't forget some lavish praise for the squad secretary," she interjected,
and quickly left.

"—and the finest squad secretary in the world!" Madzak added, loudly enough for her to hear.

"I'll second that," Kiley agreed. "She did some major work on the Winston case while I was occupied with Gloria Mendez's wake and funeral—"

"I'll see she gets credit," Madzak assured, "and I don't want to discuss
the Mendez matter with you. Any arrangement you and I make today is
contingent on you straightening yourself out with Allan Vander and IA on
that, understand?"

"Yes, sir."

They sipped their coffee and Madzak continued the main conversation.
"I'm of the opinion, after talking at length about you with Dan
Parmetter—and I've known Dan for thirty-five years; there's no better
man carrying a badge in Chicago—anyway, I'm of the opinion that you
would make a first-rate B-and-A man and an excellent addition to this
squad—but *only* if you want to; only if you've got a sincere desire to stop
being a maverick and become a working cop again. That, of course, is
something you'll have to make up your own mind about.

"Now then," the captain sat back and blew on his coffee a little, "the
other way to go is for me to just keep you occupied for a few months doing scut work, and then go to Chief Cassidy and request that you be
TADed to some other command. At that point, the chief would decide
what to do with you. Now, between you and me, I think Cassidy likes you;
he's real pissed at all the problems you've caused, but he recognizes the
value of cops like you to balance the department scales with tradition and
training on one side, and book-type intelligence and formal education on
the other. A good example is Vander's deputy, Bill Somers: He's bright,
well-spoken, polished, and knows everything that's ever been written
about law enforcement. But he's not tough, doesn't know the street, probably can't function well under the pressure of personal danger. Send him
to argue with the city council for a bigger department budget and you've
got a winner; send him through a door first on a hot bust and you might
have a problem.

"Point is, if I shift your file back to the chief's desk, you could very well
end up in a more active squad; it won't be Homicide, that's for sure, but

you could get Robbery, maybe Narcotics, Vice, maybe even something classy like the Fraud Squad. It'll be a crapshoot for you with the chief, but you could come up seven."

All the while Kiley had been listening, he had also been trying to evaluate what position to take in light of the plan he had already put into motion to avenge Nick Bianco's death. He felt there was a reasonable degree of probability that he would get away with what he intended to do; it was a well thought out plan, moving on schedule, the key players already falling into place. The *Sun-Times* that morning had included in its list of pallbearers for Frank Scarp the name of Anthony Touhy, younger brother of reputed North Side mob boss Philip Touhy. That meant Tony was back from Ireland for the funeral—so it looked to Kiley as if everything was proceeding exactly as he thought it would.

Kiley's dilemma was not what contingency plans to have if things went *wrong*; in that event, he would probably be dead and need no plans, or be in jail charged with murder, in which case he would need a lawyer, not plans. But if everything went *right*—what then? Did he just go on with his life as a policeman, an opportunity that was being offered to him here; could he do that, knowing that he had now committed murder, and was planning to do so again?

Kiley could not help wondering whether he would be able to function normally after it was all over; wondered if he would be able to manage the outward appearance and demeanor of an ordinary person, perform the tasks of his everyday work life, run on the same track that decent people, straight cops, ran on? Would he be capable of looking Captain Leo Madzak and Captain Dan Parmetter in the eye like a man, or would he shift his glance away guiltily like *suspects* did during interrogation? What he was asking himself, he realized, was whether he had any integrity left; notwithstanding his prejudices, his occasional violent eruptions of temper with criminals, his cynicism toward the world in general, did there remain a spark of decency, a hint of morality, a trace of goodness, that might sustain him in making a new beginning for himself in the wake of the blood he would have shed?

It was a question he could not answer, a prediction he could not make. His self-confidence, the self-assurance, self-reliance, that had served him so well for so long, now seemed to support him only insofar as his plan to avenge Nick was concerned. In every other facet of his existence, whatever strength of character there was within him appeared to be failing. He had lost Stella, just when he thought he might be on the verge of attaining her; he had not dealt well with Gino Bianco, sending the man's sons-in-law back bloody and humiliated; he felt terrible about the Harold Winston situation, even though he knew he had done the proper thing in arresting him; he had a troubling foreboding that he might fail Meralda Mendez in proving that her mother was not a suicide; and he was planning to involve Reggie in an illegal act, knowing how much Reggie stood to lose if caught—even though he now knew that Reggie, whom he had thought completely rehabilitated for so long, was no more an honest representation of what Kiley perceived than was anything else in his life.

So Kiley, as he listened to Leo Madzak's prognosis of what the future might hold, had no way of making a judgment call of any value. The best he could do, it seemed to him now, was take the path of least resistance and try to maintain a status quo that would give him another seventy-two hours to complete carrying out his plan.

"What do you think, Joe?" the captain asked when he finished outlining the two directions open to Kiley.

"Captain, I'd like very much to work for you," Kiley told him. "I'd like to try and make a new start with the department, and I realize that for it to be successful, I'm going to have to find a place where the past won't be held against me. To me that means being assigned to somebody like you or Captain Parmetter or somebody else from the old department. I don't seem to fit in with the newer breed, cops like Vander and Somers and the chief's deputy, Lester Ward. I need a place like B-and-A, Captain, and I need a boss like you. If you'll take me on, I won't let you down."

An expression of satisfaction settled on Madzak's face and he vigorously nodded endorsement of Kiley's decision. "Fine, Joe. Good decision. I'll get to work on a program for you. I think I'd like to send you to the FBI's bomb school back in Virginia for a month, but first I'll have to talk to Chief Cassidy about taking you off TAD status. I don't anticipate a problem there; I know he'd like to see you straighten out your career as much as Dan and I would." Madzak rose, so Kiley did also. "Vander is going to conduct your interview regarding the Mendez matter on Monday. Tomorrow's Friday; I'll try to see the chief in the morning. For the rest of today and tomorrow, why don't you review our recently closed bomb files just for familiarization purposes—"

At that moment, Aldena stuck her head in the door. "Mr. Faber just called from the state's attorney's office, Captain. Harold Winston was held to answer on one of the lesser charges: gross public vandalism.

Apparently he gave the judge a story about getting even for his daddy being fired from the transit authority. I guess the judge bought it. He turned Winston loose on twenty-five thousand bail."

Madzak and Kiley exchanged disgusted looks.

"Gross public vandalism," Madzak said. "Jesus H. Christ!"

"What does that carry?" Kiley asked.

"What is it, Aldena, one to three?" asked Madzak.

"Yes, sir. Plus restitution."

"He's a first offender with no record," Kiley evaluated.

"So he's probably looking at *probation* plus restitution," Madzak said, shaking his head. Then, having been around too long to lament such disappointments, the captain brightened. "Well, you closed the case anyway, Joe, even if he doesn't do any time. And look at it this way, at least maybe the city will get paid for some of the damages." To Aldena he said, "Get out a dozen of our most recent closed bomb cases for Detective Kiley to review, please, Aldena." To Joe: "I'll talk to you after I see the chief."

As Kiley and Aldena left the captain's office, Aldena said knowingly, "Going to bomb school, I'd guess." She looked him up and down. "You're going to have to get something to wear besides those dreary gray suits. I can't have you representing this squad at no FBI school looking like the house detective at a cheap hotel. We'll discuss your wardrobe later."

"You're the boss," Kiley said.

"You're going to do just fine in my squad, Detective," Aldena told him with a smile.

Kiley spent the rest of the morning reading case files involving bomb attempts made or carried out at a city high school, a Vietnamese convenience store that had opened in a black neighborhood, an Israeli Consulate office, a public coin-operated locker in the Greyhound Bus terminal, and a large vault in a retail Loop jewelry store during a failed robbery attempt. Kiley found the cases interesting, even with the cursory attention he was giving them, and it crossed his mind briefly that being a permanent member of the B-and-A squad might not be a bad assignment, providing everything went as he hoped it would in his plan—and provided he did not get caught afterward, or killed.

And—provided he could revert more or less to his old self after it was over.

Around noon, when most of the people in the squad room drifted out for lunch, Kiley went back to the computer section, opened his pocket notebook next to one of the monitors, and turned on the terminal. He had to try tying up the last loose ends of all the dangling threads that had unraveled in Nick Bianco's murder; he had to try and find out who the person was that Fraz Lamont knew only as Mr. O, the last remaining unidentified person who had been at the Shamrock Club meeting the night Tony Touhy killed Nick.

On the notebook page Kiley had opened was the sketchy information on the 1993 Lincoln Mark VIII owned by Prestige Automobile Leasing Company in suburban Lake Forest. All Kiley had on the car so far was the scrap of information he had managed to get from a secretary over the phone: that it was driven by one of the company's officers. Then someone named Matthew Field had come on the line and refused to divulge anything further. Kiley had initially suspected that Prestige had been either a front for some illegal mob activity, or was one of the many mob-owned legitimate businesses in the extended Chicago area. Originally he had expected to find that the driver of the Mark VIII was a ranking member of one of the three ethnic mob families who had control of the city's organized crime. Now his expectation was much higher. Because Fraz Lamont had characterized the man as an arbitrator, Kiley believed he was onto someone of much more authority in the organized crime hierarchy—possibly a person of the stature of the late Fred Scarp, who may have ascended, without fanfare or notice, to Scarp's previous lofty seat of command. Perhaps there were not, as commonly believed, three men of equal strength and dominion running everything now. Perhaps Phil Touhy, Augie Dellafranco, and Larry Morowski *all* took orders from someone else, someone who had the boss-of-bosses authority of a Lucky Luciano, an Al Capone, a Fred Scarp. Maybe there was a mob high administrator who was far smarter than those predecessors had been—because he held the power *anonymously.*

Pathing the terminal to Cook County business licenses, Kiley keyed in Prestige Automobile Leasing, and within a minute had information in the document window. Prestige was an incorporated business licensed in September 1988, with an investment base of one million dollars, all stock owned by its officers, who were: Matthew A. Field, president; Nancy Marie Field, vice-president; David M. Field, treasurer; and Natalie R. Field, secretary. The firm had a triple-A credit rating, in 1989 had received the city of Lake Forest's Honored New Business award, and in 1991 was given the Cook County Chamber of Commerce's Golden Medallion award as one of twelve model new businesses in the county.

Kiley accessed the cross-files of city, county, and state criminal records and keyed in all four names. There were no criminal records for any of them. He went into vital statistics with all four names for birth records. There were two found: Matthew Adam Field, born March 8, 1960, and David Martin Field, born May 6, 1962. Both were born at Garfield Park Community Hospital on the West Side, both the children of Craig T. and Naomi G. Field. There was no birth record for either Nancy or Natalie Field, indicating that they were either born outside the state or were the wives, not sisters, of the Field brothers.

Kiley ran the parents, Craig and Naomi, through criminal records, with negative results. Accessing business records by owner names, Kiley keyed in the Field brothers for identification with other businesses besides Prestige Auto Leasing. Five other suburban companies immediately came onto the screen: Prestige Video Sales and Rentals in Morton Grove, Prestige Camera Company in Park Ridge, Prestige Apartments in Old Orchard, Prestige Gifts in Oakton, and Prestige Travel in Evanston.

Returning to county business records, Kiley keyed in each business in turn. He found the same four names, in various orders, on the corporation documents filed for each business. David Field was president of Prestige Video; Nancy president of Prestige Camera; Natalie president of Prestige Gifts; Matthew president of Prestige Travel, David of Prestige Apartments. In each case, the other three served in corporate posts below the position of president.

Kiley went into the Cook County Bureau of Business Credit data base, entering each of the five new business names. Each business had a double-A or triple-A credit rating, with no liens against any of them. Each business was distinctly profitable.

Returning to criminal files, Kiley keyed in the name of each business to see if it was a known front for any illegal activity. He found nothing. Next he keyed in the names to the Better Business Bureau cross-files for city, county, and state records. There had been no complaints against any of them.

Sitting back in his chair in front of the monitor, Kiley sighed quietly. Everything looked impeccable; it was almost as frustrating as encountering restricted accesses. On the surface it looked like four people who were living an American dream: opening and succeeding in their own diversified small businesses. There was no apparent criminal activity being fronted, no known illegal operation in the businesses themselves, no past criminal record relating to any of the principals—nothing.

Yet—Kiley could not convince himself that there was not a connection somewhere.

Kiley accessed Cook County real property records and keyed in the names Matthew A. and Nancy Marie Field as joint owners. After ninety seconds of searching, a record came up. Matthew and Nancy Field owned a two-story, thirty-eight-hundred square-foot, ranch-style home with attached three-car garage and a thirty-foot swimming pool on a premium corner lot in Rolling Plains, a far northwest community across the line in DeKalb County. Estimated value of the property for county tax purposes was seven-hundred-forty thousand dollars.

Kiley pursed his lips in thought for a moment. That was a lot of house—but not really *too* much for a young couple with interests in six small but profitable businesses. Copying down the Rolling Plains address, he accessed the United States Government records menu. Scrolling down the list, he stopped at: CENSUS BUREAU, U. S., 1988 (UPDATED 1990), DEKALB COUNTY, ILLINOIS. Accessing the data base, Kiley keyed in the household of Matthew A. and Nancy Marie Field. The couple was shown to have three minor children: Brian, Craig, and Allison. On the chance that the other Field brother and his family might reside in the same community, Kiley keyed in David M. and Natalie R. Field. Census records showed that they had an address in Rolling Plains also, and documented two minor children: Martin and Jeffrey.

Returning to the Cook County real property records, Kiley found that the David Field family occupied a thirty-six-hundred square-foot house on a cul-de-sac lot with a twenty-eight-foot swimming pool, tax-valued at six-hundred-eighty thousand dollars. Again, not significantly out of line with respect to the probable income of the subjects. But there was still something that bothered Kiley about the whole picture. He wondered how two young men like the Field brothers had managed to start up not one, not two or three, but *six* small-to-medium-size businesses, in six separate communities, in such a relatively short period of time—and make all of them profitable. How the hell had they gotten started—particularly with a one-million-dollar investment base in Prestige Auto Leasing?

Reversing his search again, Kiley returned to criminal records and keyed in Craig T. Field, the father of the brothers. No record. Naomi G. Field, the mother. No record. Exiting criminal records, Kiley accessed county credit bureau records for Craig T. and Naomi G. The first of four pages came up in the document window. Craig Field was a baggage handler for American Airlines at O'Hare International Airport, employed as such since 1963, and had worked his way up during those years from a probationary trainee job to the position of senior supervisor. His wife Naomi was a licensed practical nurse who had worked relief shifts at the very hospital where both her sons were born, Garfield Park Community. Their credit rating over the years was occasionally slow-pay but otherwise good; they had obtained bank mortgage loans on two houses, one of which they currently occupied in the suburb of Western Springs.

Very ordinary, Kiley thought. No big family money to pass on to the two sons for investment purposes.

Scrolling the residential addresses shown on the credit report, Kiley noted that prior to Craig and Naomi Field buying their first house, which had been in Bridgeview, a suburb nearer the city, they had lived in the Archer Park district of Chicago, around 47th and Cicero. Kiley accessed Chicago Board of Education records and learned that both Matthew and David had attended Pasteur Elementary school, achieving above average but not extraordinary grades. There was no record of them attending any city high school. Kiley accessed Cook County Board of Education records, and the brothers showed up there first as students in Bridgeview Junior high school, and subsequently as graduates of Bridgeview Senior high school in 1978 and 1980 respectively. High school records reflected that each had, in his senior year, been offered an athletic scholarship to play basketball at Northwestern University, across the city in Evanston.

Northwestern was a private university and Kiley could not access its records. Turning on a screen block to cover the data he had in the document window, he left the terminal on and went over to the telephone directory library. In the directory for Evanston he found the main information number for Northwestern. Properly returning the directory to its shelf, as Aldena's sign ordered, he went to his desk and called the university. He was connected to a woman who handled records of former students, who said, "On the phone we will only verify dates and types of degrees. Anything else has to be in the form of a written request."

"That's fine," Kiley said, and gave her the two names.

In a very short time she was back on the line. "Michael Adam Field, BA in business administration, June 1982. David Martin Field, BA in business administration, June 1984."

"Thanks," Kiley said.

With the information in hand, he went back to the monitor he was using, cancelled the screen block, and sat silently pondering what he had learned—which essentially was nothing. He was not certain at this point that he was even searching in the right direction. What the hell, he wondered, made him think that Prestige Auto Leasing was dirty in the first place? The fact that this Matthew Field had refused to discuss a vehicle accident with him over the telephone? Maybe that was nothing more than company policy. Except that the secretary *had* said that the Mark VIII was—Kiley got out his notebook to double check—"an executive car driven by one of our officers."

The only officers listed on the incorporation papers of Prestige Auto Leasing were the two Field brothers and their wives. It was inconceivable to Kiley that either Matthew or David Field could be the unidentified "Mr. O" that Fraz Lamont claimed was the "arbitrator" at his last meet with the mob bosses. Yet the Mark VIII was the only car there that night whose driver remained unknown.

But, there was no connection to the case. No link.

In a quandary, Kiley closed Cook County Board of Education records, which was still in the document window, and idly went back into the vital statistics data base. The menu came on-screen and held there for further input. Kiley's eyes scanned his choices: BIRTHS, DEATHS, MARRIAGES, DIVORCES, NAME CHANGES, ADOPTIONS . . .

On impulse, Kiley selected Deaths and entered the names of Craig and Naomi Field, thinking perhaps they had died and the two sons received a large insurance settlement. But there was no record.

BIRTHS, DEATHS, MARRIAGES, DIVORCES, NAME CHANGES . . .

He selected Divorces. No records, for any of the names.

BIRTHS, DEATHS, MARRIAGES . . .

Drumming his fingers, he selected Marriages. He keyed in Matthew A. Field. Presently, marriage license record information came on. Matthew A. Field, it showed, age 24, had been party to a marriage license issued in May 1986 to marry Nancy Marie Lovat, age 23—

Kiley's mind stopped. It polarized.

Nancy Marie *Lovat?*

Quickly he accessed birth records and keyed in the name Nancy Marie Lovat. Her birth record came on. She had been born at Resurrection Hospital on September 8, 1962. Her mother was Constance Lemoyne Lovat. Father was Gordon Keith Lovat.

Kiley could only stare at the father's name.

Gordon Lovat. Commander of the Organized Crime Bureau. OCB. Mr. O.

# TWENTY-SEVEN

**J**ust after midnight on Friday, Kiley pulled his car to the curb in front of Reggie's Ribs and flashed his headlights once. The restaurant was dark except for its night-lights, but Kiley could see a shadowy figure get up from one of the tables and move to the front door. The figure came out the door, paused to double-lock it from the outside, and crossed the sidewalk to Kiley's car. Kiley unlocked the passenger door.

"'Evening, Joseph," said Reggie.

"How you doing?" Kiley asked by way of greeting.

"I'm cool," Reggie advised.

Kiley handed Reggie a pair of plastic wraparound sunglasses, the lenses and wide frames of which had been painted black with plastic model paint. "Put these on," Kiley said. "I don't want you to know where you're going."

"Okay by me," Reggie complied. With the glasses in place, he not only could not see directly ahead, he had no peripheral vision either. "Hope I don't get carsick," he said.

"You start feeling sick, you tell me right away," Kiley cautioned. "I'll pull over. Don't you puke in my car."

"I'll try not to," Reggie promised.

Kiley drove several blocks and got on the Dan Ryan Expressway, heading north. Knowing Reggie was smart enough to follow the way they were going, even with the glasses on, he turned on the radio and used the scan button to find a news broadcast. "What do you think about this situation in Haiti?" he asked, to distract Reggie from thinking about directions.

"I think they ought to give the fucking place to *Fee*-del Castro and let him kick some ass there and straighten the fucking government out," Reggie replied without contemplation.

"Oh, yeah?" Kiley was mildly surprised that Reggie had such a strong opinion. "Why do you say that?"

290

"Why, hell, Joe, them poor fucking Haitians been dealt so much shit by that Papa Doc and that Baby Doc, and then all them fucking generals and such, they *never* had a fair shake. Castro, he's a Commie, but at least he feeds the poor people."

They kept talking about Haiti. Kiley changed directions several times.

"You sure are making some strange turns, Joseph," his passenger finally commented.

"Forget that, will you?" Kiley said, a little shortly. "You're not supposed to be paying attention to directions. What do you think about this situation in Bosnia?"

"Hopeless," Reggie said, again without having to give the matter any preliminary thought. "Ought to take all the big-shot politicians on both sides, stand their asses up against a wall, and machine-gun the mother-fuckers. You see them little kids on the news had arms and legs blown off? You'd think grown-up men would see just *one* kid like that, they'd call the whole fucking war *off*." Reggie rested his head back against the seat. "I can't take seeing little kids like that, Joe. Tears me up. Every time I see one of those little kids on the news, poor little pitiful things crying so hard, I go right for the checkbook and be sending another hundred, two hundred, to the children aid organizations, you know."

Kiley glanced curiously at him. "I thought you were gambling all your money away."

"No, Joe, not all of it," Reggie replied quietly.

Since Reggie had fallen silent and did not seem to be mentally tracking directions any longer, Kiley touched the radio's scan button again, found a station carrying muted blues music, and let it remain there.

"Tha's nice," Reggie said, bobbing his chin at the radio. "B. B. King in one of his softer moments. He did a concert at the Cook County jail when I was there waitin' on my trial. Man is one of the greats."

"Yeah," agreed Kiley, who had never heard of B. B. King. Kiley could not tell through the painted glasses whether Reggie's eyes were open or not. But as long as Reggie remained quiet, Kiley decided to do likewise.

Kiley was still somewhat traumatized by the link he had found connecting OCB commander Gordon Lovat with the Mark VIII parked at the Shamrock the night Nick was killed. He would not have been more surprised initially if he had learned that Chief Cassidy was driving the car, or the mayor. Lovat, the department's top man in combatting organized crime in the city, had sat down not only with the heads of the three main ethnic mob families, but also with the undisputed leader of the most powerful street gang in Chicago. And, according to Fraz Lamont, the OCB head had been there as an "arbitrator"—which to Kiley meant a mediator, a referee: a man who had power to reconcile differences, negotiate settlements—in this case what the Disciples' share of vending machine profits would be.

In retrospect, Kiley realized that it was not such a preposterous discovery at all. Who but the highest police authority charged with controlling organized crime could have contacted, reasoned with, and persuaded, the mob bosses to do business with Fraz Lamont? Who but the man in charge of OCB could have *guaranteed* a peaceful, productive association as a result of such an alliance? Historically, Irish, Italian, and Polish mobsters had looked at blacks in general with unbounded contempt. Frequently, their identical assessment of blacks had been the only thing they had in common. In the 1940s when the late Fred Scarp had been working so diligently to bring the then warring ethnic factions to the bargaining table, he had done so by warning them that if they did not work together to control certain areas of the city, the blacks would take over and then *none* of them—not the Irish, the Italians, *or* the Poles—would share in anything. "Keep it up, you fucking assholes," Scarp often preached. "Keep fighting among yourselves over nickels and dimes, and the fucking spades are going to walk away with the dollars." When that reasoning finally got through to them, and an equitable division of the city's illegal spoils was made, Scarp had ascended to the position of boss-of-bosses, and Chicago became a better place for it. After that, mob disputes were no longer allowed to get out of hand, mob violence was no longer permitted, and strict controls were placed on the expansion of any criminal activity to the point where it would generate increased public awareness or heightened law enforcement effort toward its restraint.

The time would come, however, in the late 1970s and early 1980s, when the organized crime operation which had prospered for so long under Fred Scarp's guidance, began, during Scarp's gradual retirement process, to be challenged by the new and fearless black street gangs, beginning with the powerful El Rukns. The Rukns were the first organized blacks to get in organized crime's face—and they did it with automatic weapons. For the first time in the mob's history, it was faced with a *competitor* as opposed to a police agency, that equaled it not only in firepower but in viciousness as well. For a number of years, there was violent strife between various elements of the mob and the El Rukns, then with smaller, splinter gangs such as the Black Mambas, the V.D.s or Violent Dudes, and the Trey-Sevens, a gang laying claim to all of 37th Street. Then, ultimately, came Fraz Lamont and the Disciples. Mob profits diminished in the areas coming under control of the black gangs, but *gang* income did not increase because they did not have the business acumen to efficiently operate what they had acquired.

It may not have been immediately clear to those closest to the mob that an important element was missing in their underworld community—but it must have become very obvious *outside* that sphere. The element, of course, was a Fred Scarp figure who could draw in all the disputants involved and work at resolving differences and promoting harmony. Who better to undertake such a task than one of the highest-ranking, most honored and respected police department executives in Chicago, a man who not only had access to the heads of the mob families but also, because of his participation in command-level law enforcement meetings, had inside information on the workings of the black street gangs. Who else besides someone like Gordon Lovat? Mr. OCB himself. Mr. O.

Knowing it was true did not make it any easier for Kiley to believe it—but there was no way he could logically *dis*believe it. Too many facts were now nailed down.

Phil Touhy had learned almost at once that the surveillance of his brother Tony by Kiley and Nick was unauthorized—which permitted Touhy to come in with his lawyer and legally challenge the investigation. His information could only have come from one of a handful of people at that time—and Lovat was among them. Lovat had worked out the deal with the department to kill the investigation of Tony Touhy.

Gloria Mendez's death—her staged suicide—had to have been brought about by knowledge on the part of someone that she had provided, or was *providing*, confidential department information to Joe Kiley. Lovat, after being told by his son-in-law Matthew Field of the fake insurance call to Prestige Auto, must have become very apprehensive that Kiley was trying to identify the driver of the Mark VIII. He must have decided that it was simply too risky to allow Gloria to remain a factor in the situation, given her unlimited access to confidential records. So he had her killed.

And the logical reason for Nick Bianco's spur-of-the-moment murder must have been that he walked in on that meeting and saw Gordon Lovat there. Fraz Lamont, Kiley decided, really had *not* known the reason for Nick's killing, because Fraz Lamont had not known that Mr. O was a high-ranking police officer. Neither the mob bosses nor Lovat would have trusted the street gang leader that far. Fraz had said that none of them were strapped that night, that he didn't even know where Tony Touhy had come up with the gun to kill

Nick. He did not know that the one person there who *would* have been carrying was the "arbitrator"—because that person was a cop.

In the beginning, Kiley had set out to deal only with Nick's killer. Then circumstances had imposed on him the additional responsibility of determining the identification of and dealing with Gloria's killer. Now he knew that he also had to deal with Lovat. Every time he turned around, there seemed to be someone new who qualified as a target for his revenge.

As he was pondering the glut of perplexing facts that seemed to be ricocheting off the inside walls of his head, Kiley glanced over and saw that Reggie was once again sitting up alertly, looking straight ahead at the blackness of the painted sunglasses. Kiley frowned suspiciously.

"You got any idea where we are?" he asked.

"Kind of," Reggie admitted.

"Goddamn it, Reggie. You're not supposed to know where you're going."

"I can't help it," Reggie almost whined. "I got a natural instinct for direction, Joe. You got to remember that most of my previous work involved moving around in the dark."

"Where do you think we are right now?" Kiley quizzed. He didn't see how Reggie could possibly have kept up with all the turns they had made.

"Right now? Well, let's see," Reggie replied. "I'd say we somewhere out around Chevalier Woods, heading toward the airport."

"Dead wrong," Kiley declared. "Not even close." They had just passed an expressway sign that read: CHICAGO-O'HARE INTERNATIONAL AIRPORT 3 MI. Kiley pushed the radio scanner button again, got another news broadcast, and said, "Let's talk about Somalia. What do you think about the situation in Somalia?"

"I think if we not very careful, we going to find ourselves in another Vietnam," Reggie replied clinically. "Problem is, Joe, we got a *red*neck with a *yellow* streak in the *White* House. Mix red, yellow, and white, and you get the color of most shit. One thing this country don't need is more shit." A big commercial jet could be heard coming in low for a landing. Reggie started humming quietly to himself, a smug look on his face.

"All right," Kiley conceded, "take the fucking glasses off if you want to."

"No, I'll keep them on," Reggie decided. "Least I won't know what kind of place I'm opening. How much further?"

"Not very far," Kiley said.

Less than five minutes later, Kiley turned off the expressway and drove north for a short distance, then west again. The farther away from the expressway they got, the quieter and more deserted the night became. Kiley had been out to their destination each of the past two nights after work; he already knew exactly which route he was going to take, and he also knew the approximate times of the local police patrol around where they were going. Glancing at the dashboard clock now, he verified for himself that the timing was good: it was almost midway between times for the patrol to pass.

Presently, Kiley slowed and guided the car into a narrow, unlighted alley, turning off the headlights as he did.

"We there?" Reggie asked. Just a hint of nervousness. Wearing the glasses, Kiley decided. Without them, Reggie probably wouldn't even sweat.

Kiley stopped the car, put the gearshift in park to leave the engine on, and quickly went around to open the passenger door. Reggie was pulling on a pair of gloves.

"Come on—" Kiley whispered. He guided Reggie out of the car and a matter of only five steps to a door. "Okay, it's right in front of you—"

Reggie removed the glasses and handed them to Joe. With a penlight, he shined a needle beam on the lock.

"This is it?" he whispered incredulously. "This is the fucking door?"

"*Yeah.* Come on—" The nervousness was now in Kiley's voice.

"What the fuck is this place," Reggie asked contemptuously, "a second-hand store?" He removed a small suede case from his inside coat pocket and unzipped it. "Don't even need lock picks for this," he muttered. "Could have just brought a paper clip, or a bobby pin—" Reggie was quiet for about forty seconds, then said, "Okay."

"Okay what?" Kiley asked.

"Okay, the fucking door is open," Reggie said irascibly. "What the fuck do you think?"

Kiley reached out in the dark to assure himself that the door indeed was open. "Jesus," he said under his breath, surprised at how quickly it had been accomplished. "Okay, fix it so it won't lock," he whispered.

Kiley was aware of movement on Reggie's part, and presently heard a soft metal click. "Fixed," Reggie told him. There was the slightest movement of air as Reggie drew the door closed. Kiley handed him the glasses and he put them back on. Then Kiley led him back to the car.

Seconds later, Kiley was guiding the car out of the opposite end of the alley, turning the headlights on, and driving back toward the main road that led to the expressway.

"I hope you don't plan to take the fucking scenic route to get me home," Reggie said.

"I don't."

"Good. I need to get some sleep, got a business to run in the morning."

Reggie waited until Kiley made a turn and increased their speed enough for him to know that the car was again on an expressway, then he removed the blackened sunglasses, examined them for a moment in the dashboard light, and finally tossed them onto the backseat.

"I guess you know, Joseph, that you have got my curiosity most highly aroused," he said. "I presume you are going *back* to that place after you get rid of me."

"Do me a favor, Reggie, don't presume," Kiley said.

"What I don't dig is what you're going to do when you get *back*, that you couldn't have done when we was *there*."

"Will you just forget it?"

Reggie turned his head to look out the window. "You don't trust me," he said, trying to pout.

"If I didn't trust you, I wouldn't commit a felony with you," Kiley differed.

"Well, you don't trust me *enough*, then." Reggie sighed as dramatically as he could manage. "I prob'ly won't get no sleep all night long tonight, just wondering what that place was."

"Drop it, Reggie." Kiley's voice flattened now, its tone leveling to cold seriousness. "I do trust you—but this is a very serious thing."

"Oh, yeah? How serious?"

"As serious as it can get. Now drop it."

"Sound to me like you talking about something really bad, old friend," Reggie kidded with a smile. "I hope you not fixing to put nobody's lights out."

Kiley only glanced at Reggie, without speaking. Reggie stared hard at Kiley for a long moment, the sodium lights over the expressway giving them both an iridescent alien cast. Slowly it dawned on Reggie that he had been probing for a truth he would not have wanted to hear. He faced forward, eyes off Kiley, and concentrated his gaze on the four lanes of expressway, with Chicago's night skyline on the horizon. Neither man spoke for what seemed like a long time as that skyline grew larger and more defined. The silence became heavier with each mile, as if it was opening a fissure between them. Slowly, they each began to realize that something was happening, that this night and what had occurred was somehow affecting their relationship, that each of them had taken a step away from the other and from which there was no return. Their friendship, at least as they had known it, would never be the same again.

As they approached the Lake Street exit, near the Loop, Reggie said, "Say, Joe, instead of taking me home, run me down to Rush Street, will you? I want to find me an all-nighter and get something to eat."

"You sure?" Kiley asked. "No trouble for me to get on the Dan Ryan and run you back—"

"No, no, listen, just drop me on Rush. I'll eat and then hop a Jackson Station train out to 58th. No problem."

"Okay, if you're sure—"

"I'm sure."

Kiley exited, drove down to Michigan, crossed the river, and cut back to Rush Street. He let Reggie out at the Lennox House.

"Okay, I'll see you, my man," Reggie said from the curb.

"Yeah. Thanks for the help, Reggie. Stay loose, okay?"

"Yeah, right."

They locked eyes for a moment, then Reggie turned and walked down the street.

Kiley made an illegal U-turn and headed back for the expressway.

Forty-five minutes later, Kiley parked his car on a dark, quiet street, one block from the building with the door that Reggie had opened and left unlocked for him.

From the trunk of his car, Kiley removed a leather gym bag. He walked briskly along the silent street, keeping well in the shadows, and turned down to the mouth of the alley. Stepping into it, he stood back against the side of a building and waited a full three minutes—eyes searching what the streetlights allowed him to see, ears scanning the night for sound. When he felt assured that his presence was unknown, he proceeded down the alley to the unlocked door.

At the door, Kiley put the gym bag on the ground, blotted his forehead with a handkerchief, and pulled on a pair of surgical gloves. Picking up the gym bag, he slowly turned the knob, opening the door.

Sweating profusely, he entered.

# TWENTY-EIGHT

**A**t eleven o'clock on Saturday morning, Kiley was parked in the next block down from Our Lady of Lourdes Catholic Church in the western suburb of Madison Acres, where he had killed Fred Scarp. From a vantage point near the corner of that block, he was able to watch a constant queue of expensive cars and limousines drive up to discharge at the church entrance passengers arriving to attend funeral services for the murdered former mob boss. There were news media in evidence also: vans, video camera people, and still photographers with telephoto lenses balanced on tripods. Private uniformed security guards were managing to keep everything reasonably in order for the services, which were scheduled for eleven-thirty. From where he sat, Kiley could see florist delivery vehicles arriving one after another with wreaths and other tributes.

By eleven-twenty, most traffic had stopped and only a few late arrivals were driving up. Kiley left his car and walked up the street, past the church, and on to a small community park at the far end of the block. He sat on a bench and deliberated on the knowledge that it had actually been *him* who had brought about all the activity going on at the church at that moment. His solitary act had put in motion hundreds of people in many diverse walks of life—from organized crime mobster to florist delivery man, private security guard to parish priest, news reporter to limousine driver, mortician to airline ticket agent to grave digger to—

Whatever—he had caused it.

As he sat there, Kiley did not *regret* what he had done—at least, not regret it specifically, not regret what he had done to Fred Scarp. What he regretted was Nick being dead and all the grief and anguish he himself had directly or indirectly generated by his suggestion that he and Nick go after Ronnie Lynn's killer themselves. If he could reverse that, he would have; if he could change places in death with Nick, he would—in an instant,

298

without hesitation: he would give Nick back to Stella and the girls, set their lives right again, and keep Stella from a marriage to that low-life prick Frank Bianco. But life and death, Kiley knew, could only be advanced, not turned back, and he had to live with what he had already caused—and what he *would* cause.

After half an hour, Kiley returned to his car and sat watching until the funeral mass ended and the mourners began filing out of the church to line the broad front steps and wait while inside the extended family of Frank Scarp paid its last respects before the casket was closed. After a few minutes, Kiley saw the casket being carried out to a hearse in front of the church. Picking up his binoculars from the seat beside him, he focused on the five pallbearers he could see clearly from the car. The one in front was Phil Touhy. Directly behind him was a swarthy man with slick black hair. Augie Dellafranco, Kiley guessed. Next came a face that was etched in Kiley's mind from the pornographic tapes and photos he had seen when he had tossed the Lake Shore Drive apartment: Tony Touhy. The man directly behind the younger Touhy was unknown to Kiley, but he knew it had to be one of the two out-of-towners that the funeral notice in the previous day's *Tribune* had said would also be pallbearers: Abe Lovitz and Nate Taub, cousins and Jewish bosses of the Detroit rackets. Another swarthy man, younger, slicker, was holding up the end of the casket where Fred Scarp's head was. That would be Al Morelli, Kiley thought, the number-two man to Dellafranco.

As the casket was being placed into the hearse, Kiley saw briefly that the pallbearers on the opposite side of it were Larry Morowski, Mickey O'Shea, Jocko Hennessey, and another stranger, who had to be the other Jewish cousin from Detroit. Kiley knew nothing about Lovitz or Taub, except that they had not, to his knowledge, been at the Shamrock Club meeting or involved in Nick Bianco's killing. But they *were* in the rackets, they *were* dirty, so Kiley did not waste any time worrying about them being there. It was their choice to lie down with dogs.

As soon as the casket was in the hearse, Kiley started the engine of his car and drove away. He got on Irving Park Road and headed west along the southern edge of O'Hare Airport, and almost immediately into the suburb of Mt. Canaan. He stayed on the same road as it bisected Mt. Canaan and eventually reached New Saints Cemetery. Driving once slowly through the cemetery, he noted three open grave sites with canvas spread over the removed dirt, and padded folding chairs arranged around the graves for the deceased's family during the brief burial services. A stake driven in the ground at each location held a neatly lettered sign bearing the name of the person being buried and the time of the service.

The Scarp plot was near the east side of the cemetery; the sign at the edge of the pathway read: FREDERICO ANGELO SCARPELLI—1:30 P.M. Checking his watch, Kiley saw that it was five past one. The other burials, he knew from the signs, were at two-thirty and three-thirty, so there would be no other corteges in the cemetery while Scarp's was there.

Scanning the area, Kiley saw that just beyond the east boundary of New Saints, bordering the grounds but at a lower elevation, was the meandering Wolf River, and beyond that, at a higher point, was a drive that followed the course of the river, Wolf River Road. At most any point along its route, it presented a perfect vantage point over and down into the cemetery.

Driving out the rear gate of the grounds, which was the exit one procession of cars used while another was entering the front, Kiley cut east across the narrow, greenish river, then doubled back west following the riverbank, watchful of the cemetery across the way until he came again to the area where Fred Scarp's grave site was open. Pulling to the side of the road, Kiley parked and waited.

At one-twenty, Fred Scarp's funeral procession came slowly down the cemetery drive. The two lead vehicles, which bore the flower tributes, halted first and their drivers and two assistants quickly began transferring wreaths and other floral arrangements from the cars to the canvas-covered mound of dirt behind the open grave. When the men were finished, the two flower vehicles were pulled up out of the way and the main hearse, carrying the casket, moved into place. The nine pallbearers came forward from another car and stood waiting as all the cars in the procession halted one by one and their passengers got out and moved as an unbound group over to the grave site. The family mourners then emerged from several hearses directly behind the casket hearse, and they all made their way over to the folding chairs arranged for them.

Only then was the casket hearse's rear doors opened and the casket rolled out on ball bearings for the pallbearers to lift up for the last thirty yards of its journey. The faces of the nine men, mobsters all, were cheerless, doleful, as they carried one of their elder statesmen to his final resting place.

In his car, Kiley raised the binoculars again and focused them tight on the casket and its pallbearers.

The nine men had gone only a few steps when the casket exploded.

# TWENTY-NINE

**K**iley waited in the dark, sitting on a lawn chair he had opened, in one of the front corners of Gordon Lovat's two-car garage. Lovat's personal car, a Roadmaster station wagon, was parked on the right side of the garage, where Kiley sat; from time to time he put a foot on the wagon's rear bumper and tilted back a little to change positions. It was nearly ten o'clock on Saturday night; he had been waiting there for an hour, since shortly before nine.

Immediately after the explosion at the cemetery, Kiley had remained only a couple of minutes as the ugly black smoke cleared, focusing his binoculars on the carnage he had produced. There was, as far as he could tell, virtually nothing left of Fred Scarp's cadaver and casket except splinters and pulp. Around a patch of scorched grass, some near, some farther back, lay the bodies of the pallbearers, some of them, Kiley noted, with arms or legs blown off. Kiley could not tell who was who because all of them were seared as black as the ground on which they lay.

There was chaos all around the grave site: men shouting, women screaming, the funeral home's private security escort officers running around in confusion. It was complete bedlam and disorder, and would remain so, Kiley imagined, for quite a while. From across the cemetery where its administration building was located, Kiley saw two small electric cars racing to the scene. Before long, he knew, there would be sirens as police and medical personnel sped to the scene. Taking one last, sweeping look at the pandemonium, Kiley could not help thinking: *You were a good teacher, Hal.*

Without watching any longer, Kiley had driven away.

Now he was sitting in the garage of Gordon Lovat's condominium on Sheridan Road, waiting for the Organized Crime Bureau commander to return from a hastily called meeting of his deputy and staff at the Shop. Lovat had learned of the cemetery explosion about two hours after it

**301**

occurred. He called the meeting for six p.m. Because the incident had taken place in the suburb of Mt. Canaan, which was in DuPage County, the Mt. Canaan police and the DuPage County sheriff had jurisdiction. Lovat had quickly contacted the heads of both those departments and offered the assistance of his bureau, but the offer was declined. Because certain Chicago organized crime figures had been involved, however, Lovat knew he would be called upon by the media to analyze and comment on the incident. After conferring with his people, he decided that OCB would take an initial position that it had likely been a professional assassination committed in an effort to liquidate all current ranking mob bosses to make way for a younger group of hoodlums to move up and assume control. At a subsequent press conference, Lovat would not speculate as to who those young crime lords were, but did emphasize to the press that his offer of assistance to the Mt. Canaan authorities would remain in effect in case those departments elected to accept it. Lovat had concluded his statement with a comment that he was on his way to make a personal report on the situation to Chief John Cassidy at his home.

Kiley had learned all those facts from television news shows about the bombing, earlier reports of which had already been on the air by the time Kiley arrived home from the cemetery just before three o'clock. Preliminary information from the scene indicated that at least five pallbearers were known dead, among them North Side mob boss Philip Touhy, West Side boss Laurence Morowski, and Alfonse Morelli, chief lieutenant to Augustus Dellafranco, head of the South Side rackets. Dellafranco himself was reported alive but in critical condition with one arm and one leg blown off. No one had been injured other than the nine pallbearers, although half a dozen older men and women among the mourners had suffered shock and other emotional trauma.

As the afternoon wore on, Kiley watched a brief interview with Gordon Lovat as he arrived at the Shop. Then there was news that two other bodies had been identified as Nathan Taub, of Detroit, and local mobster Michael O'Shea, who was known to hold a major position in the Touhy crime family. Videotaped coverage from the scene showed a great deal of commotion and confusion, with much rushing about of emergency medical personnel, and many mourners being led away by uniformed officers. To fill empty time between live coverage, film clips were shown of the late Fred Scarp's rise in organized crime.

By early evening, a report was broadcast that the second Jewish mobster, Abraham Lovitz, was also dead, and that another member of Philip

Touhy's Irish mob, Jocko Hennessey, had suffered the loss of both arms above the elbow. Bad day for the mob, boys, Kiley allowed himself to think as he sipped a straight gin and waited for the one report that still had not come in. He had almost not been able to wait for that news, because several minutes later there was televised live Gordon Lovat's press conference at which he made clear the Chicago department's position regarding the situation, then cut his own participation short, turning the press over to his deputy, so he could personally brief Chief Cassidy. Lovat's departure from the press conference was Kiley's signal to leave for Lovat's condo. He had put his belt holster in place and was closing the Velcro strap on his ankle rig when the live broadcast cut away from the Shop and went back to the newsroom.

"We have just received confirmation from Mt. Canaan police Lieutenant Jerome Fitch at Forrest Hospital in that suburb that a sixth body from the shocking cemetery bombing has been identified as Anthony Francis Touhy, age thirty, the younger brother of Philip Touhy, who was pronounced dead and identified earlier this afternoon—"

"That's for you, Nick," Kiley said out loud to himself.

Now, he thought, he was going to get the man who had loaned Tony Touhy the gun to kill Nick.

It was twenty past ten when a spray of headlights swept under the closed garage door, and the automatic door opener near the garage's ceiling engaged noisily to begin lifting the door in and back. Though he had been waiting for just such an indication of Gordon Lovat's arrival for more than an hour, Kiley nevertheless was startled by the sudden light and sound. Quickly getting to his feet, he folded the lawn chair, hung it on a wall hook above where he had been sitting, and stood rigidly back out of sight in a foot-deep recessed niche next to the frame of the garage door. He drew his gun.

As Lovat drove his unmarked police car in, an automatic light came on above a door across the garage from Kiley that led into Lovat's condo. As the police car came to a halt and the overhang door began closing behind it, Kiley dropped to a crouch near the right rear tire of Lovat's station wagon. When Lovat opened the car door to get out, Kiley moved with the noise around the rear of the station wagon and assumed the same crouch at the right rear tire of the police car. He waited, barely breathing, until Gordon Lovat, keys in hand, approached the door to his condo. Then Kiley stood and put the muzzle of his gun behind Lovat's left ear.

"Freeze, Captain," he said in a quiet, even voice. "One move and I'll kill you."

"I'm not moving," Lovat said, whole body tensing, the hand with the keys suspended halfway to the door.

Reaching around him, Kiley found Lovat's gun in a shoulder holster and removed it. He put it in his coat pocket and stretched down to feel below both of Lovat's calves for a second weapon.

"I don't carry a backup," Lovat said.

"You should," Kiley told him, "if you're going to loan your gun to other people." He nudged Lovat's head with the muzzle. "Open the door."

Lovat unlocked the door and pushed it open. Kiley noticed that as Lovat worked the key, his hand did not tremble. Watch him, Kiley warned himself, he doesn't have a loose nerve in his body.

"Turn on the lights," Kiley ordered. Reaching inside, Lovat obeyed. "Hands on top of your head," Kiley said then.

"I should warn you that my wife is probably reading in the bedroom upstairs," Lovat said.

"Your wife is dead," Kiley retorted flatly. "Constance Lemoyne Lovat died on October 20, 1989, of stomach cancer." With his left hand, he took hold of the back of Lovat's lapel and guided him into the condo. From the garage, a hall led past a small laundry room and into a kitchen. "Keep turning on lights," Kiley ordered. From the kitchen, a second hall led to a dining area in one direction, and a large living room in another. Between them, a stairway led to the second floor.

"I know your voice," Lovat said, as Kiley moved him through the house to the living room.

Kiley took him to a chair and had him stand in front of it for a moment while he reached down and felt around the cushion for a gun. Then Kiley stepped away from him. "Take your hands off your head and put them on the arms of the chair. Don't move your hands unless I tell you to."

Lovat sat, turning to face Kiley for the first time.

"Detective Kiley," he said. "Of course. I might have known." A slight half-smile, half-smirk settled on his lips, as if he had suddenly become aware that a danger had passed and that this was a situation that he was going to be able to handle. "You've ruined yourself this time, Kiley," he said. "You're through as a cop."

"Don't be too sure of that, Captain," said Kiley. "Maybe it's you who's through." He took Lovat's service revolver from his pocket. "Is this the gun that killed Nick Bianco?"

"Are you out of your mind, Detective? You think *I* killed Nick Bianco?"

"I think your *gun* killed him. Your gun—in Tony Touhy's hand."

Lovat's expression of surprise was quickly replaced by sudden cognizance. "Is that what this is all about? You're still after Tony Touhy?" The captain sat forward, turning his palms up. "He's dead, Kiley—"

"I told you not to move your hands," Kiley said, cocking the hammer of his revolver.

"All right—!" Lovat responded urgently, at once sitting back with his hands on the chair arms again.

"Tony Touhy being dead isn't enough," Kiley told him evenly. "Maybe that pays for Nick; it doesn't pay for Gloria Mendez." He shook his head almost miserably. "Why the fuck did you have to kill her too? She wasn't a threat to you anymore—"

"Kiley, listen to me," Lovat said in a precise voice. "Uncock your pistol. We've got to talk, you and I, but I can't do it as long as you've got that hammer back."

"We don't have anything to talk about, Lovat," said Kiley, voice flat again. "You're a dirty cop and you were part of killing two other cops. Now it's time for you to pay. All I want to know is *why*? Why Gloria?"

"Uncock your gun, Joe, and I'll tell you." Lovat's voice eased into a thoughtful, reasoning tone.

Uncocking the gun, Kiley sat heavily on the couch facing Lovat's chair.

"What makes you think you're right about all this?" Lovat asked.

"I know I'm right about Nick because Fraz Lamont told me," Kiley replied confidently.

"Fraz Lamont? The nigger gang leader?" Lovat had to force his incredulity. "And you believed *him*?" He shook his head. "I think you've lost it, Kiley. You're over the edge."

"I think *you* lost it when you decided to kill Gloria Mendez. It wasn't necessary. She and I were ready to drop Tony Touhy in the chief's lap. All you had to do was let that punk go down and I never would have tied you in. It would have stopped right there."

"What makes you think you *have* tied me in?" Lovat asked with a smile that was sincere now. "My gun could have been stolen. I can back date a report to that effect. That'll take care of the Bianco incident. As to Mendez, well, what makes you think your spic policewoman friend didn't kill herself the way the coroner's report reads?"

"Similar bruises on the backs of both hands," Kiley said. "I think they were made from a pair of older model handcuffs that didn't close down as far as the newer ones do. Handcuffs that work fine on a man's wrist, but are a little too large for the wrists of a woman or an adolescent. Gloria Mendez was handcuffed with a pair of those old bracelets and when she struggled"—Kiley's eyes turned hard and hateful—"when she struggled because pills and liquor were being forced into her mouth, those cuffs were pulled down across the backs of her hands and left marks." Kiley's hard eyes narrowed. "Let me see your handcuffs, Captain."

"I don't carry handcuffs, Kiley. I'm not a common street cop."

"No, you're a big-shot desk cop: exactly the kind of cop who'd have an *old* pair of cuffs." Kiley glanced around. "They're around here someplace, aren't they?"

"Why don't you search the place?" Lovat suggested. "Finding an old pair of cuffs isn't going to prove a goddamned thing." Lovat shook his head. "Kiley, stop this insanity before it goes any further. I could be a lot of help to you if you'd just be reasonable."

"What kind of help?" Kiley asked wryly. "You going to set me up in business like you've done your daughter and her husband and his brother?"

Now it was Lovat's eyes that narrowed. "I think I've underestimated you, Detective. What else do you know?"

"Just about everything, I think. A few years ago you took a look at the street violence being brought about by the conflict between the three white mob families and the black street gangs. You saw that the mobs were losing their grip in the black neighborhoods, but that the black gangs that were taking over weren't smart enough to profit from their new power. Fraz Lamont himself is a very smart man, but the majority of his Disciples are on the slow side; he's got no experienced labor pool to draw from. But his people *can* intimidate. So you got to him some way, without telling him who you were, and showed him how he could control his neighborhoods and make money too. All he had to do was let the white mob boys operate under his protection for a flat fee. In effect, you showed the Disciples how the old protection racket operates. Then you arranged a meeting with Phil Touhy and the other bosses, who *did* know who you were, and you offered them not only a plan to get back the neighborhoods they had lost, but also a certain amount of immunity from OCB investigation, in return for a cut of the profits to you and a protection fee to Lamont. Touhy and the others went for it, because part of something is better than all of nothing. You set yourself up as an arbitrator to make sure any differences between the parties were settled without a fight. After you had that all arranged and the money started coming in, you started setting up businesses in the names of your daughter and son-in-law, and his brother and the brother's wife, to launder the dirty money you were getting—"

"That's ludicrous," Lovat interrupted. "It's a perfect example of what I said to you in one of the meetings following Bianco's death: You're a street cop and you have no concept of the broader picture of law enforcement in this city. There's no need to launder mob money in Chicago. We aren't talking about millions upon millions of dollars in Colombian drug money here; Phil Touhy and the others don't even *deal* in drugs. We're talking about *thousands* of dollars—five thousand here, ten thousand there—money from gambling, prostitution, hijacked merchandise: offenses that are either victimless or affect only large companies that pass the losses on to their insurance carriers. The money that went into those corporations for the kids wasn't to set up a laundering operation or anything else illegal; it was to get them started in legitimate businesses that they could pass on to *their* kids—" He stopped talking and shook his head again. "I don't know why I'm trying to explain this to you, Kiley."

"Maybe to justify why two cops had to die," Kiley said.

"Bianco and Gloria Mendez didn't die because of anything *I* did," Lovat shook his head emphatically. "They died because both of them broke the rules; both of them went beyond the book. They stepped across the line and they paid a price for it."

"Like *you've* stepped across the line?" Kiley asked.

"Not at all," Lovat declared. "What I did, Detective, was stop the street violence between the white mobs and the black gangs. What I did was the job I was *given* to do by the department. This city is a safer place today because of the deal I made between the mobs and the Disciples." Lovat suddenly leaned forward, and this time Kiley did not object. "Try to understand what I'm saying," Lovat asked with a new urgency. "I don't know what you've got in mind here tonight, but understand something: killing me to get revenge for Bianco or Mendez won't solve anything. There was a major mob assassination a few hours ago; the Touhy brothers are dead, Larry Morowski is dead, Augie Dellafranco is crippled for life. There'll be a whole new generation of mob lieutenants moving up. It's essential that the pact with Fraz Lamont be kept in place; if not, a whole new era of street violence is going to begin. If you'll just try to be reasonable, Joe, there can be a place in all of this for you—"

"I *am* being reasonable," Kiley asserted. "I can understand Nick being killed; after he walked in on your meeting at the Shamrock that night, maybe Touhy, Morowski, and the others insisted that he be killed. Maybe there was no way you could stop it. But Gloria Mendez had to be *your* call, Captain: nobody else knew about her—"

"Phil Touhy knew," Lovat contradicted. "I had already told him how I thought you and Bianco got the confidential information on Tony—"

"So Phil Touhy wanted her killed?"

"Yes—"

"Who killed her?"

"He did." Lovat swallowed. "And me." He smiled nervously. "You were right about the handcuffs. You're a smart cop, Joe. Like I said, there could be a place for you in all of this. But if you kill me, well—" Lovat spread his hands as if the result was obvious.

"I'm not going to kill you, Captain."

Kiley rose and went over to the front door. He opened it and Allan Vander walked in with his deputy, Bill Somers, and two other Internal Affairs officers. From under his coat, Kiley removed and handed to Vander a mini-microphone and wire he was wearing. He gave Lovat's gun to Somers.

"Get enough, Captain?" he asked Vander.

"More than enough," said Allan Vander.

From where he sat, Gordon Lovat stared in disbelief at Joe Kiley. "You set me up," he said incredulously. "You, a common street cop, set me up—"

Kiley paused to look at him pitilessly for a moment, then turned and walked out of the condo.

# THIRTY

**O**n Sunday, Kiley left the Shop at three in the afternoon, following a nearly six-hour marathon meeting in Chief Cassidy's office.

He felt unusually good, not tired or emotionally drained, as he thought he should be; the tension of the long meeting, instead of affecting him negatively, had done just the opposite: It had seemed to relieve him of a lot of the psychological baggage he had been carrying around since Nick's death, seemed to induce a kind of purging, promote a cleansing of his conscience, so that everything he divulged in the meeting relieved his own mental burden of that much weight.

Getting in his car, Kiley actually felt refreshed. It helped that he had an errand now that he greatly looked forward to: He was going to see Meralda Mendez to tell her that she had been right, her mother had not committed suicide, and that of the two men who killed her, one was himself dead and the other was in custody and would be charged with the crime. Kiley knew he was going to feel very good telling the girl that.

The purpose of the meeting, it had been made clear by Cassidy, was to iron out all the wrinkles of the past few weeks, beginning with the killing of Detective Bianco, and to establish a level playing field on which all facts would be examined, all mistakes corrected, all guilty parties charged, and all necessary steps taken to protect the integrity and reputation of every city and county department involved. There should not, everyone agreed with Chief Cassidy, be any holding back of information for personal reasons. Prior to the meeting, Cassidy had strongly emphasized that point to Kiley. In his private bathroom, with the door closed, Cassidy had jabbed Kiley's chest with the stiffest forefinger Kiley had ever felt outside of parochial school, and said in his most threatening tone, "I want the whole, entire, unadulterated truth from you this morning, Detective, and by God if I don't get it, I'm going to personally take you down to the academy gym, put you in the boxing ring, and kick the living shit out of you! And don't think that just because I'm sixty-three years old that I can't do it, because I by God *can*! You have caused me enough fucking grief in the last few weeks to last me the rest of the goddamned year and then some! You level with me out there or by God I'll make you wish you were never fucking born! You read me?"

"Yessir," Kiley replied meekly, contritely. Cassidy had a way of reducing men to boys.

The police chief's threat had not been necessary; telling the truth—most of the truth—was already part of Kiley's plan. He had known all along that the only way to nail Gordon Lovat was with the truth or a bullet—and doing it with a bullet would have let him die a hero and a martyr; Kiley wanted him to go out as a bad cop, and only the truth could do that.

The meeting had begun with a complete narrative by Kiley of all that had transpired beginning with the radio call to investigate a dead body behind the 4-Star Lounge, followed by his and Nick's decision to break regulations and work that case themselves because Kiley was sure that Tony Touhy had killed the dead woman, Ronnie Lynn. He related how Nick had brought Gloria Mendez into their circle of misconduct by persuading her to help them find out where Tony Touhy resided. Following that were the details of their unauthorized surveillance of both the apartment building on Lake Shore Drive and the Shamrock Club, and how shortly after that unsuccessful operation, Nick had followed Tony Touhy to that same Shamrock Club and left a message on Kiley's answering machine to tell Kiley where he was; but when Kiley had hurried there, he had been too late and had found Nick Bianco dead.

Kiley explained how he had subsequently discovered in Nick's notebook the license numbers of all the cars Nick had seen parked behind the Shamrock Club, and how, after finding records access to those license numbers restricted, Kiley had gone back to Gloria Mendez and enlisted her help again. Gloria subsequently had been challenged by Gordon Lovat when he reported her to the captain in charge of records and asked for an audit of her computer terminal. In order to try and mitigate Gloria's participation, Kiley had set out to prove that although Tony Touhy had subsequently been found innocent of Ronnie Lynn's murder, that he was, in fact, still responsible for Nick Bianco's killing. To accomplish that, Kiley had admitted that he illegally gained access to Tony Touhy's apartment, and in searching it had found Detective Bianco's badge. It had been his intention, Kiley said, to take the badge to Chief Cassidy and tell the chief everything, but before he could do so, he heard about Gloria Mendez's alleged suicide.

Through Sergeant Mendez's daughter, Kiley said he became convinced that Gloria Mendez had *not* taken her own life, but had been murdered to prevent her from further helping Kiley, and also to silence her regarding what she already knew. At that point, Kiley told the others at the meeting, he felt he had no alternative but to pursue the matter further himself, because there were now *two* police officers for whose deaths he felt at least partly responsible. He was already suspicious about how quickly Tony Touhy's older brother, Philip Touhy, had learned that the surveillance of Tony had not been authorized; then when Phil Touhy had attempted to bribe him with a job offer, Kiley felt that the facts pointed toward someone closely connected to the police department.

The only person on the list of names Kiley had whom he felt might be pressured to inform on the others at the Shamrock Club that night, he said, was the obvious outsider: Fraz Lamont. To the astonishment of everyone in Cassidy's office, Kiley related how he bluffed his way into the old Cortez Theater and obtained information from Fraz Lamont with a concocted story of Fraz being framed for Bianco's murder. After that, Kiley said, it was a matter of doing a lot of scut work on the computer to track down the unknown "Mr. O" through the Mark VIII leased from Prestige. After Kiley had gathered all his evidence, he had done the right thing and taken it to Captain Vander of Internal Affairs. IA had wired him and sent him to confront Gordon Lovat with the information he already had, in an attempt to obtain more incriminating evidence from Lovat himself. That had been accomplished

Lovat was in custody, being held on racketeering charges, but would eventually be charged with both murders; the state's attorney felt that if he could not successfully be prosecuted for Gloria Mendez's death, because of the self-incrimination rules, that he could certainly be prosecuted for Nick Bianco's death—on Fraz Lamont's testimony, if no other way. Even though Lovat had not pulled the trigger, the department's forensic people, who had worked all night, had matched the bullet from Bianco's body to Lovat's gun; so Lovat would either have to face trial for the first-degree murder of Bianco, or admit conspiracy to commit that murder by lending Tony Touhy his gun to do it. Fraz Lamont, also in custody, had been brought in by a tactical squad from the Street Gangs Bureau, which kicked in the door of his suburban estate home at three a.m. and was now holding him incognito in a division lockup somewhere, questioning him about his relationship with Mr. O, a photograph of whom he identified without knowing that it was the commander of the department's Organized Crime Bureau.

It was agreed to at the chief's meeting that the medical examiner would review his office's cause of death finding on Sergeant Mendez and issue a revised coroner's report stating that she had died "under unknown circumstances not incompatible with suicide but having more definite characteristics of a homicide—" On that basis, Captain Cleary was instructed by Chief Cassidy to open a Homicide file on Gloria Mendez, and to pursue Gordon Lovat as a suspect both in that case and in the still open Bianco case. The state's attorney agreed to act on whatever evidence Cleary could develop to corroborate the evidence they already had. Fraz Lamont would be charged as an accessory to Bianco's murder, as well as with organized racketeering violations. There was a brief discussion about whether to try to tie either Lovat or Lamont, or both, to the cemetery bombing of the previous day, but the decision was not to pursue that particular matter. The crime had occurred outside Cook County, did not directly involve the city of Chicago, therefore was not their business. The theory on the bombing was still, according to the morning news, that it had been a professional assassination to cut back some of the mob hierarchy to make room for other chieftains. Since no one had been killed or injured except organized crime figures, a general feeling of "Who cares?" was already beginning to pervade.

After the general meeting ended and the non-police department attendees had left, Chief Cassidy called down to the district patrol sergeant on duty to send two uniforms out to Manny's Deli for sandwiches. While they ate, there was an open, general discussion about how best to deal with their own situation, both internally and with the public. It was agreed that IA should be credited with bringing Lovat down; an image of the department cleaning its own house would then be maintained. Vander's deputy, Bill Somers, was promoted to acting captain and put in charge of OCB. His first job would be to find out if any of Lovat's subordinates were also dirty. Kiley was assigned TAD to work directly for Vander, and between the two of them they would develop and back date reports that would show that Kiley had been in B-and-A only as a cover for a deep covert assignment to tie Gordon Lovat with Fraz Lamont. Public Affairs would prepare a press release stating that following an undercover investigation, a police department captain had been arrested for racketeering violations and that other, possibly more serious charges, might subsequently be brought against him. Because of an ongoing inquiry, further details could not be divulged at the present time.

Kiley had managed to come out of the meeting almost without a scratch. He had been able to get away with omitting the names of Father Conley and Bernard Oznina as his accomplices in gaining access to Tony Touhy's apartment. He had covered the deputy coroner who pointed out to him the bruises on Gloria's hands. He had successfully concealed the old relationship between Nick and Gloria. And his own involvement in killing Fred Scarp and then using Reggie to get into the mortuary and plant the homemade bomb, that he had learned from Harold Winston how to fashion, was never in question. As far as Kiley could tell, he had walked away clean—without having to involve anyone who had helped him. Nick and Gloria were dead, but at least everyone who had a hand in their killings had been—or in Lovat's case, would be—punished.

Things, Kiley decided, had turned out about as well as he could reasonably have expected.

When Kiley got to the Humboldt Park neighborhood where the Mendez apartment was, he had to park a block away because it was Sunday afternoon and the neighborhood was crowded. As Kiley got out and walked down the street, he was aware of the hostile looks from the front stoops where Hispanic people sat visiting, and from the young *macho* males who loitered on the sidewalk, drinking wine coolers around their *primo* cars parked at the curb. One such group all but blocked the way as Kiley approached, one of them openly pretending to clean his fingernails with a splinter-like switchblade stiletto. The kid looked no more than Meralda's age, sixteen at the most. Ignoring the illegal knife, as well as the crowding, Kiley worked his way through the group and continued on his way. At another time he might have taken the switchblade away from the kid and kicked his ass, but not today. Today he had other priorities.

At the six-flat Kiley had visited twice before, he saw that the name Mendez was still on the bell. He had thought in passing as he drove over that Meralda might not be there any longer, that she might have gone to live with her father or other relatives. But when he rang the bell, the foyer door was buzzed open almost at once, so he entered and went upstairs. When he got to the apartment, the door was open, and a husky Latin Prince, wearing red and green, was standing in the doorway.

"Wha' jou wan', man?" he asked, with a frown that was half hostility, half confusion.

"I want to see Meralda Mendez," Kiley said.

"She's not here, man," the youth said, and started to close the door.

"Hold it," Kiley ordered, putting stiff fingers against the youth's chest and pushing him back. "I'll just take a look—"

"Hey, man, who the fuck you pushing?" the youth challenged loudly, but did not make a move on Kiley, who was a full foot taller.

Stepping into the living room, Kiley felt an immediate sense of dejection as a bolt of memory struck his mind: Gloria Mendez in jeans and an old sweatshirt, buoyant breasts shifting when she moved, sculpted ears so perfect from any angle, eyes so direct and honest—

"Wha's the pro'lem, man?" asked a taller, cleanly handsome young Prince, being followed into the room by two others, also wearing colors.

"I want to see Meralda Mendez," Kiley repeated, unbuttoning his coat in case it became necessary to rake his pistol barrel across somebody's face.

"Oh, yeah? Wha' jou wan' to see her for?" the handsome one asked.

"That's my business. Where is she?"

"I'm right here, Detective," Meralda said, entering from the kitchen, wiping her hands on a dish towel. "It's okay, Mundo," she told the handsome Prince. Kiley saw that she was wearing a tight green skirt and a deeply scooped red blouse. Colors.

"I'd like to talk to you in private, Meralda," Kiley said. "I have some news for you."

"About my mother?"

"Yes."

"Okay." She handed the towel to another Hispanic girl, similarly dressed, who had come from the kitchen behind her. "We can go out front," she told Kiley.

Meralda led Kiley back downstairs and out to the front stoop.

"You want to sit down?" she asked, sitting on the top step.

"Yeah, sure." Kiley sat next to her, feeling a little awkward. It had been a long time since he sat on a front stoop with a girl. He was trying to think of a way to tell Meralda what he was there to tell her, but before he could do so, she asked him about it.

"Did you find out that my mother did not commit suicide?" the girl asked without preliminary.

"Yes," Kiley replied quietly. "You were right about that. Your mother— she was killed, Meralda, by two men who held her and forced her to swallow the pills and whiskey. One of the men has already paid for it; he was blown up in the explosion at that cemetery yesterday—you probably heard about it on the news—"

"Yes. Which one was he?"

"The man named Philip Touhy."

"And the other one?"

"He's a policeman, Meralda. Or *was* a policeman. He's in jail and will be charged with your mother's murder."

"And you *know* these are the men who murdered Mama?"

"Yes, I know. They are the men."

"Will there be something in the newspaper saying Mama did not kill herself?"

"Yes. The coroner is going to issue a revised cause of death report."

The girl lowered her head for a moment, and in profile Kiley could see tears streaking the cheek nearest him. He wanted desperately, as he had in the funeral parlor, to put an arm around her and comfort her, but on nearby stoops there were Hispanic neighbors whom he knew were watching them, speculating about who he was, why he was there. He would have felt better, and perhaps she would have too, for a brief moment, if he *had* consoled her like that, but in the long run it would only have alienated her all the more from the people around her. That realization was part of the concern Kiley felt about her future.

"Are you living with your father now?" he asked.

"Are you kidding me?" Meralda replied cynically. "He did the same thing to me that he did to Mama: walked out. As soon as he found out I wasn't getting the insurance money, he split like a dog."

"What happened with the insurance money?" Kiley asked.

"My Aunt Lena got it in trust for me. She gives me enough to live on. I'll get what's left when I'm eighteen. Until then, I'll just stay here, where Mama and me lived."

Kiley nodded. He had no argument to offer. A sixteen-year-old Latino girl in the *barrio* was as grown-up as she needed to be in order to take care of herself. Unfortunately, that did not mean that she *would* take care of herself. It disturbed Kiley deeply that Meralda was wearing colors— something that he knew instinctively her late mother would not have tolerated.

"When did you become a Latin Princess?" he asked, trying to keep the question conversational.

"Couple of days ago," she told him. "When Papa left."

"Got your tattoo yet?"

Meralda smiled shyly. "God, no, not yet. I'm really nervous about it. Some of the girls tol' me it hurts."

"Probably does," Kiley allowed. All Latin Prince gang members had a small cross, with a single dot at each of the four ends, tattooed above their left nipple. It was a requirement for the girls also, although they were allowed to have it done farther up if they were full-breasted.

"Have you considered living with your Aunt Lena or some other relative?" Kiley asked.

"No, because I know what that would be like," she replied, shaking her head adamantly. "They'd just try to boss me around. It wouldn't work out, believe me."

"The Police League could probably help you find a good foster home with people that would be happy to have you live with them for a few years—"

"No, I don't think so, Detective." Meralda abruptly rose, so Kiley did also. "I better stay with my own, you know?" She glanced over at the door where the handsome young Mundo was now standing, waiting for her. She held out her hand. "Good-bye, Joe Kiley. Thanks for finding out about my Mama."

Kiley nodded. "Take care of yourself. If you ever need me for anything, you can just call—"

"Call the Shop," she finished it for him. "Yeah, I know. But I'll be okay. Good-bye."

On the way back to his car, Kiley felt very sad for Meralda Mendez and all the days and nights of her young life that she would now have to endure before she became the woman her mother had been.

If she ever did.

It was almost dark when Kiley arrived back at his apartment. The positive mood he had when he left the Shop that afternoon, based on how well things seemed to be turning out, had been neutralized to some extent by his meeting with Meralda and the premonition it had given him regarding her future. He had a foreshadowing of anxiety about the girl, as well as a nagging notion, not fully formed, that there should be *something* that he could do to help her. He realized that it was probably his guilt about Gloria that was generating the feeling, but that did not diminish it at all; whatever the basis, the thought was *there*: Surely he could find a way to give her some kind of moral support, at least for a few years. He made up his mind to concentrate on finding a way.

When he got into his apartment, the red light on his answering machine was flashing. Still remembering Nick's last call, he sat down on the couch and retrieved the message at once. He heard Stella's familiar voice.

"Hi, Joe, it's Stella. I guess you're out." A slight pause. "Or maybe you're not picking up because you're mad at me." Her voice broke a little. "Honest to God, Joe, I'm so confused about things, I don't know what to do. Jennie doesn't like Frank, practically won't have anything to do with him since I told her and Tessie that I'd be marrying him." She laughed briefly, without mirth. "Jennie says she's going to wait until she grows up and then she's going to marry *you*. Tessie thinks Frank is okay, but you know her: She's easily bribed, which Frank does regularly. I haven't made the commitment yet, haven't told Frank or Uncle Gino that I would. I'm just having a bad time with everything, Joe." She began crying softly. "I want Nick back. I know that'll never be, and Father Balducci says it isn't even healthy, but I can't help it—I want my Nicky back—"

Blinking away tears of his own, Kiley stopped the tape and rested his head back against the couch. Jesus Christ, forgive me, he thought, not even sure from whom he was asking forgiveness: Stella or God, or both. Stella, for Nick? God, for Nick and Gloria and Scarp and the Touhys and—

Shaking his head, he thought: No. There was too much blood on his hands to ask forgiveness from God for himself. He would burn in hell for what he had done in that cemetery, and in his heart he knew he deserved it. But if only he could help Stella—and help the girls—and help Meralda—

Sitting forward again, he turned Stella's message back on. When the crying stopped, she said, "I don't mean to hang any of this on you, Joe. I just don't have anybody to talk to about things. I know you must be pretty upset with me; I've never seen your face the way it was when you left the other night. And I don't blame you. It was so stupid of me not to realize how you felt. So the reason I'm calling is to tell you I'm sorry, Joey. I wouldn't hurt you on purpose for the world. Please give me a call so we can talk. I'll be home all Sunday night. 'Bye, Joe."

A double beep sounded, telling Kiley that she had hung up and that there were no other messages. As the machine automatically reset itself, Kiley stared into space and his mind began racing. Stella needed someone, very badly. Her girls needed someone. Meralda needed someone. And *he* needed someone.

The solution to everyone's problem suddenly seemed so clear to him. So easy. So simple.

But his mind, even though racing, was still a cop's mind, still rooted in reality. Maybe it was *too* simple. Would Stella understand it? Would Meralda? Would *anyone*?

Yet he could not dissuade the logic of it from his thoughts. The need was there, in all of them, and the resolution of it seemed to be there also, in all of them as well. The picture it presented was too magnetic to ignore. Stella and Joe, Jennie and Tessie, and Meralda, living together as a family—in Nick's house. Nick would approve. Gloria would approve. Kiley had no doubt about either.

What Kiley found so intriguing, and so compelling, was that he might be able to make it happen.

He strode into the bedroom, stripping off coat, tie, and shirt as he went. At the bathroom sink he ran hot water and lathered his face. He had shaved some twelve hours earlier, for his meeting at the Shop, but for what he had in mind now, he wanted to be fresh all over again. As he pulled the safety razor across his face, he studied himself in the mirror. There was a new kind of determination in his eyes, a determination unlike that which had been displayed in recent weeks. It was no longer a grim, unsmiling tenacity such as had motivated him to find and punish Nick's killer; now it was more a purposeful, dedicated desire to accomplish something that was beneficial, contributory; something good, for a change. He was not deluding himself for a moment that any of it would relieve him of the grave sins now staining his soul, but if it would help those for whom he cared, those for whom he felt responsible, then at least he could go to hell with that part of his conscience cleansed.

When he was cleanshaven, Kiley got into the shower and scrubbed himself under a spray of steaming water, beginning to feel very good now, very positive again, very much assured and unequivocal, as the old Joe Kiley had been before the nightmare after Ronnie Lynn's death had begun. Out of the shower, briskly toweling down, he found himself actually humming—a nameless little Irish melody that now and again he had heard his mother croon. At his closet he reached for one of his gray suits, still in a dry cleaner's bag, but his hand stopped before he lifted the hanger. His eyes swept over to a line of hanging clothes that had once been Nick's, the clothes that Stella had insisted he take. He had worn only one article, a sport coat, when he drove down to give Alma Lynn her dead sister's photographs. Now he moved his hand over and shifted through the clothes to a navy blue tweed coat with medium blue slacks on the same hanger. Without debating it, he removed the clothes, picked out a tab collar white shirt and a blue checked tie, and got dressed. With the socks he had taken off, he buffed his plain-toe black shoes a little, promising himself that he would buy some new, more stylish shoes the very next day. He would start paying more attention to his appearance, he silently vowed.

In front of the mirror, he was satisfied with what he saw. He looked pretty damned good in Nick's clothes, and never mind where Nick had bought them. Thinking briefly about calling Stella before he drove out, he decided not to. He would surprise her. If it hadn't been Sunday night with all the florists closed, he would have bought her some flowers. Or maybe not. She had only said she wanted to talk. He knew she would be pleased to see him wearing Nick's clothes. Hopefully, that would put her in a receptive frame of mind. He hoped so. She simply *had* to listen to reason tonight.

On his way out of the building, Kiley ran into his landlady, Mrs. Levine.

"My, don't you look spiffy," she said with raised eyebrows. A smallish, gray-haired woman, slightly stooped with osteoporosis, she was replacing a bulb in the first-floor hallway. "Got a heavy date, looks like. I hope it's nothing serious, so you won't move away and leave me alone and unprotected."

Kiley paused and kissed her on the forehead. "If I move, I'll find a meaner cop to replace me."

Crossing the sidewalk to his car, Kiley could only shake his head wryly. There would probably always be *something*, he thought, to make him feel guilty. It was the curse of being Irish.

Half smiling to himself, he slid behind the wheel, closed the door, and turned on the ignition.

The front end of the Buick exploded before his eyes, just as Fred Scarp's casket had done.

# THIRTY-ONE

**F**rom his wicker rocking chair on the front porch, Kiley could see the postman every morning as he came around the corner on Elm Street and stopped at the first mailbox next to the curb. The postman drove a little delivery van with the steering wheel on the right side so that he could pull up next to the mailboxes and deliver the mail without having to get out. Kiley was sitting in his rocker, waiting, every morning when the mail came. The postman, a friendly, weather-beaten man named Vernon, always brought Kiley's mail up to the porch for him because he knew Kiley still had difficulty walking.

"'Morning, Joe," Vernon said on this particular day, coming up the three steps to the porch.

"'Morning, Verne."

"Going to be another scorcher today, looks like."

"Looks like," Kiley agreed. He took the mail Vernon handed him.

"Wouldn't be so bad if it weren't for the humidity being up," Vernon analyzed. "Humidity's what does it."

"Want a cold drink, Verne?" Kiley asked.

"No, thanks anyway," Vernon said. "Just make me sweat more. Coming to the Legion game tonight?

"Maybe," Kiley said.

"Jimmy Burns is pitching," Vernon reminded. "Boy's got the best arm I've seen in ten years."

"Got a fast ball, that's for sure," agreed Kiley.

"Well, take care," Vernon went down the steps waving, and Kiley watched him continue on his route.

The mail wasn't much: electric bill, sale circular from a shoe store up on the square, national teachers association newsletter, and his Chicago paper. He had a mail subscription to the *Sun-Times*; it was always day-old news when he got it, but it helped him keep up with things back in the city.

Setting the other mail aside, on a wicker table where he had a glass of cold limeade, he opened the paper and began scanning the article headlines. On page four, he found one that seized his attention:

## LOVAT IN PLEA BARGAIN

Kiley's eyes skimmed through it to get the gist of the story; then, shaking his head slightly in disgust, he went back to the beginning and read it carefully. Gordon Lovat, former high-ranking officer in the Chicago Police Department, had negotiated through his attorneys a plea bargain arrangement with the Cook County state's attorney's office with respect to several long-standing criminal charges for which he had been indicted more than a year earlier. Originally Lovat had been implicated in the separate murders of two Chicago police officers, in addition to being charged with state and federal racketeering violations. Through a preliminary hearing and numerous pre-trial motions, it had been determined that available evidence, including testimony by Disciples gang president Frazier Lamont, could not support a case against Lovat for the murder of Sergeant Gloria Mendez, and could only support a charge of accessory before the fact in the murder of Detective Nick Bianco. In the Mendez case, Lovat's admission to an officer wearing a recording device had been ruled inadmissible after his lawyers successfully argued that he had been entrapped.

The racketeering charges Lovat faced could be proved, with Fraz Lamont's testimony—but cooperation between the state's attorney and the gang leader was dwindling as Fraz continued to be kept locked up because his Disciples had failed to come forth with money for his bail. Lamont was incensed that Gordon Lovat, accused of far more serious crimes than Fraz himself, had been free on one million dollars bail since his preliminary hearing one week after his arrest. Lamont wanted to be released on his own recognizance so that he could return to the Disciples and resume control. The state's attorney refused. Animosity began to swell between the prosecutors and Fraz Lamont's lawyer.

The plea bargain that Kiley was now reading about was that Gordon Lovat would plead guilty to accessory before the fact to voluntary manslaughter in the Bianco case; that the Mendez case would be dropped; and that the racketeering charges also would be dropped if Lovat testified against Fraz Lamont on Lamont's racketeering charges. With an added charge of racketeering committed to enhance street gang activities, Fraz

322 •••• CLARK HOWARD

Lamont could face twenty-five years in prison. Gordon Lovat, on the other hand, would receive a twelve-to-eighteen-year sentence, and probably be paroled after eight.

Kiley shook his head again. Eight fucking years for the lives of two good cops. Resting his head back, he closed his eyes for a moment. *I probably should have killed him.* Kiley could not keep the thought from his mind. He realized that Lovat would have died a martyr that way—but look what giving him to the system had done. Ten, fifteen years from now, Lovat would be free to play with his grandchildren while living quite well on the income from all the businesses his dirty money had financed for his family. While Jennie and Tessie would have grown up without their father, and with a scuzz like Frank Bianco for a stepfather; and Meralda Mendez would have—

No, Kiley ordered, he would not allow himself to even *think* about Meralda Mendez. God only knew what had become of her in the year since he last saw her. Being a part of the Latin Princes gang, she could have become common property for gangbangs; or she might have taken up with a particular member, like that handsome kid Mundo, and had a baby of her own; or she might even have been turned out to trick for the gang to produce income. Merely imagining the possible straits Meralda Mendez could be in was almost nauseating to Kiley.

Rising from the rocker, Kiley used a cane to balance himself and slowly made his way inside. He put the mail on a table in the foyer, and continued on into what Alma had once told him was originally a sun room when her father had built the house. Now it was furnished as a small bedroom with a recliner, television, and a dresser for his things. During the first several months he had lived there, after being released from the convalescent home, he had spent most of his time in the little room, sleeping alone, resting, doing his physical therapy routines. Now, he used the bed only to nap in the afternoons, usually making a slow but beneficial climb of the stairs, with Alma's help, to the big bedroom upstairs at night. But he still considered the little converted sun room to be *his* room, and retreated to it frequently during the day when he was alone.

At his dresser, Kiley retrieved a manila envelope from one of the drawers, along with a pair of scissors. In the dresser mirror he caught a glimpse of himself, but did not pause to study his face as he had done during the first months of his recuperation. The left side of his face, including the ear and most of his hair, had been burned in the explosion, and for a long time he had looked pretty hideous: a split-faced man with a normal appearance on one side, badly disfigured on the other. Plastic surgery and a nicely rebuilt ear had substantially reduced the damage, and now the left side of his face resembled, if anything, a wax museum figure. Alma said the difference wasn't even noticeable except in certain light. His answer to that was, "Yeah, natural and artificial." But his appearance no longer bothered him much, and people in the little town had long since stopped staring at him.

Sitting down in his recliner, he used the scissors to slowly and carefully cut out the news item about Gordon Lovat's plea bargain. Putting the rest of the paper next to his bed to read later, he opened the envelope and removed several dozen other clippings. For a moment, he idly sifted through them, eyes scanning the headline of each. One of the earlier ones read:

## CLUES SOUGHT IN COP BOMBING

That story, which had run several days after Kiley's car had exploded, stated that the Bomb-and-Arson squad of the police department had no significant clues in the bombing. Detective Kiley, who was on temporary attached duty in B-and-A, had worked only one bomb case, that of a man convicted of gross public vandalism, and the department had been unable as of then to connect that man with the crime. Harold Paul Winston *could* have done it; his sentence of one-to-three years had been stayed for thirty days to allow him to get his personal affairs in order before reporting to prison, and he had been free on one hundred thousand dollars bond, which had been posted by his stepfather—but Winston had an alibi for the ninety-minute window of opportunity during which the explosive device had been magnetically attached to the underside of the generator on Kiley's engine. The alibi was a ticket stub to a Loop movie theater; Winston had bought the ticket and mingled with the mixed crowd of people going in and coming out of the lobby. No one remembered seeing him leave—and he was able to recite in great detail what the feature, *Best Friends*, was about.

B-and-A had also looked into the possibility that the explosion of Kiley's car was somehow connected to the highly publicized cemetery bombing that had occurred in a nearby county the day before Kiley's bombing, but that possibility was ruled out since Detective Kiley was not involved in police matters related to organized crime. In addition, Detective Kiley had no known personal enemies who might have set the explosive.

Looking at that clipping now, Kiley grunted softly. No known personal enemies—right. That is, if Uncle Gino and his scumbag son, all of his scumbag sons-in-law, and all of his scumbag nephews were discounted. And organized crime? Who knew what *previous* orders were out on him from Phil Touhy? If Touhy and Lovat thought it necessary to kill Gloria, why not him also? As for Hal, well, the old movie ticket alibi was practically foolproof if done right. And Kiley knew that Hal did things right; just look at the quality of his bombs.

Putting that clipping aside, Kiley picked up another:

## JANITOR SENTENCED

Wallace Simpson, 31, had been given an eight-to-fifteen-year sentence on a guilty plea to voluntary manslaughter in the beating death of go-go dancer Veronica Lynn, 28. A plea bargain with the state's attorney had stipulated to the court that the defendant had been provoked by the victim and acted in a temporarily enraged manner brought on by that provocation. Simpson had no previous criminal record, which was also a strong mitigating factor. A pre-sentencing probation report had given a favorable prognosis for the defendant's rehabilitation, and recommended incarceration in a minimum security institution where he could receive educational and psychological therapeutic support. His first parole hearing would be in three years.

Another clipping read:

## DISCIPLES GANG LEADER HELD

That item reported that Frazier Lamont, leader of the Disciples, a black street gang, was being held in the central jail lockup on a variety of charges which his attorney called "ludicrous and totally in violation of his client's constitutional rights." Among those charges were: accessory to the murder of a police officer, racketeering, felonies committed in the enhancement of street gang activities, extortion, carrying a concealed weapon, resisting arrest, assaulting police officers, and several other lesser offenses. Police were also looking into the recent disappearance of a Disciples gang member, one Otis Webb, who was observed being forcibly taken from the gang's headquarters in the old Cortez Theater and had not been seen since. Lamont was being held in lieu of five hundred thousand dollars bail, and federal racketeering charges were also expected to be filed against him.

The next clipping Kiley picked up was headlined:

## RACKETEERS RECOVERING

The two survivors of the now infamous New Saints Cemetery bombing, Augustus Dellafranco and James "Jocko" Hennessey, were reported to be making satisfactory recoveries from their injuries. Dellafranco, reputed head of organized crime on Chicago's South Side, had lost his right arm and right leg in the explosion. Hennessey, a reputed member of the late Philip Touhy's North Side crime family, had lost both arms above the elbow. The men were recuperating at separate undisclosed convalescent homes in other states. Neither was expected to return to a position of leadership in Illinois organized crime activities. The cemetery bombing case was still open, but DuPage County and Mt. Canaan city law enforcement agencies reported no progress being made in the investigation. The United States Department of Justice had declined to have the FBI join in the investigation because there was no evidence of any interstate violations connected with the crime.

Translation, Kiley thought: Nobody gives a fuck.

He put the latest clipping, about Gordon Lovat's plea bargain, into the envelope with the others and put the envelope back in the dresser drawer. Glancing at the clock next to his bed, he saw that it was eleven-forty. Slowly he made his way through the dining room and into the big country kitchen of the old house. He took some leftover roast beef from the refrigerator and sliced part of it for sandwiches. As he was getting out the bread, he heard Alma's car door slam and presently she came through the back door.

"You're supposed to be resting, Joseph," she scolded mildly. She kissed him on her way to the sink to wash her hands. "Remember what the doctor said about overdoing too soon."

"Fixing lunch is not exactly overdoing," he replied.

Drying her hands on a dish towel, Alma took the bread away from him and guided him to a chair at the kitchen table. "Sit," she ordered, and took over the preparation of their lunch.

Alma came home every day at eleven-forty-five and stayed until one-fifteen. She had arranged her class schedule so that the lunch period and her daily free hour were consecutive, allowing her a long midday break. The school administration permitted it because they did not want to lose her. She had taken a leave of absence the previous semester, when she first brought Kiley home, and neither students nor parents were happy about it. Alma was probably the most popular teacher at Ripley Senior High, and the school board made it clear that whatever accommodation was necessary would be made to get her back. None of them knew how close she had come to resigning altogether. In fact, it had only been at Kiley's insistence that she resumed her teaching career. That had been six months earlier, but nearly a year since the night he woke up in the hospital and found her sitting next to his bed.

When she saw Kiley open his right eye, which was not bandaged, Alma had smiled and said softly, "Welcome back."

Kiley knew who she was—but that was all; he did not know where he was or why he was there.

"Your car blew up," Alma quietly explained. It was almost one in the morning. There was a folding cot in the room that she used to stay with him every night. During the day, she would go back to a nearby motel room to rest a little and change clothes, but most of the time she was with him. "You're in St. Benidictus Hospital," she told him that night when he first awoke. "This is the trauma unit. You've been unconscious for twelve days."

"Is my other eye gone?" he asked, alarm spreading in his awakening mind.

"No, it's just under a bandage," Alma quietly assured. She wet his lips with a towel and some water from a metal pitcher on the bed table. "Your face was burned, but your eyesight is all right."

"I can't— move anything—" He was trying to activate his fingers. Alma hovered over him, trying to reassure him with word and touch.

"You've got casts on. The concussion broke both of your collarbones and both ankles. And there was some internal damage; one of your lungs collapsed, some vertebrae were knocked out of place, that kind of stuff. But the doctors say you'll be all right. It'll just take time."

Kiley had faded back out for several minutes and woke again to find a resident doctor and several nurses around the bed. They spoke quietly, encouragingly, to him as they checked his vital signs. His uncovered right eye shifted anxiously in its socket, and only relaxed when he finally saw Alma, waiting patiently in the background for them to leave. When they at last did, she moved a chair next to his bed and sat holding his hand, talking soothingly to him as his level of consciousness rose and fell. At one point, she explained how she got there.

"My cable TV service comes from Gary, Indiana," she told him. "They carry all the local Chicago channels. I had been watching WGN almost nonstop after I heard on one of the networks that Tony Touhy had been killed in that cemetery bombing. I wondered at the time if you had anything to do with that." She paused, then asked, "Did you?"

"No," Kiley replied quietly.

"I really didn't think you did," she amended. "Anyway, the next night after the cemetery thing, just as I was getting ready for bed, I saw the report on you. I got dressed, got in my car, and drove to Chicago. I was here at the hospital before you even got out of surgery—"

Kiley dropped off again, wondering whether Stella had been there. Toward morning, Alma had answered that unasked question.

"Lots of people have been here to see you; I wrote down their names." She got a sheet of paper from his bed-table drawer. "Chief Cassidy was here; Captain Parmetter, Captain Madzak; a sweet old priest named Father Conley; a lady named Aldena Loomis; another lady named Gertrude Levine—she said she was your landlady; then there was Mrs. Bianco—she said she was your late partner's wife—widow, I guess—she was pretty curious about me, incidentally; seemed to think it was very odd that you had never mentioned me to her—"

So Stella had been there. In the hazy aftermath of awakening after twelve days, Kiley wondered what Stella would think, how she would feel, if she knew he had been leaving to come see her that night, wearing some of Nick's sharp clothes, making promises to himself to pay more attention to his personal appearance—

He didn't have to worry about keeping that promise, he thought, not with half his face burned off.

Alma remained with him for weeks, then months, keeping a room at the motel but staying at the hospital most of the time, tending to his personal needs, helping with his physical therapy when the casts came off and he began using his arms and legs again, being there for him before he went into and when he came out of the operating room after the doctors began the long process of grafting skin from his thighs onto his face. Kiley was sick a lot, nauseated, in pain, ill-tempered, and Alma was the target of some of his ire, but she never faltered, never snapped back, never deviated from being the epitome of patience, comfort, and support. Captains Parmetter and Madzak thought she was a saint and in time let Kiley know that she was much too good for the likes of him and that he was damned lucky to have her. Aldena felt the same way. Only Mrs. Levine reserved her full blessing, hoping right up to the last minute that Kiley would return as her personal policeman and that she could nurse him back to health herself. Only reluctantly did she finally give up on that hope when Alma arrived one day to pack up all of Kiley's personal belongings when he was being moved to a convalescent home outside the city.

Stella had been to see him a few times by then, and even though Alma always deferred to their privacy by leaving to run an errand or something, Stella's visits were nevertheless awkward. She and Kiley both seemed to sense a lack of comfort in each other's company that they had never felt before. They didn't know whether it was Alma's presence in his life now, or if they had finally realized that for them there simply was no future together. The last time Kiley heard from Stella Bianco was when she telephoned one Friday night to tell him that she and Frank Bianco would be getting married the following morning. That was their good-bye.

Just as it had been in the hospital, so it was in the convalescent home: Alma with a room nearby, but most of her time being spent with Kiley. She helped him exercise, eat, shower; she sat with him late at night when he couldn't sleep—when the demons of what he had done, the murders he had committed, those terrible things of which she knew nothing, came to haunt him and gnaw at his conscience and his soul. The men he had killed had been evil—all eight of them: Fred Scarp and seven of his nine pallbearers—but they had been human beings nevertheless, men with mortal souls, and the right to end their lives was reserved far beyond Joe Kiley, and that tormented him. So Alma held his hand, stroked his arm, blotted the sweat from his neck and chest, and never asked questions.

"You're putting in a lot of time with me, lady," he said one day when she had helped him walk out on the grounds for some fresh air.

"I know," she replied. "Everybody tells me you're not worth it."

"I'm not."

"Well, I'm stubborn," she told him. "I want to see for myself."

After four months in the convalescent home, during which he had his fifth and sixth skin grafts at a nearby hospital, it was finally time for Kiley to be discharged. He resisted the notion. The state disability fund was paying all his expenses, and he was still on full salary from the department. He was comfortable at the convalescent home, had a nice room, a television, the food wasn't bad at all, and people left him alone when he wanted them to. He saw no reason to go anywhere.

"You *have* to leave," Alma argued. "The doctors have told you that if you don't, you'll become a professional convalescent and *never* want to go. Now, you know that I have a great big house down in Ripley and it would be perfect for you. Six months or a year there and you could really get well—"

"No," he shook his head adamantly. "You've given up too much of your time already—"

"Joey, I *want* to help you," she insisted. Every once in a while, he noticed, she called him "Joey" like his mother had, like Stella had on occasion. "Look," Alma reasoned, "if you think I'm doing this so you'll make some kind of commitment to me, well—" she could not help smiling, "you're right. But you don't *have* to. I've fallen really hard for you, I'm sure you realize that—everyone else does; but I know that a person doesn't always get back what they give. I mean, it would be great if you grew to feel the same about me as I feel about you—but if that never happens, I wouldn't want you to fake it. All I'm saying is let's *try*. You need a place to stay until you're completely well; you need someone to help you until you can take care of yourself again. Come home with me. If it lasts, it lasts; if it doesn't, it doesn't." She took his hands in hers and her voice became very soft, a whisper. "Come home with me, Joe."

Finally, he did—but only on condition that she resume her teaching and restore some normalcy to her own life.

After lunch, they went out onto the front porch and Alma sat in the other wicker chair and they rocked together for a while.

"Jimmy Burns is pitching in the Legion game tonight," Alma said.

"Yeah, Verne told me."

"Think you'll feel up to going? You seemed to enjoy the game last week."

"I wouldn't mind going," Kiley allowed.

"If you get tired, we can leave early."

"Okay."

When it was time for her to go back to school, she kissed him long and lovingly. "See you in a few hours."

"I'll be here," he said.

Kiley waved to her as she backed out and drove away. It wasn't too bad, this small town living, he supposed. Of course, there was no *edge* to life: It was American Legion baseball, Fourth of July parades, Labor Day picnics, Christmas caroling; it was tending the garden in the summer, and grilling steaks in the backyard; stretching out in front of a crackling fire while snow fell outdoors in the winter; it was Alma playing soft melodies on the piano while he sipped gin without ice; it was reading *National Geographic* every month and *enjoying* it.

No edge—none of the sharpness of city life, no constant delineation between safety and danger, no fringes of exposure, margins of defense, no points of penetration to protect. Easy days flowed smoothly into comfortable nights. In Alma's big four-poster bed upstairs she made love to him, and to herself, in ways that were compatible with his convalescence; her imagination and dexterity were unrestrained, and his resultant pleasure euphoric.

Kiley remembered telling Alma once about the difference between people who had city blood and people who did not. He wondered of late whether that theory had any validity at all. Not in a million years would he have believed that he could power himself down enough to remain in Ripley—but then, he never counted on his Buick blowing up under him either. He realized that some of the contentment he felt was because his body was still mending, and half guessed that when—*if*—he ever regained full strength, the uncertainty of who was responsible for his bombing— Phil Touhy, Uncle Gino, Hal—might arouse in him a desire to return to the city, energize in him a need to at least *know*, if not to retaliate. Revenge did not appeal to him at the moment; he was still privately anguishing over his *last* reprisal. Secretly, he hoped that in time it would make no difference to him who had set the bomb. But he couldn't be sure how long his city blood would circulate at small-town speed.

He would just have to wait and see.